'Revelatory. Three unforgettable characters, their everyday tragedies, and the visceral ties between a woman and her sister's children. *Love Objects* is moving and deeply human, an exploration of the limits of our understanding and the depths of our compassion.'

—Kristina Olsson, author of *Shell* and *Boy, Lost*

'*Love Objects* is that rare thing: a novel of ideas which is also full of heart. Emily Maguire shines a light on elements of contemporary Australian life which are often hidden and in doing so gifts the reader with a rich and vivid world, sizzling with wit, humming with tenderness. Her characters sing on the page but more than that, they live away from the page. I see them everywhere now. It's a stunning, immersive novel that will change the conversation about class and about what possessions mean. It's important and funny and sad and beautiful and I absolutely adored it.'

—Kathryn Heyman, author of *Storm and Grace* and *Fury*

'*Love Objects* is an antidote to the clinical Kondo-world of glossy magazine layouts. Emily Maguire's characters are as messy as Aunty Nic's hallway—and every bit as layered and astonishing. She writes of their struggles and pains with dark humour and an unflinching eye, but what prevails—and makes me want to read and re-read her pages—is their tenderness and shared humanity.'

—Ailsa Piper, author of *The Attachment*

'Maguire channels contemporary life with fierce and fearless attack, targeting our deepest fears and vulnerabilities, exposing hidden shame and questioning the meaning of privacy in today's digital world. As well as wielding a forensic scalpel to human nature, she brings tender insight and compassion to those so often on the margins of society.'

—Caroline Baum, author of *Only*

'Emily Maguire pulls no punches in *Love Objects*; it is bold, furious, unapologetic and deeply insightful. This wise, brave author gave me energy and passion and rage, and made me want to write to change the world. Unforgettable.'

—Sofie Laguna, Miles Franklin-winning author of
The Eye of the Sheep and *Infinite Splendours*

'This story is full of grit, with rough edges and harsh truths, but the humanity that shines through is phenomenal. *Love Objects* has got to be one of the most big-hearted novels I've ever read. Each person fully formed, each scene and new catastrophe rooted in truth. I learned something deeper about struggling and coping against class and I looked anew at how I relate to the things I own. I finished this book in two sittings and I challenge anyone to pick it up then simply put it down. I truly believe the talent and insight on display here place Maguire in the company of greats.'

—Bri Lee, author of *Eggshell Skull* and *Beauty*

EMILY MAGUIRE is the author of six novels, including the Stella Prize and Miles Franklin Award shortlisted *An Isolated Incident*, and three non-fiction books. Her articles and essays on sex, feminism, culture and literature have been published widely, including in *The Sydney Morning Herald*, *The Australian*, *The Observer* and *The Age*. Emily works as a teacher and as a mentor to young and emerging writers and was the 2018/2019 Writer-in-Residence at the Charles Perkins Centre at the University of Sydney.

LOVE OBJECTS

EMILY MAGUIRE

ALLEN&UNWIN
SYDNEY·MELBOURNE·AUCKLAND·LONDON

First published in 2021

Allen & Unwin
83 Alexander Street
Crows Nest NSW 2065
Australia
Phone: (61 2) 8425 0100
Email: info@allenandunwin.com
Web: www.allenandunwin.com

A catalogue record for this book is available from the National Library of Australia

ISBN 978 1 76087 833 7

Set in 12.2/18.4 pt Minion Pro by Bookhouse, Sydney
Printed and bound in Australia by Griffin Press, part of Ovato

10 9 8 7 6 5 4 3 2 1

The paper in this book is FSC® certified. FSC® promotes environmentally responsible, socially beneficial and economically viable management of the world's forests.

LOVE
OBJECTS

ONE

NIC

Nic's shoes had always worn unevenly. *Pigeon-toed* was what the ballet teacher, who was actually just an ordinary mum who had lived in France for a year when she was younger, had called her. *Such a pretty face, but those feet!* the fake-French ballet teacher would cry, patting six-year-old Nic's smooth cheeks and gazing not at the terrible feet but away from them at the school hall rafters. What would she say now? Nic wonders, watching each foot press its inside into the asphalt as it stepped. *Such a sagging face! At last a match for your sloppy feet!*

Sagging face, sloppy feet, arse outgrowing its pants, right hip which has, in the three years since she's turned forty, woken her most nights with its urgent ache. Not all bad, though, or else Jase from the stockroom, who goes to the gym every morning before work and wears tight shorts and tighter singlets to show how well that regime is working for him, wouldn't whistle appreciatively and call her gorgeous when she passed him, and Reg the store's night manager wouldn't stand far closer than polite in the break room and ask her for the thousandth time if she wouldn't consider joining the night shift so he'd have something good to look at during the long quiet hours between six and closing.

Night shift is better money, but aside from having to dodge Reg there's the matter of transport. Nic isn't a panicky person; not like her sister Michelle, who sees rapists and meth heads where there are only passing motorists and harmless neighbourhood kids. Still, even the calmest and most reasonable woman doesn't take twenty-minute walks alone after midnight. Or accept the no-doubt-insistent offer of a lift from the creepy manager finishing work at the same time.

Besides, if she got home after midnight she wouldn't get to sleep before one, but would have to rise at six anyway to make sure the cats didn't howl the neighbourhood awake in hunger.

Besides, if she didn't walk home in the bright, clear light of afternoon she would miss so much.

Like the newly pasted telegraph pole poster telling whoever passes to LOOSE WEIGHT NOW!!!! She tears a tab off and slips it into her uniform pocket to nestle with the SECRETS OF YOUR SOUL TAROT business card she picked up from the shopping centre information desk this morning and the kebab shop receipt with today's queue number 14 in thick black texta on the top. On second thought, she unsticks the whole poster, working carefully so the bits of tape come away with the paper. Folds it in three so the tabs are safely tucked away.

Like the way this pair of sneakers looks ready to chuck on the inside edge and yet near new on the outer. Is it time to swap them with one of the pairs she bought in Kmart's January sale or should she wait until the canvas wears right through? First sight of skin, that was the marker.

Like the fact the diamond chip in Mum's engagement ring is not sparkling as it should in the late afternoon sun. Michelle, who wears Mum's plain gold wedding band, told Nic to keep it sparkly with a monthly bath of half hydrogen peroxide, half Windex solution, but that was typical Michelle over-fussiness. Dishwashing liquid, warm water, soft toothbrush, good as new. She'll do it tonight while watching *Married at First Sight*.

Like the peeling polish on her left index fingernail. A raw pink spot at the edge of an otherwise perfectly glossy lavender finish. How long had it been that way? All day she looks at her own hands without seeing them. Product-scanning robots. Only on the walk home do they become part of her again; only now can she see their messiness and feel the shame of it. She should have expected this. The lavender polish had been gloopy and her usual solution of acetone drops had not sufficiently thinned it. She'd known it and now look!

Like the mustard-coloured envelope slipped under the windscreen wipers of a shiny black Jeep in the no-parking zone outside of the nursing home. Some people had so much money they treated a ticket as a minor fee for the convenience of parking wherever they damn well liked. Never used to see those kinds of people in Leichhardt. The owner of this car probably didn't even know anyone in the home. Another scavenger tracking which old ladies were due to die next, leaving their unrenovated 1960s houses to be bought cheap, flipped and sold within a month for millions.

Nic plucks the parking fine from beneath the wiper blade and drops it into her handbag, next to the empty Coke bottle from lunch and the Thermomix pamphlet from the pop-up stall outside the shopping centre toilets.

If she walked home at night she would not see treasures like the doll's bonnet (she at first thinks *baby's* bonnet, but not even a newborn's head could be so tiny, surely?) that winks at her from under the swings in the pocket park three doors from her house. It must have been dropped only that afternoon, so unblemished by dust or dog piss or cigarette ash is the white brocade. When she holds it up close, she can see that a length of shiny satin ribbon meant to act as an under-chin tie has been attached to each side, but unevenly and in a jagged stitch. A handmade bonnet, imperfectly made but so clean and crisp it hurts her heart to think how the one who sewed it would feel about its casual discarding. She pulls a scrunched plastic bag from her jacket pocket, shakes it smooth and gently places the bonnet inside.

So much she would miss if she were to walk home in the dark with only the too-far-apart streetlights to guide her.

The letterbox is satisfyingly stuffed. Nic sifts through the pile as she approaches the front door: new catalogues from Target and Bunnings and Aldi, a voucher book from a local pizza shop and a couple of real estate ads. Rosa D'Angelo's place down the street has a price guide of $2.2 million. Rosa used to wrap her torso in newspapers to keep warm during the winter. The last time Nic visited, a month or so before Rosa died, there'd been a pot of beef bones boiling on her stove. The butcher gave her the bones for free because her late husband had worked with his grandfather forty years ago.

Shouting rudely from among the real estate brochures is a page torn from a school exercise book: perfect, pale-blue lines marred by angry block letters.

PLEASE STOP FEEDING STRAY CATS!!! IT MAKES THEM GATHER IN OUR STREET AND THEY FIGHT AND CLIMB ON OUR CARS WHERE THEY LEAVE MARKS. I KNOW YOU THINK YOU'RE DOING A NICE THING BUT PLEASE THINK OF YOUR NEIGHBOURS.

THANK YOU!

Instant heat, like she's sitting under the hairdresser's lamp. Thought she'd seen the last of this nastiness when she quit the neighbourhood Facebook group. She reads the note over, rage rising. Anonymous, too, the coward. She returns to the letterbox, glares a challenge up and down the street. Nobody is out. Nobody watching from behind glass, either, far as she can tell. Well. When she figures out who it is she will *anonymously* dump a tin of Fancy Feast chicken liver on their precious car. *Anonymously* scatter dry kibble all over their lawn. Because if it's someone with a car who can't tolerate cat paw prints it will be someone who lives in one of the new places built on the blocks that used to hold two or three houses like hers. It'll be one of them and they all have lawns—showy, tree- and shrub- and flower-less expanses of green. The buzz and whine of mowers around here on Saturday mornings is louder these days than the planes overhead.

Returning to her front porch, she slips the foul note into the middle of the stack of catalogues, smothering the nasty slip of paper with colour and gloss. Imagine being ALL CAPS angry at a sleepy, well-fed cat! Miserable fuckers.

Nic unlocks the door and turns to her side to squeeze through, careful not to catch her clothes or bag on the swinging latch. Inside, she takes a moment to adjust to the gloom. The light bulb blew weeks or months ago, and every day at this time she curses herself for not changing it, but then her eyes recover from the transition and she sidles smoothly past the newspaper stacks and into the kitchen and doesn't think of it again until the next re-entry.

Her niece Lena says that beating yourself up for failing to reach your goals is a waste of energy; recommit or ditch the goal but no negative self-talk about what you woulda-shoulda-coulda. Lena was usually talking about her diet, which week by week seemed increasingly strict and easy to fail at: no sugar, no dairy, no gluten, no artificial sweeteners, no caffeine. If she ate something she shouldn't, she would ask herself: is it important to me to stick to this rule? If it was, she forgave herself the mistake and promised herself she'd do better. If it wasn't, she would decide to ditch the restriction.

Lena had never, to Nic's knowledge, made the latter choice, but that doesn't mean Nic can't. To hell with changing the hallway light bulb, she decides, edging her way through the kitchen. If it worked she would only worry about forgetting to switch it off, then worry about the electricity bill being even more than it was already.

She feels immediately lighter. Lena's been a wise old thing since she was a baby. Proven by the fact she's always liked me more than her own mother, Nic would say if either mother or daughter were here right now. Lena would tell her not to be such a bitch, but wouldn't mean it; Michelle would laugh, and she wouldn't mean that either.

Nic adds the catalogues to the stack beside the microwave and the vouchers to the one on the front left hotplate. She puts today's newspaper on the kitchen table, where it slips about for a few seconds before settling nicely. It would sit on the kitchen table until she had a chance to finish reading it, and if that hasn't happened by bedtime she will put it with its colleagues in the hallway, waiting for a day when she has more time, better concentration.

Nic opens her handbag, sees the plastic bag within, thrills at the baby doll bonnet. The problem, though, is where to put it. It is such a new and special thing that it has no place.

The kitchen is out of the question. It's for paperwork and food containers and recipes and medicines, for things that need processing or dealing with or eating or discarding, for life's ephemera (a word from Lena's vocabulary homework a decade ago and which Nic loves so much she uses at every opportunity).

She scuffs her way through to the living room, holding the bonnet in both hands. It would be safe from physical harm atop one of the towers of DVDs or VHS tapes lining the right-hand wall, but it'd be lonely surrounded by hard plastic with only the dull grey popcorn ceiling above. The toy crates were a better choice. There, the bonnet could nestle against other things made to be fondled by tiny hands, other things left behind by a child too spoilt or ignorant to appreciate what she had. The top toys on the top crates had views clear out into the street—or would if Nic opened the curtains. Even with them closed, they were able to enjoy the filtered sunlight for much of the day and the friendly glow of the streetlights after dark.

Nic lays the bonnet on top of the centre crate, which is full enough that the new addition perches like a crown with the clear air and views it deserves. She takes a careful step back. Something is making her heart hammer. What what what what? She returns to the crate. There! Little Bo-Peep with her crinkly blonde hair and wonky staff lined with tiny teeth marks is suffocating! Nic snatches up the bonnet. 'Sorry, sorry.' She repositions the doll, tiny chin on the edge of the crate so she is looking out to the street. 'I was only resting it there, to see. You're okay now.'

Bonnet in hand, Nic surveys the room as her heartbeat returns to normal. The TV cabinet is for trophies and ornaments, vases and decorative jars. Pretty things, yes, but hard: all metal, plastic and glass. Any of the sofas in here would make appropriately soft beds for the bonnet, but it is such a small, dear thing that it would easily get lost among the cushions and throws and blankets.

Back in the hallway she shuffles along the left-hand wall, pausing at the break in the newspaper stacks that leads to Lena's room. She's long thought of it that way, even though it was originally her own room, shared with Michelle, and then, after Michelle moved out and Mum died, it was the guest room and both kids would use it on their sleepovers, first snuggled together in the single bed then, older, fighting over who would get the bed and who the makeshift mattress of couch cushions on the floor. Around the time Will turned twelve, sleepovers with school friends became more attractive than sleepovers with Aunty Nic, and so it became Lena's room, indisputably. Not every weekend, but a lot. Not every night in the school holidays, but most.

Until the horror year. The year Michelle's husband Joe died and Will—sweet, kind, tough little Will, in training to be a child-care worker, for goodness sake!—went to prison. And Michelle, as though deliberately testing how much loss the human spirit could take, swept fourteen-year-old Lena away to live in Brisbane. And Nic had to let her go. No such thing as custody rights to your sister's kid. No matter how destroyed you are by her absence.

She has her back now, though. A serious, fiery twenty-year-old so smart it amazes Nic that the girl would want to spend any time with a dullard like her at all. But she does! Miraculously, she really does seem to enjoy hanging with her old aunty, insisting, now that she is living in Sydney again, that they have lunch together every Sunday.

I should clear this room out, Nic thinks, pushing open the door, taking a cautious step inside. Tell her there's always a bed for her here. It wouldn't be so hard: the rag dolls and teddy bears and lions and puppies could move onto her own bed. The books—well, some of them could stay. It'd just be a matter of sorting through them, so only the most worthy remained. Only enough to fit neatly in the walnut-stained bookshelf, which is itself a beautiful, Lena-worthy thing currently hidden by all the non-Lena-worthy books stacked on and over and around it.

The clothes would be trickier to rehome. Some in plastic washing baskets, moving boxes and black garbage bags, others making multi-coloured soft statues or waterfalling off the furniture. Could she shift some of them to the living room? The lounge blankets wouldn't mind the weight of clothing on them, surely. If she put only woollen jumpers and fleecy tracksuits out there it'd be like blankets for the blankets, wouldn't it? But blankets don't need to be blanketed. It would insult and offend and anyway, if they were gone, if the toys and the books and the clothes were gone, that would still leave the other things, the precious painful needed beautiful awful beloved things over there in the wardrobe in the corner, and what could she do with those that wouldn't hurt them hurt her hurt hurt hurt—

Nic squishes down between the bags. The pillowy weight of clothes presses into her. Cuddles her. It is easier to regain her breath sitting here. *In: one, two, three. Hold: one, two, three. Out: one, two, three.* Lena would not want to sleep here, anyway. It's too far on the bus to get back to uni, where she often has early classes, and too far from the supermarket, where she often works late. *In: one, two, three. Hold: one, two, three. Out: one, two, three.* Meeting for lunch on a Sunday was perfect for them both. No need to complicate things out of nostalgia. *In: one, two, three. Hold: one, two, three. Out: one, two, three.*

Nic rubs the satin ribbons of the bonnet with her thumbs and forefingers. This is too delicate an object for this room of heavy love and heavier pain. The bonnet needs a simpler space.

Breath normal, Nic gets to her feet and steps into the hallway, turns right and, after four more stacks, right again into her bedroom. It's the only space left, save the bathroom, which is unthinkable; all that moisture and heat, the easily spilt lotions and beauty products. The toilet with its gaping maw! No, her room, the best and safest place. Standing here it is immediately obvious. That hook on the wall over the dresser. It once held a painting of a white horse being fed by a girl with a brown ponytail, but that fell a long time ago and now lives somewhere behind the dresser, which is fine because the moment being captured between girl and horse is so intimate and tender it made Nic feel embarrassed to look at it. It made her think of the shock of hate she saw in the big tabby's eyes when it caught her watching while it lay on its side and let its kittens suck on its teats. This is not for you, the cat's eyes told her, and she'd scurried away, appalled at her own trespass. That was how the painting made her feel, and for years she'd avoid looking up at it, but then it dropped itself behind the dresser of its own accord and they'd all lived happily together— Nic, girl, horse and empty hook—ever since.

But now it is evident that the hook is tired of being alone and unused. What is it for if not to support and display something of interest and beauty? Poor thing, sticking out there all naked and unemployed. And here in her hand the thing that would make the hook know she had not abandoned it, only kept it free waiting for its true match.

A burst of happiness surprises her. Like whenever she looked at her buzzing phone and saw Lena's name glowing up at her. She squeezes between the nail salon chairs and steps over a box of records, nudging aside the piles of *Women's Weekly* and *Who* magazines. Holding the bonnet in her left hand, she uses her right to move the fishbowl filled with copper coins onto the top of the stacked jewellery boxes to its left. She assesses the cleared space. Her calves are not as narrow as they once were, more's the pity. 'Sorry, darl,' she tells the unplugged clock radio, moving it to rest on the Sydney Olympic Games commemorative Weet-Bix tin. It looks good up there, and the hair ties and ribbons and scrunchies in the tin will not be bothered by its presence. Perhaps they will feel even safer with that extra weight on top. Yes! Serendipity. Lena's favourite word when she was nine. It felt like this: like joy that had been waiting for you to catch up to it.

Space enough now. She shivers with excitement, lifts a leg experimentally. No, that won't be happening. No way she can get onto the dresser unboosted. She tests the closest pile with her foot; magazines slide against each other beneath the barely applied pressure. She apologises, withdraws. The records are too easily damaged to put her weight on. She could go back to the living room and empty one of the toy crates, but that seems unfair. She has already messed with their serenity this afternoon.

Of course! Like the empty hook, the exercise bike has been hiding in plain sight. Over there, under the window, a little further from the dresser than is ideal, but with only a few shoeboxes, a hairdryer and three small lamps between her and it. Easy. She reaches the bike without disturbing anything. Its bars are a tangle of bag straps, but the seat and frame are miraculously clear. She hoists herself up, sits for a second while she evaluates the task. If she can reach the top of the mirror frame on the dresser she can use it to steady herself as she leaps across. It isn't even as far as she jumps to reach her bed each night, but that is at ground level and soft mounds of clothing form a crash mat if she misses. There is further to fall here and the landing ground a variety of hard, irregularly shaped things.

But that won't happen. The bonnet urges her on. She is standing more steadily than she thought possible on the bike frame. 'Sorry, but I have to.' She tosses the bonnet onto the dresser. Keeping her eyes on the hook, she reaches across and gets a firm grip on the mirror. One foot up on the seat, waits a beat then squishes the other beside it. She wobbles and her heart is going nuts, but she breathes calmly and keeps hold of the mirror, eyes on the hook. Go on. Go on now. And she does, just steps out, and her foot connects with the wood and then the other follows and something clicks in her hip and she stumbles a step and loses her stomach, but then there she is, up on the dresser, eye level with the hook, the bonnet at her feet.

A simple thing from here: she picks up the bonnet, brushes away invisible dust, runs her fingers over the satin ribbons one final time. 'Welcome, beautiful,' she says and drapes it over the hook. Her whole body hums with the rightness of it. Like it's 1996 and she's in the back seat of Tony's Datsun again. Like it's 1999 and she's holding Lena for the first time. Like it's 2003 and she's being held by her dying mother and the fear that she is unlovable even to the woman who gave birth to her dissipates and is replaced with surety of her worth. Some things your body just knows.

Her body, humming like this, alive and delighted, missteps. She is on the dresser and then she is not. She is falling backwards, twisting. On the ground, fast. So much blood so quickly. The sound of the lamp smashing must have been muffled by her flesh, but smashed it has, under her. Into her. Her right ankle screams differently to her gouged arm. Her left leg different again. So many varieties of pain to feel all at once. She thinks about what to do next and then doesn't think at all.

LENA

After two months of perving at Josh from across the lecture theatre, Lena finally managed to speak with him on the way out of Education in the Twenty-first Century one Wednesday afternoon. 'Nice presentation,' she said, and he smiled like someone used to receiving praise and said, 'Thanks. Can't wait to see what you come up with.' She'd done her presentation the week before and had made eye contact with him several times throughout, so his response was a bummer, but on the following Friday he approached her after class and complimented her on an answer she'd given earlier and they small-talked all the way out to the east lawn, where she turned left towards the bus stop and he right towards his college. Every Wednesday and Friday for three weeks they repeated the ritual, exchanging slightly more information each time.

In the fourth week, Josh was absent on Wednesday, but on Friday he came and sat right beside her. Several times he almost brushed her arm with his, confirming her suspicion that if he ever touched her it would be incredibly difficult to concentrate on anything else except the thought of touching him again. The lecture was a total loss, learning-wise.

When they reached the place of their usual separation on the east lawn that day, he said, 'You in a rush?' And without waiting for an answer sat down on the grass and held his hand out to her to join him and she did, like it was a normal thing to do, just take the hand of a man you'd been fantasising about for the last three months and sit easily beside him on the lawn of a university you'd fantasised about attending for the six or so years since you knew it existed and then talk on that lawn with that man as though you were the kind of girl to whom all this was *nothing*.

She missed her bus and the next one, which meant she would barely make it to work on time, and even then only if she managed to squeeze on board the 5.35, which was always packed with city office workers on their glum and pushy way home. It'd be worth it, though. Josh had told her that talking to her was addictive, and then he hugged her long and hard and pressed his impossibly smooth cheek against hers before pulling back and looking into her eyes for one, two, three, four, five seconds. 'See you next week, Harris,' he said, and when she looked back from the edge of the lawn he was still there watching.

At Sunday lunch Aunty Nic had noticed she was buzzy. Forced her to disclose that she was in the grip of a serious and very fun crush.

'We're only in one class together because he's actually a third year.'

'So he's your age then?' Nic asked.

Lena was old for a first year. Not old like the mums returning to uni now their kids had left home or the senior citizens using their retirement to pack in an extra degree; not so old that you could tell just by looking that she wasn't fresh out of high school. Coming from interstate it was easy to glide over the gap. Her answer to the inevitable *where-did-you-go* was a school none of them had heard of and so there was no follow up of *oh-my-god-you-must-know-my-tennis-friend-Janie.*

Admitting she'd spent two years redoing her leaving certificate at TAFE to earn entry to uni was out of the question. And for a primary teaching degree, of all things! A shameful, last resort of a course, according to most of her classmates. The profession you entered because you didn't get the marks to enter any of the good ones. Imagine if they knew how Lena had strived for this. How brain-foggingly, vertebra-crunchingly, wrist-crackingly hard it had been to get these unimpressive marks. The only acceptable thing to say about going into teaching was that you were passionate about education, but, actually, she had hated every minute of school and now she was out the idea of voluntarily going back there and standing in front of a class of kids made her feel nothing but tired. She was doing teaching because it was as close as you could get to a guaranteed full-time job with sick pay and holidays and superannuation. She was lucky the public school system was desperate enough for teachers that even a thickhead like her could make the cut. After two years at TAFE, anyway.

'Nah, Josh is old for his year, too,' Lena told Nic. 'He took three years off after his HSC and travelled. He's been to, like, Italy and Greece and everywhere.'

'Kissed on the dick, hey?' Nic said it loudly, like she said everything, and Lena felt the cafe bristling with judgement. Couldn't bear to actually look around and check.

'Yep,' Lena said quietly, hoping to lower Nic's volume by example. 'His family owns half the state. The country half. All of the soy or wheat or something. I don't know. He lives in the college that all the prime ministers lived in.'

'All except Julia.'

'Obviously.'

Lena pulled up Josh's Instagram page, found the pic of him on horseback he'd posted during winter break. Nic whistled, long and low. Not too loud, at least. 'That's a pair of thighs right there.'

Before that, Lena had never noticed Josh's thighs specifically, but the following Wednesday in class her gaze kept drifting down and to the left, taking in the surprising thickness of them. Most boys here, she realised now, had thighs barely thicker than their calves. Their legs giant khaki-cotton-wrapped matchsticks. Josh had thighs like the boys she grew up with. Footy-playing thighs, but without the bent nose and thick neck that usually went with them. Was it horseriding that did that for him? If so, it must be a regular part of his life. Something else that had never occurred to her: that the photo wasn't a show-off holiday shot, like the one her mum had taken on their only ever trip to Wonderland Sydney, right before it closed for good, her and Will gripping the wheel of the Snowy River Rampage raft with expressions of goofy concentration. Josh on a horse was normal. It was like a picture of her on the stinking 412 bus! What was his life? God.

Also: he dressed exactly like all the other boys from his college, managing to somehow look like he'd just rolled out of bed and put on the first combo of clothes he stumbled over, but also like he could be a men's style influencer on Instagram. But there was no way Josh was buying his pants at the same places as the other boys. A pair of pants to fit his neat waist and cuppable arse would be burst open Hulk-style by his thighs.

A piece of scrunched paper landed on her lap and she looked up into his leering face. 'Eyes up here, Harris. Geez.'

Oh god, oh god, oh god, oh god. She stared straight ahead at the lecturer, resisting the urge to run from the room. To leave the state!

She slid her silenced phone from her pocket and texted Nic: *Josh just caught me perving on his thighs. Now I'm dead and it's all your fault.* Nic wouldn't answer right away; she'd be behind the register still. Just as well. She'd probably text back something really dirty and Lena would lose it. Lose it worse than she already had.

Her screen flashed. New text. From Josh. Shit. She didn't even know he had her number. With the most who-gives-a-fuck expression she could possibly fake, she tapped it open.

Oh. God. Help. Me.

A photo. Of his crotch. Wearing the same palest-of-pale green pants he was wearing today. Sitting on the same fuzzy burgundy-coloured lecture theatre seat he was sitting on right now. Evidently taken in this room, today, while she was beside him trying not to think about his thighs. While he had an obvious—proud, even—hard-on.

Lena shoved the phone in her pocket. It vibrated immediately. Fuck. She held it by her side and glanced down. Josh again: *Obviously don't mind you looking . . .*

The urge to run out of the room intensified and was then overtaken by a hot flash of inspiration. Before she could second-guess herself, she typed: *I was admiring your pants, creep. Kmart's spring collection?*

She kept her eyes ahead. Waited for the buzz which, when it came, caused an echoing vibration between her legs.

Unfortch have to get my strides custom made

Off the rack are too tight in the crotch

Lena shot back a vomit emoji bracketed by eye-roll emojis but was thinking of how three years ago she had to get her year twelve formal dress altered because she'd lost so much weight since she'd bought it in the July sales and it cost forty-five dollars and that was just to take in the waist and bust of a dress that already existed. And also thinking that she couldn't wait to get out of here and take another look at that photo because it *did* look impressive.

Bet you'd like to have a feel

Of the fabric I mean

It's really soft

The fabric is

RUOK ur face is red

The room erupted. People standing and shoving laptops and books into bags. 'Hey, can I borrow your notes?' she said, so fucking nonchalant. 'Some idiot was distracting me and I missed, like, everything.'

'Sorry, Harris, can't help you.' They were walking out together, like always. 'Spent the whole time thinking about this girl I'm into. Maybe you can give me some advice, actually.'

'I can try.'

'So we've been hanging out a bit, after class or whatever. I think she might be interested in taking things further, but I'm kind of nervous about asking her.'

'You don't strike me as the nervous type.'

'That's the thing. I'm not usually. But this girl's different. I can't figure her out.'

'Different how?'

'Well, like, she's super smart, but she hardly ever speaks up in class. And she's super beautiful but seems shy about her looks. Always covering up. Hair in her face.' He stopped and so did she. With both hands he pushed her hair behind her shoulders, then plucked at her sleeves. 'Wears big baggy jackets on warm days.'

The sun had no right being so hot this late in the afternoon. He had no right.

'Sounds as though you don't like her much at all,' she said, stepping back. 'Maybe even wish she was a different girl altogether. Good thing you haven't pushed things further, I think.'

'Harris, I—'

'Gonna miss my bus. See ya.'

On the ride home her phone buzzed, making her stomach flip, but it was only Aunty Nic: *Sorry you died without taking a ride on those thighs, darling. What a wasted life.*

Friday he sat beside her and complimented her jacket and she said, 'Thanks, I love how it covers everything up so no one can see how beautiful I am.' And he said, 'Smart. Otherwise all kinds of creeps might think it's okay to send you crotch shots while you're trying to focus on a lecture.' And they smiled at each other and didn't talk for the rest of class, but afterwards, walking with him across the lawn, she steeled herself with the thought of dying without riding those thighs and slipped off her jacket.

Predictably, his gaze fell to her chest. She was okay with that. Not as busty as the other women in her family, at least not since she'd lost all her chub, but not flat either. And this bra under this fitted V-neck tee gave her cleavage worthy of his gawping. She willed him to keep looking at her tits, but he was too well-trained. He looked up at her face, smiled, but gently now, let his gaze sweep over her uncovered top half.

And there it was: the flinch as he took in the ropy purple keloid snaking up her forearm.

The scar was a Rorschach test. If it repulsed someone, she was repulsed by them; if it excited them, she knew to be cautious. Occasionally she came across someone who was distressed by it and was reminded of her brother Will and torn between irritation and warmth.

'Knife fight?'

'Something like that.'

'Can I touch it?' His hand already reaching.

She nodded and he ran a finger along its length. 'Does it hurt?'

'Nah. It's old.'

'Yeah? It looks kind of fresh. Angry.' He let his hand rest on her arm, purple scar tissue flashing through the gaps between his fingers.

'It wasn't stitched properly at the time so it healed all ugly like that. Ugly but painless.'

'I've got something like that I can show you. Purple, angry-looking, big, ugly thing. But totally painless. Some might even say pleasurable.'

Lena laughed. 'You're such a sleaze.'

'Seriously, though. Thanks for letting me see.' He squeezed her arm. 'I feel like you trust me.'

''Cause I showed you my naked forearm? That demonstrates trust where you come from?'

He smiled, cool as anything, dropped his hands to his sides. 'Hey, tell me something I don't know about you.'

'That's everything. You know nothing about me.'

'Hence me asking.'

'Hmmm, where to start? I'm a first year student at the University of—'

'Where were you born, smartarse?'

She side-eyed him. 'In a rose garden.'

'Okay. Didn't see that coming. Hey, you wanna sit.' It wasn't a question; he was already dropping to the ground.

'It's kind of awful out here,' Lena said. Bushfire haze from the north had settled over the city earlier in the week, making her throat itch and her eyes stream every time she stepped outside. 'I feel like I've smoked a pack of ciggies just crossing the lawn.'

'You city kids are so soft. Where I'm from we run marathons in smoke like this.'

'Explains a lot.'

'Sit down and finish the story, Harris. Where was this rose garden?'

Lena sat, burning eyes and throat be damned. 'My parent's backyard. Mum went into labour during a party and everyone was too drunk to drive so they called an ambulance, but it took forever and I arrived before it did. My aunty and nan helped Mum through it, and Dad sat cross-legged in front of a rosebush and played his guitar. He didn't even stop when I was out. Aunty Nic was the first one to hold me. "Born amongst roses and music. What a happy life you'll have, my love," she said. At least, that's all according to family legend.'

'Your family has legends. Wouldn't have guessed it.'

What the fuck is that supposed to mean? she wanted to say, but that would only make his point for him. 'Oh, yes. Volumes of legends,' she said, easing herself onto her side, so she could look at his face and he could look at her cleavage. 'You could fill a book with stories of my maternal grandfather alone.'

'Yeah? Give me the back-cover summary.'

'Conman, showman, bookie, war hero.' Murderer, she left out. 'He lived twenty lives in his fifty years.'

'He died young.'

'All the men in my family do.' An image of Dad, his face blurred by tubes. Where were they all going? He only had one mouth, two nostrils. Had they made extra holes in him somewhere? 'So the legends foretell and so it is.'

'You mean prophecies. Legends tell of the past, prophecies of the future.'

'Legends can foretell.'

'I think you'll find—'

'Any retelling of past events can also foretell future ones.' She knew boys hated it when you cut them off, but for fuck's sake, he was being painful. She sat up straight, tucking her legs beneath her, looking down at him. 'Like, if I told you that the five o'clock bus had been at least ten minutes late every day this year, you'd agree I shouldn't bother rushing to the bus stop on the dot.'

'But that's learning from lived experience. Legends aren't lived experience. They form a specific function in normalising—'

'Legend has it that the men in my family die young because the women in my family become murderous when mansplained to.'

'As I understand it, mansplaining is when a man tells a woman something she already knows.' He smiled, lazily pulled himself up to sit eye to eye. 'I, on the other hand, am telling you something you clearly don't.' He placed a hand on her knee, triggering an electric pulse direct to her cunt. 'So simmer down, little lady.'

'You're a cocky bastard, aren't you?'

He raised those goddamn eyebrows again, moved his hand so very, very slightly upwards. *Shit.*

'A cocky bastard who's going to make me miss my bus.'

'It'll be late. Legend foretells it.'

'It's already five past.' She moved as if to stand, but also to see what his hand would do. It moved with her leg, sliding to rest on her mid inner thigh. She looked at it there, then looked him right in the face, the smug fuck.

'The next one's not until five thirty-five.'

'So you've got half an hour to kill.'

And then it happened, easy. One instant Josh was looking at her, holding her thigh, and the next they were making out like they'd been doing it their whole lives. After one second or forever he broke the kiss. Kept his mouth right there, though. 'We need to stop,' he said, grazing her lips with his.

'Okay.'

They were kissing again. More intensely, which two seconds ago she didn't know was possible.

Air between them as he rolled away. She couldn't stop herself glancing at his crotch to confirm that what had been grinding into her thigh was indeed a hard-on and not an oddly shaped phone. Her last boyfriend would have shot after two minutes of such hard-core frottage. There it was, though, clearly outlined by the soft stone-coloured cotton of his skinny-fit chinos. *Jesus.* Nakedness would be less obscene.

'We're going to get done for indecent behaviour,' he said, sitting up and holding his knees to his chest, ruining her view.

Lena looked around. There were fewer people on the lawn than usual, thanks to the toxic air, and none of them were paying any attention. Josh was right, though. Another minute and she'd be opening his pants. Two minutes and her shorts would be at her ankles.

'Is your room close?' She knew it was. Millionaires' kids couldn't be expected to walk more than a few minutes to get to class.

'Just over there.' He gestured vaguely. 'But it's kind of . . . Not a great scene right now.'

It'd been all over the news a few weeks back. Vicious hazing of first years and sexual assault as a competitive sport for everyone else. It hadn't occurred to Lena until now that Josh might have been involved in any of that. He was smug and mouthy, but too gentle, too *clean* to be capable of forcing some seventeen-year-old boy to drink beer off his balls or taking his turn raping an unconscious girl slick with other boys' semen. And he'd shown such self-control now, putting a stop to things. No. He slept at the college but was not of it.

'Your parents at home?' he asked.

'Mum might be; wouldn't know. She's, like, ten thousand k's away.'

'You don't live with your olds? Cool. So can we . . . ?'

She imagined for a millisecond walking him the six blocks to her room in the non-college women's-only residence, a character-less, 1970s red-brick complex known variously as Lesbo Manor, the Convent and Povvo House. 'Nah. Housemates. It'd be awkward.'

He exhaled heavily. 'Maybe another time. When your house-mates are out or something.'

Would it be so bad, having him see where she lived? She tried to imagine him in the dim stairwell, eyes straining to adjust after the brightness of the afternoon, nose twitching at the mustiness, hand jolting away from the inexplicably greasy railing. Past the shared bathroom to her door, jiggle the key until the lock gives and then Josh standing there looking at the fold-up card table piled with textbooks and the clothes horse strewn with undies and socks drying under the barely-cracked-open window. The nun's single bed made up with a blue-and-yellow-gingham sheet

29

set which Aunty Nic gave her as a moving-in gift. Over her pillow, the corkboard covered with pics of Mum and Will and Nic and a couple of Dad and lots of Lena with her arms around friends, all of them pulling ugly faces. The cupboard-sized kitchenette that always smelt like old eggs, though she hadn't cooked them there even once.

Josh drummed his fingers on his thighs. Long, long, pale pink fingers with neat, perfectly manicured nails. A lady doctor's nails. She imagined those hands on the stairwell guardrail again, the greasiness that you could feel for hours even though you scrubbed and there was nothing there. She had imagined those fingers sliding into her so many nights. They were always this clean and dry, this unsullied.

He leant across and kissed her, so light it was almost a breath. 'Another time then, Harris.'

'Yeah.'

'Unless . . .' His lips nipped hers as he spoke.

'What?'

'I've got mates in other colleges. Ones they're not surveilling so heavily. We could maybe . . .'

'You think?'

Josh's phone was out and those fingers flying. They kissed until his phone buzzed. Probably less than a minute but long enough for her to decide that she would be fine with doing it in a toilet stall. Happy to do it. Thrilled.

He checked his phone. Smirked. 'Johnno's come through. Good man. He'll meet us there, let us in.'

'What'd you tell him?'

'The truth. That I had a thirsty-as-fuck girl all up on my dick and needed a place to take her.'

Lena flushed with shame. But not so much to wash away the desire. She heard Aunty Nic in her head. *Forget being a good girl. Be a happy girl, Leen.*

'So let's go then.'

On the way, she texted work that she'd been struck with the gastro that was going around. She'd never chucked a sickie before and her manager knew she was scraping by, desperate for every shift. He would believe the lie, no question. She would worry about making up the extra cash after she'd ridden herself sane again.

—

The friend—Johnno—greeted her by name and shook her hand. From the corner of her eye she saw him give Josh a double thumbs-up. Gross that this made her feel proud, but it was what it was.

The room was twice the size of hers and had its own bathroom—she could see the toilet and the edge of an open shower door from where she stood near the built-in wardrobe. The room smelt of vanilla. She heard they had professional cleaners here, every week. Her building had no cleaners and a large fine on moving out if you'd failed to maintain the place appropriately.

When Johnno was gone and the door locked behind him, Josh motioned towards the bed. Of course it was a double, and neatly made: soft-looking navy blue sheets with white trim, a paler blue blanket folded across the bottom. She sat on the edge and began to take off her shoes. Before the first sneaker had hit the floor Josh had half lifted, half pushed her so her head was on the pillow and was wrestling her shorts and undies down. He plunged cold fingers into her, while his other hand unzipped his pants.

'Fuck, you're wet.'

Lena reached for him, but he grabbed her wrist, pushed it over her head and held it there. His fingers pulled out and in an instant his dick took their place.

'Wait.' She held his hip with her free hand, trying to still his thrusts.

'So wet, girl, fucken drippin' for my dick, aren't you, huh?'

'Josh, stop for a sec, please.'

'So fucken juicy in here. I don't know how long I can handle pounding a pussy this wet.'

'Stop!' She braced everything, went stiff as a board. He kept pounding. She slapped his face.

'Fuck!' He jerked away, out. 'What's your fucking problem?'

'You weren't listening! You just started up without—'

'What? A written invitation? Did we not come up here to fuck?'

'Not without a condom, you shithead.'

He exhaled. 'Oh. So you do want to fuck?'

'Yes. If you put on a condom.' She half sat, touched his cheek where she'd slapped him. 'And you've got to listen. You can't just keep at it when I say stop.'

'It felt like you were into it.'

'I was, I am, but—do you have one or not?'

He groaned. 'You're killing me here. I want to feel you.' His fingers on her cunt again, teasing the lips, dipping into the opening. 'Without rubber.'

'You can keep doing that as long as you like. But if you stick your dick in you need to—'

'God. All right!' He strode to the desk, pulling off his t-shirt as he went. He let his pants drop to the floor and stepped out of his boxers as he grabbed a foil packet from the top drawer without even looking. Obviously he'd done this before. Obviously. Stupid to be bothered by that. It's not like she thought he was a virgin or anything. He was twenty-three, had travelled the world. Thought nothing of asking a mate if he could hook up in his bed. Obviously she wasn't the first.

And actually, she decided, as she watched the way he expertly rolled the condom onto his really very impressive dick and strode back towards her on those ridiculous muscular thighs, she didn't care. So she was one in a line. Big fucking deal. It was a line worth being in.

'Okay?' He was back on the bed, pushing her thighs apart. 'Can we do this now?'

He didn't wait for an answer, but he didn't need to. She'd grabbed his arse and pulled him in already. After a minute, he said, 'Take your shirt off. I need to see those fine tits.'

She wrestled her top off and while it was still tangled over her head he popped her left breast out of the bra and started sucking on her nipple. She didn't want him to stop but the underwire was cutting into her something wicked. She shook off the t-shirt finally and managed to unhook the bra. The release was instant and she moaned a little in relief.

'Ah, yeah, look at those fucking things. I wanna see those titties bounce, girl. Get on up and ride my dick like a cowgirl.'

'Can you chill with the porn talk?'

He grimaced. 'But you'll do it, right? Get on top?'

Lena had never done it like that before, but now was a good time to start. At least if he mouthed off again she could hold a pillow over his face.

Okay. Yeah, this was the go. This was definitely the go. She was never going to fuck on her back again. Every stroke in her control, depth just right, speed exactly as she liked it, and he was looking up at her with awe, making a sound in the back of his throat that was actually the sexiest thing she'd ever heard. Later she might ask him to make that noise without touching her because she bet it'd make her come all on its own, but right now she was going to have to speed up and let this wave—

'Yeah, bitch, you really know how to ride a cock. Never ridden one big as this, though, have you? That dripping pussy of yours is gonna get split in two and you'll still keep going because you can't get enough—'

She slammed her hand over his mouth. 'Shut up, you gross shit.' He bit her palm, but softly. She was so close, if he could just not interrupt she could get there. He kept biting at her hand, which was, as it turned out, even sexier than the throat noise. The sexiest thing she'd ever experienced, in fact. No, wait, *this* was, his hand suddenly on her clit, applying pressure exactly as she did it to herself when she needed to come fast so she could get to sleep. She pushed her fingers into his mouth and he sucked and bit them while she came as hard as she knew she would as soon as he'd touched her knee for the first time an hour ago. She covered her face with both hands, smearing her cheeks with his saliva.

Made of jelly now, she let him roll over on top of her and finish with a half-minute of jackhammering and *fucking-wet-cunt-dirty-whore*. He collapsed on her, sweat-soaked and panting, kissing her collarbones and cheeks and eyes. 'Lena, oh shit, oh Lena, oh shit. Fuck, you're amazing. Lena. God.'

———

Back in her room she texted her only real uni friend, Annie:
🍆🔒💋

Wait. What?

☞✊ Josh T. 🎆

Serious? And really 🎆?

💯

Are you home for once? Im coming over right now

👍

———

In the first week of classes, Lena had noticed Annie in all of her lectures but one. Not surprising, she realised later, since most primary teaching students had to do all the same first-year subjects. There were loads of them all in the same classes. But Annie was noticeable in a way none of the others were. She looked like a

35

movie star trying to prove her acting chops by playing a disadvantaged, plain teenager. The casting notes would have described the type they wanted for the role as *stunning but doesn't know it. Despite her threadbare clothes and unbrushed hair, she possesses a rare and striking beauty.*

Even as she thought all that, Lena was taken in. Annie might have been the most beautiful person she had ever seen, but she was also clearly a poor person who didn't know how not to show it. She wore the kind of thin, white cotton t-shirt you bought at the supermarket in a pack of three for fifteen dollars. Her jeans looked like she'd dug them out of the reject pile at the Salvos: early nineties marble-wash and two sizes too big so the waist had to be pulled in like the top of a paper bag. She carried a canvas knapsack that looked like it had been with her right through high school, and used the embarrassing uni-logoed water bottle the student union handed out for free during Orientation Week. Her yellow thongs looked like freebies, too: there had once been a brand name emblazoned in white down the side but the rubber had worn away too much to make it out.

All this gave Lena the confidence to approach her and ask if she wanted to grab coffee between classes and compare notes from week one. During that first conversation, Lena commented on Annie's perfectly painted toenails and Annie said she felt feral if she went more than a week without a pedicure. Lena told Annie that her aunty was the same with her fingernails; she'd go out with no make-up and unwashed hair, but never, ever without polish on her nails. Lena had never understood why she cared so much about that one detail, but seeing how Annie's immaculate grooming made her clothes and shoes into necessary but irrelevant wrapping was revelatory. Perfect nails on top of an expensive outfit made you look like you were trying too hard, but on someone who clearly didn't care about (or couldn't afford) nice clothes they gave a touch of class, a promise that this was a woman who took care of what mattered.

After that first meeting, Lena and Annie often sat together in class and at lunch, grabbed coffee between lectures. When they had to work in pairs or groups in tutes they looked to each other at once. Several times they'd hit the uni pub together, and on two of those occasions chucked up almost in unison on the way home. Home being Lena's shitty room, which was where Annie crashed on the pub nights, complaining that it was too far to her own *digs*.

It took Lena months to learn that Annie had a studio apartment in the city, in a new, prestigious, luxury security building with a basement gym and a rooftop pool. She made this discovery after the two of them had carried their friendship out of the university for the first time and gotten messy drunk in a city dive bar offering three-dollar shots to ladies until midnight. Lena had been too smashed to notice the outside of the building Annie led her to, but sometime between stumbling past an indulgently smiling, avuncular front desk attendant and emerging from an impossibly long elevator ride directly into a room with a view of the Harbour Bridge, she sobered up enough to realise Annie was a fucking fake. What kind she didn't know. Like, was she an upper-class sex worker or was this a *21 Jump Street* sitch?

'What the fuck?' she asked, and Annie laughed as though they were both in on the joke. She explained that her parents paid for the place. The family home was only over the bridge, but they wanted Annie to have the independence of living out of home. Without actually living on campus, with all the orgies and drug rings, obviously.

'Or the cockroaches and lukewarm showers,' Lena said, and Annie fell about laughing again.

'God, imagine if they knew I stayed in your res! They'd hold a fricking intervention. They don't get that you can lively simply and be, like, fine.'

And Lena finally understood that she was not the one who had magnanimously befriended the clueless poor girl.

But by then they were involved in joint projects in half their classes and, anyway, really did kind of like each other, and so they'd stayed friends, even though Lena avoided going to the uni pub with Annie so as to never again have to see her soft bare feet with their immaculate—*professionally*, not home-pedicured—toes padding over Lena's mysteriously, stubbornly sticky floor to reach the never-fully-dry shared bathroom to piss in the never-not-stale-smelling toilet.

Annie didn't seem to notice the change in dynamic. She kept being the same friend to Lena she'd always been. Which made sense, since she'd always known who was who and what was what between them. It was Lena who had to catch up, act natural, as though talking about her scummy, desperate college hook-ups to someone who'd lost their virginity to an actual baron while on international exchange in Germany was normal.

But now, Lena felt so fucking good, so fucking *right* with the world, that she'd happily invite the whole of Annie's extended family into this shitty room. Who cared what your place was like when you'd just been fucked like a goddamn queen?

For her part, Annie seemed unbothered to be back on Lena's creaky bed, her hair swishing against the grimy wall. Seemed extremely bothered by the fact Lena had been expertly laid by the hottest member of the Australian squattocracy.

'Look, I'm happy you got yours, Leen, I really am, but the thing is? Every boy in that college? A literal dog.'

'Absolutely positive it was a human man I just rode.'

'Nope. A literal dog, generated by a long, long line of literal dogs. That's how they're so good at tricking people into thinking they're human. All that knowledge passed down from dog father to dog son. I feel responsible, I really do. I knew you were crushing, but if I thought you'd move this fast and . . . Well, it's done now. Just put it down to experience and move on with gratitude that he didn't give you chlamydia or something.' Annie's eyes widened and she lurched forward, her always-straight back like a gently falling plank, the front of her paper-thin white t-shirt hovering millimetres over the bedspread as she gripped Lena's knees. 'Shit, Leen, what if he gave you chlamydia or something! You need to get tested, like *now*.'

'Oh my god. Calm down. We used a condom.'

'I would seriously get checked anyway. Those boys are *nasty*.'

'I actually can't believe how much you're flipping out over this.'

'I can't believe you're not! You know what they're like over there. The whole country knows what they're like. A bunch of shit-smearing, bullying, racist rapists.'

'Not all of them. Not Josh. If you knew him you'd see that.'

'I bloody hope you're right.'

'I am. Believe me. I'm an excellent judge of character.'

Finally a smile. 'You did befriend me, after all.'

'Exactly.'

'Okay, slut. You've got the night off work and a fine post-orgasm glow. We going to get hammered or what?'

Having skived off work she would be broker than usual next week. But that was next week and Annie was right: she was glowing, didn't even need to look in a mirror to know it. Time to celebrate her Josh-infusion.

NIC

There is something under the bed that she cannot make out. It's silver-ish. Silver but dull. Silver but dull is grey, isn't it? This thing is not grey, though. Silver, yes, and sort of sharp-looking? Two sharp points she can see over the top of a box she has not looked in for years. Not sharp like knives; sharp in shape but not likely to do any damage. Plastic, probably, which explains the dullness of the silver. Dull colour, dull blades. Okay, yes. Silver, plastic, two sharp points that appear not to be smooth along their sides. Little nodules or bumps or—

How could she have let this happen? Let it get so she doesn't recognise one of the things in an instant. Shouldn't even need an instant, should know with her eyes closed and in another room—out of the house even—what each of the things is and where it lives.

Tears tickle her cheeks but she cannot move her arm to wipe them away. Hasn't this already happened? The crying and the wanting to wipe the tears and then the flashes going off inside her head and the learning that moving is not a thing she is supposed to do. If she does her brain will cancel her consciousness. But if she can't move her arms, maybe she can flop her whole body over so at least she'll be on her belly and might have a better view of the forgotten thing. Upside down and sideways of course it made no sense. Nic tells her body to roll and it does and the flashes are red and when she next remembers she was trying to see the object better the room is dark and she can see nothing except inky shapes.

She wakes with the light and right away she knows she is looking at the Princess Diana 1983 Sydney tour souvenir tiara. A morning like this one, the rude brightness making her squinch her eyes. Mummy singing, *We're off to see the princess, the princess. We're off to see the princess, and the princess will see us* as she arranged Nic's hair in the kind of elaborate looped braids that she was daily envious of other girls for having, that she had never considered for one second her own mother could make. Mummy's hair was freshly blonded and pushed back off her face with a black velvet ribbon. She wore blue eyeshadow and pale pink lipstick and a high-necked white lace shirt. *You look like a famous lady*, Nic said, and Mummy laughed and kissed her face and she felt like a girl on TV.

It took so long to get to the Opera House, on and off trains, and all the time Mummy singing that little song and not even caring that people were staring, and then it was so long waiting in the sun with sparks shooting off the water at her eyes and she was scared she would wet herself like a baby and scared she'd miss the princess if she told Mummy she needed to wee. Finally a roar went up and Mummy was jumping up and down and squealing. All Nic could see was adult knees and calves and she began to panic, but Mummy laughed and said, 'It's okay, Nicky baby,' and bent low so Nic could climb on her shoulders, but it wasn't like with Daddy, the clambering and then the tummy-flipping fast swoop upwards. She didn't say that, though, because talking about Daddy made Mummy sad and angry at the same time and today was a magical day of joy, even if Mummy was currently saying swears as she stumbled, still crouched, to the side and almost dropped Nic when she tried to stand. *Please, let me help*, a man they didn't know but who was standing very close said, and Mummy told Nic to pop down and said, *Oh, that's so kind, she gets heavier every day*, and then the man crouched and she had to climb on his weird wide shoulders and balance herself by touching his hair that looked wet and felt like two-minute noodles straight from the packet.

Has there ever been a disappointment like that first one? She looked and looked, searching for the princess with golden hair piled high on her head and a dress so sparkling it would hurt to look at it. What she saw, finally, was an ordinary lady, with hair like Mummy's and a dress like Nan would wear. *You're much prettier than the princess*, she said to Mummy and the man said, *She's right, if you don't mind me saying*, and Mummy giggled and then the princess was out of sight and the man said, *The trains will be packed for the next little while. How about we have a drink?* And so they went to a dark shop and Nic was allowed to go to the toilet with Mummy (as she remembers this she notices her crotch and thighs are wet and cold and she realises her bladder must have

43

let go) but then she had to wait outside while Mummy and the man drank wine. The man gave her five dollars and told her she could buy anything she wanted, but he didn't know she already had three dollars from Nan in her pocket and that is what she used to buy the souvenir tiara from the table covered in glitter and streamers. She put it on her head and then she used the man's five dollars to buy the biggest Pepsi you could get and the biggest bag of red frogs and the biggest bucket of chips, and she ate and drank it all and then vomited all over the man's feet when he and Mummy came out after a hundred hours. On the train home Mummy cuddled her and kissed her forehead and said, *What a beautiful tiara, aren't you a lucky girl,* and she thought how she would have to keep it very safe so Daddy could see her wearing it when he finally got home.

Not the kind of thing you forget if you are not an out-of-control, stupid, thoughtless woman. Her oldest thing, probably, if you don't count the ring and photo albums she inherited from Mum. Her oldest own thing, that she had managed to protect from Mum and Michelle all through childhood. (Where was Michelle that day? She would have been four or five, must have been with them. Nic cannot remember her presence at all.) It was so small and brittle and yet had survived almost as long as she had. Though her current situation had revealed unknown levels of breakability in her own structure and it was becoming increasingly likely that the tiara would outlast her in the end. The soon end.

—

There are other things to remember with while she waits. A handbag squished between the end of the bed and the washing baskets filling the space from bed to cupboard. When had it fallen and why hadn't she noticed? Burgundy leather—real leather, soft all over and softer still in the creases. Lots of creases because it had lived a long life before Nic rescued it from a garage sale three blocks away towards the shopping centre. It had been shoved in a cardboard box along with a man's striped business shirt with all the buttons missing, a pale pink satin negligee with lace trim and a matching pair of old-fashioned fluffy mules, a white cotton apron printed with large, bright oranges, and a child's painting smock—yellow, and speckled with all the other colours. Nic had been planning to take only the handbag, since its opened zipper— a silent screaming mouth—had called to her, but halfway across the lawn towards the payment table she felt the terrible pull in her guts that meant she was doing something wrong. *Listen to your gut*, Mum always said, and Nic had never gone wrong doing so. She returned to the box, placed the handbag back among its friends, carried the whole thing over to the table.

'How old are your kids?' the man said as she handed over the ten dollars.

'No kids.' Confused but not offended. 'Niece and nephew, but they're—'

'Ah, you're vying for best aunty award, hey?'

She smiled, didn't know why. At home, examining each item more carefully, she understood the box was for children to play dress-ups and she flushed with heat. Imagine if she'd told him her niece and nephew were teenagers and lived in another state. He'd have known her for what she was. Childless old dope, buying other people's junk.

She'd sat for a bit, stroking the burgundy leather. It soothed her, made her sorry. Not junk, not at all. *Magic.* She could see the sweet baby calf in the green field, huge eyes blinking up at its mama as it feeds, grows tall and wide and strong, the farmer protecting its skin from insects and barbed wire and brands, and at the end of its life, the cherished, perfect skin is turned over to artists to create their tribute. A whole team of people working together for weeks or months, tanning and treating and dying and stretching. Brushing and buffing and stitching with such tenderness. How much time passed between the birth of that calf and this moment? How much labour and care and ingenuity and skill? When she stroked it, she felt the traces of all those other hands. The wonder of that!

And the smock—she shook it out in front of her with one hand, the other still resting on the leather—better than any piece of art she'd seen hanging on a wall. She could see the woman who bought it new—a young mum she'd have been, maybe twenty or twenty-one when she fell pregnant, and still fresh-faced and smiling as she chose the smock her suddenly hip-height baby would pack in a small green backpack for her first day at school. She could see the child: looking like Lena at five, hair always stringy, cheeks always red, chubby arms and legs always in motion. This child who looked like Lena but wasn't her, proud as punch slipping the yellow smock over her head to get busy with the work she'd come to this place, the *school*, to do. But then—disaster! She becomes distracted by a table mate's impossibly pretty painting of a horse and she allows her paintbrush to drip drip drip bright blue all over the yellow smock. Panic swells and tears start but then the teacher bends down and holds her hand and tells her that the smock is *for* getting paint on. And she remembers that's exactly what Mummy said and so must be right. Still . . . it seems wrong to allow paint on your clothes. A test, then. With the teacher smiling on, she deliberately drags the brush over her belly. The girl across from her says, *You're in big trouble now.* But the teacher laughs and says, *See? It's fine. Now get back to your painting and don't worry anymore about the smock.* And she paints a horse that isn't as good as the other child's and then a dog that is white and fluffy and then green trees and then purple ones because she can. At the end of Art Time her smock is prettier than it was when she took it from her bag and she can't wait to tell Mummy how well she did.

Imagine throwing that out! It hurt Nic's heart to think of the iciness that hid inside even the warmest-looking people sometimes. Thank god she had found the smock, could make things right. She would frame it. (There was a frame in Lena's room just waiting for the right thing to fill it, another smaller one on top of the TV cabinet. She would introduce the smock to each, see how it fit, see which brought out its cheerful yellow background and bold globs of paint better.)

The negligee was too small for her but she had been planning to try the paleo diet thing a work friend was doing and then she would feel more confident about flirting back with Jase and possibly even bumping bits with him and wouldn't this sexy little

47

pink thing be perfect for that? It was as slippery as the handbag was soft. She imagined Jase's hands sliding over her body, how he'd comment on the smoothness of her curves. She would be wearing the mules, too, of course. They were a little tight, but she wouldn't be taking a hike in them; just a ride. Ha. And after, the man's shirt. Nothing sexier than an unbuttoned man's shirt over a naked woman. Tony said that once when she had chucked on his green-and-white-striped McDonald's uniform shirt to cover her chest while she held her own top, which had been soaked in beer kicked over while they were going at it, in front of the car's heater to dry.

And the apron, ah, well she would save that for when the kids came back from Queensland. She imagined their sweet little faces (oh, not so little anymore, fine, but still sweet) looking up from their places at her table as she presented them with the home-made apple pies she'd baked specially for them.

A sob is stuck painfully somewhere deep in her body, caught on broken bone or flesh. The night of the garage sale she washed the negligee and the shirt and put them . . . And the mules are . . . The apron is in the kitchen, surely, waiting for the day the kids return. But when had she last seen it? She scans the room in her mind: where are those bright oranges? Buried under what? For shame, for shame. The painting smock had never been framed. The frames she tried were all wrong and she had planned to find another. In the meantime she'd put it . . . put it . . . Ah! Yes! This she knew. The painting smock is in Lena's room, folded on the top of the bookshelf. When she gets up she will fetch it immediately, hang it on the wall frameless, its utterly beautiful self.

When she can get up. For now, to ease the shame at having misplaced the other beauties from that day, she gazes at the burgundy handbag. It deserves better than being squished in there, but it seems unharmed. If she could reach a little further, skitter forward a tad, she might be able to touch it. She heaves, that unexpressed sob punishing her attempts. She heaves again and stops.

LENA

On Saturday morning, hungover but feeling happier than she had in forever, Lena texted Josh from bed: *I had heaps of fun yesterday*

Texted Nic: *So much to tell you tomorrow. Thigh-boy* 👍

Texted Lou, her best friend back in Brisbane: *U know the boy I was telling you about?* 😺💀❄️

After a minute, Lou answered: *YES GIRL*

After three damn hours Josh replied: *Same*

It wasn't until she was falling asleep after a whole afternoon and evening of trying to study while frantically texting with Lou and Annie about that one-word text from Josh that she realised she'd never heard back from Nic.

The message tone of her phone woke her at 3 a.m. She read Annie's text with one eye still closed. It made no sense. She opened both eyes and read it again: *fuck leen shithed recoded u*

Another message: *some1 sent to Mo he showd me*

cant see face but must of told bcos every1 here saying its u

here @Lawsons

I told every1 bullshit that as if ud fuck him but they know ur my girl & Im cryin a bit so obvs

Lena put her phone under the pillow and sat cross-legged in the dark, ran the mangled messages over and over, willing them to reveal a different meaning.

Josh recoded me.

Recoded me but not my face.

Sent my recoded body to Mo.

Everyone knows it's me.

Who has been recoded.

The recoding is making Annie cry.

Because I'm her girl.

Not Josh's girl, because he is the one who did this.

What did he do? She ran her own recording—organic, precious until now—through her mind, saw the thumbs-up between the boys when she and Josh arrived in Johnno's room. Did they both glance to the side just before the thumbs-up? Look at the desk for a split second? Thumbs-up about something there to the side, not about her at all. The desk where Josh went to get the condom. There was a laptop computer and maybe it was open and facing the bed instead of lying flat but who notices things like that in the moment?

She ran to the window and flung it open as far as it would go, which wasn't far at all. For safety, they'd said at orientation. Then, she'd imagined the bible-thick gap keeping danger out; now she saw it differently. She sat on the floor, tried to get enough fresh air from the narrow opening above. When she couldn't stand not doing so, she returned to the bed and snatched her phone from under the pillow.

Seven new messages. At 3.14 in the morning.

One from a girl in her Mathematics and Numeracy tute who she'd exchanged maybe five sentences with all year. *Thought you'd want to know*, with an attachment which Lena clicked on immediately, because whether she wanted to know or not she goddamn well *did*.

The clip was shorter than their encounter had been, the whole video only two minutes and twenty-five seconds, but it stuttered and buffered because the reception in this stupid fucking shithole was rooted. When the thing finally started playing more than one second at a time, it became clear that there had been two cameras in the room. One on the desk, filming the entire thing from the side. Another must have been on the bedside table, his phone, probably, angled to film her breasts front on when she was on top. It was a smooth editing job, not just splicing the two different angles together, but seamlessly excising the bit where she stopped him until he put on a condom and when she asked him to stop saying all that nasty shit. He'd also erased the end, where he said her name so tenderly and kissed her neck and face. Instead, there was a three-second scene in which she's in the background pulling on her undies. He faces the camera, sweaty-chested, dick hanging, face covered by a giant smile emoji. He holds up seven fingers, turns to look at her arse, then shrugs and folds one finger down. An animation of a bikini-clad woman holding a scorecard bearing the number 6 fills the screen.

Lena replayed the video, muting the sound this time. It was remarkable that he'd managed to keep their faces off camera throughout. No amount of editing could achieve that. Some serious thought had gone into the camera placement and choreography. She could see now how he kept repositioning her so that her body filled the screen and her face—though not the back of her head with its wildly swinging ponytail—was always out of shot. Was this intended as a kindness or as protection against legal action? How would that work? You can't tell it's her so no harm done?

In either case, he was clearly as big an idiot as he was an arse-hole. For a minute and twenty-nine seconds he has her grinding away on top of him, and for at least a third of those eighty-nine seconds, the footage is taken from the side so the goddamn instantly recognisable keloid scar is rippling its way up and down her arm.

Her phone kept dinging. She switched it to silent; it buzzed and buzzed. She read every message, answered none. At ten she showered and washed her hair and got dressed for lunch. If anyone knew how to deal with a catastrophe like this it was Aunty Nic. Of course, it was possible that on hearing the story Nic would catch a taxi out to the college to saw Josh's balls off with her nail file. Lena would do her best to discourage this, but only because she would miss this weekly lunch if her aunt was sent to jail.

Lena was early, which was not unusual. It was also not unusual for her to be late, such was the reality of Sydney buses. Aunty Nic relied on the buses, too, and so was always either early or late as well. Today she was late. At five past, Lena allowed herself to check her phone. Twelve messages but none from Nic. At quarter past she checked again—six more—and then shot a text to Nic to check she was close.

At 12.20 she tried to call, but the phone went to voicemail. The waiter hovered. Lena sipped the water he'd brought when she arrived. She spent ten minutes deleting obscene messages from her Facebook account, then another ten going through her friends list and deleting any randoms. Every minute or so the phone would buzz to let her know someone else had messaged her. If it wasn't from Nic—and it never was—she deleted it unread. The place filled up with couples and families and the scent of garlic and onion and roasted tomatoes. Lena tried calling again—straight through to voicemail. She opened the Transport NSW app, hoping to find a notice about a strike or major roadworks on Nic's route. For once, it seemed all the buses were running on time.

Annie had watched the video, obviously, before she'd texted in the middle of the night. Annie who had shiny black hair like in a shampoo commercial and perfectly arched eyebrows and not a single other hair on her body. Annie who didn't let herself orgasm during sex because it would mean losing control in front of a man.

Who else had watched it? Who else that she knew, that knew her?

The waiter asked if she wanted to order yet, his glance moving between her empty water glass and the empty chair across from her. Lena told him she would wait and his expression was pure hate but only for a split second before it morphed back into professional blankness. When he was gone, she called her mum.

'Is it the end of days? A blue moon? What is this miracle occurrence, a phone call from my daughter?'

'Hilarious, Mum. I just wanted to know if you've heard from Nic lately.'

'She calls even less than you do. Why?'

'We were meant to meet for lunch but she's, like, an hour late.'

'Did you call her?'

Lena pulled a face at the phone. 'Not answering.'

A pause. 'Well, you know what she's like.'

'She's very reliable, actually.'

'Nicole? Please. She's so . . . you know.'

'I don't, Mum. But it doesn't matter. You haven't heard from her. That's all I needed to know.'

'Don't be like that, Leenie.'

Lena's nose and eyes tingled. After everything she'd been through the last twelve hours, it was speaking to her mother for thirty fucking seconds that was going to make her cry. 'Mum, I've gotta go. I'll talk to you later.' She hung up, spent a minute breathing the tears away, made an apologetic face at the waiter and fled towards the bus stop.

A text from Mum: *It was nice to hear from you. Wish you'd had more time to talk . . .*

If Mum ever found out about the video, that would be the end. She was the most judgemental and least forgiving person ever, and Josh was *exactly* the kind of bloke her mum had warned her about.

'Never trust a man who spends more time on his hair than you do,' Mum'd say. And, 'Never trust a man whose clothes cost more than your car.' *I don't have a car, so that's everyone*, Lena'd bite back, and her mum would usually say, 'You know what I mean,' but once, after a big fight with the Dick, she said, 'Exactly.'

The thing is, until she started uni Lena never even met any boys like that. She couldn't have defied her mother, in this way at least, if she tried. But at uni they were everywhere. These beautiful, beautiful boys whose hair looked like it hadn't been touched since they rolled out of bed, until you got close enough to smell the expensive wax and mousse and serum. Boys whose t-shirts cost more than her weekly pay. Boys whose girlfriends dressed like the librarian in a shitty teen movie. Either that or like they'd rummaged through the St Vinnie's bin to piece together an outfit. Girls like Annie, who could dress like they were homeless because nobody would ever actually think they were. As Nic said, second-hand clothes were like day drinking, government handouts and having a lawyer: classy if you're rich, proof you're trash if you're poor.

—

On the bus to Nic's place, Lena opened Instagram. A bunch of new comments on her latest post, a photo of her that Annie took on the pub terrace on Friday. The setting sun behind her left shoulder is a fireball burning through dense grey smoke. *Enjoying Sydney's lovely fresh air,* she'd written.

The first new comment said, *u should post box shots here ud have heaps more followers.* The next said, *more tits less face.*

She closed the app. It could be unrelated. Drive-by gross comments were part of being female online.

But the timing.

She reopened the app, deleted the comments and then, after a few seconds, the picture. It hurt; she had liked that one: the flattering apocalyptic light, the way her hair sat just right over her shoulders. The winking now-ness of the comment. But her top was very low cut, her lips definitely pouting.

She scrolled down her older pics. Every photo of herself looked provocative, lips wet and pouting, cleavage showing. She started deleting them one by one; stopped, went to settings, deleted her account.

If only you could delete your whole life, start a fresh one, pseudonymous and with locked-down privacy settings. She heard Mum's voice in her head: *Careful what you wish for.* Because she had asked for her life to be deleted, once. She'd been fourteen, still reeling from losing her dad to cancer, and then Mum tells her that Will didn't get a warning like she'd promised. He was going to jail. Like actual adult jail even though he was barely eighteen and sweet and kind. And it just felt *unbearable.* That she would lose him as well as Dad and that she'd have to go back to school, where everyone was already looking at her funny because her dad was dead, and would now look at her like an absolute loser freak because her brother was a crim. She had begged to be allowed to change schools, somewhere far enough away that nobody would know about her. She hadn't imagined Mum'd take her to a whole other state.

It had been better, though. Not good, especially since they had to live with Mum's obscenely fast rebound husband, but better. As Mum explained to Aunty Nic, Lena needed a chance to meet people for the first time without them already thinking they knew her. *I want her to be seen for who she is in her own right, not just the girl with a dead brother and father in jail.* And Lena, who had been eavesdropping from the kitchen, couldn't help it, had to shout a correction: *My father is not in jail! My brother is not dead!* And it was years before she understood that Mum had been talking about herself and Nic: their dad, their brother. They knew what it was to have someone else's reputation precede you.

This was generational progress, then. Well done, Lena. First in the family to go to uni, first daughter and sister to fuck up her reputation all on her own.

NIC

Time is a closed circle. What was that? Something Lena had told her, a line from a book or maybe a TV show, one of those streaming ones that was as entertaining to watch, and took as much concentration, as the business segment of the news, which Nic sat through on her lazier nights because she had lost her remote control and it was only ten minutes to get through between the end of the proper news and the next program.

Lena had explained what it meant over lunch, and Nic had felt at the time she understood and that her outlook would be changed by this understanding. She hadn't thought of it since and now she can't for the life of her (funny expression in the circumstances) remember what it was all about. Still, it loops through her mind. Aren't all circles closed? It's what makes a circle a circle and not an arc, a crown a crown and not a tiara.

Time is a closed circle.

She already knew that time—or perception of time—was relative. Busy days at work last half as long as quiet ones, and the time spent watching TV fled twice as fast as even the busy-days time at work. Except for the business segment of the news part, during which she experienced ten minutes as thirty. But the thing that is happening now, has been happening since she fell, is different. Time is neither fast nor slow. If it weren't for the changing light, and the fact that her crotch is sometimes wet and sometimes dry, she might believe time had stopped altogether. Is that what death is? An eternal present?

She has heard that phrase before, too. Lena again, most likely. How could someone from this family be so damn smart? The girl is a miracle.

The light, and the dryness of her pants, seem to be on a loop, but not everything. For one, the blood was wet and hot and then cold and sticky and has been unchangingly dry for minutes or maybe hours. Not days, she thinks. Probably not. Hunger had whispered and then screamed and then fallen silent, at which point thirst's long-present whine became unbearably loud. It too has gone and not come back.

The pain has not changed much, but she used to feel that escaping it was a matter of urgency whereas now its existence seems inevitable. She knows there was a time before the pain but can't remember what it was like. This, now, is what it feels like to be.

———

There is something about this new way of being that is worse than the physical pain and that is the presence of Steve. He has not existed as anything other than an occasional stabbing thought for over twenty years and she has worked hard to control her exposure to even that version of him. Not because she doesn't love him but because she does, too much, and it is unbearable— people use that word to mean hard, but she means actually not possible to be borne—to have him in her thoughts but not in her life. She has not let him go entirely. She keeps what remains of him in a safe place she can visit every so often when she needs reassurance that he was ever real.

But now here she is and so is he. Not a physical presence, but might as well be. She can see him, although her eyes are closed and he, her older brother, is younger than her, which is confusing and obscene. He is supposed to be a decade her senior, as he was when she met him, a twenty-two-year-old streak of trouble bursting into their family. A product of her dad's early oat-sowing, the adults said, which made her think of her dad in a field, scattering seed and walking away. And Steve sprouting up from there, coming into being, big brown eyes blinking, wondering how exactly he'd come to be alive and all alone among the oats. She never stopped thinking of him that way, a creature brought into the world without care; a boy waking up alone, realising no one is with him, no one is coming.

Poor Steve, who turned up at the door one night, the scrap of paper with their address trembling between his fingers, which had the nails bitten below the quick, just like Nic's. He told them over tea how on his eighteenth birthday his mum had told him his real dad's name. It had taken two years to find him, a few months to adjust to the knowledge the man was in prison, then another couple of years of letters and phone calls before he'd been told about the two half-sisters who'd been living twenty minutes away their whole lives. So here he was.

Mum was kind to Steve, told him he was always welcome, but she didn't ever look at him, not properly. Nic noticed it first, mentioned it to Michelle, who told her she was stupid but then, weeks later, announced it herself as though she'd been the one to see. Announced it to Steve, not to Mum. Steve stuck his finger up, walked out of the room. Nic realised he'd probably always noticed it, the not looking. It was Nan who explained why, though she didn't know that's what she was doing. She met him at Christmas lunch that first year they knew him and straightaway said, 'Geez, you're the spit of your dad.'

Nic saw it then, too. Steve's face was exactly like Dad's face in the wedding photo Mum kept in the top drawer of her bedside table. It was the only photo of Dad in the house. She was sure. She had looked and looked. And even though going into Mum's room when she wasn't home was forbidden, she *had* to, because if she didn't look at the photo regularly she would forget what Dad looked like and then he might turn up at the school gate one day and she would walk right past him! He might start following her down the street and she'd turn and scream at him to piss off, like she'd been taught to do if a strange man bothered her.

Fat lot of good all her sneaky looking had done. She hadn't recognised Dad's face even when it was sitting right across from her at family dinners for months. The good thing, though, was that now she knew the faces matched she didn't need to sneak into Mum's room to remind herself. She only needed to look and look and look at her half-brother. Her *brother*. She gorged herself on his face the way he gorged himself on Mum's spag bol. A few times he asked her what she was gawping at and she said the truth, that she was gawping at his face. He told her she was a weird kid but he said it in a voice that meant he loved her.

Her intimate knowledge of Steve's face meant she was the first to know something was wrong. Long before Mum noticed money missing from her purse, long before the TV and video player disappeared and they didn't hear from Steve for weeks, before Michelle came home and found him on the floor and when she woke him he sicked up on her and called her the worst names, long before Mum changed the locks, told him she could help him find a rehab place but she couldn't let him put her girls at risk any longer. Long before all that, before his skin turned grey and his eyes yellow, Nic knew something was wrong because his face went from being an open door to a closed one. She hadn't known you could do that, become private from the inside out.

The last time she saw him she asked him straight out to *let her in*. She hated the way it sounded like something from bloody *Home and Away* but she didn't know what else to do. Years of hinting and hanging around and hoping hadn't made a bit of difference. *I want to help but I don't know how,* she'd said. They were sitting on the red-brick fence outside of the block of flats he said he lived in. He never let her inside and she didn't know if it was because he didn't actually live there or he did and it was too awful to let her see. *If you'd just tell me what's going on with you,* she'd said. The TV-soap words brought TV-soap tears. *Please, Steve. Let me in.*

But she was alone in the scene. He went further inside himself and everything she said after that made more space between them.

———

There is a new sound breaking through. New and familiar at the same time. Nic concentrates, trying to make sense of its rhythm and pitch. *I know this.* Too fast to be her heartbeat. Too far outside of her body to be an intensification of the thud in her head.

It stops. Maybe it had never been. It was hard to know, like when she thought the cats were here asking for their breakfast. She's still not sure if that was real. They weren't in the room, that much is clear, but were they crying right outside, missing their morning delivery, or were they only crying in her muddled mind? She can't remember if it happened more than once, if it was at the same time as the light changing outside. Can't remember anything except the way the sound of them gave her a surge of hope. Such a racket. Someone would notice. And then nothing.

Until the new, maybe not new, noise. A thumping not from inside. Is it still there? Has it always been?

Steve is still here, in her head. She understands why. In those last few years of his life she tried to show him he wasn't as alone as he felt. But he was, in the end. It was a month before he was found. Imagine that. She wishes she wouldn't, but she can't help it. Imagine is the wrong word, implying an act of will: *use your imagination.* She's not using anything, not trying, the images come to her: the hours before his death, the moment of, the hours, days, weeks afterwards. The hours before his death were like this, except she has him with her and he had no one.

———

Her name, loud. Knocking! Obviously, it's knocking. Again and again, knocking on the door. Again and again and again, her name. Nic tries to call in response but this isn't real; only another nightmare in which you scream and scream but nothing comes out.

———

Light and noise and bright, sharp pain. Her voice has returned but different from how she remembered it. Croaky and old. Has time sped up after all? She might be a hundred with a croak like that, with bones shattering into stabbing shards just from the careful prodding of gentle gloved hands.

Lena does not seem to have aged, though it is difficult to tell while her face is all scrunched up. Nic hasn't seen her like this since her father's funeral. Twenty-year-old Lena cries just like thirteen-year-old Lena, with total abandon. It broke her heart. Had done, is doing. Time is a flat circle. Flat. That was it. Of course. Closed! Honestly.

'Time is a flat circle,' she says and Lena stops sobbing, bursts out laughing, but then the laughing becomes sobbing so quickly that Nic isn't sure it has ever not been.

'Try not to speak, Nicole.' A voice she doesn't know, coming from somewhere above the blue gloves. Gentle, calm. 'Concentrate on taking nice, even breaths, okay? Not too deep. I know that hurts. Shallow is okay, but slow it down. In . . . and out . . . In . . . and out . . . That's much better. I need you to keep that going, okay? You can forget about everything else. Leave it all to us. But keep the breathing nice and even, nice and slow. In . . . and out . . . In . . . and out . . . No, we're not sleeping now, Nicole. I really need you to work hard on those breaths for me. It's so important that you . . .'

LENA

Lena spent Sunday night on a camp bed in the hospital's family rest area. Even had the rubber mattress not farted every time she moved, even had the hospital blanket not scratched her neck and chest, she still wouldn't have slept. Her mind was too busy repeatedly forcing her through the nightmare-scape behind Nic's front door. Again and again she relived those first disorientating seconds entering the house behind the officers, wondering why the hallway was half the size it should be; wondering if, like Alice, she had grown gigantic. And why was Donald Duck grinning at her from the living room, his terrible white head seeming to float in mid-air? Something snagged her sleeve and that something appeared to be a mannequin arm but that didn't make sense. None of it did. She stumbled through this space that she used to skip through, elbows colliding with unidentifiable shapes, hips scraping walls that shouldn't have been so close or soft.

And at the end of this bewildering journey there was Aunty Nic, the only member of her family who wasn't neurotic and brittle and *insane*. There she was begging the cops to pass her tiara. The woman Lena had accused of fastidiousness because she carried wet wipes at all times, would whip one out to clean the cafe's spotless cutlery before eating her lunch, another to wipe her hands afterwards—*that* woman was sprawled out, seemingly unbothered by the crust of snot above her lips or the piss stain on her pants. She was extremely agitated, though, that the cop had knocked over a Cinderella-themed lamp with his knee.

While the lamp-knocking cop tried to get Nic to tell him how long it had been since she'd fallen, the other one, a woman around Nic's age, took Lena out to the hallway and suggested they clear a route for the ambos to get through.

'They'll be here in under ten, so no time to be precious,' she said, moving quickly up and down the hallway, switching on the lights of the adjoining rooms. She began lifting stacks of newspaper and tossing them into the kitchen. Lena stumbled her way to the front of the hall and began on the stacks there, lifting as many papers as her arms could hold and throwing them into the living room, where they floated to rest on a Salvos warehouse full of soft furnishings.

The ambulance arrived just as Lena and the cop were pushing the last stacks out of the way. They let her ride along and she wanted to reach out and stroke Nic's face, but her hands were streaked black, her nails gunked up with sticky dust. She'd tucked them under her bum and willed herself not to cry.

By the time Nic had been examined and admitted, and Lena had taken care of the paperwork as best she could and waited another forty minutes for someone to give her access to the family area, she was so exhausted she could barely blink. Yet sleep wouldn't come. If her brain paused its looping of the nightmare tunnel of Nic's hallway it was only to splice in the smiley-face emoji and six fingers from the video. And accompanying the pictures a commentary track, running the whole time:

nastiest bitch in the series yet

tits are good but the rest is 😿

Noise it makes when it cums 🔥🔥🔥

fuck dude cover that wound no one wants to see that shit

A+ serious good bouncing there

Love these whores so cock drunk they don't know whats happening 😵‍💫

look at em titties go

—

Nic was still unconscious on Monday morning. After three different nurses had told Lena to go home, she did, but only to pack a bag with toiletries, a week's worth of undies and t-shirts, her phone charger and work uniform. She wanted desperately to call in sick, but she'd taken Friday off in order to fuck the worst person in the world and store policy demanded a doctor's certificate for missing two shifts in a row. Besides, she couldn't afford to lose another night's pay.

In the end, it was a relief to be busy. A new promo catalogue had gone out that morning and people were stocking up on frozen pizzas and toilet paper like the zombie apocalypse was imminent. There were whole minutes throughout her shift when the porn loop forgot to play. Though it only took a customer looking at her too intently for it to start up again. Was the man buying the maximum-allowed six tins of premium baby formula attached to one of the dripping dicks she'd been sent through the uni messaging system? Was the bloke who forgot his PIN three times and had to yell out to his girlfriend to come and pay the same one who'd commented that Josh wasted the opportunity to *ass-fuck the nasty bitch*?

On Tuesday morning Nic was moved from ICU to a general care ward, which signified improvement. To Lena she looked the same as when they brought her in: bruised, grey-skinned, unconscious. Apparently the nature of her unconsciousness had changed, though, to one in which a standard level of observation and treatment was sufficient. As Nic's *care partner* (or *next of kin*, as the older nurses said) Lena had been allowed to spend as much time as she wanted in the ICU, but in the general ward she had to confine herself to visiting hours. Perhaps she'd like to go home and get some rest? Pick up some of her mother's personal items so she'd be more comfy for the rest of her stay?

She stopped correcting people about her relationship to Nic. No one cared who she was as long as her name matched that next to *care partner* on the paperwork. She also didn't bother explaining that going 'home' to the giant complex of residential, research and educational buildings in which every single room contained a device on which someone was watching her fuck a douchebag would not be restful and that her chances of finding anything that could make anyone *comfy* at Nic's was impossible. Instead she walked half an hour through dry, ashy heat to the nearest Kmart, where she spent next week's alcohol budget on a pair of pink cotton PJs, a six pack of undies, bedsocks, a toothbrush and toothpaste, and hand cream.

Back at the hospital she put away the shopping in Nic's bedside unit, touched her sunken cheek to see if she'd wake, got an unhelpful update (*doing just as we'd expect*) from the ward nurse, then retreated to the hospital cafeteria. She poured herself a glass of water from the green plastic jug set out for customers, chose a table at the back, and sat facing the room so that her screen was hidden from passers-by. Starting with the links people had sent her and then using search terms tagged on the posts, she tracked the video through the internet, saving the address of each site as she went. As she looked, she came across others in the 'series' made by Josh and his college mates. They were all in that same room, that same bed, using the same two camera angles, edited to conceal faces. Lena couldn't bring herself to watch the others in full; she skipped through rapidly to see if any of the women were identifiable. They weren't, to her. But she bet there were plenty of people who knew a girl with a splattering of moles in just that configuration on her chest and that anyone who'd ever seen the lower back of that other girl would recognise the birthmark shaped like a wonky wineglass.

As for the men, Lena was sure none of them were Josh. During the fucking it was hard to tell—especially skipping through fast, as she was—but that bit at the end, the bit she watched in full in every case—showed the whole body, with only the face blanked out. None of them had Josh's thick thighs and narrow waist, none his precise, briefly beloved way of moving.

She hated how jealous it made her to see girl after girl receive 7s and 8s. Hated the glow of relief when a girl got 4 or 5. Hated most of all the sick compulsion to read all the comments, to wonder along with them whether it was the *wild bush* or *bee sting tits* that caused an otherwise hot girl to be marked down or if it was the *power sucking* and *firm ass* that caused a *total dog* to be scored higher.

—

In between following the tracks of her shame, she kept Mum and Will up to date on what was happening with Nic. With Will she could be blunt, but with Mum she had to be careful. The sisters had a relationship Mum described as *volatile* and Nic called *shit*. They'd never been especially close, as far as Lena could figure, but things had only got truly volatile (shit) when Nan died and left the Family Home to her eldest.

Mum and Nic always said it like that—the Family Home—with capital letters. Maybe underlined and bolded as well. You'd think they were talking about some grand estate with a separate wing for each family member and stables and servants' quarters ranging around it, rather than a 1960s two-bedroom brick cottage without even a driveway or inside laundry.

The legend. Lore? *Fuck off, Josh.* The *legend* told that a year or so after Nic and Michelle's dad went to prison for the murder of his friend, a man with a jagged scar on his cheek and a blond ponytail turned up at the rental flat. He gave the girls a bag of chicken Twisties each and their mum told them to watch the cartoons and eat their treat and don't bother the grown-ups. *The Smurfs* wasn't even at the first ad break before the man patted them on their heads on his way out the door and their mum, who had done nothing but cry and talk on the phone since Dad went away, sat on the floor between them and took a handful of Michelle's Twisties and, when she started to complain, she took a handful of Nic's, and she gobbled them both at once leaving yellow dust all over her chin and hands and then sang 'Everything is Going to Be Alright', tickling them both until they joined in.

Soon after, the three of them moved into the house their mum bought with the money the ponytailed man had given her. A house in Leichhardt in 1982 was not too far out of reach for working people, but the Millers were mostly not working people and so a house was beyond their wildest. Fast forward twenty years, Nic and Michelle's mum is diagnosed with stage 4 bowel cancer. She makes a will, signing the house over to her eldest, with the caveat that it would always be there for her other daughter to live in if she needed and that if Nic ever sold it the proceeds would be shared between the two of them.

Michelle was furious. Said their mum obviously felt sorry for Nic because she was clearly Not Quite Right and would never get married or have a house of her own, but why should *she* miss out just because she wasn't a dim-witted old maid? Immediately after the funeral she started pressuring Nic to sell the house so the money could be divided between them. Nic, deep in grief

(*As if I wasn't!* Mum would protest to Lena and Will), declared that it was the Family Home and it would be dishonouring their mother to sell it. She told her sister the door was always open. Told her the kids, especially, would always have a home there. But it would be sold *over her dead body*.

Lena's mum kept track of housing prices in Leichhardt. Every time there was an increase it'd spark another skirmish between the sisters. It was hard not to take Mum's side on this one. By the time they were in their teens, selling the house would have brought ten times the money paid for it in the eighties. Still not enough for them each to have bought a house in Sydney, but a sizeable deposit on an apartment in the outer suburbs maybe.

But Nic held firm. The Family Home was hers to preserve.

The thing was, Mum wouldn't have sold it either if it had been her name on the title. She would've proudly taken on the mantle of Protector of the Family Home. Would have done a good job with it, too, killer housekeeper that she was. Used to drive Lena crazy, the need to iron everything—even tea towels and pillow-cases, for fuck's sake! The way she'd tut and redo the vacuuming if Lena hadn't taken care to do it in straight rows working with the nap of the carpet. If there were streak marks on the windows, on the mopped floors, they'd have to be redone, too. Every shitty rented flat or house they'd ever lived in had perfectly hemmed curtains on the windows, a precisely pressed tablecloth on the table, matching cushions on the couch.

If Mum had inherited Nan's house they wouldn't have had to pay rent all that time Dad was sick off work and Will might not have resorted to selling weed. Which would have meant no prison, no move to Queensland. Lena's interstate uni escape plan would have taken her to Melbourne or Adelaide. She would never have met Josh, never had the correct rating for her imperfect arse become the subject of heated internet discussion threads. The Leichhardt house would be a clean, safe place to return to in uni breaks instead of the stinking, filthy site of her aunty's recent near death.

—

When Mum got angry about the house she believed should have been theirs, the unfairness of it all, Dad would remind her that people who dwelt on the past were scared of the future. He said the same thing whenever Lena or Will asked about his childhood and family, or about Mum's dad or brother.

We don't dwell on the past in this family, he'd say. *We're too excited about the golden future.*

How do you know the future will be golden? Lena would ask, knowing his answer, loving to hear it.

With you in it? How could it be anything else?

It was a spell he cast. Turned the past into a dark fairy tale they need never relive. Why would they when they had made it through to the happily ever after, unscarred and unscathed?

But when the wizard dies the spell is broken. You see that while you refused to dwell in the past, the past has never stopped dwelling in you. You are bursting with it, can't get near the golden future without leaking history all over it.

NIC

Nic wakes and knows she is in hospital. Her mouth and throat are dry but other than that nothing hurts, which is a good sign. Also, though, she can't seem to sit up, which is not so good.

'Good morning, Nic!' A man's voice, young and cheerful. 'What a delight to finally see those pretty eyes of yours.'

'I fell.' The voice coming from her but not hers.

'That's what they tell me. Never mind. We'll have you patched up in no time. Now I'm going to lift the top of your bed a touch and then we'll see if we can't get you a nice cool drink while we wait for the doctor.'

She begins to move upwards and for a terrible second thinks she'll throw up, but then the motion stops and she is looking at the back of a small, dark-haired man murmuring into a blue wall phone. 'Righto.' He turns and smiles. He's older than you'd think from his voice, maybe even as old as her. It's mesmerising how easily he moves: gliding out the door and back in holding a white plastic cup, and across to her bed where he helps her sip it while chatting about the spooky bushfire sky and how many extra admissions they're having down in A&E due to smoke inhalation.

'Pharmacy downstairs sold a month's worth of face masks in one day. They won't help much—wrong kind for smoke particles—but people like to feel they're doing something rather than nothing, don't they? Now, as for you, gorgeous, a doc'll be up to chat with you soon, and tomorrow or the next day you'll have a visit with the social worker. But the absolute priority visitor is the lovely Miss Lena. I'm going to give her a call right now, if that's okay with you?'

'Lena knows I'm here?'

'Lena has been *living* here, watching over you.'

'How long have I been . . . ?'

'Three nights, I believe. And though you probably don't remember it, you've been working very hard the whole time. You are a healing machine, Nic.'

Do machines usually feel this tired? she wants to ask, but she can't muster the energy. She hopes the nurse knows to wake her again when Lena comes.

———

She wakes to someone taking blood from her arm.

She wakes to someone telling her to swallow a pill with water.

She wakes and drinks some tea and a nurse tells her things she should probably care about but can't.

She wakes and notices a TV at the end of the bed, finds the

remote and switches it on, but there is no sound and her eyes close in protest at the tiny white subtitles.

She wakes and the silent TV is showing footage that could've been taken any summer in the past ten years: flame eating into a line of trees, a yellow-clad firey aiming a piddling stream at a wall of blazing bush, a helicopter dumping a swimming pool's worth of water onto a cloud of smoke. The subtitles tell her it's not like any other summer (not even summer yet, not for weeks). On the map they show the east coast as one long fire line, starting less than an hour's drive from where Nic lies and extending all the way up to North Queensland. She tries to remember where Will is, if it's far enough north to be out of harm's way.

She wakes and her girl is right there, close enough to touch, looking like she's swapped sleep for poking herself in the eyes, but still the sweetest sight in the world.

'They told me you'd been mooching around here.' Her voice still unfamiliar, husky. 'Don't you have anything better to do?'

'Nah. Air con, free cups of tea, comfy little camp bed set-up down the hall. Hot doctors. It's been tops.' Lena sounding the same as ever.

'Well, the fun stops now. I'm awake and on the mend. No reason for you to hang about.'

Lena's fingertips on the back of her hand, a millimetre from the cannula. 'You scared the crap out of me.'

'Sorry, darlin'. A lot of fuss about nothing. A silly stumble.'

'Nic, if I hadn't found you, you woulda died.'

'There's my little drama queen. It was only a—' A cough, dry and sharp, stops her speaking for a bit.

Lena pushes a plastic cup close to her face. 'Here. Want me to get you some tea? Might be more soothing.'

Nic swallows some water, coughs again, sips and lets it settle. Whole time Lena watching her like she's going to choke.

'The nurse who was here earlier—little bloke . . .'

'Kon, yeah, he's the best.'

'He said that there'd be a social worker in to see me. Does that sound right to you? A social worker?'

Lena nods. 'Yeah, the doctor mentioned that. They need to do certain checks and stuff to make sure you're not in danger.'

'Isn't that what the bloody nurses are poking at me ten times an hour for?'

'Yeah, but this is . . . It's to do with you not being in danger when you leave here. Because the police had to come and rescue you.' Lena's tone firm, like she's dealing with a scummy customer claiming she hadn't been given the right change. 'They've reported or registered or whatever they call it . . . There needs to be this whole assessment process with a social worker and all that. For your own safety.'

So much heat all at once in her face and chest. 'Bloody ridiculous. Talking about me like I'm a child. Or a geriatric! And to a kid, as if you'd know anything.'

'I'm not . . . You've been asleep and I'm the only one here. Who else were they meant to talk to?'

'It's degrading!'

'Mum said she can fly down if—'

'If I want to be further degraded? Yeah, that's all I need. God.'

'Okay. Is there someone else then? If you don't want me here, I mean? Is there someone else you want me to call?' Tears running down Lena's face and, ah, this is pain right here. Broken bones are nothing. Suck it up, woman. Suck it up.

'No. No. Sorry. Thank you for being here,' she manages to say.

'It's going to be all right. You'll see the social worker, tell them you'll clean the place up, go on your way. This is a blip.'

That last phrase something she has said to Lena many a time. A bad fight with a friend, rejection by a boy she'd been crushing on, the failure to get the marks for uni at the end of year twelve. *This is a blip, Leen. In a coupla months you'll look back and see it in perspective. Your life is going to be so big, and this—this is just the tiniest little blip.*

Lena leaves after a while, telling her to get some sleep. Nic knows she's been doing nothing but, yet she can't imagine how, here, in this room with its cold green floor stretching stretching stretching out between the metal beds, six of them but each smaller than even a single bed should be, not nearly substantial enough to hold their own against that greedy floor, the ravenous space. Even with the various machines and stands and bits and pieces around each bed there is too much nothing, and nothing is *loud*. The corridor leading off in each direction for what sounded like a very, very long way makes it worse. Every word spoken or cried, shoe slapping tile, piss hitting toilet, needle piercing skin is happening right into her ear. The noises burrow deep, gnaw at her bones.

And the bed itself, back to that. Too small for the room, too big for a woman alone. She longs for her pillows and books, her photo albums and soft toys and cardigans and coats and all the other things that have made their home in her endlessly generous and stalwart queen over the years. How long has it been since she'd spent the night in a different bed? Fifteen years? More. The last one she could remember belonged to a bloke she'd gone out with on and off in the early 2000s. Murray. Yes. He was nice, that man. It hadn't ended badly or really, when she thinks about it, at all. That is, there had never been a decision to finish whatever it was they were doing. It just hadn't continued. The eating dinner and sharing a six pack and conversation and then bumping bits together in his bed and waking up in the morning and saying sweet things in embarrassed voices had all been nice. But not nice enough to make an active effort to keep doing it. There had been a last time which she didn't know was a last time. He just didn't call for a while and neither did she, and eventually she realised— as he must have, as well—that too much time had passed for a call to be the easy thing it had once been.

There had been a couple of attempts at finding love since then. None went particularly well nor particularly badly. Just never enough feeling to make it worth the trouble. Beds had been rolled about on but not slept in, not all night, since Murray. She didn't know why. And no men had slept in hers. No men, no anyone, had crossed her doorstep in years.

Until the fall. The uniformed strangers. Lena, crying.

Stop. It's not a thing that needs thinking of right now. The thing that she is thinking of is the experience of sleeping in a strange bed, a strange room, strange building. Not even considering how disturbing it is to be surrounded by all these people: nurses constantly grabbing at you to check this, adjust that; and the other patients, all of them seemingly on different schedules so that the minute after one finally stops the yapping or moaning another starts; and then the visitors who cry or laugh or drone on and bloody on about the most banal bullshit. An hour or so ago there was an old fella somewhere out of her line of sight who would not shut up about a book he was reading. Napoleon this and Nelson that and in between ten different lectures about ten different warships. Normally she'd have yelled at him to pipe down and give 'em all some peace but the fall has knocked the boldness out of her. She feels too small and exposed as it is. A newborn kitten, defenceless against the loud, bright, hugeness of the world.

'That's hospitals for you,' the nice nurse—Kon—says breezily when she complains about the racket. She realises that not only has she not slept away from home in over fifteen years but she has never had a hospital stay. When she was born, she supposes, but not in her recallable life.

Miraculous that she never ended up here as a kid, when you think of all the out-of-date food, car rides with drunk drivers and no seatbelts, scavenged bikes without helmets, cigarettes left to burn out in the living room ashtray, father with a temper enough to kill a man. Lucky, but not so surprising, to have avoided it since. Or unlucky and quite surprising if you consider the reason most women her age had at least one stay in hospital.

Michelle had been in those two times, at least: Will, a tough little sweetheart from the first. Barely cried or fussed from the minute he popped out. Once, when he was a couple of months old, Michelle had come around for a cuppa with Nic and Mum. Will was such a good sleeper, they slid his carrier under the table while they drank tea and chatted. When it was time for Michelle to leave, none of them remembered the new fella, left him sleeping out of sight. Poor Michelle had been in a mad panic, roaring back in after ten minutes to find Nic and Mum watching telly, oblivious to the little bub, awake but silently smiling away under the table still. God, they'd laughed about it later, when Will was old enough to laugh along with them. No trouble at all, this one. You'd forget he was even there. Literally!

Lena, though, she was a different kind of kid altogether. Centre of attention from day dot. Couldn't even wait to get to the birthing suite if it meant missing out on a party. She heard music and laughing and hurled herself into the middle of it all, immediately became the focus, the purpose of everything.

The tea lady had been in earlier. 'Shall I leave a couple of extra bickies for your daughter?' she'd asked, and Nic had shaken her head to say no, because Lena didn't eat sugar or wheat or anything processed, and because, no, she wasn't coming back in today, and, no, she wasn't her daughter.

'Well, I'll leave them in case you want them yourself then, love.'

Love, which is what people called the elderly and infirm. *Love*, coming from someone fifty if she was a day.

At least she'd guessed Lena as Nic's daughter rather than grand-daughter, like one of the nurses' aides did the other night. Not that a woman her age couldn't be a grandmother; she knew plenty who were. But their grandkids were in nappies, their strollers pushed by kids of Lena's age or younger. Either Nic looked sixty or she looked like the type to have had a baby in her early teens and raised that baby to herself pop one out soon after her body was able. She'd prefer the latter. Women who'd had their kids while kids themselves tended to be both fun and practical (except her sister who was un-fun and practical). Mostly they were the kinds of women who would get smashed and sing karaoke with you at 4 a.m. but who also knew how to change a tyre, fight a parking fine and hem a pair of dress pants. So, yeah, not so bad to be in their gang, but Nic knows it isn't what the young aide had been thinking. She hadn't been thinking at all; just looked at the crumpled old lady in the bed compared with the fresh-faced kid on the chair by her side and leapt to the obvious.

Daughter, though, that was nice if people thought that. For a long while she did assume she'd end up a mum. It was just what happened at some point as you grew into an adult. Except if you didn't have a husband or steady bloke and you were getting on, *your eggs drying up, biological clock running out of tick*, as the breakfast shows said; then it wasn't something that just happened, it was something you had to decide on doing and then spend a bunch of money and time on trying to make happen. That or screw every bloke who looks at you sideways, lying that you're on the pill or stabbing pinholes in the condoms. She's heard of women who went about it that way. It was a nasty approach, for sure, but she understood it. People with thousands of dollars for donor implantations and all the rest could afford to be honest and ethical. The likes of Nic needed to be sneaky sometimes.

Anyway, she'd thought about it on and off. Then noticed she only thought about it when one of those segments came on the telly or one of the mags ran a story telling her she should be thinking about it. If she clicked the channel over or flipped the page the thought dissolved. So it didn't happen and she didn't make it happen and here she is, old enough to be a grandmother (to a *baby*, thanks very much) and without much prospect of that ever happening.

When Lena has kids (*if*, Nic corrects herself, while still believing *when*) they would practically be her grandchildren, wouldn't they? Just as Lena is practically her daughter, has been from the minute she was born right through to this week, when she'd sat in the hospital with such dedication and care that onlookers like the tea lady assumed they must once have been of the same flesh. The flesh was irrelevant. Lena was her own child in every way that mattered.

Yeah, bullshit, you sad old cow. If that were true, Michelle wouldn't have been able to take her away for all those years.

—

Her store manager calls in the afternoon. (Is it afternoon? She keeps dozing off and when she wakes the light and noise are the same as when she fell asleep.) Lena has apparently spoken to him already and explained Nic's condition, and he's calling to tell her not to give work a second thought until she's back on her feet. She's hardly taken a sick day in all these years and has a bunch of annual leave accrued, if it comes to that. They can talk about putting her on reduced duties when she's ready.

She thanks him, says she'll be back as soon as she can, doesn't tell him she misses the damn place almost as much as she misses her house. For all the frustration and agitation the shop causes her, it is still the place—apart from home—where she feels most relaxed, most in control. She has her locker in the back, her mug in the kitchen, her own checkout—number 5—which the night and weekend girls know to return to her settings when they are finished. She has seniority and, more importantly, the respect of her co-workers. She is the one they come to first if their register isn't reconciling or they need to change a shift or ask for time off. She can't solve any of that stuff directly, but she knows which manager is the best to approach for which problem and what turn of phrase or explanation will be most likely to get a good result.

She wishes this lot here could see how she is at work, how important and respected. Then they might speak to her properly, let her know what she has to do to get home.

LENA

Nic waking up made Lena feel—for a minute at least—happier than she thought she would ever feel again, but it also meant she no longer had an excuse to stay at the hospital. Awful though it had been, Nic's accident had allowed her to avoid the scene of the crime. Was that too dramatic a way to think of it? No, it felt right. She had been criminally fucking stupid and the evidence of that was being replicated second by second.

The bus was packed and the air conditioning struggled. Three stops past the hospital a blur of children in navy school uniforms boarded as one. The temperature and noise level were immediately unbearable. She needed those noise-cancelling headphones that Annie wore around her neck like a pharaoh's collar. What did a person who could afford to Uber everywhere need with those things? They should be subsidised for everyone who spent more than three hours a week on public transport. Think of the public health benefits of preventing rocketing blood pressure, anxiety and random punching attacks. Like, right now, Lena's blood was pounding in her ears as if in an attempt to block out the vaguely threatening tittering of the school kids, and when a few of them got off and their racket receded, the far worse assault of wet, rhythmic sniffing right behind her head. She wondered if anyone'd ever studied how many strokes happen on public transport and/or in close proximity to someone who doesn't know how to use a fucking tissue.

A woman three rows in front of Lena was watching a video with the sound on full. Buy some goddamn earbuds! Or switch on subtitles. Or, fuck, wait until you get home? What could be so urgent? The sound filtering through to Lena was gibberish, a tinny rising and falling of voices. She imagined storming down the aisle, snatching the phone from the woman, throwing it to the floor and stomping on it over and over until it was just shards of glass and plastic, a tangle of tiny wires.

Back in Brisbane one time, a man diagonally across from her on the train put his legs out on the seat beside her, propped a tablet on his knees and started watching a video. She couldn't see the screen but from the panting and groans it became obvious within seconds it was porn. She was blocked in by his thick, bare legs; nobody else in the half-full carriage seemed to be bothered, if they noticed at all, seeing as most of them had done what this creep hadn't and stuck earbuds in or headphones on. She thought about telling him to turn it down. Thought about standing and making him move his legs. She thought she might be overreacting; it wasn't like he was wanking or anything. She snuck a glance at his face; calm, focused, like he was watching an instruction video: how to poach an egg perfectly every time. Lena wished someone would walk past and see, tell him it was inappropriate. Her mother's favourite word, which always drove Lena crazy but now she wished for Mum and her prissiness, her sense of propriety. *Excuse me, but watching that in public is inappropriate*, Mum would say.

Lena tested the moment out in her mind, watching the inner suburbs fly by. *Excuse me? Can you switch that off? It's inappropriate.* She couldn't get her mind to show her what would happen next. You are not someone who tells strange men on public transport what to do or not do, she thought. You are not Mum, even in this best of ways.

Then she thought, What would Aunty Nic do? And she knew right away. She cleared her throat. The man looked at her, a challenge in his eyes. *Go on, tell me not to watch my porn.* She smiled, lifted a hand, stuck her middle finger up her nose. He grimaced as she turned it around, really having a good old dig up there.

'Filthy dog,' he muttered, closing his laptop.

'Oops. Probably something I should only do in private, hey?'

The man legged it out of the carriage and Lena wiped her hand on her jeans and then texted the woman who inspired her.

Now, on this bus full of sniffers and sneezers, screeching kids and unmuted cat videos, feeling like her head was going to explode, she tried the trick again: What would Aunty Nic do?

No answer, only images: the bruised old woman in the hospital bed; the urine-stained, ranting one, half buried by junk and tat.

While she'd been hiding in the hospital, Sydney's jacarandas had burst into flower and the campus and surrounding streets were flushed purple. The sight of them infused her with optimism. She'd forgotten this about Sydney; how the blossoming of the jacarandas signalled the winding down of the school year, the almost-here summer holidays. This lightness, this buzz of child-like excitement was merely Pavlovian. The sight of the college building Josh had taken her to, disguised as an innocent sandstone backdrop to three giant jacarandas, corrected her falsely lifted mood. There was nothing to look forward to here.

She'd been in her room ten minutes, was preparing to make the trek down the hallway to the shower, when there was a knock on her door. The RA who had run her orientation in February. Julie, Julia, Julianne? A peroxided pixie cut, eighties-style blue eyeshadow. She wore baggy pyjama bottoms, candy pink stripes on a white background. Her yellow t-shirt hung to mid-thigh.

'Lena! You're here for once. Can we chat?'

'Okay.' Lena motioned to the desk chair, perched herself on the edge of her single bed. Her shower bag—an absurd, shiny hot pink sack hanging on a hessian rope, a gift from Mum—by her side. She hadn't turned on the light when she'd come in and the day was fading fast. The dim quiet made it feel like a sick room. Switching on the light now would only encourage the RA to linger. Let her sit in the growing dark for as long as she could stand it.

'So, this is awkward . . .' Juli-whatever looked at her own twisting hands. 'I've been made aware of this, um, this *material* that's circulating?'

Lena listened to her own breaths, in and out. Normal.

'Material featuring you?'

Unprecedented quiet. Why no stomping in the hallway? No shouting from downstairs or hammering on neighbours' doors? No tinny music or shrill ringtones or Skype trills. Not even a bird calling its babies in for the night. She picked up the shower bag, couldn't believe the loudness of the squeak its skin made against hers.

'You do know what I'm talking about, don't you? Lena?'

She wound the hessian rope around and around the fingers of her left hand. Remembered that the RA's name was Juliette-but-you-can-call-me-Jules and that she was from South Australia. It's why her accent was so posh, Annie had said, confusing Lena, who thought that Jules and Annie sounded so alike you would mistake one for the other through a closed door, but Annie was Sydney born and bred. Confused her, too, because why did being South Australian make you speak posh? She realised she knew nothing about South Australia or people from there at all and, as with so many of the things she didn't know, she felt this was a thing that most people *did* know. It wasn't like asking in class for the definition of *metacognition* or *phonology*. It wasn't the kind of question people meant when they said *there are no stupid questions.*

'I know you haven't attended any of your classes this week, haven't been returning to your accommodation. You're not in trouble. I mean, that's not—I'm not here to tell you off or anything. You don't have to be so . . . Look, I'm trying to reach out, Lena. To find out what I—*we*—can do to help you. I spoke to the university liaison and he—'

'Who asked you to do that?'

'I didn't identify you—not that it would . . . It's confidential, anyway. I wanted to find out what could be done for you. He advised making an appointment with the student welfare office. Speak to a counsellor?'

The hessian was permanently wet. What a stupid material to make a shower bag rope from. Never properly dried, its fibres swelling and shrinking, swelling and shrinking, always damp and scratchy. She wound it tighter and tighter; it couldn't be broken was the thing. Her circulation would be stopped, her damn fingers would drop off, before the rope gave the slightest bit.

'Is that something you'd like me to do, Lena? Make an appointment with—'

'No.'

'Okay. So . . .'

It was properly dark now. Lena wanted to say, *Get the fuck out of my room*, but she had never been good at saying things like that. To her mum, to the Dick, to Will, sure. But with them she knew she was in the right. Everyone else, it was harder to know. People in general weren't like her and her family. It made it difficult to know how to handle things.

'I understand this is hard to talk about.'

If she understood that why did she persist? Again, Lena wanted to say the words but they wouldn't come. She sat like a goddamn mute. Because what was the right response? There was a stranger in her room wanting to talk to her about how it felt to be fucked over and over again for an audience.

'Wait,' Lena said. 'Have you seen it?'

'The material was shown to me by—'

'You watched it?'

'Not in any *prurient* way. I needed to know what we're dealing with. What the nature of the situation—'

'Get the fuck out of my room.'

'Lena, please, I only—'

She stood. The bag dropped to the floor, her hand singing in relief. 'Get the fuck out of my room. Now.'

And the RA did. Not another word. Not a backward glance. How easy was that? She didn't even feel bad about it. About telling the bitch to leave, that is. All the rest of it . . . Bad didn't come close. If she could tell herself to get the fuck out, she would. Stupid ugly desperate whore. Get the fuck out.

———

Lena slept badly, woke a few times thinking she was still at the hospital, remembered she wasn't, remembered as she had every night at the hospital when she woke that whatever time it was there were people watching her fucking Josh, some of them jerking off to it, many of them laughing or pretending, like Jules, to be sorry for her. By the time morning broke she had accepted she must go to class. It was just like after Dad died. People would stare openly. Other people would pretend not to stare but in a way that made the effort obvious. A few would broach the subject with squinted-up eyes and a tone that would make you want to punch them, hard. They'd say, *I heard. I'm so sorry. I'm here for you.* And what she would do was ignore the stares, say, *Thanks.*

I appreciate that. What I really want is to get on with things, get back to normal. And she would. It was like after that singer pissed herself on stage during a televised show. She just kept showing up at things and, in time, everyone moved on.

So: Introduction to Classroom Management at 10 a.m. She dressed low-key—jeans, t-shirt, grey hoodie—but took time with her hair and make-up so she looked well rested and natural and like nothing in the world could be wrong. Even so, she arrived early, hoping to avoid walking into a roomful of people who had probably seen her bare tits, heard her pathetic panting. But the building was locked—the lecturer had no idea why, had to stomp off to find someone from maintenance.

By five to ten more than half the class was there, leaning solitary against the wall or forming jostling knots around the door. Some murmuring, others laughing loudly. Lena tried being one of the wall leaners, earbuds in, eyes closed. The surety that the murmurs, the laughs were about her grew each second. Eyes open, pretending to focus on her phone, then really focusing on her phone because there was a message from Nic saying, *Social worker at 12. Will you be in class? Okay if you are just thought I'd ask.*

She closed her eyes again, pressed her skull into the wall. How had she never seen what a useless child Nic was? Even without the house of horrors she should have realised. What kind of forty-something woman paints her nails like she's taking art direction from a kindergartener? How can you be that old and not only have no partner but no evident history of ever having had one? No kids. Same shit job her whole adult life. Texts her uni student niece every single day, hangs out with her on weekends. And lucky she does, because otherwise she would have lain alone in that shit-pile until she rotted. What kind of person can go days with no one noticing they're not around, not even answering the phone? Have no one to visit them in hospital? No one to call on for backup before a difficult appointment?

But Lena had always known Nic was a child, hadn't she? That she'd been able to think like one, at least. When six-year-old Lena was scared of the dark, Nic didn't tell her to stop being silly like Mum did; she said of course the dark was scary, because you couldn't see what was there. *You're being very logical. So we'll leave on the hall light and then any nasties thinking of sneaking through won't even bother.* When nine-year-old Lena cried because she hadn't been invited to Sara Frost's Pretty Princess Pamper Party, Mum said, *Good. Pedicures and facials for nine-year-olds is the most ridiculous thing I've ever heard.* But Aunty Nic booked the two of them into a proper grown-up beauty salon and they took a thousand photos of themselves with face masks and head wraps and holding glasses of champagne (whisked out of Lena's hand as soon as the shots were taken) while the girls who went to the party only had pictures with clear nail polish and babyish pink lemonade.

It had always been the way: Mum had taught her about budgeting; Nic had shown her how blowing fifty dollars on a high tea made you feel like you had thousands in the bank. Mum had shown her how to use pads and then tampons, warned her it'd be a pain every month for the next forty years so better get used to it now; Nic had told her that she now had a monthly free pass to sleep in, binge on chocolate, skip her turn at making dinner and, if she had a male teacher or boss, get out of pretty much anything. *Tell 'em you're bleeding like a stuck pig and they'll jam their fingers in their ears while begging you to go home and lie down.*

Every step of the way, Mum had taught her how to survive in the world as it was, and Nic had shown her how to make the world as it was a bit more fun. Was that what all that bloody *stuff* was about? Trying to make things more fun? Was it just what happened when someone who thought like a kid made an adult wage? *I'll take this and this and this and this and one of those.*

A social worker might be exactly what Nic needed. Help her face up to the way she'd been living. But also, it might be that the social worker would be like fucking *Jules* and would sit there and put on a syrupy, kind, sympathetic voice when the whole time the details of Nic's humiliation are looping entertainingly through her mind. She would be saying, *I only want to help*, and thinking, *Can't wait to tell the girls at yoga about the disgusting mess this crazy bitch was living in.*

Nic would say, *Get the fuck out*, no problem at all. But the thing is, the social worker wouldn't have to get out, because the room was not Nic's. And even if the social worker did get the fuck out, someone else would come and they, too, would talk in syrupy tones like Nic's life was their business, her shame their problem to solve.

Lena had a break between twelve fifteen and one. She'd have to slip out of this lecture early. Slip out. Fat chance. Wherever you sat, an early escape drew jealous or judgemental eyes. And once they realised who it was . . . Their eyes were on her now, she felt them, searing through her closed lids. Her closed lids were giving them the opportunity. Practically a fucking invitation, leaning against the wall, her nasty body stretched out like that, so they could take a proper look.

Skinnier than she looks on screen

Can't see her ugly scar at least

Needs to show her tits more, best thing about her

Get the fuck out. She opened her eyes, caught no one looking, felt them start up again, taking in her flat arse, the one that had her graded down to a 6, as she walked as normally as she could away from the building. *Family emergency*, she told herself, practising—as if anyone would ask. *There's no one else who could be there to handle it.*

NIC

The social worker looks no older than Lena but is dressed like she's on a filming break from *Real Housewives of Sydney*: skin-tight black jeans, open-toed leopard-print stilettos, a fuchsia singlet with leopard-print bra straps peeking out. Her black, arse-length hair is unnaturally straight and shiny, and her nails are, Nic has to admit, both edgy and immaculate: rounded tips, deep, true navy blue polish, satin-finish, not gloss. She tucks her own split and naked nails into her clenched palms.

'We're meeting today because concerns have been raised about the circumstances in which you were injured,' the social worker says from behind a desk piled with papers. The walls are plastered with posters about DEPRESSION and ANXIETY and BORDERLINE PERSONALITY DISORDER, about SUICIDE and HANDWASHING and NATURAL MOOD BOOSTERS. There's a calendar displaying all of last year against a backdrop of sunflowers. A newspaper clipping whose headline is too small to read. A child's drawing of a family with purple faces and hair in front of a house as small as the purple dog.

'I'd love it if you'd tell me in your own words, Nicole, how you came to hurt yourself?'

On their last Sunday lunch date, Nic and Lena had eaten salads as big as their heads and drunk prosecco and flirted with the hot young waiter who brought them limoncello on the house and asked when they'd return, and Lena had spoken in excited whispers about this boy she was crushing on and Nic had told Lena about Jase from the stockroom and shocked them both by admitting she wouldn't mind a ride. When they were paying, the flirty waiter had asked if they were sisters and Nic had rolled her eyes, said she could never get on so well with her actual sister.

And now, here is Lena, grey-skinned and baggy-eyed, smile like a slapped-on sticker. A middle-aged, careworn daughter nodding encouragingly at her decrepit parent to go ahead and tell the nice lady what happened.

'I climbed on the desk so I could hang something on a hook.' She hears and hates the wobble in her voice. 'I misjudged the edge and fell. Big whoop. I can't be the only person to have fallen off some furniture while trying to reach something high.'

'Of course,' the social worker coos, making deep sympathetic arches of her brows, 'accidents like yours happen quite often. What we're concerned about is the circumstances in which you were found. The space in which you fell is what we could describe as cluttered or congested.' She inclines her head as though she has asked a question. When no one answers, a look of disappointment crosses her face and she presses her beautiful fingertips together and continues: 'We're concerned that the clutter may have exacerbated the damage caused by the fall.' Another pause, during which she looks down at her desk, nods gently as though all is explained there. 'It certainly made it very difficult, Nicole, for the emergency services to reach you quickly.'

'It wasn't *very* difficult,' Lena says. 'I mean, it took a couple of minutes to clear the hallway for the, um, stretcher and that. No big deal, really.'

The social worker turns her pity-filled gaze away from Nic towards the speaker of these true and necessary words: *no big deal*. Lena knows! And she's young and clever and in one piece so will be heard.

'I'm only going off the report I've been given,' the social worker says. 'And it indicates that the clutter was a complication during patient retrieval. In any case, ah—' she looks down at the papers on her desk '—Lena, we're concerned, as well, that the cluttered nature of your aunt's living space presents several ongoing hazards, increasing the likelihood of another fall or of items falling on her. There's also the fact her home represents an unacceptable fire risk due to the amount of flammable materials accumulated and the inaccessibility of electrical connections and power cords in case of emergency.'

If she could walk away she would. She can't even slam her fist on the desk. Maybe she could raise her hand and stick up a finger, but it would hurt. Speech is all she has and her weak and whiny voice adds to the humiliation: 'Am I really being lectured and threatened because my house is messy? Is that what we've come to in this country?'

The woman smiles at her, not unkindly. 'Nobody is lecturing you or threatening you, we're merely con—'

'Concerned, yes, you keep saying. And I do consider being told I'm not allowed to return to my own home a threat, actually. What else can you call it? Wait, don't tell me! *Concern.*'

'There are services available to help you, but you need to be willing to let them. Let *us.*'

'What kinds of services?' Lena asks.

The social worker hands a pamphlet across the desk. Nic manages to read *Treating Hoarding Disorder* before Lena flips it over on her lap.

'That's a more long-term approach for your aunt. In the shorter term, we can look at getting some commercial cleaners in. Some councils offer a subsidy in cases where there's a threat to public health.'

'Public health! Are you fucking kidding me?' There's her voice! Hearing it is like a steadying hand of a friend on her back. 'There is nothing unhealthy about my home! I'm not one of these mad people with thirty-five-year-old steaks in the fridge and cockroaches swarming over the toilet seat. It's fucking *pristine.* I spend half my pay on Pine O Cleen and Glen 20 and all the rest. More hygienic than this bloody place, I'll tell you that. Need to wear a contamination suit to go for a piss in here!'

'Nic.' Lena's hand stroking hers. 'Calm, yeah?'

'Nah, actually. This is a bloody insult and I've had enough of it. Public health! I'm leaving here *today*. Call the police if you want. I'd love to see them arrest me for having a messy house. Bring it on.' She tries to reverse the wheelchair; it moves a skidge then hits the wall.

'Nic, can we just—'

'I can see you're upset, Nicole,' the social worker says. 'I tell you what: I'm going to go and get us all a nice cup of tea. While I'm doing that, you two have a chat about the way forward.' She hands Lena a little stack of pamphlets from her desk. 'Some more ideas there. I'll be back to talk through some solutions.'

Nic waits until the clicking of those ridiculous shoes has faded into the hallway. 'Lena, please. Get me out of here before she comes back. I can't take it.'

'I really think—'

'At least move your bloody chair so I can get myself out. I'm done with this conversation.' She rolls herself as far back as she can, rams the wall, not entirely by accident.

Lena squeezes her arm, not hard, but enough to still her. 'Nic, they won't let you leave until we sort this. Even if your place wasn't . . . No matter what it's like, you can't be on your own right now. I know this sucks, but it's just how it is. Let the doctors take care of you here a bit longer. While you're getting better, I'll organise the cleaners so the social worker will get off your back.'

'No! I don't want anyone in my house. I can't stand the thought, Lena. Please. *Please.* Don't let them get bloody cleaners in. I've seen those TV shows. I know how it goes. All my stuff'll be piled up on the front lawn for the neighbours to gawk at.' The tears are coming and sweat is tormenting the cut on her forehead and she is trapped—actually trapped—in this grim little office. 'Just kill me now if you're going to let them do that to me.'

'Okay. Okay.' Lena sighs, rubs her eyes. 'Let me do it then. No cleaners, nothing on the front lawn. Just me making sure there's enough clear floor space for you to get around safely.'

She has let things get out of hand. She realises that. But to have Lena clean up after her is too much. It's supposed to be Nic helping *her*, sorting out her blips and stumbles.

'I could stay there for a bit while I'm tidying. I need a break from the res hall anyway. It's driving me nuts.'

The morphine is wearing off. Her spine reverting to molten steel. The pain will become too much very soon.

'It's the best way forward. Seriously.'

Lena back at the house. Maybe it won't be so bad. It's her house, too, Nic has always said. Both the kids and Michelle. How had she let herself forget that? It was Mum's house, meant for them all. Lena could make it good again, the family home.

'How will you know what to do with everything? What if you chuck something that I need?'

Lena's face relaxes, which makes everything easier. 'I won't. I promise. Anything important I'll keep for you to look through later.'

'This is the problem! You can't see.' Nic's heart is racing again, the blood flooding her temples. Lights shudder behind her eyelids. 'It's all important! Why would I have it otherwise?'

'What about the newspapers in the hallway? They're digitised these days, you know. Anything you want to find in those papers, you can look it up online.'

Like she's an idiot luddite! There's no way Lena can understand that the stacks lining her hallway are not about *finding* anything. She could never tell her brilliant niece about the night she went to pub trivia with Lala from work and blazed like a fireball through the TV and Music categories and everyone was cheering for her but then it was Current Events and she didn't know a single answer except who the prime minister was, and even then she was wrong, not in her answer, but in excitedly leaning forward to write the answer, because everyone else knew it was only there as a joke question because of the recent political turmoil. That she thought she was smart for knowing the PM's name when even the slurring, cockeyed bloke with half his teeth missing cackled at the question. Even him in on the gag while she's earnestly filling in the form.

How can Lena, whose brain is like a miracle and who goes every day to a place that literally exists only to create and share knowledge, possibly understand?

The social worker comes back into the room with a cardboard tray holding three styrofoam cups, a teabag string dangling from each. 'How'd we go, ladies?'

'I think we've come up with a plan,' Lena says.

'Wonderful. Let's hear it.' The woman puts cups in front of Lena and Nic.

If she could reach without too much pain she would knock the boiling water all over the desk. 'The pain is very bad,' she says instead. 'I need to lie down.'

'Of course. As long as you're happy for Lena to fill me in, we should be able to do without you.'

'You okay with that, Nic?'

Of course she isn't. Doesn't matter, does it? She nods.

The social worker mumbles into her desk phone and in a few minutes an orderly appears and wheels her from the room.

'It'll be all right, I promise,' Lena says as she leaves.

My arse it will, Nic thinks. My fat arse.

Back in the ward, Nic soothes herself by imagining returning to work the way she used to, as a kid, think about the upcoming school holidays. She sees herself walking (easily, smoothly) towards the front of the store, greeting Jo and Ahmad and Mel and Maria and Lala, all gathered around the security grille waiting for the manager to arrive and open up for the day. They exchange bits of gossip and complaints about the weather or the bus or train. Ahmad and Maria might have some news to share about their kids, Jo and Mel and Lala about their grandkids. Nic might boast about Lena's latest triumph or show off her newest manicure.

The manager arrives and they all stand about awkwardly not looking at his bum crack as he squats to unlock the grate. It clangs clangs clangs up up up and they file in, taking off coats if it's winter, fanning their faces in summer, waiting for the air con to kick in, which will happen four minutes after the power board is switched on. The lights come on right away and this—this—this—this is the bit which makes Nic's tummy lurch with excitement. Sometimes in her mental run-through she gives in to temptation and skips the waiting and the chitchat, jumping straight to this moment, but it's better when she makes herself hang on. Like foreplay, it is.

So, the main event. Nic walks through the store on her way to the staffroom, ten minutes until opening. The store is bright and clean and though not quiet—the staff are chattering around her and the manager is running through the specials and promotions for the day—it is quieter than it will be again until closing. On her left, the row of registers stretching to the far side of the store; from this angle she can see the neat racks of magazines fronting the area where customers will queue. She can't make out the individual magazines from here, but she knows if she were to turn right and walk in front of the registers she would find *Women's Weekly* and *Woman's Day* and *Who* and *New Weekly* and *House and Garden* and *Women's Health*. Maybe a special edition cookbook attached to one of the main titles, or a seasonal collector's edition.

She keeps walking straight ahead down one of the three extra-wide aisles that divide the store into departments. On her right is Ladies Wear, and as long as she's not running late she'll allow herself a few minutes browsing. It's important to know what's in stock. On any given day she might find a new range of sundresses, four different prints and ranging from sizes 6 to 24. Or a restock of the oversized t-shirts with retro band logos on them. Guns N' Roses and Metallica and Def Leppard popular with both ironic teens and sincere fans like her. Today, she imagines the first of the winter stock coming through: thick woollen jumpers in rich jewel tones, and corduroy pants in dark berry and chocolate brown. She runs her hands over the fabric of the pants, pinches the thickness of the jumpers between her fingers, feels a surge of warmth and comfort.

But time is getting on—the others are already in the staffroom securing bags in lockers, finishing takeaway coffees. Nic walks on, glancing longingly at the Children's Wear version of the new winter gear—darling corduroy pants with nappy-accommodating oversize seats; plush jumpers which look much like the adult ones but she knows will be made from one of the new-era synthetics that are flame-retardant and softer than wool but just as warm.

Onwards, past Shoes on her right and Electronics on her left. Ah, it makes her heart sing that they still sell DVDs and CDs. Funny how almost everyone who buys these supposed relics comments on their backwardness. *Ah, yeah, I'm old school, hey. I know everyone's doing Netflix or whatever but I can't be bothered with all that.* And Nic says, *I know what you mean,* and they feel like a rebel, a true iconoclast, not knowing they're the eighth person that day who's said it.

Almost at the back of the store now, she looks far to her left, past Electronics, where the edges of the next aisle are visible: Toys. Her very favourite, which is why she never walks that way if she can help it because how would she ever leave them? The delicate-faced baby dolls in slippery satin dresses and the bright, bold building blocks and darker, metallic engineering-inspired ones. The games with their boxes promising hours of fun for the whole family, and the army and spaceman toys which all have angry faces but sweet little moulded arms and legs, not to mention the tiny clothes—camouflage and space suits and all kinds of things with arm and leg holes smaller than her pinkie finger. The preciousness is too much. She looks away towards the edges of the abutting section—Homewares—another danger zone what with all the crates and filing solutions and pillows and lamps and—

Too much, too much, she's reached the end. She steps into the relative darkness of the staffroom—no fluoro lights in here, just a single regular bulb in the centre of the room. Her workmates are adjusting their collars and pinning on their badges, and she does the same. In a minute she'll be up front opening her register, and a new kind of thrill will begin as she waits in place and the objects come past her, surprise surprise surprise. A whole day of that—now a pair of bamboo-fibre undies, now a cookbook and striped apron gift pack. Now here's a box of glass tumblers with a blue tint and now look at this rattan and synthetic mix welcome mat. Now a crimson lipstick, now a skein of pale blue wool, now a pair of men's slippers, tartan with non-slip soles. A Chupa Chup, a fan heater, a birthday card with a duck on the front, a corkscrew, a packet of paperclips, a battery-operated fire engine, a chequerboard-patterned phone cover, a framed print of a sailboat against a stormy sea, a child's easel, a pair of safety scissors, opaque winter-weight tights, an amber lampshade, a box of home hair dye (burgundy), a shiny red backpack, a ceramic flower pot, a cheese grater, four pillows and four plain white pillowcases, an espresso machine, a tube of toothpaste. Each one passing through her hands, each one lending her a bit of its spirit, showing her, even if for only a millisecond, what might be possible.

She's drifting in this lovely place when Lena texts to say: *How messy was HER office, hey? Might have to report her to the authorities. Those 👠👠 combined with all that paper, disaster waiting to happen.*

She blows a kiss at the phone, knows Lena is still her girl, will back her against these lunatics.

LENA

The front of the house was too neat. She'd seen enough *Current Affair* segments on hoarders to know that the courtyard should be cluttered with wheelless shopping trolleys and dead pot plants and washing tubs and bicycles without seats or tyres and maybe a couple of bird corpses and a rat skeleton. There should be mail piled up on the front porch, the edges chewed by snails and covered in slug juice. It should smell bad enough that even passing on the footpath you need to cover your face with a scarf and hold your breath.

But no. The pavers were even and recently swept, the hedge tidy. The front stairs were clear, as was the porch. You'd never, ever know that walking through the front door would be stepping into a nightmare realm. It was a trick front. A trap.

Like Josh.

The tiny scratches around the front door lock were the only indication that anything disturbing had happened here at all. An easily picked lock, the police said. As they were leaving, they told

Lena she should look at getting it replaced with something sturdier. Given the state of the place it'd be a better idea to remove it altogether. Leave the door swinging open. Welcome, Neighbourhood Burglars. Take whatever you like. Please.

In the hallway, Lena dumped the sleeping bag and backpack of clothes and toiletries that she'd lugged on and off the bus. She coughed violently, swiped at her streaming eyes. It was barely 8 a.m. but the air was murderously hot and smoky already. Not much better inside. A desperate inhale between coughs lined her throat with dust. She rifled through her bag, grabbed her empty water bottle.

The kitchen was blocked by the newspapers she'd helped clear from the hallway the other day. They coated her hands in black powder as she pushed them out of her way. Why were Nic's papers so fucking dirty? Lena handled newspapers all the time and they never left her with more than slightly gritty-feeling fingers, and that was only if she was unusually sweaty in the first place. Most nights it was cool by the time she carried them. Last job of her shift, clearing the low shelf to the left of the cigarette counter of that day's leftovers. Sometimes there were few enough she could sweep them up in one hand as she passed. Other times she needed a trolley to lug them out to the recycling. She never wondered why until the day she arrived for her shift and noticed the counter already clear, a handwritten sign declaring PAPERS SOLD OUT SORRY.

'That woman drove her kids into a dam,' Kim at the ciggie counter said. 'People can't get enough of it.' After that, when there were few papers to clear at the end of the night, Lena would take one for herself to read on the bus home. Always something bloody and tragic on the front, with kids or a pretty girl. Occasionally a terror attack somewhere famous, like Paris or London. Sometimes the front-page stories were horrifying enough that she couldn't sleep. A couple of months ago a man out in WA killed his whole family. She'd lain awake all night thinking about how there were times up in Brisbane when she had churned with rage at the Dick, and sometimes at Mum, too, for inflicting him on their family. Still never occurred to her to murder them in their beds. Punch the Dick in his dick, yes. Drive his car to a cliff top and release the handbrake before leaping clear, sure. But not while he was inside it or anything.

Did the Dick ever think about killing them all? Sometimes when he was angry he'd yell in a way that made Lena imagine a cartoon fist about to burst from his mouth. But the worst that ever happened was a spittle shower. He was a dick, but not the physically violent kind. Though maybe people weren't until they were.

Neither Mum nor Dad ever laid an angry hand on them growing up. Not even a smack on the bum. Mum definitely wanted to sometimes. Many times she'd walked away from Lena or Will or both of them, naughty—screaming, fighting kids. Kids who'd drawn on the walls or made mud soup in the only good saucepan or broken each other's Christmas toys. Mum would speak calmly even as her face turned pink then red. They'd laugh at her. *Oooh, look out, Will, she's gonna blow.* But she never did. She'd go outside, close the door on them. When they were little they measured her fury in how many cigarettes she smoked before she came back in. Once she'd quit they'd watch at the window as she paced.

Working off the cheese, they'd call it and laugh. God, they were shits. They didn't know.

Knowing was what kept Lena awake the night she read about the man in WA. His picture had been in the papers, but three or four hours into the sleepless night Lena noticed that the figure she was imagining stalking through that house with a shotgun had her grandpa's face. She'd only ever seen him in photos, this man who they weren't allowed to know about until they were teenagers and then, once Mum told them, they weren't allowed to talk about ever again. They'd googled him, of course, once they knew there was something worth googling. Will tried to be all protective—*Lena, trust me, you don't want to read this*—but she'd elbowed him out of the way and read the article herself. It wasn't even that bad. The article that was. Not graphic, anyway. A friendship gone sour, a fight the other man thought ended when he broke his ex-mate's nose. Then Lena's grandpa returned with his nose taped up and a knife in his fist and finished it his way.

Nothing like the crime in WA, then. So why did her mind insist on conflating the two, and so vividly she couldn't sleep? Why her inability to push away the image of the girls in My Little Pony t-shirts in the picture on Mum's mantelpiece—eight-year-old Nic taller, fatter, smilier; serious, skinny, six-year-old Michelle tucked under her arm—in bed in the farmhouse from the paper, their dad coming through the door with his gun, shooting one in her sleep and then, when the other woke at the noise, shooting her as she screamed and screamed. Why couldn't she stop obsessing over which one he killed first, which one had to see her sister's body? I hope Mum was first, Lena's brain kicked, because Aunty

Nic was older, could've handled it better. But, then, Aunty Nic would've understood more, so maybe it was better that she went in her sleep, Mum still so young she might not have had time to comprehend the size of the betrayal, the irrevocability of the horror.

This didn't happen, she'd told herself, leaning out of bed and grabbing her phone and opening a news site to see the picture again. See, idiot? Those faces belong to strangers. The thing in your head never happened. Not to them.

Was that why Nic kept all these papers? Lena wondered now, rubbing her hands together to dislodge the grime. So she could refute the midnight horrors by returning to the documentary record, reassuring herself that though terrible things have happened—keep happening, will always be happening—they are not happening to her?

But how would that work, like, actually? The three or four papers on the top of each stack might be accessible, at least until the tower got above head height. When Lena and the cop had cleared them all for the ambulance they'd had to push the top stacks off the towers, leaping out of the way to avoid being hit as they came tumbling down. It hadn't occurred to her in the nightmare moment to wonder how those stacks, each one made up of maybe fifty papers bound with string, had got so high in the first place. Lena hadn't noticed a stepladder anywhere, but that didn't mean anything. There could be a whole fucking industrial lift in here and she wouldn't have seen it.

She finished clearing the kitchen doorway of newspapers, making a mental note to check if the council around here did extra recycling pick-ups. There was a narrow path from where she stood in the hallway to the sink under the kitchen window, passing the table on the left and the fridge and stove on the right. She tried to picture Nic in this space, stumbling through sleepy-eyed in the morning to make some toast, or dashing in during the ad breaks at night to boil the kettle. It was impossible: there could be no stumbling or dashing, here, only steady, watchful motion. Like walking across the stone bridge over the creek behind her mate Lou's place in Brisbane. Wide enough as long as you don't slip or turn an ankle.

The sink was filled with plastic takeaway containers—clean, by the looks of them. Nic had always been fastidious around food. When they slept over as kids they had to eat at the table off new plastic plates. As soon as they were finished, Nic would throw the leftovers and plates in the bin, wipe the table and their hands with antiseptic spray that smelt like pine trees and stung the broken skin around your nails. Then she'd take the bin bag outside. Later, if she'd bought ice creams, they'd sit on the front steps and gobble them down, throwing the wrappers and sticks straight into the outside bin. Lena had mentioned it to her mum once and she'd rolled her eyes and said, *Thank god she doesn't have kids*, which was a thing Mum said about Nic *all the time*, even though she seemed perfectly happy to leave her own kids with her for days or even weeks.

Lena was glad for that particular weirdness right now. If Nic had been a food hoarder or even let her dirty dishes pile up, she really didn't think she'd be able to deal with it. Her gag reflex was overdeveloped. Pity she didn't go down on Josh; might have spewed all over his deceitful dick.

Stop! Focus.

The windowsill over the sink was cluttered with empty soft drink and wine bottles. Over the top of them she could just make out the corner of the Hills hoist that, on scorching hot days, she and Will would hook their hands on to and swing in a circle while Aunty Nic aimed the hose at a central point. Reaching that point, feeling the cold slap of water before quickly moving on, was better somehow than standing still and having Nic spray them all over.

There used to be a door from this room to the backyard and laundry. She guessed there still was, somewhere in that corner between the end of the sink and the entrance to the living room. Behind the stacked cardboard boxes, which were themselves almost concealed by a pedestal fan, a breadmaker, a blender, two irons and an assortment of other small appliances and their tangled, grimy cords.

She ran the tap a minute, splashed her face with water, drank greedily from her hands, then refilled the water bottle. She opened the fridge, hoping there'd be something cold in there she could chug before she continued.

There was not. Nothing to chug, nothing cold.

On the top shelf—raised as high as the notches on the side would allow—were a dozen or more small dark amber bottles, some with fading prescription labels, some with Chemists' Own labels advertising their contents. Among them were stacked boxes of Panadol, Nurofen and Codral, as well as at least twenty other packets of medications Lena hadn't heard of, wound-up bandages, boxes of bandaids and, poking up between the rungs of the shelf, tubes of what looked like medicated cream. Fat, full tubes; scrunched-up-at-one-end tubes; squeezed-completely-flat tubes.

The shelf below held enough single-serve packets of mustard, ketchup, salt, pepper, soy sauce, wasabi, chilli sauce, sugar and Splenda to service a medium-sized restaurant for a month. Each condiment had its own section, though the slipperiness of the packages and the sheer bulk of the lot of it meant that there was considerable overlap, ketchup sachets having fallen onto Splenda stacks, sugar onto salt, soy sauce onto chilli. Still, enough care had been taken that the space was divided into mostly uninter-rupted chunks of colour: red, yellow, brown, green and white.

Between the middle shelf and the vegetable drawers were tissues. On the left, four regular-sized boxes stacked two by two, on the right at least forty purse-sized packets.

The left-hand vegetable drawer was filled to the brim with boxes of toothpicks, matches, travel-sized sewing kits and other small packets and boxes Lena couldn't bear to examine. The right-hand drawer held an astonishing range of condoms, with tubes of lubricant and several different brands of pregnancy test mixed in.

The freezer was stacked with ice cube trays. All of them empty, many of them broken.

'I'm being pranked,' Lena muttered, groping behind the fridge until she found the plug, which was firmly pushed into the socket. She flicked the switch and waited to hear the whir of the cooling unit start up. Nothing.

By the time she had emptied the fridge (out-of-date medicine, creams and condoms straight into a garbage bag, along with all the condiments and all but one box or bottle of everything else), it was clear the fridge was not getting any cooler. She took out her phone, off since she'd been woken in the night by obscene messages from men she didn't know, turned it on, bit her lip while the banked-up messages buzzed onto the device. She deleted them all unread and then texted Nic: *Is your fridge broken?*

While she waited for a reply, she sprayed the inside of the fridge with disinfectant, wiped it down, sprayed and wiped again, then a final time with hot water.

There's a fridge in the living room

Okay, Lena wrote. *But does the one in the kitchen work?*

Not for years

Bloody hell. Lena stepped over the piles of who-the-fuck-knew-what to get to the living room and felt new panic rising. What was all this? Just fabric and boxes and, and, and, *what?* Finally she made it out: snuggled in between an armchair and a stack of video tapes, and bearing the weight of what looked like five or six clumsily folded blankets, was a tiny white fridge, smaller than the bar fridge in her room at uni. She picked her way over and wrenched it open. Two small cans of off-brand cola, two bottles of Fanta, a bottle of spring water, one of orange juice and a small carton of chocolate milk. All of it blissfully chilled.

Lena drank the water and then a cola, crouched right there in front of the open door. The fizz burnt her throat and made her eyes tear up but the cold was like a miracle. Soon the sugar and caffeine would hit and might just get her through another hour of this hell. And then?

Her phone buzzed.

Josh.

The cola almost came right back up. Not that it would matter. Cola spew would blend right in to this filthy rag of a carpet.

Do u hate me?

Three seconds of her heart hammering and then:

Wouldnt blame u

Know I don't deserve it but would luv to talk

She typed *go to hell*, deleted it, forwarded his messages to Annie and Lou instead. She waited for their counsel, crouched in front of the little fridge with its children's party mix of drinks.

Annie and Lou were of one mind: fuck him and the horse he rode in on. Delete the messages, delete his contact details, block his number.

She would. Later. Right now, she'd noticed there was a path, of sorts, running from where she crouched to the armchair in front of the TV. Shit, Nic, could you be more of a stereotype?

Lena stood and, careful not to disturb the stacks of who-the-fuck-knows on either side, made her way to the chair, an old-fashioned recliner covered in chocolate brown velour, with crocheted granny blankets draped over its back and arms. This, at least, was familiar. Aunty Nic would settle herself in here after dinner, Will and Lena or, later, Lena alone on the sofa beside her. Sometimes Nic'd start gently snoring, and Lena would crawl onto her lap and tickle her face until she woke and returned fire, tickling Lena into ecstatic hysterics. Only now, looking back, did Lena understand that the snoring had been fake.

The fluoro yellow crocheted sock velcroed to the arm of the chair was filled with a nail file, a bottle of nail polish remover, lavender polish, clear top coat and a purse pack of tissues. The whereabouts of the remote control it was supposed to hold was a mystery. At her feet was an old-school portable CD player. She pressed play and glam rock screamed into the room. She pressed stop, flipped the player open: *Open Up and Say . . . Ahh!* Poison. Ugh. When it came to music her mum and aunty were bogans through and through.

Her phone buzzed, buzzed, buzzed and she ignored it like a dripping nose. Sniff sniff sniff.

She needed a strategy. Already she'd wasted time and energy scrubbing out a fridge that was destined for landfill. She needed to take stock of her situation, plan, prioritise. From the armchair she could see the television, which sat in a cabinet almost hidden by the stuff it held. Like the back shelf of an op shop, it was cluttered with a horrifying array of worthless, dust-gathering porcelain figurines. Garishly bright frogs and wonky-eyed cats, dogs with threatening grins and yellow ducklings with creepily realistic webbed feet. Little shepherd girls reading books or weeping or bending over lambs or puppies or looking out over the rest of the miserable creatures on the shelf. A dozen or so figurines of Pregnant Mary and Mother Mary kept company with a bunch of fat Buddhas, mostly laughing but a few, seeming to understand the gravity of the situation, stared heavy-lidded at their own feet. Between, behind, in front, over and under the figurines were vases of every colour, shape and size, along with—*for fuck's sake, Nic*—trophies for sports Lena was pretty certain no one in the family, let alone Nic herself, had ever played: cricket, rugby, soccer and volleyball.

The wall to the right of the TV was lined with colourful crates and opaque plastic organiser boxes. Lena counted sixteen without even moving her head. They ran all the way to the back of the room, in some places stacked right to the ceiling. A few rag dolls, some CDs and various office supplies spilt out here and there. The space between where she was and the at-least-neatly-stacked stuff around the walls was chaos. She could see at least five tables of various sizes piled high with paper and books and cardboard boxes like you got at the fruit and veg market. There were some more armchairs and lounges piled high with blankets and towels. Or probably, based on the sharp edges poking through, covered in other stuff over which had been thrown blankets and towels. The floor, where she could see it at all, had a light coating of papers and fabric.

Lena sank into the armchair. She could use up the entire roll of garbage bags, fill each one to bursting, and it would make no visible difference in here.

Her phone buzzed. She opened the message without thinking, was punished with a picture of an erect dick, gripped by a pale, hairless hand. *wanna fuck i last much longer than that college fag*

She blocked the number, was startled by her phone ringing in her hand. Mum. She contemplated not answering, knew the phone would keep buzzing at her until she did.

'Lena. Jesus. What the hell have you got yourself into? Do I need to come down there?'

'What are you talking about?' Cool, calm, voice of a virgin who's never been filmed so much as flipping her hair in a boy's direction.

'I'm talking about you letting Nic turn you into her personal home cleaning service.'

Relief like a shot of vodka through her. 'Mum, it's fine. I'm just making sure her place is safe for her to come home to on crutches.'

A deep, long sigh. 'How bad is it? Really, Lena. Tell me the truth.'

'It's . . . pretty cluttered.'

'Jesus. That woman is a bloody disgrace. S'cuse my French, but bloody hell. She has no right to drag you into her—'

'She hasn't dragged me. I want to help. And she's your sister. Have some compassion.'

'I used to, believe me. I had buckets of it. That woman drained every one of 'em. And now she's doing it to my daughter. I won't have it.'

'Well, it's not up to you. I'm an adult.'

'You're a sucker.'

'Better a sucker than a bitch who turns her back on family in need.'

'I'm a bitch, am I? Lovely.'

'When it comes to Nic, yeah, you are.'

'She's never been able to understand that you're not *hers*.'

'I'm not *anyone's*. I make my own choices.'

'I'm trying to protect you.'

'I don't need protection.'

Another deep sigh. 'Yeah, you say that, but . . . I'm your mum. I worry about you. I don't want you taken advantage of. She does that, you know. She's a leech. Living for nothing all these years and—'

121

'Mum, I've gotta go. There's a lot to do here and I've still got uni and work and everything.'

'Do you want me to come down? I can ask at work. They owe me some time.'

The day her mother saw what Nic had done to the place was the day the only bit of property owned by anyone in their broken, fucked-up family would be burnt to the ground. Better at least wait to find out if it's insured before letting that happen.

'Nah, don't. It's really not that bad. It's good, actually, having my own space for a bit. No housemates.'

A pause. 'Yeah, okay. But I'm serious, Leen. If it gets too much, if she starts asking you for, I don't know, anything else, you say no and call me and I'll handle her. You've got your own life to live—you can't be—'

'Okay, Mum. See ya.' She hung up.

Four texts had arrived while she'd been talking. Two dicks, a *Mum said Aunty Nic's got you cleaning her house?* from Will, and a *Can you do 4–12 tonight?* from her manager. She deleted the dicks, sent an eye-roll to Will and a thumbs-up to work.

Seven hours until she'd have to leave. Six-and-a-half before she'd need to be in the shower. She could get heaps done in that time. The whole kitchen would be good. That way she could at least make coffee tomorrow before she started.

First, though, she made a careful lap of the entire place. Though lap was the wrong word. There was a zigzag, barely there path running from the lounge room to the hall. From that relatively clear space she opened the door to the spare room and her stomach filled with cement. When she'd visited Lou the first time she'd been astounded to realise that Lou's bedroom had *always been that*. The bed was the one Lou had slept in since her early teens, when it replaced the one she had slept in since she was a toddler, which had replaced her cot. The pale cream walls with butter yellow trim used to be pink with purple trim after they were cream with pink trim, but they were the same walls. The antique hardwood dresser had been there since before Lou was born, handed down to her parents to place there in anticipation of the daughter they knew would come. Lou moved to the overstuffed armchair by the window at a certain time in the afternoon because she knew the winter sunshine would warm her there, just as it always had. There was a photo in the hallway just outside the room of Lou aged maybe six or seven sitting in the exact chair she sat on talking to Lena, with what appeared to be the same shaft of sunlight bouncing off her shoulder. It seemed, to Lena, like time travel.

Lena had never had a room of her own for more than a year or two at a time. Even then, those rooms were never really hers, as she was reminded whenever she wanted to change the colour of the walls or stick posters on them. *If you mark the walls they'll take it out of our bond*, Mum'd chant.

This room at Aunty Nic's was one she woke in from age three to thirteen. Not every morning or anywhere near that, but at some point, at many points, in each of those years it was this grey popcorn ceiling she saw when she opened her eyes, this tan loop-pile carpet her cold morning toes pressed into, this mirror-fronted built-in wardrobe she checked for monsters then ghosts then serial killers before sliding the doors closed and climbing into this bed. And now ... now, goddamn it, this room was just another warehouse for Nic's shit. The hope—one she hadn't known she held until this moment—that she might crawl into the creaky old bed tonight, curl up and watch the headlights of passing cars dance across the wall until sleep swamped her, was smashed. She kicked the bag of clothes nearest to her foot; it shuddered but remained in place, held tight by the boxes, bags, baskets surrounding it.

Back down the hall, a glance into Nic's room and with it the concrete loosening nausea swimming in. There was clear space from the door to the stained carpet marking the spot where Nic had lain, leaking.

Lena continued to the bathroom, stood in the doorway for long minutes staring at the full-to-the-brim bathtub, the cluttered shelves over the sink. The shower stall at least seemed useable. The toilet, too.

Back out and into the kitchen. She would start with the table to give her some clear space to work with. The closest pile of papers was also the smallest, reaching only to her bellybutton. On top was a flyer asking for help finding a lost bulldog. The pet's puffy, wet-eyed face looked the way Lena imagined her own did right now. The back of the paper was sticky—Nic had clearly ripped it off a telegraph pole. Why? Had she seen the dog and planned to call the owners? But no, underneath this poster was another: a poodle this time. Below, a lost budgie, a tabby, a Persian. Dogs, birds, cats all the way down. The thought hit Lena like a fist to the chest: had Nic taken all these animals, kept the 'lost' posters the way a serial killer collects newspaper clippings of their crimes? Were there live or—Jesus, no—*dead* animals hidden somewhere in this house?

Calm down.

Checking with you as promised: can I chuck the lost pet posters on kitchen table?

The phone rang immediately. Nic, panting as though she'd run flights of stairs: 'Leave all that, Lena. I need it.'

'Some of these notices look years old. What do you need them for?'

Heavy breaths. 'What if I see one of the pets? I won't know who to call!'

'But—'

'Lena, they're out there. Lost. Alone. Probably hungry. How will I know who to call if I find them? Please. Think about it.'

This Nic—wild with panic, delusion and fear, panting, weeping, helpless, mad—this Nic she could imagine in this house. This Nic she had never met.

'Okay, yes. I get it. It's fine. I'll leave them. How are you feeling today?'

'This whole thing is so stupid. You shouldn't be there. You don't know what you're doing. Please, just leave it, okay? Please.'

'Yes, yes. Of course. Whatever you want. I'm sorry I upset you. Try to calm down. Drink some water. Maybe have a sleep. It's all fine, here.'

'Will you leave?'

'Leave?'

'My things. My house. I need you to leave, Lena. I can't bear it.'

'Okay.'

'Do you promise?'

'I promise. Don't worry.'

She hung up, pushed the stack of posters into a garbage bag, started on the next pile.

———

The kitchen cupboards were filled with cookbooks. It was like a history of food trends: *The Women's Weekly Cookbook, Campbell's Easy Summer Recipes* and *Margaret Fulton* cookbooks Lena remembered from childhood, along with *Microwave Cooking With Style, 50 One-pot Meals* and *In the Kitchen with Rosie: Oprah's Favorite Recipes*. A bunch of low-fat and heart-health books, high-fibre, Mediterranean, low-carb, organic. Some were very recent: paleo and keto. In between were more timeless collections: Italian, Cantonese, Potatoes and Pasta, Vegetarian and Vegan, Soups, Desserts. There was one, still in its plastic wrap, written by an Instagram diet guru Lena had told Nic about only a month or so ago. She imagined her aunt going straight from their lunch together, finding and purchasing the book. Did she think, as she handed over her credit card, about how she'd invite Lena over and surprise her with Caris's clean-eating feast? Did she think, *I'll just have to tidy the kitchen a little* . . . Did she imagine the two of them in this room, eating slices of Paleo Apple Spice Coffee Cake, their laughter echoing in the clear, empty space that surrounded them?

She bent and wrenched open the oven. You couldn't see its walls or racks. Couldn't see through to the back. Enough paper in there to burn down the neighbourhood.

People have died of sadness, Lena knew. Was this what it felt like, just before?

———

Will, she texted, *how have we gone all these years and not known our aunty is completely and utterly batshit crazy?*

Speak for yourself, he replied. *I've long known EVERYONE in our family is batshit.*

I'm serious tho! There's a stack of books on feng shui and home decorating stashed . . . wait for it . . . behind the DUNNY!

That's hilarious

It's devastating

Devastating but hilarious

Our family motto

TWO

WILL

Will woke to the stench of stale piss mingled with fresh bleach and the sound of men grunting, boots stomping, meaty hands slapping steel bars. Opened his eyes to light designed to stop you having a single second more sleep than legally mandated. For a woozy moment he thought he was back in prison.

The moment passed, his head cleared, and he knew he was in a forty-five-dollar single room out the back of a Mackay pub. It was his third morning waking to the eye-watering Queensland sun blitzing through the broken venetians and the racket of FIFO workers using the shared bathroom across the hall.

Not prison. But not home either. Home (Mercy's home) smelt like Haymish's sweet milky morning breath in his face, sounded like Taylah's attempt at a whisper (louder than her normal speaking voice) saying, *Hay, stop bothering them and finish your Rice Bubbles*, looked like Mercy's sleep-crusted eyes fluttering open closed open closed, her lopsided smile twitching as Haymish's surprising weight landed on the bed, then Taylah's, and the four of them became one tangled pile of laughter and love. Home was being woken by another man's kids who felt so like his he forgot to worry about losing them.

He checked his phone for messages from Mercy and found five from Lena and one from Mum. A voice that could've belonged to a screw bellowed from the hall that all rooms needed to be vacated by nine. Will loud-mumbled acknowledgement, became aware as he did so that the toothache he'd had for a week had morphed from dull and intermittent to intense and constant.

He read through Lena's texts:

Remember that pogo ball we used to fight over? STILL HERE

Big box of floppy disks. Would there even be computers left that can read them?

Heap of old tapes I think are from our 'radio show'. Remember??! I think it's them. Can't find a working tape deck to check

Each text made his toothache a little worse and he'd used up the half-pack of codeine he'd brought from home (Mercy's home) to help him sleep these last three nights.

FOUR not-working tape decks and counting

Huge box of tiny tapes from an ANSWERING MACHINE! Not kidding, huge box!! Who keeps answering machine tapes!!! Hours and hours of people saying giveusacallback

He usually heard Lena's voice in his head when he read her texts but this last string was silent, toneless, even with the over-punctuation and capitals and shit. He stared at the stripes of sunlight on the lino, tried to figure out if she'd say *giveusacallback* all breezy and inviting like Dad or stern like Mum. For a while as a kid he'd had a bedroom with venetian blinds like these ones, had enjoyed playing with the angle of the slats to create different line patterns on the floor. He imagined telling that to Haymish and Taylah. *That's what we did for fun back in my day. None of this PlayStation business, just good old-fashioned venetian blind string pulling to keep us entertained.* Mercy'd laugh, say, *Yeah, those long gone olden days when you were young,* and the kids wouldn't realise she was being cheeky because she was a decade older than Will, would have been married to her ex already when he was a kid flicking the blinds.

The text from Mum said, *Im not going to nag but I really wish youd come home. Rick and I would love to have you here.*

Had to mention Rick the Dick, didn't she? It'd been the same on the phone yesterday. Will had been seriously considering taking up her offer to buy him a ticket to Brisbane. She'd said all the right things: how she was sorry about Mercy and his job; that she hoped he'd be able to stay in touch with those lovely kids who obviously adored him; that she knew he'd find more work quickly, but maybe this was a good opportunity to head south for a bit and hang out with his old mum. *I've missed you so much, boyo,* she'd said. But then, as if the Dick was standing at her side, poking her ribs, she corrected herself: *Rick and I both miss you.*

To which Will had said, *Yeah, what does he miss about me?* because they'd spent all of five minutes together, for fuck's sake. The Dick had swept in and taken advantage of Mum while she was still grieving then whisked her and Lena off to Brisbane so fast Will was probably still being processed at Silverwater when their flight was landing. Four months later, when Will was released, he'd spent an unbearable couple of weeks trying to reconnect with Mum and Lena while the Dick lurked around insisting on his importance.

I know I can't replace your father but

I know you've been away but we're a family and I want

I know you've had a rough trot but I think it's time you

Will didn't care how the sentences ended. It didn't matter. Dad was dead. Mum seemed happy, Lena seemed okay. There was no point in him sticking around to disrupt the new family that had been formed in his absence.

An absence which was, ironically, caused by his love of family, of his need to do what he could to help Dad. Not cure him, that was never on the table. By the time the stubborn dickhead went to the doctor he was riddled with tumours. No hope, just months of watching the bits of him that weren't cancer shrivel. But Will knew there was something that would help with the grinding, gruelling nausea at least. Everyone knew it, if they were being honest, but Will was the only one with the guts to make it happen. Get the old man some medicine that actually worked. Let him sit up straight and eat dinner and watch telly. Let him be a human fucking being for a bit before he died.

Had to be paid for, though, didn't it? And Mum was barely making rent on her cleaner's wage. Dad's treatment was meant to be all Medicare but there were always extras. Will asked around, found the right people. Got himself dropped right into the supply chain. Dad's needs met plus a little cash on top. Perfect solution.

He could've stopped once Dad died. Should've. But he just . . . he didn't, was all. Maybe if he'd realised turning eighteen meant he could now be in serious, adult shit. But it didn't occur to him.

It had felt for so long as though no one was paying attention to anything he did that he'd stopped being careful.

Three days past his eighteenth birthday, one block down from the training college where he had almost completed his Early Childhood Education Cert III, he saw, over the shoulder of his buyer, a cop approaching. He had this weird feeling of *oh, right, yeah, this.* Not inevitability, like this was always going to happen; familiarity, like it had already happened. The words the police officer spoke to tell him he was under arrest? Never heard that set of words in that order before. His wrists had never felt the pinch of handcuffs, his neck and shoulder muscles never tensed in the specific way required of the cuffing position. New, too, the feeling of a firm but gentle hand on the top of his head, guiding and protecting at the same time, as he bent awkwardly to slide into the police car. All new and, on one level, surprising, fascinating even. But *oh, right, yeah, this* underscored it all.

Only years later, when he heard a radio segment about inherited trauma, did it click into place for him. His grandpa had died in prison after more than a decade inside. His uncle Steve had done a few stretches, as had some great-uncles and great-great-uncles. The men of his line—his mother's line, not that of his poor dad, although who knew really? Dad'd been out of touch with his family since he was a kid—these men had prison in their blood.

Will had prison in his blood, and now he also had it in his memory and on his record, waiting to fuck him over. Stealing away dreams and jobs and relationships and sleep.

His phone buzzed, Lena again.

I could die in this hoard and it would be a close thing whether the neighbours noticed the smell of rot or you noticed I'd stopped texting you first

He couldn't hear her, didn't know if she was being ironic or silly or genuine. Couldn't think of a single thing to text back to let her know he was listening. Reading, whatever. Didn't have the first fucking clue as to what was required of him right now.

Dad would know. That thought, the drumbeat of his adult life. He knew there was a danger of romanticising the dead, knew he wouldn't be the first bloke to mythologise his own dad into some kind of too-good-for-this-earth hero, but for real, he hadn't ever met a man who was as good at life as his dad was. A man who could move confidently through a room, knowing when to hug, when to kiss a cheek, when to shake a hand or rest one firmly on a shoulder. A man you wanted at your party because he could make small talk and tell jokes and knew exactly what song to put on to kick things up a notch. Knew when a joke was a human-ising gift rather than glib distraction. A man who stopped fights, never started them. Who women trusted to mind their kids and sometimes mind them when they were too pissed to mind them-selves. Who his own kids loved so much they would have died of grief when they lost him if only he hadn't made them promise not to. Whose kids respected him so much they'd never break a promise, even one so bloody bloody bloody hard to keep.

The question Will never thought to ask him, but which he thought about all the time these days: how did he know to do all that, to be such a good man, when he didn't have a dad himself to teach him? It was one of those questions Google couldn't help you with. How come my fatherless dad was so good at being a man? How come I'm so bad at it?

'Five minutes!' the not-a-screw-but-could-be hollered through the door and that was helpful, because Will knew then that what was required of him was to pick his shorts off the floor and slide them onto his legs, find his t-shirt and pull it over his head. To shove his feet into his sneakers and tie them up. Wallet into one pocket, phone into the other, overstuffed backpack from floor to shoulders.

Three minutes, tops, to clear himself out.

—

A smoke haze sat over the pub dining room thanks to the wide-open, full-length windows. You could see ash particles moving through the sunbeams over the food station, mingling with steam as the barmaid from last night slopped baked beans into the bain-marie. 'Beautiful one day, can't fucking breathe the next,' she said.

'Geez, they work you hard here. Didn't you only knock off five minutes ago?'

'Feels like it, yeah.' She cradled the empty pot like a pregnant belly, looked him up and down. 'You've pulled up all right this morning.'

Was she taking the piss or were her standards that low? He hadn't showered or looked in a mirror for three days, had been drinking and popping codeine like a man with no family, no job, no hope. Which he was. If this was her idea of 'all right' then he worried for her, he really did.

'Got any coffee?' he asked.

Her face closed down. She nodded towards the bar. 'Usual place.'

One of the old-timers who lived out back was stationed next to the coffee urn. 'Cobraball fire's out of control, residents of Yepoon evacuated, six thousand hectares burnt in Livingstone Shire,' he said, speaking to the mostly empty room rather than Will personally. He continued as Will carried his food and coffee over to a cleanish-looking table, reporting in the same flat tone on the status of a bunch of towns Will had never heard of. Only on the third mention of the out-of-control Cobraball fire did Will realise the bugger was reading the ticker-tape alerts from the silenced TV over the bar.

Eating his soggy beans and dry scrambled eggs Will scrolled through Mercy's Facebook page, clicked a link she shared about some meteorologists in the Arctic who had been trapped with a bunch of polar bears on a tiny ice island as the rest of the ground literally melted away around them. In the comments someone said, *Why is this news? Glaciers have been melting at unimaginable rates for years*, and Will muttered that it was probably the meteor-ologists trapped with the bears bit that made it newsworthy, but there was no Mercy to hear him and he shuddered because the blokes inside who muttered to themselves were lost causes. The kind of men you'd hear had drowned in their own spew or thrown themselves off a balcony within a week of being released, of being unwatched.

The next comment said, *ha ha no sympathy had it coming*. The bears or the scientists? Us, maybe. We have it coming. It was what Mercy always said, that the human race was getting what it deserved. She said it with something close to excitement and it made Will queasy, this way of talking about climate catastrophe like it was justice. *What about Haymish and Taylah?* he'd asked her once. It was last summer, fifth day in a row over forty degrees. *Do they deserve to live in a world where the temperature will stop them going outside for months at a time?* She'd rolled her eyes at him. *I'm taking about the human race being generally shit custodians of the planet. Don't be so literal.* When he asked if Haymish and Taylah weren't part of the human race, she got properly shitty with him, told him he could cool it with worrying about *her* kids, thanks very much. Her KO move, reminding him they weren't his to worry about.

Back on Mercy's Facebook page, one of her friends had written under the polar bear link: *Babe, this article's 3 years old FYI.*

And Mercy had written back, *Oops! Bad news comes so fast it's easy to miss things when they happen, hey?*

And he really, really wanted to write: *WHY DO YOU SOUND SO FUCKING CHEERFUL ABOUT IT???* But that was the kind of comment a lost cause, aggressive ex-con, *not* stepfather material kind of person would make and so he didn't.

Instead, he navigated to a job search site and scrolled through the current vacancies in the area. There were a couple of warehouse and labouring possibilities, but even the thought of clicking APPLY NOW exhausted him. His first job out of prison had been up at the mines. Just labouring, but better money than you'd get doing the same work anywhere else. Plus there'd been room and board provided, every second weekend off to do what you liked in town. It'd been hard work but an easy life and he'd managed almost four years before he'd pushed his luck on the detox time after a weekend bender and returned a positive alcohol test on the Monday morning.

The best job he could get after that was collecting trolleys at a shopping centre in town, but that ended when the HR department followed up on his non-supplied police check and he had to admit he'd been in prison. They said it wasn't his record that was the problem but his lying about it. Always be one or the other, though, wouldn't it?

Mercy was furious on his behalf. They're not legally allowed to ask, she reckoned, unless it's a place where you need a Working with Children Check, and even then a drug offence isn't necessarily a deal breaker. She said this like it was helpful, though she knew that the only job he'd ever wanted to do absolutely needed a WWCC and that given the choice between an employee with a drug conviction and one without, anyone with half a brain would pick the second. Not to mention the fact that the question's illegality was a technicality at best. What was he going to do? Drag the centre through the courts for unfair hiring practices? 'Scuse me while I withdraw the ten thousand bucks to pay my lawyers.

Her righteous anger on his behalf was pretty bloody great, though. They'd been seeing each other for a couple of months at that point, having first hooked up at the shopping centre Christmas party, and he assumed she was in it for the sex, because, let's be real, what else could a gorgeous, super-smart pharmacist mum-of-two want with an uneducated, bogan, ex-drug dealer trolley boy? But when she went off her head about his getting fired and got her dad to help him find another job, it was honestly the most loved he'd felt in years. Maybe ever. He grew a whole foot taller just listening to her defend him. He'd moved in a week later, adjusted easily to life with two sweet, funny, needy little kids. Which is not to say he didn't look forward to the one week a month they were with their dad and Mercy ground him almost to dust (happy, grateful, lovestruck dust) with all the fucking.

Anyway, turned out his initial instincts were spot on and the happy family bullshit was, well, bullshit, and here he was now, retrenched from the warehouse and fired from his role as Mercy's fuck toy/live-in babysitter and therefore unable to ask her dad to help sweep his past under another HR rug, and so it was back to sitting across from blank-faced recruiters buzzing with anxiety about if and when he should disclose that he'd been locked up.

Lena's name popped up on his screen and he clicked through to the new message:

Shit. Maybe you're the one who's dead and rotting and that's why you're ignoring me. Soz if true. My bad

That one he heard. It made him laugh out loud (like a self-talking lost cause?) and it gave him the next step. He took a gulp of lukewarm coffee, dug his nails into his palms while the wave of tooth pain crested, navigated away from the job ads, then used almost every dollar left in his account to book a one-way ticket to Sydney, leaving that arvo.

Meanwhile, old mate in the corner had switched up his routine: *No rain on the radar,* he reported. *Hot, gusty winds forecast across the state. No relief in sight.*

LENA

Three hours into Lena's Friday night shift, right when she was due her tea break, a man buying a kilo of extra-lean pork mince and a four pack of top-of-the-range toilet paper asked her if he knew her from somewhere.

'Don't think so,' she said. 'Do you need a bag?'

'Yeah, give us a bag, thanks. I do know you, though. I'm sure.'

Lena made herself look him in the face. Early twenties, pale skin, dark-blond goatee. Could be a student. Or just the kind of bloke who spends time swapping amateur porn with other blokes on the internet. 'Probably seen me in here. I work a lot. That's eleven forty-five. Cash or card?'

'Nah, I never come here.' He put his head on the side. 'You on Tinder?'

'No. Eleven forty-five.' She pushed the EFTPOS machine towards him.

He slapped his card against the reader, looking down at her chest. 'How come you don't wear a name tag?'

She resisted the impulse to cross her arms over her breasts. 'Lost it.'

'So you'll have to tell me your name then.'

'Jane. Is there anything else? I need to close my register.' She turned to her cash drawer, never wished so hard in her life for a queue to form.

'Nice to meet you, Jane. I'm Zac.' Out of the corner of her eye she saw him pick up his bag and then hold his phone out towards her. She would not look.

'I'll keep an eye out for you,' he said. 'Message you next time you pop up on here.'

She was going to throw up. Or scream. She pulled a Handi Wipe from the container under her counter, wiped up the moisture that had seeped out of his meat pack before she'd bagged it. It wasn't much. A patch of sweat. She scrubbed at the belt, taking off months-old grime. Kept going until she could be sure he'd left.

In the tearoom, she told Barb about the man. Laughingly, like it was a clumsy pick-up attempt because probably that's what it was.

'I dunno how you do it, you young ones,' Barb said. 'All this online dating palaver. I'd never have gotten hitched if I'd had to do all this selfie swiping stuff, worrying the next customer coming through has already had a good look at me and my proclivities on his phone.'

'I don't do any of that,' Lena said. 'He didn't know me at all. Just being a creep.'

A couple of shelf-stockers passed by. One mumbled something to the other and they laughed, side-eyeing Lena. The taller one saw her looking, stuck his tongue through a V of his fingers.

She stood, fire all through her. 'You got something to say?'

'To you? Nah, love.'

'You sure? Because it seemed like you did just now.'

'Calm down,' the other bloke said.

'Let 'em be.' Barb touched her arm.

'I'll let 'em be when they stop talking shit and making obscene gestures.'

'Obscene gestures?' He threw his hands in the air then brought them down in a chopping motion on either side of his crotch, pushing his groin towards her. 'Like this, you mean?'

'For god's sake,' Barb said.

'Get the fuck away from me.' Funny how easy it was to say now. It was as if saying it to the RA had unstopped the bottle and all the fuck-offs fermenting inside were bubbling out. 'Just fuck right off, I mean it.'

'Could report you to management for talking like that.'

'Report this.' Lena stuck her finger up.

They left, laughing. Barb said something about not rising to the bait. Lena couldn't listen. The whole world was bait. She couldn't move without getting hooked through the guts.

—

I think people at work know
  What happened? from Annie.
  Just comments and looks and stuff. Sleazy shit
  Fuck em, from Lou.

Go to Human Resources, Annie wrote. *Tell them you're being harassed #metoo. They'll shit themselves*

Human resources! Would that be ancient Yvette who still collated the timesheets by hand, or the snappy bitch of an office assistant who spoke like organising the electronic funds transfer was fucking rocket science, met any questions about late or wrong payments with an exasperated sigh and a lecture about how complicated the system was? Maybe it was the store manager, a man Lena had never seen let alone spoken to, or his 2IC, who was known to the women of the store as the Creeper?

Nic would get it.

Nic was not an option.

Think I'll just quit. Like right now. Just walk out

That's what I'm talkin about! Fuck. Them. From Annie.

That's my girl. Walk with your head held high, said Lou.

But later that night, Lou texted again: *Sorry about the work sitch. That must suck*

What doesn't these days?

You, girl. You do not. Hang in there

———

Back at Nic's, three hours earlier than she should have been and with a whole new series of messages to delete—these from her manager—ex-manager—she turned on the TV, watched without registering what she was seeing for a long while. Slowly some of the content leaked into her consciousness. A reality show where old English people brought fancy shit down from their attics and presented it to other old English people who declared it was worth hundreds or thousands of pounds and then, as often as not, the owners declared they would keep it because of its sentimental value and Lena thought, *Bullshit, that ugly fucking figurine will be up on eBay before the credits roll.*

Oh. An obvious solution. She'd always been a bit slow. Not stupid, though. She knew there wouldn't be any items worth thousands in this mess, but there were so very, very many items that even a buck or two for each would add up nicely.

—

It took an hour or so to figure out the best way to go about it. The hallway was the only clear space so that was where she worked. Spare light bulbs seemed to be the one consumer item Nic didn't buy in bulk, so Lena had to pull one out of a bedroom lamp and then risk ending up beside her aunt in hospital by standing on her toes on a rickety chair to change it. Light on, body in one piece, Poison sing-screaming, she got to work. Wet wipes and phone (on airplane mode) on one side, garbage bags on the other, she started on the first crate, pulling out an item at a time. If it was unbroken, untorn and unfaded, she wiped or shook it clear of dust, laid it to best advantage on the actually pretty nice retro-looking floorboards and snapped a photo. These items made a neat, single-depth line against the wall. Broken, torn or faded beyond repair went into a garbage bag. Those items needing a button sewed, a crack glued or other minor repairs went back into the crate or box of origin to be dealt with later.

Much of what she photographed was, in her opinion, useless crap, but she'd spent enough time scrawling through Gumtree and eBay and Etsy to know that people sold and bought useless crap all the damn time. The key was to make the price low enough that people felt they were getting a bargain, but high enough that they didn't realise they were actually doing you a favour by getting rid of your garbage for you.

When there was no more room in the line across the wall, she started on the other side. When that was filled she moved to the armchair, disconnected from airplane mode and created a new web-based email account and vendor profile. She uploaded the pictures and descriptions, making sure to note that pick-up was free, delivery would be Australia Post rates.

Yellow t-shirt, ladies, size S. Good condition. $3

Orange terry-towelling shorts with white racing stripes, men's, size 34. As-new condition. $3

Red-and-white-striped sundress, ladies, size XL. Never worn. Tags still attached. $5

Canvas tote bag with retro-style drawing of a cat in sunglasses. Good condition. $2

White leather handbag, 80s-style with tassels. Leather in good condition, zipper broken. $3

Dark brown teddy bear wearing red bow tie, 45 cm, brand-new, tags still attached. $6

Original Cabbage Patch Doll, red curly hair, very loved, with some smudges on cheek and one shoe missing. $4

Little Bo-Peep plastic toy. Teeth marks on staff, otherwise good condition. $1

Set of four blue-and-white-gingham cotton placemats, never used, labels attached. $2

Set of twenty-four *Cleo* Magazines from 1980 through to 1990. Make an offer.

Child-sized pale blue plastic clothes hangers. 50c each or 10 for $4

25 jam jars, various sizes, some with labels attached, all with lids. Clean. $6

Kmart-brand white canvas shoes. Ladies. Size 9. Never worn. Tag attached. $5

Girl's summer nightie. Cotton/polyester blend. Pink with *Frozen* picture. Good condition. $2.

Pet rock, light brown, 3 cm, plastic eyes. $1.

Pet rock, dark brown, 3 cm, plastic eyes. $1

Pet rock, dark brown, 5 cm, plastic eyes. $1

Pet rock, white and brown marble effect, 3 cm, plastic eyes. $1

Pet rock, red and brown marble effect, 3 cm, plastic eyes. $1

Pet rock, tan and black marble effect, 3 cm, plastic eyes. $1

Mousepad, 35 cm x 30 cm, cartoon mouse print. $1

Mousepad, 35 cm x 30 cm, cartoon kangaroo print. $1

Mousepad, 35 cm x 30 cm, cartoon duck print. $1

Mousepad, 35cm x 30 cm, Rubik's cube print. $1

Mousepad, 35 cm x 30 cm, Disney princess print. $1

12 Officeworks-branded mousepads, still in original wrapping, 35 cm x 30 cm, light grey. $1 each or 12 for $10

Red, patent-leather dress shoes, 4 cm heel. Ladies. Size 7. Good condition, slight scuffing on sole. $2

Lanyard holder (black plastic) with retractable 45 cm red strap. 10 for $3

6-piece bone-coloured plastic chopstick set, new, sealed plastic box. $5

Christmas tree brooch. 5 cm x 5 cm. Plastic front, gold pin backing. $1

Jumbo box of 100 multi-coloured hair ties, never used. $3

She didn't judge, didn't assess in any more detail than was necessary to communicate the condition. What she couldn't help doing, however, was adding up in her head the amount of money she would make if every single item sold. Chump change. Keep her in 7-Eleven coffee but not much more.

When Annie's grandma had died earlier this year, the family auctioned off her estate, which did not mean—as Lena had stupidly, embarrassingly thought—a block of land, but all the shit inside her Paddington terrace and Milton farmhouse. The proceeds were put into trusts for Annie and her siblings and cousins. Lena didn't know what trusts were either, had to google it when Annie went to the loo. She still didn't understand, really, but the gist was a heap of money gets planted somewhere to grow into lots more money and then you can have it. It was a big family, but still, Annie's share would buy her a house on the North Shore once she finished uni and moved on from her city pad.

What would Annie say about Aunty Nic's estate? Yeah, Lena could tell her, I'm thinking of investing in a large cappuccino next week if the estate sale goes to plan. I think the interest will be strong—I mean, look at this beautiful artefact: an early twenty-first-century mass-produced office stapler, blue plastic, standard-sized, used, but works like new. Likely to fetch as much as $1.

A message pinged into her vendor mailbox.

HeelMan94: *tell me about the red shoes*

Lena retyped the description she'd already used.

what do they smell like?

Like nothing. They're barely worn, very clean

do you have some that smell like your feet? any colour but lots of foot sweat smell please. i'll pay double

Then, before she could answer: *actually i'd prefer to wait for a few days so you can wear the red ones for awhile. tell me how much. i'll pay extra if you send me pics of your feet in them while i wait*

Lena hit the block button. Went back and deleted the shoe post, but not before she saw that twelve people were 'watching'.

—

Exhausted, hands red raw and itchy from handling dust and polyester and rubber and plastic, aching from cleaning and folding, Lena walked up and down the hallway, surveying the goods. What would it take to pack up and post this shit even if it did sell? Inviting all these dicks to creep onto her alternate online identity in the meanwhile, risk having someone like HeelMan94 turn up at the door if she arranged an in-person pick-up.

She deleted all the posts she'd made, deleted the account. Took out a new roll of garbage bags and filled one after another after another, placing each newly swollen bag against the wall until there was a satisfyingly neat row, three bags high, ready for the skip that was coming tomorrow morning. She'd had to use Nic's credit card to pay for it, which she felt shit about, but the bloody thing cost four nights' work and since the Mastercard had literally fallen into her hands while she'd been searching for Nic's Medicare card, as requested by the hospital, she figured it was a sign.

———

Finally encased in her sleeping bag, Lena steeled herself to scroll through all the messages that had arrived since she'd last looked. She should forward some of these dick pics to the shoe creep, that'd be fun. Or maybe forward them to each other, a dick exchange, though most of the dick senders blocked their numbers.

Better idea: *Think these came to me by mistake*, she wrote to Josh, then forward forward forward every last unwanted cock.

Closing down all the apps she noticed it was 3.25 a.m. The row of bags against the wall was less satisfying now she realised it was the result of six goddamn hours of work.

On the other hand, she felt even better about bombarding Josh with penises since he would either be woken by all the pinging dicks or wake up to a phone turned filthy with them.

NIC

'Lena not coming today?' Kon asks while checking Nic's bandages at the end of his shift.

'Don't think so. She's got a lot on.' Nic wonders if he knows what the social worker said, what Lena promised. It seems to her that nobody communicates with each other here except for notes about dressings and medication scribbled on a chart. Every nurse or doctor she speaks to seems not to know anything about her circumstances beyond the chart. Except Kon, who is either the only human on staff or, if she's being fair, somehow has fewer patients or less admin work to attend to and so can spend a few minutes chatting every time he comes around.

'I bet. I don't think any of my nieces or nephews would be able to find five minutes to visit me in your situation.'

'You have nieces and nephews? How many?'

Kon pretends to count on his fingers, throws his hands up when he reaches ten. 'Dozen or more. Lost count. I'm one of eight and the rest of them have been breeding for Australia, so it's hard to keep track.'

'You're not close to them? The kids, I mean?'

'Oh, now and then. You know how it is. You're their favourite one day and they don't want to know you the next. Maybe it's me, though. I never liked kids that much—even when I was one.'

'Lena's the same way. I mean, she's fine with older kids—going to be a teacher and all, so you'd hope so. But she's not keen on babies, toddlers and that. Says she can't stand to be around people content to sit in their own poo for hours.'

'Right? Sitting in their own poo, face covered in snot and slop and god knows what and will scream the place down if you try to clean them up. Disgusting little creatures.' As he says this, Kon washes the hands that have just re-dressed her infected leg wound. She doesn't believe for a minute he'd be repulsed by a messy baby. He wouldn't know how *not* to be tender. Look how he'd distracted her from being swabbed and stung and bandaged! Banter as anaesthetic, Michelle used to call it. Taught Nic how to launch into a slightly shocking story or controversial opinion right before the splinter had to come out or the mercurochrome had to be dabbed on.

'Not that I've given up on world's best uncle title, mind you.' Kon adjusted the blanket over her newly dressed leg. 'Once these kids reach legal age it's my time to shine. No PlayStation at my place, but I've got a well-stocked home bar and a hell of a music system.'

'You have a lot of parties?'

'Not formal, capital P parties. But there's always something simmering, people coming and going. It's a hub, I like to think. Mates know they can come and hang out, stay over if they need to. Open house, pretty much. More the merrier.'

'That was my place once—but for the kids. When Lena and her brother were little. They were always around and often had a little friend along. No home bar but a truly impressive selection of sugary breakfast cereals.' It hurts to think about it, but in a nice way. Best years of her life, those were. She could have that again, couldn't she? For adults now, like Kon had described? She can picture it, actually: a nice little chrome and red vinyl bar up the back corner of the living room. Two or three shelves on the wall behind with bottles of whisky and bourbon, Midori and brandy and vodka and gin. She has some cocktail recipe books she can display. And all the different kinds of glasses: highballs and tumblers, flutes and coupes. Then over the other side of the room, next to the TV, a proper, grown-up stereo. And some candles—or, no, retro lamps here and there around the space making it all soft and sexy and atmospheric.

What she can't picture is who will be there to enjoy the soft and sexy atmosphere. It stings, the thought of all the unused space between the bar and the stereo, the sparkling emptiness of the glasses, permanent fullness of the bottles. She wants to ask Kon what came first for him: the welcoming home or the friends needing welcome? There had been times over the years when acquaintances were on the verge of becoming friends and it was her turn to reciprocate their dinner or barbecue or drinks invitations, and when she didn't the relationship drifted back to a nodding one. Three times this had happened. More maybe, but she doesn't want to think about them too much. It wasn't the fault of her house. If they'd been good enough friends she would've made the effort to clean up for them. If they'd been good enough friends they wouldn't have cared if she didn't.

'Can I ask you something?'

Kon has been fiddling with her drip and jotting things down on her chart for the last couple of minutes. The pen is in his mouth as he fiddles some more. He makes a noise she interprets as *yes*.

'Say you had to get rid of some of your things. Say, I don't know, like a third of your stuff.'

'Mmm.' He stops fiddling for a second then continues, but Nic feels the change in his listening, knows he must be aware of her situation. Feels unable to turn back.

'Out of all the people who come and go at your place, all of them and all your brothers and sisters, nieces and nephews, work-mates and neighbours and just . . . out of everyone you know, is there anyone you'd trust to do that for you? Like, to choose what stays and what goes?'

Kon smiles. 'Sure. I can think of, oh, ten, fifteen people. Maybe more.'

'Really?' Does she even know that many people? If she counts everyone at work, including the casuals, then maybe. 'You wouldn't worry that their idea of the important stuff will be different to yours?'

He considers it. 'There's this artist in London, right? He got all of his stuff together. Like, everything. Chairs and towels and empty chip packets. His own art and pieces from friends. Photos, letters. His bloody *car*, which was a Saab or something. And he destroyed it all. Like, every single thing he owned.'

'Drugs?'

'Don't know if he had any, but if he did they'd have been in there.'

'No, I mean was he on drugs? Is that why he did it?'

'No, no. It was art. He did it in the middle of Oxford Street. Invited people to watch. Put on a boiler suit, played some Bowie and smashed it all up into nothing. It took weeks.'

'What a terrible thing to do. You'd have to be a psychopath.'

'Well, he was being deliberately provocative. Challenging people to think about consumerism and identity and all that. Like, who are we without our possessions?'

'If he wanted to know who he was without his possessions, he could have given them away.'

'Yeah, but that's not art. It's just, like, a life experiment.'

'I guess. Sounds like a dickhead, though.'

'Probably he is, but here's the interesting thing: the public was mostly on board—critics, too. It was all, *Down with consumerism, smash up that big-screen TV, pulverise those state-of-the-art speakers*, but when it came to the love letters and photos, the art, they were like, *No, that's inhuman. Those things aren't objects. How could you?*'

Nic is still, concentrating on her breathing. The story feels like a trap but she doesn't know what kind or when it will spring.

'I think it tells you that most people agree about what's important. Most people found the destruction of those particular items painful, considered them a different category.'

To anyone with a brain—with a fucking *heart*—it all would have been painful, she wants to say. A *Saab!* In her whole life she will not earn enough money to have a bloody Saab. Or a TV not from Kmart. Or half the shit the wanker destroyed.

'What did he do with it all, after? The smashed-up stuff?'

'I don't know, actually. Chucked it, I guess.'

'Yeah, but where? Like, it must have been a lot to get rid of. He would've needed a couple of trailers at least.'

Kon laughs. 'Big important artist. Bet he had someone else to worry about those details.'

'That'd be nice, wouldn't it? Someone else to worry about all the details.'

'Ah, well, that's the one good thing about being stuck here. You get to relax and live like a London performance artist for a bit.'

'Lucky me,' Nic says.

She wants to know what the artist did when he was finished destroying everything. When he went home and realised he didn't have a bed to sleep on or a plate to eat off, no toothbrush or soap or loo paper. But Kon is already wishing her a good night and saying he'll see her tomorrow.

WILL

Mercy had been very clear she didn't want him contacting her.

Clean break. Easier for everyone.

Walk away with sweet memories, no bitterness.

This is exactly why we need to—

No, I won't get into this with you.

I can't believe you're trying this, Will. There's no such thing as access rights to your ex-girlfriend's kids.

Clean. Break.

Move. The. Fuck. On.

Which was fine. Easy. Every time he was tempted to call or message her he simply shoved his tongue as hard as he could against the screaming raw nerves around his rotting tooth and every thought he'd ever had was obliterated. If this went on long enough his brain might automatically make the connection between her name and agonising, most likely pus-filled infection sites, which would be helpful in curbing his tendency to mope and crawl and plead after a break-up.

On the other hand, he might die of blood poisoning. Which would also prevent moping etc. Win-win.

Whether because of imminent blood poisoning, mopiness or his usual general dumb-fuckery, he managed to stuff up his flight schedule, left himself only twenty minutes to make the connection in Brisbane, which, since the flight was delayed by an hour out of Mackay, was a big fucking problem. Of course there were no more flights to Sydney that night. Of course. The airline desk attendant was sweet and seemed genuinely sorry for him. If he'd tried he probably could have swung an invitation into the airline lounge. He couldn't remember how, though. To try. He spent the night at Brisbane Airport's gate 41, the discomfort of the row of plastic seats he attempted to lie on distracting him for whole minutes at a time from the pain in his mouth.

When the airport pharmacy opened at 7 a.m. he tried to buy some codeine, was reminded he needed a prescription and had to settle for Panadol. He swallowed a double dose as soon as he got on the plane, and another two halfway through the flight. The box told him the contents could be toxic if you exceeded the recommended dose, but at least if he ended up in hospital with paracetamol poisoning he might get some decent pain meds.

By the time he'd boarded the Sydney airport train he concluded he'd been sold a placebo. The pain was immense and he couldn't resist sticking a finger in there every so often to try to press the throbbing down. An old lady across the aisle made a point of muttering under her breath each time and he genuinely felt bad about grossing her out, but it was that painful he couldn't help himself.

As a distraction he flicked through the photos Lena had sent. He focused in hard, zooming and dragging multiple times on each, feeling a tickle of satisfaction when he managed to recognise a chair or toy or framed picture in among the visual noise. He was reminded of the window of Kerrie's Gifts back in Mackay. From across the street it was a jungle scene, but painted in gold and blue and pink and yellow instead of shades of green. Up close, you began to see where one object ended and another began and then, with concentration, you could make out what some of those objects were: garish Venetian-style masks hung off teddy bears which sat on side tables which were perched over ceramic dolls which were nestled next to wooden crucifixes and glass vases and lamps and some of all that half draped in scarves and tablecloths, and in any tiny gaps glimpses of the shop beyond, shelves and shelves of more of the same.

Except in Lena's photos, only a third or so of the stuff was identifiable, even when he zoomed right in. A lot of the space was taken up by bags—garbage bags and canvas shopping totes and a few of those plastic-hessian stripy things you saw homeless men dragging around at Roma Street station. He hoped the bags were Lena's work and that they would all be gone by the time he arrived, but he knew that was unlikely. Most of them were wedged tightly against other bags, against furniture or stacks of paper. They were storage, not garbage. But storage for what? Clothes, probably, but also things with sharp angles that poked through the sides, small appliances and boxes and . . . and . . . what? He racked his brain.

Will owned exactly the amount of stuff that fit into the backpack at his feet. He knew he was an extreme case, but still. He went through Mercy's house, mentally opened all the cupboard doors, scanned the shelves. More pots and pans and plates and glasses than they ever used in the kitchen. Board games they never played in the hall cupboard, a drawer full of tangled cords and cables that had never been needed but seemed like they might one day. Mercy and the kids had more clothes than they wore, but no more than fit in the wardrobes. What else was there? What did people have? Books, maybe? Like, what do you call them—ornaments?

The old woman across from him muttered *disgusting* and he dropped his spit-covered hand in his lap. 'Sorry,' he said, because he was. 'Toothache.'

'Have you seen a dentist?' She sounded like his mum. Exasperated at having to ask such an obvious question.

'Yeah, nah. Bit broke, you know.'

The woman closed her eyes, sighed. He was in for a real lecture now. 'You got a Medicare card?' In a tone that suggested she expected him to say *no*, because that's how evidently incompetent at adulthood he was.

'Yeah. Dentists don't take—'

'Go to a doctor, love. Bulk billing. Not a dentist but better than shoving your filthy paws in there making it worse.'

He tried to smile, but it hurt quite a bit. 'Yeah, good idea.'

She muttered something about common sense, went back to squinting disapprovingly around the carriage, looking for someone else to shame into taking basic, obvious action to sort out their shit.

At the Railway Square walk-in medical centre the receptionist said the wait might be an hour. He settled into an uncomfortably soft chair and scrolled through his social media feeds, then on to the news app, where he found himself looking into the face of a fifty-thousand-year-old wolf pup uncovered after massive permafrost melts in Canada. *Another day in which the Sydney skyline is invisible, thanks to unprecedented levels of bushfire smoke blanketing the city*, said the breakfast program playing on the TV over his head.

Twenty-four hours ago he'd been in a Mackay pub tasting locally produced catastrophic bushfire smoke with every spoonful of beans, and though he'd travelled almost two thousand kilometres by bus, two planes and a train, the background commentary as he held in his palm a recent photo of an animal last seen in the Ice Age was still of locally produced catastrophic bushfire smoke. Was this what vertigo felt like? Or was it simple dread, this sense of plummeting and spinning at the same time, with no surety you will ever land?

It wasn't just this story, this pup. All over the world things meant to stay buried were being uncovered because people had forgotten they were part of the world even as they couldn't stop devouring it. In Russia, a long-frozen reindeer carcass suddenly thawed and the nineteenth-century anthrax that had killed it took the opportunity to infect a twenty-first-century child and not a single flight was cancelled, not a single carbon-spewing factory closed.

Last year a Czech river revealed centuries-old low water marks made on stones. One said, *If you see me, weep.* Nobody did, though, far as Will could tell. They tweeted it, reposted it, reported it in the last minute of the TV news, letting the credits roll over the footage of the rock, so dry it was hard to believe water had ever touched it. The etched warning didn't look frightening at all if you couldn't read Czech. It could have said anything. It could have said, *Everything is fine. Carry on exactly as you are.* Everyone, including Will, acted as though it did.

———

At the ninety-minute mark he approached the desk, waited for the receptionist to stop typing and look at him. When she didn't he cleared his throat, asked if it'd be much longer. The woman sighed loudly, demanded his name, rolled her chair over to a different monitor, sighed again. 'There are three people ahead of you,' she said.

'It's just I've already been waiting for—'

'The people ahead of you have been waiting longer.' She slid back to her original position, recommenced typing.

He sat back down, ashamed. Nobody else had stood to question the waiting time. Nobody else thought they deserved special treatment.

At the two-hour mark he caved, washed down two more Panadol with water from the cooler next to the front door. The white cardboard cups were so tiny he needed to refill and tip the contents into his mouth five times before the tablets went down all the way, and still his throat felt bruised from the effort. He was going in for a sixth refill when his name was called. He dropped the cup, fumbled to pick it up as the doctor repeated his name. 'Here,' he called, sounding like an idiot kid in class. Couldn't see anywhere to put the cup, scrunched it in his hand and tried to keep up with the bald, skinny doctor race-walking down the corridor.

Before Will had managed to sit, the doctor was asking what the problem was.

'Um, I've got this toothache . . .'

'Seen a dentist?' The doctor was as absorbed in his screen as the receptionist had been in hers.

'Nah, um, that's the thing, why I'm—I can't afford to yet but I thought maybe you could, um, in the meantime, something for the pain.'

The doctor pushed back from his desk, swivelled in his chair to face Will with widespread legs, elbows on his knees, gaze steady. 'Something for the pain?'

'Yeah. It's, um, pretty bad. Keeping me up and that. I hoped you could—'

'Tried Panadol?'

'Yeah, that's what I'm taking now. I had some codeine—'

'You have codeine?'

'I had some left over but it's gone so I—'

'Left over from what?'

Will's face flashed with heat. He knew from Mercy and her pharmacist mates that asking directly for the strong stuff was a red flag. So was acting nervous or on edge. Like, say, dropping a cup of water, scrunching and un-scrunching a bit of rubbish in your hand and turning red when questioned. He focused on breathing slowly, relaxing his shoulders.

'My girlfriend had them left over from something. I haven't been prescribed anything.'

The doctor kept watching his face. Didn't move.

Don't babble. Don't fidget. You haven't done anything wrong. 'The pain is sort of here.' Will cupped his cheek. 'It's been a week or so, getting steadily worse.'

'But you haven't seen a dentist?'

'No, like I said, I don't have the money right now. I've just, um—' *Stop!* 'I was retrenched last week and my financial situation is . . .'

The doctor flicked his eyes at the computer screen. 'You're a long way from home.'

'Oh, yeah, um. I'm staying with family here.'

The doctor looked pointedly at the stuffed backpack at Will's feet. Will was immediately aware of his faded board shorts, threadbare t-shirt, greasy ponytail and five days of stubble. Knew the shadows under his eyes must show the nights of disturbed and shallow sleep. He felt tears coming, sucked in a few fast breaths to clear them away.

'I will be staying with family. On my way there now. After this. Just arrived this morning from Queensland. Long trip, you know. Overnight as it happened, because of flight delays and, um, travelling's tiring, yeah, but I'm on my way to my, um, aunty's place now. She's in Leichhardt and I didn't know if there's, like, ah, a bulk-billing place there anymore, so I thought I better, you know, while I'm in the city still, find somewhere to get some, um—' *Stop it!* Deep breath. 'To get this sorted.' He cupped his cheek again.

'Let's see then.' The doctor snapped on a pair of gloves, rolled forward, shone a torch inside Will's gaping mouth, prodded at the pain with surprisingly gentle fingers, rolled away, discarded his gloves, began typing.

'Any allergies?'

'Nah.'

'There's some indication of infection. I'm prescribing you an antibiotic to help with that. If the pain continues, though, you will need to see a dentist to sort out the underlying cause.'

'Right, thanks.' Don't ask for pain meds. Don't ask for pain meds.

The doctor handed him the prescription. 'Anything else?'

'No, um, yeah, it's just the pain is—'

'I understand you have some pain. The problem, Will, is that you've never attended this practice before. Your home address is in another state. I don't know your medical history, have no way of knowing how many prescriptions you've already collected or how much codeine or whatever else you may have hoarded. And in any case, the level of inflammation does not lead me to think prescription pain relief is necessary. Over-the-counter should be sufficient to tough it out.'

Fucking hot face, fucking goddamn prickle of tears. He couldn't speak and didn't know what he'd say if he could. He nodded, left the doctor's office with the prescription in one hand and the scrunched-up cup in the other.

At the pharmacy counter he swallowed his last trickle of pride and asked how much the prescription would cost. Twelve bucks. There was fifteen, maybe, left in his account and he still needed to get to Leichhardt. If he skipped the antibiotics he could buy three packs of off-brand ibuprofen for nine dollars and then he'd definitely have enough left for the bus fare. Probably.

'Mr Harris?' The pharmacist was tapping the counter. He was aware of the line forming behind him.

He nodded, let the woman take the script away to prepare. There'd be painkillers of some sort at Aunty Nic's. Maybe even some good stuff. Could be Aunty Nic had a hoard of the kind the prick of a doctor was referring to. A whole pile of opioids or narcotics ready to tumble out of some high, forgotten cupboard Lena hadn't cleared out yet.

Boarding the bus at Railway Square his adrenaline surged. When he asked the driver the fare to Norton Street, the man rolled his eyes, pointed at a machine further down the aisle. Told him to tap. Again, there was a line forming behind him and he felt the collective impatience at his taking a whole goddamn five seconds to ask a question needling his spine.

There was a time he wouldn't have thought twice about boarding a bus without the fare. On the rare occasions an inspector boarded you'd duck, get off at the next stop, no worries. Different once you were a grown man, couldn't easily slither through the packed aisle, jump over shopping bags and dodge prams, slip out the back door before the inspector made his way to you. Different when you had a record, and no idea which of the tiny infractions so-called civilised society might accuse you of would be over-looked, which a cause to drag you back to court.

Anyway, he tapped his debit card on the machine like he saw others doing and it chirped in the same way it had for the people in front of him which probably meant he was okay.

While he'd been waiting at the medical centre he'd worked out that keeping his mouth slightly open helped. He felt like a creep sitting there gaping, but figured it was better than poking himself in the gums every few minutes. Probably. The view out the window onto Parramatta Road might have made him gape anyway. He'd been away less than seven years but everything had changed. Empty shopfronts and graffiti-covered building sites where there used to be bridal shops and bakeries, towers of apartments where there used to be delis and 1940s terraces. A low-rise unit block they'd lived in for a few years when he was at primary school was now a pole dancing studio, the building they moved to after that was gone altogether, a block of dirt and rubble protected by a chain-wire fence and signs warning tres-passers there were attack dogs on site.

On Norton Street, the Coles where he and his mates stole Mars Bars and batteries and condoms was still there, but on either side nail salons and massage shops had replaced the Italian cafes and delis. The primary school looked the same as it had when they'd jump the fence at night to lie on the grass, which was softer and cleaner than the grass anywhere else in the suburb. Looked the same but there'd be an alarm system now, for sure, maybe secu-rity guards. Boys like they'd been would have to find somewhere else to watch the stars and smoke and talk shit. Were there still boys like that here? It seemed unlikely what with all the Pilates studios and artisan bread shops.

Walking from the bus stop through the back streets of the suburb was like walking back in time, though (except for the top-of-the-range cars parked in front of every second driveway, *Stop WestConnex* signs on every third lawn, construction racket from every fourth or fifth house). But lilly pilly hedges and red-brick walls still outnumbered security fences, and jacarandas and silky wisteria still dripped onto the footpaths. Still the waft of garlic and roasting tomatoes, the roar of planes overhead. Houses he'd been inside once or twice or dozens of times, yards where he'd smoked his first cigarette, drunk his first bourbon, had his first—first ten or twenty, probably—kisses.

In one street, he passed two houses of now-dead school mates and the turn-off for the street of another. One car crash, one accidental OD and one on purpose. All in this neighbourhood, all before they were sixteen or seventeen. Thanks to the shit show of prison followed by years at a FIFO site that attracted the desperate and reckless he knew other dead young men, too many to say off the top of his head. He'd have to actually run through their names and count, and he wouldn't be doing that, thanks very much.

But these three he knew without thinking, without remembering. They were there same as Dad, too much alive in this place to ever not be here. Macca, jug ears and a stinking mutt of a dog always at his heels (though not in the car when it melded finally with the telegraph pole). Stokes, short but with a Hollywood smile that made every girl ready to kick off her undies and every bloke keen to smash his teeth into his throat. No one did, though, because he was always up to his not-real-high neck in both pussy and pills, and happy to pass on his extras to the other fellas. Forgot he had to take the children's dose, they all joked at his funeral. Sam had been laughing the loudest. Held a deflating beach ball he'd found melting into the ground somewhere, said, *Hey, look, I'm Stokes with an eccy.*

Sam downed his entire prescription three weeks later. What the prescription was Will didn't know. People just said it like that—*took the lot, whole prescription*—as though you were meant to know.

Prescription. Fuck. He stopped in the middle of the foot-path, slapped his loose short pockets as if the packet could have somehow made its way in there without him knowing, unzipped the backpack and ferreted around with both hands even though he knew he had not opened the damn thing since the airport. When had he last held the pharmacy bag? Boarding the bus it had been in his right hand. He'd balanced it on top of the backpack while he fumbled his debit card out of his wallet with the whole hostile line bristling behind him. Balanced it there and then tapped his card and, still holding the card and his wallet in one hand and the backpack with the other, clomped down the aisle to an empty seat. He'd dropped the backpack while he put the card in the wallet and the wallet in his pocket, and then?

Someone would find it later today, he guessed, skidding out from under the seats as the bus took a corner. Check if there was anything good inside before chucking it in the bin or dropping it back on the floor, stomping it flat for the hell of it.

At the corner of Aunty Nic's street it occurred to him that spending twenty-four hours travelling while grieving several relationships, panicking about the future and nursing a terrible toothache was pretty dumb. Doing all that in order to revisit the city where he watched his dad die and where his last known address was a state prison was completely fucking stupid.

But then there was the reason he came. Lena. Seeing her would slow his plummet, maybe even reverse its course. For all the shit memories he had of Sydney, he also had plenty of good ones, and most of them featured his sister. Not her alone; the four of them. As a family they were the kind of happy you didn't realise was rare until it ended and you got a taste of what life was like for most people, most of the time. They were an ordinary, squabbling over the TV, struggling to pay the bills, annoying the shit out of each other at the dinner table, really, really, really fucking happy family. They loved each other and a lot of the time *liked* each other as well. It was a miracle unnoted until it was over.

He could never get that back, obviously. But maybe something new and almost as good, now he and Lena were free, independent adults. No Mum hovering anxiously, no Rick the Dick forcing himself into their space, pretending to get their decades-old family jokes. Just the two of them against the world. It could be great. A fresh start. Exactly what he needed.

LENA

Salvation arrived at 8 a.m. in the form of a bright yellow skip bin taking up three car spaces on the road outside the house. Within an hour of signing the delivery docket Lena had cleared the house of eighteen bursting-at-the-seams bags. Drop in a garbage ocean, but a boost all the same to see the speed with which it was possible to get rid of stuff once there was somewhere to chuck it.

She had just hauled the second non-functioning vacuum cleaner of the day into the skip when the road moved beneath her feet and black spots appeared on the yellow steel. She closed her eyes, eased forward until she could press her head and palms against the skip, and waited for everything to stop moving.

She breathed in metallic tang, breathed out the sickly sweet fruitiness of ketosis. Lou had taught her to recognise the smell, celebrate its achievement. It meant her body was cannibalising itself, using its fat stores to survive. Problem was that she needed to do more than survive today. She needed to complete another ten hours or so of hard labour. Also, she didn't have much in the way of fat stores left after nine months of eating lunch like Annie (miso soup, sashimi, garden salad without dressing) and skipping dinner because who can afford it when you've spent fifteen dollars on a frigging tasteless lunch salad? Eating like a rich girl while still being a poor one had not only helped her become as thin and wan as a model, it had taught her a lesson that extended into every aspect of life: If you get used to wanting less, you'll always have enough.

She'd forgotten this briefly, gone ahead and let herself have what she wanted without restraint or caution. If she'd known the voice in her head urging her on belonged to a woman so greedy she would almost die under the weight of her belongings, she may have resisted. May not have ended up in an exponentially replicating video, the epitome of a shameless whore who just can't get enough.

When the world felt stable again, Lena returned to the house and scoffed a stale protein bar from the bottom of her backpack. Her ungrateful stomach grumbled and cramped while she started work emptying the bath. Could start her own shitty supermarket, right here. Come get your out-of-date, slimy-labelled, store-brand shampoo and conditioner, your leaking, sticky tubs of hair gel. Buy three jars of palm-oil-and-paraben-laden face cream and get a jumbo bottle of environmentally disastrous micro-beaded body wash for free.

She stopped to piss, wondering whether 'organic and all-natural avocado body butter' was edible, saw that her undies were splattered with blood. She hadn't had her period for months—another benefit of the skinny rich girl diet—but *of course* it had to come now.

You win, body, you win. I'll leave this house stocked with everything except what I need to go spend money I don't have on things I don't want. Fucking perfect.

—

As she stepped out on to the porch, a man pushing a stroller with one hand and gripping a leash attached to the torso of a rapidly toddling child with the other glanced at Lena, then focused. His eyes said, *Don't I know you?* Or maybe it was: *What are you doing there?* He slowed, calling for the child to stop, tugging on the leash as he moved towards Lena. His smile said, *ugly bitches are the best at riding dick theyre so grateful.*

She fumbled with the door, which had closed and locked behind her. It took her too many seconds to remember that the key was in her pocket, and by the time she had it in the lock the man was calling to her. Not loud, close.

'Hey! Hi! Something happened to Nic?'

Lena turned, took him in. Smooth baby face but with grey streaking through his thick black hair. One arm pulled behind his back by the straining toddler.

'I'm Andre. I live across the street. Up a bit and across.' He jerked his head to the left. 'Haven't seen Nic for a bit. Wife and I were just saying, hope nothin's happened to her?'

'Oh. No. Actually, yes, sort of. She had a bad fall last week. I'm Lena. Her niece. I'm just—'

'Lena! The brains of the family. We know all about you and your high distinctions and everything. A fall, hey? That's no good. You're here to take care of her?'

'Yeah. I mean, she's in the hospital at the moment. Probably for a bit longer.'

'Geez. Poor thing. We wondered because, well, she sometimes watches the rug rats for us. I texted her the other day but she never—I feel awful now. Shoulda come and checked up in person.'

'She babysits for you? Here?' Lena could imagine the straining toddler climbing one of those living room stacks, falling hard on her soft little head. And the baby? Would it even be able to breathe in that thick, dusty air?

'At ours. The little one sleeps through and this one—ha, not that you'd know from her current feral state, but she crashes out early and stays out mostly. So it's not, like, a lot of work for your aunty. We're not taking advantage or anything. I trim the hedges, sweep up the leaves and that for her.' He spread his free arm out, taking in the non-expansive expanse of it.

'I was just thinking how neat it was out here.'

He smiled, bit of pride there. 'Nice having neighbours you can rely on, help each other out. Not many in this street, sorry to say. Nic's one of the good ones, but. So you just here to get some things for her or—'

'Daddy! Stop talking! Come on come on come on come on!'

Andre laughed, waved a hand at his little girl.

'I'm staying for a bit,' Lena said. 'Getting the place, ah, cleaned up for when she comes back. She'll need a bit more room to get around.'

'Good on you. She's that proud of you, hey. Must be stoked you're doing all this for her.'

'Daddy! I need you now! Come on come on come on come ooooooooon.'

Andre grinned, turning towards the stroller in the driveway and the straining child. 'Better get this one to the play centre before she screams the neighbourhood down. But hey, let us know if you need a hand with anything. I work nights, so anything during the day. And after five my wife Mel's home. She loves Nic, so, yeah. Number forty-eight. All right, chicken, I'm coming. See ya, Lena.'

⌒

The supermarket aisles reverberated with a child's full-throated screams. Lena scanned the shelf labels beneath the tampons. The yellow-stickered ones, super-sized and with applicators, were almost half the price of her preferred slim regulars. The difference would buy a tub of cottage cheese and a tin of tuna. Maybe a bag of salad, too, if the cottage cheese was on special like last week.

Probably there had been tampons in the piles of stuff she'd thrown out from the kitchen the other day. There had been so many overstuffed plastic bags in the cupboards and under the table that she'd stopped opening them. What was the point when nine out of ten items went right into a different plastic bag ready to be tossed?

This, right now was the point. The blood stiffening her undies while she calculated the unit price of discount tampons.

Probably some of the bags she'd tossed from Nic's room had brand-new undies in her size, too. There had been a lot of clothing, tags still attached.

From behind her came a *tut-tut*, which she didn't know was even a real thing that people did. She spun, ready to unload on the cow *tutting* her slow tampon contemplation, but the cow— actually a tiny, grey-faced woman with Amy Winehouse hair—was shooting daggers at the screaming, thrashing child who'd just been wheeled into the aisle by a serene-faced woman in a West Tigers jersey.

'A good slap'd sort that out,' the cow said as the trolley rolled past. If the Tigers fan heard, she didn't show it, continuing up the aisle and stopping in front of the painkillers. Then, as though her hearing worked on delay, her head snapped towards Lena and she blinked, looked back at the pills, peeked to the side as though she wasn't.

I didn't say it, Lena wanted to tell her. Instead she knocked the cheap, giant tampons into her basket and took off for the tinned food aisle.

At the checkout, the toddler was doing its best to maintain the rage one aisle over. It was like those old battery ads with the drumming bunny; the kid kept kicking the sides of the trolley and shaking its fist, howling incomprehensibly at the floor, but ever slower, ever quieter. Winding down down down.

Lena felt the mother's eyes on her. She glanced over . . . Yep, still staring. Fuck. Did the woman think the slapping comment had come from her or . . . Fuck fuck fuck. Even here? Even fucking everywhere. That's the point of the internet, hey.

If the checkout chick hadn't already started scanning her shopping she would've taken off. She willed the girl to go faster, shoving the items into her backpack as soon as they were through, smashing her card against the reader before the girl could mumble *Nineforty-sixcashorcard.*

She had one foot out the door when she heard her name. She turned and saw the trolley—with half-a-dozen canvas shopping bags and the toddler now slumped, hiccupping, with eyes half closed—wheeling straight for her.

'Lena! Bloody hell! Lena Harris! It's been like eighty-seven years!'

Jersey tight against enormous breasts and several fat rolls, slicked-back blonde ponytail, black roots regrown to her ears. Something familiar about those green-grey eyes, though, and the dimples now she was smiling.

'Shit! Kylie?'

'In the flesh, mate.'

'Shit!' Lena laughed, slapped a hand over her mouth.

'You're blocking the entryway, girls,' a man's voice said, and without looking or responding the two of them moved out into the shopping centre, Kylie gripping Lena's arm with her left hand, steering the trolley with the other until they were clustered against a railing.

'How do you look the exact fucking same as when you were thirteen?' Kylie said.

'Bullshit.'

'Nah, you're right. Your skin is way better. Still got no tits or arse, though. How've you managed that?'

'Who's this?' Lena nodded toward the dozing, snot-encrusted child.

'Lacey. Fucking menace, she is. Nah, for real, though, she's a great kid. Just going through the terrible twos and all that. So how come you're here? Like, on holidays or back for good?'

'For good, I guess. I mean, I came back down for uni, but—'

'You were always smart as fuck. Hey, listen, I've gotta get this little monster home, but why don't you come with us? I'll get her settled and then we can catch up properly.'

'Oh, I should really . . .' She shrugged her backpack, pointlessly.

'Someone waiting for you?'

'Nah. Not really.'

'So come on then.' Kylie started walking and Lena followed. When they came to the automatic doors, she wheeled the trolley right out on to the street and kept going, chattering away about what Jo and Nash and the rest of the old school crew were up to. It was three minutes or so before Kylie stopped out the front of a shudderingly familiar block. Four separate six-storey red-brick buildings, each divided into thirty units with a shared balcony connecting them. The ground in between was concrete and determined weeds, VB cans and ciggie butts and faded choc-olate wrappers. It was like a TV executive's idea of how poor people lived.

Kylie scooped up her kid in one arm, grabbed shopping bags with both hands. Lena went to take some for her, but she was already marching up the path towards the middle building, the trolley left to fend for itself on the street.

'You still with your mum, hey?' Lena asked.

'Fuck, no. I've got a place of my own one floor up.'

'Cool. She's still here then? Your mum?'

'Yep. They'll get her out of here in a body bag if they ever get her out at all.'

These were the flats Lena thought of when that tower in London caught fire a few years back. It was much taller than the building she was following Kylie to, but the shape and feel of it—the paper-thin interior walls, the concrete external stairs and landings—had made her think of the place she'd spent so many summer days as a kid.

Kylie climbed the three flights of stairs surprisingly quickly for a fat woman carrying a toddler and a week's worth of groceries. Lena, half the size including her backpack, struggled to keep up, her lungs burning by the top of the first flight. By the second her knees were creaking, the left one threatening to give out as she reached Kylie's floor.

'Bit puffed, mate?'

'Yeah.' Lena stood against the railing, catching her breath as Kylie unlocked the door to the unit at the far end of the landing. 'This air's so shit. Too much crap in the lungs, I reckon.' Which might have been true, but also she felt her body becoming her father's in the first months of his illness. The clicking and cracking that signalled he had stood or bent or knelt or sat; the breath-lessness after walking from car to front door. Not the cancer turning his strong, young body ancient. Not directly, at least.

Malnutrition, the doctor said, and she never knew whose idea it was but a regime of pot smoking was decided on and Will sent to procure the supplies, and Dad was better then, for a bit.

Lena followed Kylie into the gloom, confused for a second by the thick, sweet smell of pot as though her thoughts had taken form. At the back of the room, a man in a tall black beanie leant over a state-of-the-art bong, coloured glass and engraved brass attachments, twice the height of the two-litre bottle of Pepsi sitting next to it.

'Ty, this is Lena. Lena, Ty.' Kylie dumped the shopping in a doorway to her left and then placed the sleeping child on the overstuffed brown velvet sofa next to the bong and its user.

'Hey.'

'Hey,' Lena said.

Ty was older than them. Older than Will. Maybe even as old as her mum or Nic. It was hard to tell for sure with his face cloaked in shadow and smoke.

'Leen and me were mates when we were small. She's just moved back from Queensland.'

'Fuck the Cockroaches,' Ty said, but with so little spirit Lena wondered why he bothered.

Lena asked to use the bathroom, took her backpack with the tampons. The toilet door had a laminated poster on it saying *Best Seat in the House* in fancy black font. Inside was a matching poster: *Hello, Sweet Cheeks.* There'd been a stack of similar posters at Nic's. Cheap laminated prints saying things like *This Home Has Endless Love and Laundry, Life is Short, Lick the Bowl* and *Siri, Pour More Wine.* She wished she hadn't chucked them now. They'd be a good gift for Kylie.

She returned to the living room to find Kylie sitting on the floor in front of the lounge. She patted the carpet beside her, and Lena sat.

'So tell us what you've been up to.'

'Oh, well, you know. Like I said, came back down to go to uni . . .'

'Ha. Fucking Queensland don't even have any unis. Explains a lot.'

'Ignore him. He's an idiot.'

'Least I'm not a Queenslander.'

'Yeah, so uni, hey? You doing teaching? Tara's doing teaching. Maybe she's finished by now. I dunno. You remember Tara? Always scratching her arms until bits of skin flew off?' Kylie shuddered, rubbing her own bare arms.

'She had eczema.'

'Yeah? Fuck, I thought she was just addicted to scratching and that.'

'Mighta been on the ice,' Ty said. 'Seen a fella scratch right through to his insides once on that shit.'

Kylie rolled her eyes at Lena, saying, 'Yeah, Ty, she was on ice at the age of ten.'

'Could be, could be.'

'Anyway, I know she was going to uni to do teaching because she came into Mac's—you know the chicken place up at the centre? Yeah, so I work there a couple nights a week—and she came in one time, like three years ago or something, and she said how she'd gotten into the teaching course and that. She looked pretty pleased with herself. Can't remember if her arms were scratched up or not. That'd be a bit shit for a teacher to have skin flying off and that, hey?'

'The treatment for eczema is heaps better now,' Lena said, although she had no idea if it was true. She was sinking into a pleasure she'd long forgotten—being the clever one, being appreciated for that.

'Good to know. So what are you going to teach? Like the little ones or . . . ?'

'Yeah, primary. But actually, maybe not. I'm thinking of dropping out.'

'How come?

'Lots of reasons. I haven't been going much, exams are starting and . . . I dunno. It just feels kinda pointless, you know?'

'Fuck, what doesn't, mate?' Kylie said, but then reached behind and stroked the sleeping child's arm and smiled a little.

'Yeah, so, weird thing, though. You remember my aunty Nic?'

'Yes! She always had rainbow Paddle Pops in the freezer. And she painted our nails for us, like all different colours and with glitter and that. We used to pretend she was our mum. How's she doing?'

'Turns out she's, like, a total hoarder these days.'

'Fuck, for real? Mrs Kidd in the block one over's a hoarder. Department's been trying to get her out for ages, hey, but she's got some lawyer or social worker or something, this smart bitch who keeps fending them off. They tried to get some cleaners in a while back. Poor Mrs Kidd. Screamed her fucking head off the whole time, cops came and all. Remember that, Ty? When the cops were up at Mrs Kidd's?'

'They were looking for her husband.'

'No, they weren't. That's a stupid shit rumour.'

'Yeah, well how come he just stopped turning up at the pub one night and then after that the mad old thing starts filling her house with so much shit no one can get inside? I'll tell youse why. Because she's knocked him off and his body's hidden somewhere under all that crap. He'll be dust before anyone gets to him.'

'Maybe he took off because of all the shit. Didn't want to live in it anymore.'

Ty shook his head. 'The shit came after he disappeared, I'm telling you. He's in there somewhere.'

'Grief,' Lena said.

Kylie raised her eyebrows.

'Just . . . maybe he left her and then she started to just, like, keep stuff because she was sad and that.'

'That what happened to Aunty Nic? Her bloke leave her?'

Lena shrugged. 'I don't know what happened. Don't think she had a bloke, though. Not anyone serious anyways.'

'What does she say about it?'

'Doesn't think there's anything wrong. Forbid me from cleaning up. Mum and Will reckon I should leave it, but they're not here. They don't get how—'

'Will! God, I had the biggest crush on him when we were kids. Such a babe. How's he going anyway? Staying out of trouble?'

'Yeah, he's good. Been up in North Queensland pretty much since he got out. Got himself a girlfriend, coupla stepkids. Living the dream, he reckons.'

'Good for him. For real, stoked to hear he's come through okay. Bloody Will, hey? Speaking of, do you want—' Kylie cringed. '*Not* speaking of Will. Just, I was gonna ask if you wanted a smoke.'

Lena laughed. 'I'll tell him his name makes you think of that now.'

'Shit, I'm a dick. Forget I said it. But have a smoke if you want. Ty'll give you some.'

'I'm good. You go ahead, but.'

'Nah, I don't touch it. Not since . . .' Kylie tipped her head towards Lacey. 'Gotta stay sharp with a little one. Especially round here. All the stairs and balconies and bloody druggies and everything.'

'That's right,' Ty added, before sucking back again.

'You want something to eat? I'm starving.' Kylie crawled across the floor and rummaged through the bags she'd dumped earlier, emerging with a pack of Doritos the size of her child. 'Help yourself.'

'Nah, I'm good.'

'Go on, you're skinny as a rake, mate. You should eat up.'

'Nah, really. I should go, actually. Call in at the hospital before I head back to the hoard.' Lena stood, shook out her creaking knees. 'Hey, I love that poster.' Muhammad Ali in full glorious flight, white letters across his chest: *The harder the battle, the sweeter the victory.* 'I should get that tattooed on my forehead.'

Ty looked up. 'I know a bloke can do it for you. Cheap and that. If you want.'

Kylie laughed, squeezed her eyes shut for a second. 'Yeah, Leen. Ty'll hook you up for a cheap forehead tatt whenever you want.'

Lena was overcome with the urge to hug Kylie, but instead she tapped Ty on the shoulder as she headed for the door. 'Hey, good to meet ya.'

'Wait, wait, wait. Lemme give you my number.' Kylie moving faster than seemed right, again, reaching towards Lena with open hand. 'Give us your phone.'

Lena's phone hadn't stopped vibrating in her pocket this whole time. What was waiting there when she pulled it out?

'Dead battery. Gimme yours.'

Kylie handed it over before she'd finished asking. A newer model than Lena's but with a spider web crack over the top half of the screen. Lena added her number. Said goodbye. Kylie closed the space between them in an instant, gave her a rough, hard, fast hug and then disappeared back into the apartment.

At the bottom of the stairs Lena leant against the wall, waiting for her legs to catch up to her heart. When was the last time anyone other than Nic had hugged her? Josh, when he said goodbye to her after they fucked. And before that? Annie a few times when she was smashed. Mum, saying goodbye at the train station more than nine months ago.

Her phone buzzed and she pulled it out. A fuckload of notifications, but at the top, just arrived from Kylie: *Glad your back nerd i bawled my eyes out when you left shutup but i did stay in touch xxxxxxx*

Lena scanned through the messages that had banked up in the hour she'd been in the supermarket and at Kylie's. A missed call from Will. One text each from Lou, Annie and Mum. Eight unknown numbers. Three unlisted numbers. Two from Nic. Four from Josh.

I guess you've blocked me and I'm sending this into a void. Have to try

Can't stop thinking about you

If you'd give me a chance to explain

Just meet with me one time then Ill never contact you again if thats what you really want. Please

She stared at the phone. How could she speak to Nic without telling her about the giant yellow skip, to Mum and Will without admitting she'd quit her job and, by the way, was an accidental porn star, to Annie or Lou without letting on how broken and disgusting and ashamed she felt? How could she respond to Josh with anything except a raw, guttural scream?

She deleted everything. Called no one back. Decided to skip the hospital for the second day in a row. When your whole life has become unspeakable, you'd best avoid speaking.

WILL

Will was waiting on Aunty Nic's porch when Lena started up the path. He'd been planning to leap up and shout, *Surprise!* but her expression as she approached was pure terror, like there was an axe murderer charging at her. He barked with laughter, snapped a series of fast photos as recognition hit.

'Will? Holy fuck! You bastard! Why didn't you tell me you were coming?'

'Wanted to surprise you. Which, mission accomplished. Your face, mate. Bloody unreal.'

Truth was he felt a bit shocked-and-awed himself now he was looking at her up close and personal. When he'd said goodbye to Lena in Brisbane she was a sturdy, sun-browned fourteen-year-old. He'd seen plenty of photos of her since, knew she'd got skinnier as she grew taller, but none of the photos captured this frailty. Her collarbones stabbed up between the straps of her dirt-streaked pink singlet; a pair of navy school shorts hung low and baggy off her bony hips. And that goddamn vicious purple scar, more obvious than ever against the unnatural, wintry paleness of her skin.

He swallowed the gut-cramping panic the scar always produced in him, gestured to the front door. 'Can we go inside before the lung cancer sets in or what?'

'Yeah, 'course.' Her huge, wet eyes blinked fast. She unlocked the door, hesitated. 'Actually, just let me put this shopping away and then we'll go see Nic. She'll be so excited.'

Lena turned on her heel and Will followed her into the house. It looked about the same as in the pictures Lena had sent, which was weird given the skip he'd walked past on the way in had been half full.

'You ready?'

'Yeah, but . . .' He put his backpack on the floor at his feet. 'Can we take a minute to catch up first. I haven't seen you in—'

'Nic's expecting me.'

'—six years,' he finished.

'We'll catch up later. Come on.' She squeezed past him, out the door. 'Make sure the lock clicks shut,' she called, already on the footpath, moving away from him.

⸻

Aunty Nic was in a different hospital from the one Dad had died in. This one was on an inner-city street so chaotic that making it from the bus stop to the front door was like a game of *Frogger*. Motorbikes and delivery vans and SUVs screamed to a stop milliseconds before slamming into Lena as she dominated the crossing, seemingly oblivious to it all. Will kept stopping before the vehicles did, not sure they wouldn't speed through, leaving a vaguely man-shaped smear on the road. By the time he reached the entrance Lena was tapping her foot. 'Keep up, country boy,' she said.

Once through the sandstone arches and across the granite and stained-glass foyer the hospital felt remarkably familiar. The same poster chiding lazy lift-riders about the missed opportunity to be good to their hearts by taking the stairs. Same creepy instrumental versions of Elvis Presley songs playing just loud enough that you can't ignore it, interrupted by the same decibels-louder pre-recorded announcements about proper hand-washing and the fines applicable to anyone found smoking in the building. Same aggressively chemical scent in the public areas, not always disguising the reek of piss or shit or vomit or blood wafting from the wards.

Outside Aunty Nic's room, Lena reminded Will not to say anything about the house. 'As far as she knows, I left and never went back.' He thought it was stupid to lie about it—she was going to find out sooner or later—but this was Lena's show; he was merely the supporting actor.

If Lena hadn't been there it would've taken him an age to figure out which of the six seemingly comatose, elderly white people was Nic. But Lena went straight to the middle bed on the right-hand wall, plonked herself in the visitor's chair. 'Wakey, wakey, Nic. Big surprise for you today. Huge!'

The eyes opened, blinked a few times and there, instantly, undeniably, was Aunty Nic. For a terrible second he was sure he'd burst into tears, instead he said, *'Haven't you been in the wars?'* like an awkward grandpa talking to a toddler. Lena had taken the only chair, so he hovered a minute and then perched on the end of the bed, millimetres from the blanketed lump of his aunty's left foot.

'Surprise all right! Geez, I would've taken a dive from my dressing table years ago if I thought I'd earn a visit from the one and only Mr Will Harris.' She said it in the same light-as-air tone she used the last time they saw each other, the day before his sentencing. She'd hugged him tight and told him it was a blip, that no judge in his right mind would put away a kid like him for supplying a little pot, whatever that legal aid moppet said. Mum said Nic was exactly right, which made him relax all the muscles he'd been tensing since his arrest. They never agreed on anything, so this must be, like, inarguable. Aunty Nic said she wasn't even going to come to court because she'd just see him at home after.

And here, nearly seven years later, he was the one to come to her, the one asking *her* how she was coping.

Aunty Nic flicked the question away, sending tubes shuddering, making Lena suck in her breath and gently press the hand back down to the bed before running her fingers over the cannulas, checking they remained attached.

'Stop fussing,' Aunty Nic said, then to Will, 'Tell me everything! How's Queensland? What is it you've been doing up there? Something in the mines?'

'Nah, nah. That was a while back. Lately I've been in a ware-house. Packing and transporting produce. Getting it from the farms out to grocery stores and that.'

'And where is this again? I know Lena told me.'

Will himself has told her more than once in the odd, rare text or Facebook message.

'Mackay,' Lena said now.

'Yeah. Actually, though, I was let go last week. The drought and the fires and all. Not so much produce to be moved at the moment, so . . .'

Lena made a sorry face, whether for the job loss or for not having bothered to ask for his news he didn't know.

'Best bit is,' he said, before either could ask if he was okay, 'couple of days after I lost my job, Mercy asked me to move out. Talk about kicking a man when he's down, hey?'

'Bloody hell. I'm sorry,' Aunty Nic said and actually sounded it. 'Do you reckon it's for good? I mean, people fight, need space and that. Doesn't mean it's over, does it?'

'Yeah, nah. I reckon it is, though.' As he said it he knew it was true. His jaw clenched and pain erased the world. When it ebbed and his vision returned both of them were looking at him with anxious, crinkled faces. 'It's fine,' he told them. 'I mean, I'm sad and . . . I'm gonna miss the kids something chronic, but . . . I'm fine. I'll be fine.'

'We should've known something was up, shouldn't we?' Aunty Nic said to Lena, fake jolly-jolly voice. 'Knew he wouldn't come all this way just because I had a little tumble.'

He had to walk out of the room then. It was just a bit too fucking much.

———

He wandered the hallways with half a plan to find a doctor and ask for some proper painkillers, but it quickly became obvious that the doctors and nurses—he wasn't sure he could tell the difference—occupied a different dimension. They were in his field of vision, but he was never in theirs. He observed that a few civilians had somehow learnt how to flag them down and draw them through a portal to communicate with the lowly realm for a minute at a time but then *whoosh*, off they went again, and you could be bleeding to death from all your orifices at once and they wouldn't see it. Literally bleeding to death, he reckoned, but if you didn't know the correct signal, every one of these green-and-blue-clipboard-and-lanyard-wielding figures would float on by, oblivious.

———

Lena didn't ask why he'd taken off. Didn't ask him anything. Looked at her phone the whole bus ride, angled so he couldn't see the screen. *Boyfriend?* he asked at one point, and she shot him a look that would kill any other man. It made him smile, though. He lived for those looks growing up. Making your little sister's face do that was the ultimate Achievement Unlocked.

Back at the house she slid a builder's dust mask over her nose and mouth. 'I spent yesterday in Nic's room,' she said, her voice muffled. 'There's space enough to move there now. You can take over. Concentrate on getting the floor clear.' She handed him two rolls of garbage bags. 'Green for rubbish, white for clothes or anything else that can go into the charity bins. When I say rubbish, I mean shit that's broken, faded, useless. Shit no one would want, even for free. You'll be filling five green for every white, trust me. Appliances, framed stuff, anything big, can go straight into the skip as is. Paper recycling bin is already full, so magazines and paper products go in the skip, too. Put anything that looks precious or important on the kitchen table—I started a pile there already. I'll go through it later.'

'Leen, wait. Can't we get some lunch or something? Catch up?'

'I've got too much to do. You go eat if you have to.' Lena plonked herself on the floor in front of a plastic storage container, pulled out a stack of CDs, dumped them into a green garbage bag by her side.

'Seriously?'

'Sorry. I really can't stop, though,' she said, not stopping.

'Right. Okay. But hey, do ya want me to sort through those CDs before you chuck 'em? Might be something good in there.'

'There's nothing good, Will.'

'Maybe not to you, but something Aunty Nic likes. Or I'd like. Or that we could sell.'

'Think like that and we will never, ever be done here.'

'So you're just chucking everything?'

'Pretty much.'

'Would Aunty Nic be okay with that?'

Lena pulled the mask down so it hung at her throat. 'She will not be okay with any of this. It doesn't matter. If we don't clear enough space they won't let her come home.'

'We can make space without chucking everything, surely. She's just gotta be able to move around easily, yeah? A few CDs aren't going to make a difference.'

Lena stood, pulled the CDs back out of the garbage bag and handed the stack to Will. 'Go for your life.' She gestured to the dozen or more clear plastic storage tubs lining the wall, and stomped out of the room.

He flicked through the CDs—*Panpipe Classics*, *Music to Dream To*, *Classics for Bedtime*. Fair call, Leen. He dropped them back into the garbage bag, dug into the container for the next lot. *75 Best Nursery Rhymes*. The cover left a film of sticky dust on his fingers. He chucked it and the six or seven beneath it into the bag, sung out to Leena that he could do with a rag or something for the dust.

She didn't answer, and after a bit he pulled off his t-shirt and began using that to wipe his hands, and the occasional promising-looking item. Didn't matter if the shirt got wrecked. It was a crappy old freebie, hardware store logo front and back. He'd worn it because it was the softest t-shirt he owned. Had to dress comfy for travel. Didn't notice when he put it on that moths had feasted on a section near the back hem and that the neckline was fraying in the front. No bloody wonder Mercy'd had enough. Look at the state of him, when she always made such an effort.

———

Over the next couple of hours Will sorted through six plastic storage containers in between glaring at his still and silent phone. There were dozens of records (mostly rubbish compilations but a couple of classics—Bowie! Springsteen! Patti Smith!—that he put aside for himself), four containers of wrapping paper (used and neatly folded as well as brand-new rolls) and six of Christmas decorations and lights. Underneath a plastic tub of sewing patterns—none of them looked more recent than 1985—there was a sewing machine, still in its sealed-up box. He wanted to ask Lena if Aunty Nic sewed and, if not, what did she reckon an unused but possibly quite old sewing machine was worth, but she was getting saltier and saltier every time he opened his mouth. She had, at least, chucked a pack of ibuprofen at him when he asked if she had any painkillers, but she'd looked super angry about it. He pushed the machine to the side and carried on.

Next: three tubs of yarn and one full of knitting needles and patterns. Definitely never seen his aunty knitting, never received a knitted gift from her (thank god). Knitting gear could be chucked. Or sold. Would anyone buy this stuff? It looked all right. Lena had said anything useless and this wool was definitely useable. Shit. He shoved the knitting gear next to the sewing machine. He'd deal with the definitely-getting-thrown-out stuff first and then make decisions about the rest.

———

'Will?' Lena yelled from some distant pile, ten years or half a day since he'd arrived. 'Did you want to order some food? There's fuck-all here.'

'Yeah, um, thing is I don't have any cash and my account is kind of—'

A sigh heavy enough to bring down walls. 'I'll get it. But it'll have to be cheap-arse Dominos.'

Will's whole mouth spasmed at the thought of the chewy crust, the acidic sauce. He told her not to bother for him. He wasn't hungry. 'Cool. Same,' she said. 'Just thought I'd offer.'

He could howl with hunger. Fucking roar with it. He pulled out his phone (nothing from Mercy) and googled *Free dentist Sydney*. The first page of results all had the word 'pain' before the word free, which sounded good, but not without cost, which was what he needed. He dialled the first on the list anyway, walking out into the front yard as it rang. Smelt like someone had doused a bonfire the second before he'd stepped outside. The phone was answered by a machine, so he tried the next number and then the next. Finally he got through to an emergency dental service. They could see him immediately but it would cost a minimum of $245 for the consultation. More depending on what treatment was needed.

Back inside, he looked at the gaps in the hoard like a man waking from a coma. The newly revealed baseboards and window-sill were coated in what must be years of accumulated grime and laced with cobwebs. Some were grey and stringy, but others appeared freshly woven. Must be spider families scuttling all over the place, shocked by their exposure after living in peace for generations. Living well, it would seem from the black and brown flecks of half-eaten bugs scattered beneath the webs.

The carpet looked almost new in some places, protected from wear and tear and sun-fading; in other places it had been stained by unknown forces, worn through to the under-fibres by pressure or nibbling. And the air was getting worse, not better, the more he cleared out. Like every item had been holding a lungful of dust ready to release into the room when it was moved. He'd blown his nose earlier and the tissue came away bloodied, like he'd been punched.

Will pushed aside several empty plastic crates and leant over a waist-height stack of still-full ones to reach the window. The curtain was caught on something, and when he yanked it the whole thing came down, rod and all, sprinkling insect remains and scat as it fell. With it out of the way he was able to unlatch the window, but it stuck like it'd been glued in place.

'What are you doing?'

'Playing basketball.' He turned to his side, put his shoulder to the sash. His feet were too far from the wall. There was no way to get a proper grip.

'The air outside is worse than in here.'

'Impossible.' He stepped back, moved four crates from under the window to in front of the TV. Lena watched from the kitchen doorway, her arms crossed, face blank. Why had he imagined she'd be happy to see him? Hadn't they got on best of all when they'd been minimum nine hundred k's apart?

'I was out there, like, literally one minute ago, Leen. It's not that bad.' Now he was closer to the window he was able to get his shoulder right in under the sash, his hand flush on the lower glass. He took a deep breath, heaved. Nudged the window up a centimetre.

'Fine. Go ahead and poison the air I have to sleep in. Why should you give a shit?'

Will paused in his shoving, rested his forehead against the cool, weirdly sticky glass, remembered the time when he was ten or so and Lena had thrown a massive tantrum about some trivial shit and was sobbing into her pillow while Mum comforted her. Will had turned to Dad, sitting next to him on the lounge watching cricket, and said, *She's such a whiny cunt. Like she's permanently on her period.*

Dad, his eyes still on the telly, said, *You're gonna need to repeat that, because I can't possibly have heard what I think I heard*, and Will could read the tone of his voice and knew he was in big trouble. He mumbled something about being sick of Lena carrying on all the time. Dad turned the TV off. Told Will to look at him, which Will tried to do but couldn't.

Three things, Dad said. *One. I don't know who you heard that period thing from but you need to know that periods don't start until girls are teenagers, or near enough. Your sister is six years old. Saying she's on her period makes you sound really, really dumb.*

Two. Only ignorant, backward idiots who hate women think talking about periods is funny or insulting.

By now Will had his defence, was busting to spit it out, but he knew it would work better if he waited until Dad was finished, so he held it in.

Three. If I ever, ever hear you use that word again—you know the one I'm talking about—I'll knock your teeth out. If I hear you use it about your sister, I'll cut out your tongue, too.

This last bit shook him. Dad never hit them, never even threatened it. The worst punishment they ever got was having to go to their room for an hour or miss out on dessert. But Dad was saying, *Do you understand me, Will? Do you?* And so Will took a deep breath and said, *Yes,* then, with the thrill of the righteous, added, *How come you didn't knock Muzza's teeth out?*

Dad blinked and Will went on. *'Cause he said it. That's where I heard it from. The other week out the back when Linda yelled at him and stormed off home Muzza said, She's such a—what I said. All of that. But you never told him off for it.*

Will shivered with pleasure at Dad's face. Almost said, *Ha ha, gotcha.* Muzza was one of Dad's *good* mates. He had lots of mates, but only half-a-dozen *good* mates, the ones who came around most weekends and who Dad went to the pub and the footy with on the regular. Muzza was maybe even a *best* mate, though Will had never heard him called that. But he was around more than most of the others, and on Anzac Day Dad took him to the march and then let him spend the day drinking until he cried and then passed out in the backyard and that seemed like a *best* mate kind of thing to do.

Dad stared at Will so long that the pleasurable shiver was replaced with fear. He could still hear Lena's sobbing down the hall. Maybe he should start yelling, get Mum running back out here. But no, Dad closed his eyes a sec, said, *Yeah, well, that wasn't*

*right him saying that. Not right at all. But he's not my son. It's not
my job to teach him how to behave.*

Will nodded, knew he wasn't really in trouble anymore. Dad
turned the TV back on and they watched it a bit longer before
Dad said, *It's okay to be annoyed with your sister. With anyone. But
you've gotta try to say things straight and calm. Kind, too, if you
can. Men like Muzza, they never learnt how to talk right to people.*

You said you'd knock my teeth out. That's not calm or kind.

A laugh, kind of. *Can't get away with anything, can I?*

Later, Lena came and snuggled on the lounge between Dad
and Will, and Dad kissed her forehead and told her the score.
Will felt crappy about what he'd said then. She was just a little
kid with a lot of feelings. And if Dad could stay calm and kind
about that then so could he.

'You're right,' he said now, pushing the window back down,
giving up the tiny ground he'd gained. 'We'll keep it shut.'

'Do you what you want. I don't care.' And she was gone again.

———

He was supposed to sleep in Aunty Nic's room, which had been
more cleared out than the others. But there was a stain on the
carpet he knew came from her body. Lena had done her best, but
blood and piss don't ever come out, not fully. Ask anyone who's
worked prison laundry. The bed was clean, fresh sheets and all,
but even with the light off the stains across the room bothered
him. The longer he lay there the more the residue seemed to be
seeping into him. He thought about little Taylah and Haymish, how

often he'd cleaned up their leaking body fluids or got up to change wet sheets and pyjama pants in the middle of the night. Hadn't bothered him one bit. Little kid piss was nothing. In prison the smell of other men's leakages was constant. The disinfectant made it worse, its chemical stench burning your nostrils and making them more sensitive than ever to the piss and shit and come, the sweat and unwashed hair and balls.

This was not like that. The room smelt a little musty but nothing animal, nothing invasive or infectious. But still. Someone had bled and pissed on the carpet a metre away from where he lay. Not just someone. Aunty Nic. Family. Made it worse somehow. Will imagined his own uncreated, until this moment unimagined, nephew having to sleep in a room in which he himself had lost control of his functions. Imagined the pity and disgust the kid would feel for poor old Uncle Will. The shame socked him in the chest.

He took the quilt and pillow, inched his way to the door, giving the stain a wide berth. The spare room. He could clear the things from the bed onto the floor tonight, clean up properly in the morning.

'What's wrong?' Lena said.

Will spun, tripping on the dangling quilt, taking a moment to find his balance again. She was on the sofa, her phone screen illuminating a face so old and haunted-looking his breath caught in his throat.

'What?' The phone dropped on her lap, her face in darkness and so bearable.

'Yeah, sorry, Leen. Can't sleep in there.'

'There's nowhere else.'

'What about—'

'Spare room? Yeah, good luck.'

He opened the door with difficulty, switched on the light as the small avalanche he'd started settled. Right. Was there even a bed in there anymore? It'd take a day's clearing before he could say one way or the other. God, he used to daydream about this shitty little room. After Mum told him she was moving to Brisbane with Rick the Dick and tried to get him to commit to coming up when he was released, he said to her, *You know, I think I'll stay in Sydney. Aunty Nic has always said the house was ours, too*, and Mum had said something cynical and mean, but he thought that was just her way when it came to her sister. He spent a lot of time thinking about how he'd fix up this front bedroom, paint the whole house while he was at it. After that he could clear the backyard and plant some vegies. Get a Weber and a little outdoor table. It helped, thinking it through; like designing a simple, comforting path he could take to reach the rest of his life.

He returned to the living room. Lena didn't look up from her phone. 'Can we swap? You sleep in Aunty Nic's room.'

She sighed. 'Why?'

'I don't like it in there.'

'Are you joking?'

'I find it creepy, okay? And you obviously don't, so stop being a bitch and go sleep there.'

'Wow. I was about to, but now you've called me a bitch you can sleep on the footpath for all I care.'

'Why are you like this?'

'Born this way, I guess.'

'Seriously. I came all this way to help you and you can't do one little thing so I can get some rest.'

'Fine.' She stood so fast, it was like she'd never been on the sofa at all. 'Thank you so much, mighty saviour. Of course you should sleep wherever you like, whereas I who have been dealing with this shit alone all week should immediately move to make way.'

'Leen, come on. I don't get why you . . .'

It was pointless; she was gone, stomping herself and her sleeping bag down the hall and slamming the door. *Cunt*, he said under his breath. Let Dad rise up and kick his teeth in. He'd bloody welcome it.

—

Before he'd woken properly, still cocooned in blankets on the lounge, pressing his tongue to his tooth, wondering if Mercy was awake and if she was thinking, as he was, of the way they were together in the early mornings, half asleep and warm and seemingly unable to get close enough to each other, wondering this while a tiny raw part of him did what it always did in the moments after waking and waited with a deep, sick sense of disbelief for the rise-and-muster bell. Still in this state of pain and longing and dread, but on the far edge of it, beginning to think of shaking off the night and the dawn and sitting up, a weight fell on his feet and with it the sound of his little sister sobbing.

'Leen? What? What's happened?'

She was a scrunched-up, quivering ball at the far end of the sofa. He couldn't move his feet without disturbing her, but he couldn't do much without moving them. She let herself be rocked and dropped, didn't let up on the sobbing.

Her phone was clutched tightly in her left hand, as per usual, but there was something else in her right hand. A moment of disorientation. Back in time, yes, but also space. This object that still existed but in a place it had never been. Will reached for it, was surprised at the tenacity with which she held on and then the suddenness with which she let go. It fell hard onto her thigh. Will grabbed it, turned it over in his hand. Dad's vice grips.

'Shit.'

'Yeah.'

'Where?'

'In her wardrobe. Box up the back. All of his stuff's there. His tools. I didn't know at first. That they were his. But once I saw that . . .'

Will ran his hands over the initials engraved on the underside of one arm. The rest of the metal was so scarred you wouldn't know the letters were there, unless they'd been pointed out to you, proudly, by the man who'd carved them. First tool Dad'd bought with his own money. The stuff in his bucket before then had been handed down or loaned to him by older mates. But he'd taken his first pay envelope straight down the hardware and, though he'd thought about getting cheap versions of half-a-dozen tools, when he laid eyes on the shiny red-handled vice grips he changed his mind instantly. Had to have them. Over the years he'd lost them many a time, he told the kids, but they always found their way back to him. It's how he knew it was the right decision; they were made for each other.

'How come Aunty Nic . . . ?'

Lena shook her head, swiped the back of her hand roughly across her face. 'She helped us pack and clean up before we moved. Her and Mum fought the whole time. Bet there's other stuff here that she nicked.'

'You think she nicked these? Maybe Mum—'

'Why would Mum give her Dad's tools?'

'I dunno. Why would Nic steal Dad's tools?'

'Seriously? Look around! She's nuts.'

'I guess, but . . . I mean, she wasn't like this then, was she? Her place was neat. Not like Mum-neat, but normal.'

Lena's phone buzzed and she flinched as though it had transmitted a tiny electric shock through her arm. She kept staring at the vice grips. After a while, he said, 'Anyway, I'm glad she took them. Probably would've been chucked out otherwise. Now we've got something else of Dad's to remember him.'

She was up and off the sofa in a second. 'I don't need a chunk of metal to remember him!'

'Good. You won't mind if I keep these then.'

'It's sad, you know. Needing an object to remember someone you loved. Your own father.'

'Didn't say I *needed* it to remember him. Just that it's nice to have.'

She kicked a garbage bag, as hard as she could judging by the way her whole body shook and staggered. It moved maybe a centimetre, stopped from going any further by the other bags surrounding it.

Will pressed the vice grips to his jaw. The initial contact killed but the cold was soothing. He'd never thought to ask what happened to Dad's stuff. Last of his worries at the time. It was sick-making to think of Dad's tools dumped into the stinking abyss of the council tip or accumulating dust in a cardboard box at Vinnies. Or, god, his clothes! They were bloody terrible, Dad's clothes. A family joke that Will was never quite sure if Dad was in on or not. He could see the stack on the ironing board, folded and ready to be put away: couple pairs of fading footy shorts, a thick stack of flannies, that one dressy shirt he got from the Country Road clearance sale, three identical pairs of Kmart jeans that Mum said made his bum disappear. No one would want any of that shit. Will didn't own enough clothes to fill a small backpack and even he didn't want it.

But.

Still.

But, still, though he had spent yesterday loading a giant street bin full of someone else's useless shit, and he would do the same today and tomorrow, still, if Dad's stupid, embarrassing clothes were here he would fall on them like they were laced with morphine. And this tool in his hand? This beaten-up, useless, worthless fucking thing he'd not given a single thought to until it was in front of his face? He would hold on to it until the day he died and if anyone ever tried to throw it away he would use it to bash their smug, sensible brains in.

NIC

Nic is woken by a text from Michelle asking how she is, texts back that she's great, thanks for asking. *Your lovely kids have been taking good care of me*, she adds, meaning it but also knowing it'll grate Michelle's cheese to think of them all together.

They are lovely kids, aren't they? Michelle writes.

Nic flicks back some love hearts.

But are you doing better?

Thumbs-up.

Thumbs-up returned.

This is as warm an exchange as the two of them have had in years. They're not estranged, but not *not* estranged either. Michelle will never forgive Nic for inheriting Mum's house; Nic will never forgive Michelle for moving to Queensland. But they both love Lena and Lena loves them both and so, for her sake, they attempt civility and occasionally even warmth.

Nic finds it funny that she has so much in common with her workmates who've been through bitter divorces. They swap stories of biting their tongues in front of the kids rather than let them know their parent is a piece of shit, of having to make polite enquiries about the health of the person who ruined their lives.

Of course, it's Michelle who would find Nic's inclusion in the divorced parents club funniest of all. Michelle is fond of calling Nic an Old Maid; has said, devastatingly, that she's been one since puberty. To Michelle this is the ultimate burn. She had her first boyfriend at eleven, first pregnancy scare at thirteen, first marriage proposal at sixteen. Nic, meanwhile, drifted through most of her teens happily unaware that boys or sex or babies or marriages might have anything to do with her at all.

There was this teacher, for example, who tried to seduce her when she was fifteen, but she didn't realise this is what he'd been doing until she was seventeen. She'd thought at the time he was another adult wanting to prove he was a good person by giving special attention to the girl whose dad was in prison. She didn't know that there were a half-dozen of them at the school with parents locked up, because none of them, including her, would ever talk about it, and so his targeting of her with daily compliments and questions about her weekend and offers to help on assignments that weren't even for the subject that he taught (PE, for god's sake) was not, or not only, because of that misfortune. She didn't know either that adult men weren't supposed to talk about the smoothness of teenage girls' legs or notice their painted nails or stroke their hair and tell them how silky it was. Which isn't to say she enjoyed it—it made her skin crawl, made her spin on her heel and duck into empty classrooms when she saw him coming—but she didn't see it as *meaning* anything. It was just what some adults were like.

At some point the teacher stopped. It hadn't been bad enough that you'd notice it stopping right away. Just after a while she saw him standing too close to Elissa James, who was backed up against the closed door of a classroom and his face had that *I'm really listening to you* intensity that creeped her out so much and she thought, *Ugh, poor Elissa, her dad must have been arrested or her mum OD'd or something,* and when Elissa left school soon after Nic assumed that she'd been right, something awful had happened at home. Then she didn't think about the teacher or Elissa or any of it again until a year or so later when it was all over the news that Elissa was expecting the teacher's kid. Her parents and his wife wanted him prosecuted but Elissa was eighteen and wouldn't cooperate in any inquiry about what had happened before that, so there was nothing anyone could do.

'That coulda been me,' Nic told Michelle while they were watching the story on *60 Minutes*.

'You wish.'

'He wished. He tried it on me before her.'

'Yeah, right. Look how pretty she is.'

'She's no prettier than Nicky,' Mum, who had crept in behind them, said. 'Quite plain, really. That's what creeps like him look for, though. Girls who'll be grateful for the attention.'

Michelle smirked at that, but Nic felt good. She'd not felt a bit of gratitude to the old perve. Not a teensy-tiny bit.

The first time she noticed she was wanted and that she wanted someone else was when she was twenty. Tony. He was a mess of a man—always drunk or high or both, always broke. Often in debt to people who thought nothing of pulling a knife to settle an argument or smashing someone in the back of the head with a rock over a perceived disrespectful look. The latter happened to a friend of Tony's. The man, whose name she couldn't remember, lived but was, as they said, *not all there* after that. The former, well, that actually happened to Tony—he was fine, the knife nicked his breastbone, gave him a proper scar—but it also happened to another man fifteen years earlier and that man died. In that case, the knifeman wasn't someone Tony owed money to but her own daddy. The two cases had nothing to do with each other except in the murk of Nic's guts whenever Tony begged money off her to pay someone who might otherwise get nasty.

The begging didn't bother her so much. She was richer than she ever imagined being, having a job at the local discount department store which paid just okay normally but time and a half on nights and weekends, which was mostly when she worked back then. She was living with Mum still, paying a bit of rent and helping with the bills, but nothing like she would have to pay if she moved out—and why would she when Michelle was gone, already moved in with Joe, and Mum kept to her own self and it was an easy stroll to work and with Tony to pick her up after late shifts.

So if Tony needed fifty bucks here and a hundred there it wasn't a big deal. But she knew already at twenty that people don't change, not really. If anything, they become more and more themselves. Eventually he would run up a debt that she couldn't pay and the knife would not nick his breastbone but sink deep into his heart or guts. Or he would, as he sometimes threatened when he was drunk and trying to prove how big his balls were (as though she didn't know their exact size, having rolled them in her mouth with great care), use a knife of his own to put a stop to the hounding.

The thing that kept her hanging in there as long as she did was that they loved each other. It was a difficult thing to explain and so she didn't try. But from the first time he'd caught her eye across the pool table she'd felt it—oh! This!—and that night they'd kissed in the car park, him pushing her against the brick wall and her wanting him to, and her favourite red top which she hand-washed in the sink with shampoo because it was that delicate all snagged in the back from rubbing against those rough bricks and she didn't even care because it was the night she met her person, the one who made her feel the way she didn't know a big-hipped, plain-faced daughter of a killer could feel. Like a girl in a movie. Like *the* girl, the one that you know will be happy ever after because how could anyone not cherish the living hell out of her?

It's hard to let go of someone who makes you feel that way. Her friend Asha said *there's plenty more fish in the sea* and *you're hot you'll find someone else in a minute* and *you can do so much better* and she knew it was true but also that, in a way, it wasn't. Because they loved each other and what was better than that? What could be?

But she was nothing if not sensible and self-sufficient and other shit that girls like her had to be even (especially) when someone was making them feel like they were a different kind of girl, the kind who would always be taken care of. She ended it. He begged.

Cried. Shouted. Carved her name into his arm with a penknife. This last made it easier to go.

There had been other men she liked and who liked her. A couple who she might have married if they'd asked, but they didn't, and she wasn't mad enough about them to push the issue. It was more like, well, if he wants to I can't see the harm. That was all in her twenties, though. By her thirties she was asked out less often and accepted few of those who did ask. She'd had enough sex to know that at least half the time it wasn't worth the effort, and when it was it could make you loopy, make you feel like your life wasn't whole anymore without the sex and the man. How many women, in her own bloody family alone, had let that loopiness become their driving force? How many good women ruined by being unable to let go of a really good fuck?

She has tried to get this through to Lena. Enjoy yourself but don't get caught up. Be open to romance but don't chase it. Know you're worth fifty of almost every man alive, and if you meet the rare bloke who's your equal don't you dare be grateful for his attention. At least no more than he is for yours.

She remembers now that Lena had a crush on some rich looker from uni before all this nonsense began. Sends her a quick text: *Whatever happened with thigh-boy? Any progress?*

Lena doesn't answer right away, which is fine, but when she does text a few hours later it's to say she won't be in today—too much exam prep. Nic takes the silence to mean things didn't work out with the farm stud. It's the family way: no answer is the answer. Nothing to talk about, move on.

WILL

For three days Will and Lena worked side by side, filling bags and lugging them to the skip, and that entire time she didn't go more than three minutes at a stretch without checking her damn phone. Conversations longer than the interval between checks were out of the question. Pretty much the only time she spoke was to yell at him for sorting through a pile of something instead of chucking the lot or to remind him how pressed for time they were if he dared to stop for long enough to take a sip of water or wipe the sweat off his forehead.

But whenever he got close to blowing up and telling her to bloody well wake up to herself, she'd come to him with those wide, wet eyes holding out a thing she'd uncovered—a Twister mat, a box of worn-down crayons, a pair of tiny rollerskates— and she'd say, *Remember, remember,* and he always did, and for a stretch they were kids again, nearly sick with laughter at twisting their bodies over the game board while Aunty Nic bent low to examine, pretended to be stern as she advised that Lena's left foot wasn't exactly on red and Will's right hand was off the edge of the blue. They were kids colouring the free cartoon place-mats from Maccas and then sniffing the crayons because a boy at Will's school said you could get high from doing that, and when Aunty Nic caught them she told them that boy had crayons for brains and they used that insult ever since. Kids again, playing out the backyard in the summer, Lena on those bloody skates, Will pretending not to care that she had a pair and he didn't. Pretending not to be interested in her at all, only in the (admittedly cool) handheld solar-powered video game he'd got instead of rollerskates. And then Lena stacked it and instead of crying she laughed and couldn't stop, which made Will laugh, too. Both of them cracking up while her knees bled through the new holes in her jeans. Aunty Nic came out with some first-aid stuff and said, *I saw from the kitchen. One minute looping around and the next—whoops—arse over tit*, which made it even funnier, though it was hard to explain that to Mum when she went crook later about the jeans being torn and stained with mercurochrome.

Then Lena's phone would buzz or vibrate, her giggles or tears would stop, and she'd snap back into this alien, furious, closed-up girl, slam the childhood memory into a garbage bag.

Mum texted to ask if he was looking for work while he was in Sydney. She was worried he'd sink into habitual unemployment, become like so many of the people she grew up with. He spent ten minutes dutifully scrolling through local job postings before clicking on a link titled *So You've Been Made Redundant?* which advised him to *Use the opportunity to rediscover and follow your passion*. It reminded him of the prison orientation video which said to *view your time in custody as an opportunity to make positive life changes*. When the video finished an intake officer asked him about work skills and education, and Will said he'd love to use this opportunity to continue his childcare studies. In response he was handed a piece of paper detailing his laundry duty schedule.

It's possible the officer thought he was being a smartarse. Not many blokes in childcare, it was true. He himself hadn't considered it an option until the end of year ten, when his friend Jas left school to do her Cert III at a private college in Parra. It was like she'd shown him a hidden window in a locked and stuffy room. Mum said he'd try anything to get out of school, Dad said it was one thing to do a bit of babysitting, another to become a professional *manny*, but Aunty Nic was on his side, helped him look up the different courses at the library near her work. He couldn't afford the fees, but. Not even for the subsidised TAFE course. So one more year at school, this time working as a trolley boy at Coles during the week and a burger flipper at Hungry Jack's on the weekends. He saved enough for the fees, finished year eleven feeling like a fucking superhero, though he told the other kids at school he was leaving to start a mechanics apprenticeship. Northern Beaches, he told them, so they wouldn't try to visit his alleged employer and reveal the lie.

Best nine months of his life, it was. Class four days a week, with him the only bloke in a room full of girls. They all tried to make him their best friend at first. Thought he was gay just for being there. When they figured out he wasn't, a few backed off but most of the others were into it. Straight bloke, loved kids, down to fuck and not too bad at it, thanks very much.

And then. Then he sold weed to a fourteen-year-old in full view of a police officer and there was no *positive life change* that could make that un-happen. *Follow your passion*? Might as well tell him to reverse global warming. Love to, internet job coach, love to. Lend me your time machine, yeah?

Yes, Mum. Couple of possibilities to follow up on here, he texted.

Great!!! Mum replied. *Just FYI, if it doesn't work out there Rick is looking for someone to do basic maintenance etc at the car yard. Only part time but at least you'd be here in beautiful Brissie with us!! We'd so love to see you . . .*

If you see me, weep, he wrote. Deleted it. Typed five rows of 👍 even though he knew the sarcasm would be lost on her.

On the third day at Aunty Nic's, he failed to finish even half of the Vegemite sandwich Lena had made him for lunch, and she yelled that he couldn't blame her if it was shit since he hadn't given her any money for food and she was nearly out and so had to buy day-old bread instead of fresh. He wanted to tell her that it wasn't the bread, it was the eye-watering sting of Vegemite on an open mouth wound, but she had already stormed out. After that, too hungry and worn down to feel shame, he called the emergency dentist from the other night and asked if there was any way—any way at all at all at all—he could be treated today and pay later.

No, was the short answer. The receptionist gave him another number to ring which turned out to be for a practice that provided free dental care *if* you had a pension or Centrelink concession card. Didn't matter he was eligible for free care based on his unemployed status; if he hadn't done the paperwork and had it processed in time for the toothache he was shit out of luck. Also, the queue was quite long. Might be months, unless there was a cancellation. A hospital training clinic might be a possibility, he was told, and given more numbers. He called every one of them, was put on three waiting lists, felt slightly more positive but also in agony.

And although he was truly fucking starving, swore he could feel his muscles cannibalising themselves as he worked, he was relieved when Lena didn't raise the topic of dinner that night. There was nothing he could imagine eating that wouldn't cause him to throw up with the pain.

NIC

Nic's blood itches. She knows she can't say that out loud, knows it sounds like a confused-old-dear thing to say and if there's one thing she can't bloody have it's for the people here to receive confirmation that she is, indeed, a confused old dear.

But how else to describe this feeling? Like the itch is both deep and on the move. Like even if you could find a way to get inside your arteries and scratch you couldn't ever get to it. A flowing itch. An itchy stream.

Her pain meds have been reduced, she knows. She knows that. Is not confused or incompetent or vulnerable or any of the things she's heard them say. She knows where she is and why. Knows what's going into her arm and what she's taking by mouth. She knows the possible side effects, the ones to accept and the ones to alert the nurses about. She knows all that and none of it accounts for this deep, thick, surging itchiness.

She pays attention: it is worse when it is light and quiet. When she can see and hear the unfilled spaces around her bed. It is worse when the blanket falls and she can't reach it, and she has to lie exposed to the air until someone comes along and says, *Oopsie daisy, let's get you cosied up again.* Worse when she can't sleep and she imagines her little house dark and empty, abandoned. It makes her feel like when she was little and they watched a TV show about Chernobyl and she got so upset she couldn't breathe. Mum rubbed her back and told her that it was far, far away, that the nuclear fallout wouldn't even come close, that she didn't need to be scared. Mum didn't understand that Nic wasn't scared; she was heartbroken. Everyone in that city took off and just *left* everything there. All the books and dolls and shoes and chairs and tables. The spoons and bowls and pencils and swimming caps and prams and pillows and photos. The pipes, salt shakers, eyeglasses, nails, hair brushes, clocks, compasses and coins. The buttons and wheels and fans made of feathers. All alive in there, still. Alive and utterly forgotten.

—

Will comes by during morning visiting hours, says Lena is busy studying. As he says it his eyes cut to the side so she knows he is lying. That he has the same comically obvious tell as he did at five years old floods her with so much love she barely minds that he's bullshitting her. He chatters away about how awful it is outside, how lucky she is to be in this cool, clear air, how everyone's wondering if the fires'll ever be out.

The nurse she privately calls the Meanest One comes to check her blood pressure and temperature. Will introduces himself and the scowl dissolves. *It's so lovely of you to come and visit*, in a voice entirely unlike the rasp Nic is used to. Even her hands feel warmer and gentler as she performs her checks. So, this is unchanged, too: Will's ability to charm and cheer without even trying. It's a gift she didn't even know she could hope for, her Will come back after so long, older but still very much himself.

As she leaves, the Meanest One comments on the obvious family resemblance and Nic immediately renames her the Best and Most Observant One. Michelle likes to say her kids have grown up to be *all Joe* and Nic understands that she misses her husband and searches him out in the faces of her children. It's not true, though. Will and Lena's faces are *her* family's faces, one hundred per cent. Both have Mum's high forehead and deep-set brown eyes. Lena has Dad's dimple and Will has his lashes, so thick and dark you'd think he was wearing mascara. Both of them have Michelle's lips, the top one almost as full as the bottom. And like their mother they both unconsciously puff their lips out when they're concentrating or overtired. Will's smile is Steve's is Dad's. And Lena's smile is Nic's own, everyone says it. Only their lankiness gives them away as not pure Miller. Her family all pears and apples, not a string bean among them until these two.

'So, Lena's preparing for exams and what about you? What've you been up to?'

'Ah, you know.' Those sliding eyes again!

'Catching up with old mates?'

'Nah. To be honest, Aunty Nic, I've just kind of been moping a bit. A lot.'

'Sorry to hear that. Feel like talking about it? I've got all the time in the world.' She gestures to herself, stuck in bed, but his gaze is on the far wall.

'Yeah, nah. I mean, not much to say. It just . . . it blindsided me, you know. The break-up. I'd been on a bit of a bender. Me and the other blokes who'd been laid off, we really . . .' He shakes his head, cringes as if the hangover's still there. 'Anyway, I came home messy as, slept most of the next day, get up late in the arvo and Mercy's waiting for me in the kitchen, tells me it's been fun, but time's up.'

'Because you got blotto one time? Seems harsh. Unless it wasn't just the one time?'

'Yeah, see, that's the thing. I never got smashed like that since we've been together. Total one-off and I'd just lost my job, so, you know, give me a fucking break. But once I shut up and listened to her properly, you know, she wasn't even talking about my coming home maggoted. She was saying she'd been feeling for a while that it was time to split but had been waiting until the kids were at her ex's to talk to me. He's FIFO, so it's always a while between their week with him and, she said, you know, the timing's unfortunate, because of me losing the job and that, but . . .'

'Oh, Will. And you didn't know? Didn't feel anything was wrong?'

'Nah. Yeah. I don't know. I was always more serious about us than her, I think. She didn't like . . .' He wets his lips, cringes again. 'She didn't like how I was with the kids.'

'What? You're great with kids. Always have been.'

He nods, barely. 'She said I acted like they were mine.'

Like cold water over her face. She is alert, heart racing. 'Isn't that a good way for a stepdad to act?'

'I'm not their stepdad, though. She'd said it a few times. *You're not their dad, Will. They already have a dad, Will.* I didn't . . . I s'pose I didn't really get what she was saying. I just . . . I love 'em, you know?'

'Yeah.' She should say something more. Comfort him or offer wisdom. But his pain is so big it's broken free of his body and is pushing up against her chest.

'There was this one arvo I keep thinking about. Coupla months back. Haymish'd been having a hard time at school. He's small for his age, you know. Bright as, but looks four instead of six. Some kids were giving him a hard time. Name-calling, leaving him out of games at lunch and that. Mercy talks to his teacher about it, and she says she'll have a word to the kids, remind them to be kind.

'A few days later, Mercy gets a call at work. Haymish has crawled into the art cupboard and won't come out. Merce's stuck at work— no one else to mind the pharmacy—but I've finished for the day, so I go up to the school. Little fella comes out as soon as he sees me. Big cuddles, his face all wet. Tells me what's been happening.

'Apparently the kids who got told off for being mean are punishing him for dobbing. Being real nice in front of the teacher and then kicking him or knocking his stuff off the desk when she's not looking. That lunchtime a kid had kicked him in the shins while another kid took his sandwich and stomped it into the dirt.'

She takes it all back, the gratitude for Will's unchanged nature. He is too transparent, too raw. How has he got to this age, been through the things he has, and remained this soft and open?

What was it Steve used to say about her face when she gaped up at him adoringly? A thumb without a nail. That was her. Is Will.

'I'm fuming by this time, but trying to be all cool and adult and stuff. The principal calls us into her office, poor little Haymish clinging to my side, and while I tell this woman what's happened she's all sympathetic, nodding and frowning. But then she says to Hay, *Oh dear, it sounds like your friends got a little bit carried away at playtime today!* And I—ah, shit, Aunty Nic, you're going to side with Mercy on this. *I* bloody side with Mercy on this.'

He takes a loud breath, taps a beat on the bed.

'I stood up, calm as anything, and I swept my arm across her desk. Knocked all the paper and pens and shit off. Walked around the side and did it again so the computer crashed to the floor. Poor little Haymish's nearly hyperventilating in the corner, principal's dead silent. I go, *Oh, sorry, I got a bit carried away with the playing and all.* Then I lift Hay up in one arm, open the door with the other and walk out.'

'Bloody hell, Will.'

'Yeah. That's what Merce said. And the rest. And I get it. It caused trouble for her. The school calling her in, asking all these questions about this young thug she's got living with her kids.'

'You're not a—'

'Anyway, what she said the other day, how it's been fun but blah blah blah, I reckon she's been building up to it since the thing at the school. Weighing up if the fun we were having was enough to make something like that forgivable. If she liked me enough to make up for being such a shit influence on her kids.' He makes a what-can-you-do gesture, shifts in his seat.

'Will. Listen. Listen to me. That boy? Haymish? He will remember that for the rest of his life. What you did, how you stuck up for him. It'll matter to him forever.'

He flicks a hand. 'Maybe. Or maybe I've been Rick the Dick in this situation. Maybe Hay and Taylah will remember me as the try-hard, bogan ex-con who thought doing it with their mum made him their dad.'

'Stop it!' Her voice is too loud. Will blinks at her, then down at his hands. 'Don't talk about yourself like that. I can't stand it.'

His lips twist, droop. 'Whatever,' he says, standing. 'I better let you get some rest. Sitting here raving on about my problems while you're—'

'No, it's fine. You don't need to—'

'Should get going anyway. Stuff to do.'

He leaves and right away her blood is itching worse than ever. There's something that would make this better if she could only think of it. She should know. What makes someone better. What will help. An original Western Suburbs jersey she bought at good old Tempe tip a few years back. Yes! Thought to herself at the time it'd be good for Will and it would, it will. What else? That Nintendo console some spoilt dickhead put out last hard rubbish night. She just needed to find some controllers and give it a clean and it'd be perfect. Take his mind off it all. Oh! And what about the stack of self-help books she'd bought at the big Dymocks sale a couple of years back? One was about resilience, she remembers, another about self-esteem. She'd felt embarrassed buying them, but as she told the kid ringing them up, life can be hard and sooner or later someone she knew would need them.

'Nicole, can we chat a minute?' The social worker is suddenly there by her bed. No clip-cloppy high-heels today. She's padded in as soft and sure as a nurse. She grabs the remote and switches off the TV even though Nic had it on mute, subtitles only. 'I'm told you're doing really, really well.'

'Apparently not well enough to let me leave.'

'That's what I wanted to talk to you about. I've been speaking to your niece and she tells me that your home is in a safe condition for you to return to, which is fantastic news.'

Nic says nothing. Silently thanks Lena for convincing this professional busybody that all is well.

'I'm heading over there later today just to—'

'Heading where?'

She flashes her teeth. What is she smiling at, for god's sake? 'Your house. Lena is going to meet me there so I can complete a walk-through. Soon as I'm done, I'll sign here.' She holds up the green binder. 'Then all you need is your doctor's sign-off and we'll have you out of here. Could be as early as tomorrow. How's that sound?'

'I haven't agreed to . . .' Her voice is barely audible, damn it. She reaches for her water, sends the plastic cup flying.

The social worker sidesteps the splash, murmurs reassurance that she'll get someone in to clean it up and bring fresh water.

'So I'll pop back and see you later today, let you know how we got on, okay?'

It sounds like a question but the social worker doesn't wait for an answer, turns and leaves. Nic goes for her phone, sees it's dead, yells out like she's been shot. An aide rushes in, rolls his eyes when she asks him to help with the charger, but he finds it quickly, plugs in her phone within reach.

She dials Lena's number, which goes straight to voicemail. Hands shaking like buggery, she manages to type: *DONT LET THE SOCIAL WORKER IN CALL ME WHEN YOU GET THIS.*

Seconds, minutes, half an hour with no response. She sips the water a nurse's aide has brought her. She dials, texts, dials, texts. Tries Will's phone but it goes straight to message, too. Drinks some more water to cool her panic. The only time Lena doesn't answer is if she's at work, but it's midday and Lena never starts before four. She might be in class, but even so she'd see the texts, would notice the urgency and type something back.

Is it possible Lena's intentionally ignoring her? Because why? Because what the social worker said is true? Because she's been lying and conspiring all this week while Nic has trusted that—

A vice closes around her ribs. Pain like she's never known. Not even when she fell. And there's no air at all. Like the squeeze on her middle has pushed something thick and sticky into her throat. Nic slams her hand down on the call button. She can't die and leave the social worker to wander around her home. Can't die without knowing what has happened to Lena, why she's abandoned her like this.

LENA

The social worker—Ada—was the same woman they'd met with in the hospital, but standing in Nic's hallway she looked too young and tiny to have any kind of responsible job. The sneakers, Lena noticed. Off-white, canvas, no socks. The other day she'd worn a near identical outfit of tight pants and brightly coloured singlet but with shiny high heels. Extraordinary that all it took to transform an officious hospital social worker into a high schooler was a change of shoes.

'I saw the skip out front. Looks pretty full,' Ada said, as Lena closed the front door behind her.

Will appeared from the living room, where he'd been help-fully napping since he returned from visiting Nic. 'Yeah, probably should have ordered the biggest one. Hey, I'm Will. The nephew. Thanks heaps for coming today and for looking out for Aunty Nic so well. We really appreciate it.'

For a second Lena was poleaxed with pain and love. It was still a shock, him being here. Over the past six years he'd been this calming, supportive presence who was never actually, you know, *present*. After his release he'd come to live with them in Brisbane and, although no one said it out loud, it was kind of awful. Prison had changed him, which sounds obvious, but it had been such a short time. Barely four months he was in and low security and all. Mum and the Dick had reassured her over and over that the kind of jail he went to was nothing like on TV. Will's experience wouldn't be much worse than a strict school camp. Three meals a day, exercise, recreation time. Just that he had to share space with randoms and he couldn't leave when he wanted.

But when he came back he was a different boy, man, whatever. He looked weirdly younger. Maybe all the time out of the sun, maybe his too-short hair, maybe the nervous stillness with which he held himself. Younger except around his eyes, which seemed permanently squinted, as though his face had frozen on its way to a cringe. After a month or so of trying to pretend everything was as it had always been, that the only thing different was the Dick lived with them instead of Dad and that here the sun tried to kill you for nine months of the year instead of three, Will took off to chase a job a mate had told him about further north.

It was easier to be close again once he left. Once she didn't have to look at his stiff neck and crinkled eyes. Text messages speeding back and forth across the state, exchanging jokes and complaints and secrets. Six years of that and now he was here, broader across the shoulders and more tanned than she'd ever seen him. Hair past his shoulders, beard growing in. Here in Nic's hallway, talking to the social worker like he's known her his whole life. This man so relaxed and confident that he made others feel relaxed and confident too. The broken brother who had gone away and turned into Dad.

'You've obviously been working super hard here.' Ada touched Will's arm as she said it, smiled like she was really, truly proud of him.

'Nah, not really. Lena's done most of it,' Will said, but with a one-shouldered shrug that communicated the opposite.

'As you can see the hallway is completely clear,' Lena said.

Ada managed to drag her attention from Will, noted something on her clipboard, took a few photos with her phone. 'How's your aunt's bedroom?'

Lena led her past the closed spare-room door and into Nic's room. She wished the social worker could've seen it last week, to appreciate the miracle Lena had performed in here. Three pieces of furniture—bed, bedside table, dressing table—each cleared of everything but the essentials. The bed made up with pink and white rose-covered sheets, a pastel pink quilt, two pillows in matching cases. It had taken the better part of an hour sorting through the mountains of linen to find matching pieces and then to shake out all the wrinkles and smooth them over the bed. Worth the effort though; it looked cosy and soft and clean. A perfect welcome home.

The bedside table held a single touch-operated lamp (six more-or-less identical items were in the skip alongside five different kinds of desktop lamps). The dressing table top was completely clear, its four drawers emptied of a hundred things that nobody needed and then neatly refilled with: 1) moisturiser, lip balm, hairbrush and a scrunchie; 2) seven pairs of clean underwear; 3) seven pairs of clean socks; 4) two pairs of clean pyjamas.

Apart from the closed, organised, built-in-wardrobe there was nothing—*nothing*—else in the room.

Ada moved (easily! freely!) around taking pictures. 'This is where Nicole fell, yes?'

'Yeah. Off the dressing table. It had a lot of stuff on it then, though. And she fell on a whole heap of hard stuff, not the floor like this.'

'You can see where she bled and that, just here.' Will pointed out the area of carpet Lena had scrubbed and re-scrubbed until the stain was unnoticeable. Unless you really wanted it noticed and so pointed it out.

'It's been cleaned, though? The whole carpet, I mean.'

'Yep,' Lena said.

'Not, like, by a cleaning company or anything, though,' Will said. 'Just leave-in shampoo and some good old elbow grease.'

Lena wanted to slap him with her chafed and flaking hands, but Ada obviously liked him and wanted him to like her so he was, in one way at least, being useful.

'It's quite bare in here,' Ada said.

'Isn't that the point? So there's nothing for her to—'

'Sure, sure. But did you read the literature I gave you?'

Lena had not. She had, in fact, chucked it all in the bin before she left the hospital. It was a matter of pride, not to mention survival, that she brought nothing new into this house.

'The thing is,' Ada went on, talking mostly to Will anyway, 'Nicole is likely to experience some distress when she comes home and finds all her things have been removed. I'm concerned for her welfare when she finds her space so bare.'

'I don't . . .' Lena took a breath, staving off tears. 'I thought the concern for her welfare was because the space was too full. Isn't this—' she waved an arm over the beautiful, clean, clear space '—isn't this what you wanted?'

Ada smiled kindly. 'It's not a matter of what I want, Lena. It's about ensuring Nicole has a safe home to return to. We need to balance her physical safety with her emotional and psychological safety. For someone with hoarding disorder—'

'Wait, is that an actual thing? Hoarding disorder?' Will asked.

Ada looked so disappointed she might as well have been Lena's mother. 'This was all in the literature I sent home with your sister.'

'Nic herself says the only thing she cares about is getting back home. So can you just tell me, please, if the house passes and, if it doesn't, exactly what I need to do to get it right?'

Ada nodded. 'Let's take a look at the rest.'

In the bathroom she turned all the taps on and off, flushed the toilet, tried to slide the bathmat under her feet before taking more photos. The kitchen caused some tense moments as Lena explained the fridge situation. When Ada asked about the (emptied and scrubbed clean) oven, Lena lied that there was a repairman coming tomorrow to check it was safe to use, which seemed to make the social worker inordinately happy. More photos then into the living room, which was 'not ideal' because of the cord running across the floor to the bar fridge, the blankets piled up on the lounge, the still over-full cabinet behind the TV and the crates (a quarter of what there had been!) under the windows and across the back wall.

'Maybe for the best, though,' Ada said. 'Enough clutter to help Nicole feel secure but not enough to impact her safety.'

'So we shouldn't keep going in here?' Lena asked. She had hoped to get rid of the rest of the crates at least before the skip got picked up in a few hours.

'I wouldn't. The more Nicole can feel that her home is unchanged, the easier the readjustment will be.'

'It's actually very, very changed, though,' Lena pointed out.

Ada looked sceptical. 'Well, it's not empty by any means, so . . .'

'So that's good, yeah? Middle ground and all that.' Will was like a goddamn puppy, bouncing up and down for approval.

'Maybe. You do need to be prepared for—oh!' Ada had reached for the door of the spare room before Lena could stop her. She froze, silent, hand still on the knob, door only half open, which was as far as it would go. Now you get what it's been like, Lena wanted to say. Now you can see what I've been dealing with!

'Yeah, we haven't worried about that one,' Will said, right at Ada's shoulder. 'Aunty Nic doesn't use it day to day, so we figured it wasn't a priority.'

'As if you know what Aunty Nic does day to day,' Lena muttered. Will had the gall to look hurt.

The thing is, Lena would have liked to have cleared at least some of the floor of the spare room, but after only half an hour in there it had become obvious that this was the room in which Nic kept her most meaningful junk. Some of it not even junk, to be fair. Boxes of cards and letters. Photos, in envelopes and loose, in albums and frames. Clothes not all shoved in bags, but some folded carefully and placed in boxes alongside other mementoes. One box held a folded dress which Lena immediately recognised as the outfit Nic wore to Dad's funeral. When Lena pulled it out to be sure—yes, it was distinctive, black jersey with embroidered daisies around the hem and collar—she saw beneath it the order of service and a brochure from the funeral home. There were other papers that Lena didn't look at because she had spotted, peeking from underneath them all, a flash of yellow. She yanked it out, the bright cotton sundress she'd worn because it was Dad's favourite. At the chapel, confronting the sea of black, she'd been shot through with shame. Worse, horror. Like a nightmare where you get on the bus naked. Mum was no good that day and Will was surrounded by mates, tall serious young men wearing borrowed suits and expensive sunglasses, so it was Nic who chased after her as she ran towards the car park. Nic who told her to wait in the car, ran back to the chapel, returned only minutes later with a men's suit jacket and a black patent leather belt. She helped Lena belt the jacket in so it looked, at a glance, anyway, like a sophisticated suit-style mini-dress. Nic took off her own shoes and black pantyhose, urged Lena to put them on, wadded tissues in the shoes to help the fit, showed Lena how to tuck the waist-band of the hose into the bottom of her bra to keep them from rolling down. Nic took Lena's white sandals. The straps cut into the flesh on top of her feet but, she pointed out, they didn't look so odd with her black dress since there were, after all, those white daisies tying it all together. And after, when everyone came back to the house, Lena had changed into her own black jeans and shirt

234

and handed the yellow dress to Nic along with the items she had to return. *I don't want to see it ever again,* she'd said.

If Lena had kept going in the spare room there would have been other things she didn't want to see, again or for the first time. She chose not to. Closed the door. Hoped it might stay closed forever.

'Is that right, Lena?' Ada asked. 'This room isn't in regular use?'

'No. I mean, yes, that's right, it isn't.'

Ada took some photos, closed the door. 'Okay,' she said. 'Thanks for showing me around.'

'Did we pass?'

That kind smile again. Pity stabbed Lena in the throat. The shit this tiny, kind woman had to deal with every day.

'I have to report back to my supervisor, who'll have the final sign-off. But I don't think it'll be a problem. The level of clutter is non-critical.'

'Woohoo!' Will said. 'High five!'

Lena ignored his raised hand. Ada slapped it with a giggle and Lena instantly liked her more and trusted her judgement less.

'Are you sure? Like, if you think your supervisor might say no is there anything we can do now to—'

'You've done a great job, Lena. Both of you. Nicole's lucky to have family like you. So many people in this situation have to rely on contract cleaners and they just . . .' Ada swept her arm across the empty space. 'Everything gone.'

Sounds wonderful, Lena thought.

'Poor buggers,' Will said. 'It must be awful to have no one.'

After Ada had left, an hour before the skip was due to be picked up, Will said maybe they'd gone too far.

'Excuse me?'

'With chucking stuff out. Like, maybe we got carried away and—'

'Please, Will. Can you not?'

'It's just that Ada said—'

'Don't.' Lena pushed past him to get inside Nic's room. She closed the door, looked again at the results of her extraordinary week's work.

More anonymous and strictly utilitarian than her room at uni. Like some 1950s boarding house for unwed mothers, where the sparseness of the surroundings is both punishment for your sins and an attempt to make you too depressed to consider escape. All it needed was a wooden crucifix on the wall and a worn leather-bound Bible on the bedside table.

Her phone had been silently vibrating in her pocket throughout Ada's tour of the house. She pulled it out, glanced at the screen full of messages from Unknown Caller, from Annie, from Lou, from Mum. And from Nic. Nic saying DONT and PLEASE and I DIDNT AGREE. She threw the phone hard against the opposite wall. A sickening, expensive crack and then it lay face down on the carpet, shimmying a half-centimetre every time a new message arrived.

—

In the rundown but blessedly un-junkyard like backyard, which was now accessible via the previously blocked kitchen door thanks to Lena's *going too far and getting carried away*, she gathered a loose bouquet of flowers and greenery. Most of it probably weeds, technically, but it looked pretty. Bursts of yellow and orange and a spray of white. In the kitchen, she trimmed the stems, chose a tall tumbler from the sparkling clean cupboards she'd carefully stocked with the best of the hoarded crockery, and half filled it with water. She carried the arrangement into Nic's room and placed it on the dressing table. Pulled out her goddamn cracked phone and texted Nic: *Sorry, my phone broke! Everything is fine here tho. Spoke to that Ada chick and she said we're good to bring you home tomorrow! Off to work now but can't wait to see you tomoz xox*

WILL

A couple of hours before they were due to collect Nic, Will googled *hoarding disorder*, cringing because he hadn't thought to do it before. *Why do I have to be the one to think of everything?* Mercy said all the time, and he used to not know what she was on about until he did, and then that, too, became a thing she'd had to think of first.

He'd only thought of it at all because his tooth had seared him awake while it was still dark and he had taken the last of the ibuprofen and was back on the sofa under the quilt, trying to distract himself from the barely diminished pain. He read the 'Hoarding Disorder' Wikipedia page and then one from a social services mob, tried to see Aunty Nic in any of it. But how would he? He hardly knew her anymore. Was she indecisive and anxious? Socially isolated? Did she have OCD? But here was something: a traumatic event. She'd had a couple of those, he knew. But who hadn't? Still, could be a thing to consider.

The toilet flushed, water ran on and off, a pool of yellow light cast out into the hallway.

'Hey, Leen,' he called. 'When did Uncle Steve die?'

'What are you on about?' She was in the doorway, scowling, hand on hip like a cartoon of an angry mother.

'Just wondering what might have triggered all this.'

'Steve died when I was a baby.'

It annoyed him, her dropping of the Uncle, the Aunty. Like she thought she was on par with them, grown. 'Do you reckon that might—'

'Obviously not. We practically lived here as kids, long after he died. She was fine.'

'Yeah. But it's weird Mum and Aunty Nic never spoke about him. Maybe there's something—' But she had stomped away already.

It wasn't that Uncle Steve was a secret. Will had always known his mum had a half-brother who was much older and who had died young. But the tidbits of info mum dropped about him when pushed made things less rather than more clear. *What was he like?* Will asked once, and Mum said, *He always brought me and your aunty a bag of mixed lollies from the corner shop and a box of Roses for our mum.* When he asked what Steve did for a job, Mum said he worked in a tool shop, but another time she said he worked in a factory and another time that he was a cleaner, and when Will wanted to know why he had so many jobs she said, *Not everyone works in the same place their whole life,* which didn't answer the question but did seem like a dig at Aunty Nic, who had worked at the same place since she was a teenager.

It wasn't until the morning after fourteen-year-old Will came home from a mate's place with a vicious case of the giggles and bloodshot eyes that Mum sat him and Lena down and told them their uncle had died from a drug overdose. She didn't say which drug, or that his death came after a decade of addiction, including short stints in jail and rehab—these details were filled in later. At the time, she made it sound as though Steve, like Will, had smoked weed one night with a mate and that was the end of him.

Later, after Will's arrest, Aunty Nic had asked him if he was an addict, if that was why he'd been dealing. He told her truthfully that he didn't even use, and she'd sucked in all her breath and let it out again and started talking about something else altogether. Some dumbarse reality TV show. Even at the time he'd known that was fucking weird. Her nephew facing serious drug charges and she's rabbiting on about some bloody cooking comp. When he mentioned the weirdness to Mum she'd said, *My sister is not good at handling hard things*, and then hugged him for the thousandth time that night.

Mum wasn't that great at hard things either. Never talked about her brother, never talked about her dad, but at least when Will and Lena's dad died she let them ask as many questions as they needed, always did her best to answer, even though it was obvious how hard it was for her to speak without crying. But, then, his death was innocent. His life, too, as far as Will knew. Too short to have done much damage.

Aunty Nic had scripts to be filled so Will ducked into the hospital pharmacy while Lena helped her out to the street to wait for the Uber. He asked the pharmacist if she could fill the repeats as well but she barely bothered to say no, just repeated the doctor's instructions for Nic's medication regime. He thanked her, bought some more piss-weak painkillers for himself (all on Aunty Nic's Mastercard, which Lena had handed over like it was her own), took a double dose right there in the useless fucking emporium of public health.

When he got to the car, Lena was in the front seat next to the driver, leaving Will to sit beside Aunty Nic in the back.

'You all right there?' he asked, because she sat like she was balancing her tailbone on a tightrope.

'I'm good, but listen, there's something I've been worried about. Lena doesn't know this, but . . .'

Lena's head whipped around. 'What don't I know?' Like a meerkat she was, eyes bulging, hyper alert. Meerkat or ice addict.

Aunty Nic half raised her right arm. She might have meant to reach out and touch Lena's shoulder or to wave off the question, but the actual gesture she managed was a pointless flapping. Title of my autobiography, Will thought.

'You know a lot about animals, right?'

She must have been high still. What he wouldn't do right now to get dosed with whatever they'd given her.

'Um, not really.'

'You've been living in the country! All the farms and that. You must know something about animals.'

'Yeah, nah, I was in town. Not really any animals. Unless you count pets, I s'pose.'

'What are you worrying about animals for?' Lena asked, but Aunty Nic didn't take any notice. She kept her glassy-eyed focus on Will.

'It's just I have these cats and—'

'Nic! You don't have any cats! What are you—'

'Let me talk to my nephew, please, Lena. Will, listen, I have these cats. They visit me every morning for their breakfast. I don't know where they get their other meals from, but breakfast is always at my place.'

'Nic!' Lena made eye contact with Will, pulled a drunk face like they used to behind Mum's back when she had more than one glass of wine.

'Now, I'm not worried they've starved. They're scrappy little street fighters, you know. They'll have survived all right without me, I know that. But—I know this is silly—but . . . have they forgotten me, do you think? When I take out their food tomorrow morning, will they even come for it? Do they forget so quickly, cats?'

Lena was laughing silently, as was the driver. Both of their faces turning red under the pressure.

'Nah, cats have great memories,' Will said. 'Like elephants.'

'Really? That good?'

'Almost as good, yeah. Plus, they're great communicators, cats. One of 'em will pass by tomorrow morning and see you out there with the brekky and before you know it the whole lot of them will have heard and be over with their bibs on.'

'Ah, good, good.' She smiled at the air in front of her face. 'I knew you'd know.'

———

Will helped Aunty Nic out of the car while Lena got her bag and crutches from the boot. The pharmacy bag nestled his thigh through his shorts. Tease.

The three of them made slow progress to the front door. A man called out from across the street and they waited, Aunty Nic leaning hard on her crutches, Will and Lena hovering either side, while he bounded across to them. Kissed Aunty Nic on both cheeks. Told her how good it was to have her home. He greeted Lena like an old friend, shook Will's hand warmly when introduced.

'How are my little chickens doing?' Aunty Nic asked the man.

Will was ready to whisper that she was experiencing medicated delusions of animal visitations but the man's answer made it clear that the chickens were children belonging to him. Real children that Aunty Nic cared for sometimes. Children who missed her and couldn't wait until she was well enough to come play again, apparently.

When the neighbour left, Lena transformed back into the meerkat. Ready to run, or stick her head in a hole. Or scratch and bite. She pushed the door open, skittered into the hallway, let Aunty Nic swing herself over the threshold, Will right behind.

For a moment it was good. Will closed the door. His aunty said, 'Home!' like it was New York City. Her head fell back and he leapt forward but she was just looking up at the ceiling. 'You fixed the light,' she said. Then she was looking everywhere at once. Almost coming off her crutches as she smacked a hand against the wall.

'What have you . . .' she said. 'What did you do?'

Her words came fast and violent, then. Lena's, too. Like lightning striking each of them in turn, taking off flesh and splintering bone in the process. Within seconds, both women were sobbing. Within five minutes, Lena had fled outside and his aunty was crumpled on her bedroom floor, her face shiny with tears and snot.

'Do you understand what's happened here?' Her eyes enormous and wounded, her whole body shaking and shaking. 'She's . . . She said she wouldn't . . . Oh, it's . . . I can't even tell you what this feels like. I can't even say it.'

'I think if we get you up on to the bed you'll be—'

'Rape! It feels like I've been raped. The violation of it, Will! She's just stripped away everything, violated me. There's nothing left.'

Don't be hysterical. You weren't meant to say that to women, Mercy had taught him. There was a whole history which they all apparently knew and were scarred by even if you, the one using the word, had no fucking idea. Anyway, you weren't meant to label people's emotions. Just respond to the material facts of the situation.

'There's lots left,' he pointed out. 'Heaps. Look at—'

'You don't know what you're talking about!'

'Aunty Nic, I wish you'd—'

'I should call the police on her, the little thief. Bet she's made a fortune selling off my stuff. Is it drugs? You've seen how skinny she's gotten, how puffy around the eyes. Taking advantage of an injured woman and sold off all my things for her meth or whatever.' She pounded the floor with her fists. 'How can I live?'

'I think once you calm down—'

'Stop! I don't need to be patronised and and and—just stop, Will. Go away. Go.'

He backed from the room slowly, unsure of whether it was okay to leave her alone in such a terrible state. Her sobs followed him right down the hallway.

He found Lena on the front step, scrolling through her phone, the whites of her eyes streaked the same colour as the eerie red sun.

'I keep thinking about that skip,' she said. 'How quickly we filled it.'

He'd been thinking of that, too. The relief of having it taken away, problem solved—as long as you didn't picture where it was going, which was to landfill. How when it got there it would contribute to the increasing toxification of the earth as the mercury and cadmium, the solvents and acids and lead, the PVC and arsenic locked away in all those electronics and bits of plastic crap leaked into the soil. And when it rained, water would turn the chemicals into leachate, which did what it sounded like, leached right into the ground, poisoning the soil and water.

Taylah had taught him all that. Or he'd taught himself after he'd stayed up half the night reading in-depth after helping Taylah with her Earth Day project. Imagine if she could see what he'd done here, see his hypocrisy and blatant disregard for the planet. The shame of it made him want to crawl into the skip himself.

'I just . . . How can someone accumulate so much stuff?' Lena went on. 'In such a short time, too. It's like she was trying to bury herself. And now she's angry we've dug her out.'

'Maybe it's that—' Will stopped. The need in Lena's face made him want to flee. He thought of Dad, took a breath, tasted ash. 'I get stressed a lot about the environment and that, you know? Like really freaked and . . . I was talking to Mercy about it, about how fucked up it is that the planet is dying and nobody seems to know what to do to fix it, and—'

'Will, understand I do not want a lecture about fucking climate change right now.'

'I'm not talking about climate change, just this thing Mercy said. That the scariest thing isn't that the planet is dying and we don't know how to fix it. We do know, actually. How to slow it down, or make it less terrible anyway. The scariest thing is that so many people don't give a fuck that it's dying because giving a fuck means they might have to give some shit up, and being less comfortable in the short term is a worse prospect to them than a dead planet in the long term. Or middle term, even.'

Lena had been thumbing her phone while he was talking but she was obviously listening because she said. 'The planet's going to be fine, though.'

'You serious?'

'Yep. We're not killing the planet. Just making it uninhabitable for ourselves.'

'Fucking hell, Lena. Always looking on the bright side, you are.'

She smiled a little at that. Properly. So fast it could have been a tic, but he was pretty sure it was a smile. That he caused in his sister. As wins went it wasn't huge, but he'd take it.

'Point is, maybe Aunty Nic hasn't been, like, deliberately burying herself. It's just the unfortunate consequence of making herself comfortable.'

'You've seen the pictures when I first got in here. You can't think that was comfortable.'

'To her, maybe. Or she'd become so used to it she couldn't see it anymore. Hey, give us your phone a sec.'

'Use your own.'

'I wanna show her the photos you took.'

'She hates me enough as it is.'

'What if she's got some warped idea about how it was? If she sees the, like, objective reality, she might understand what a good thing you've done.'

Lena looked at him. 'You think it was a good thing?'

'Leen, you probably saved her life and then you made it possible for her to move back home. There's no question it was a good thing. But it's a good thing in the way that taking away an addict's supply is a good thing. In the long run she'll thank you, but first she's got to come to terms with how bad things were. The photos will help, I think.'

Lena swiped at her eyes although Will couldn't see any tears. She fiddled with her phone, started to hand it over before folding it back into her palm. 'My screen's all cracked. I'll forward you the rest of the photos.'

'It's cracked? Bad?'

Lena nodded, kept thumbing the screen. He felt the vibrations in his pocket as the photos arrived.

—

Back in Aunty Nic's bedroom Will held his screen in front of her face, swiped through the photos. Lena was in the doorway, like a roo stock-still in a field, ready to bound off the second you make a move towards it.

'No. No. I didn't leave it that way. Not at all.' Nic waved the phone away. 'Don't you see? She trashed the place and now she's trying to put the blame on me. God. What did I do to deserve this? Lena! You were my—' She let out a wrenching moan. 'She's been my best friend,' she choked out at last, talking directly to him. 'I thought she was, anyway. I can't believe she'd do this to me.'

'Aunty Nic, I think if you maybe have a bit of a rest and then—'

'Get out of my sight.' She said it calmly.

He stood there, trying to think of the right thing to do. From the corner of his eye he saw Lena disappear.

'Are you deaf? I told you to go.'

—

In the hallway Will tried not to cry like a fucking child. There was this story about Aunty Nic that he and Lena loved as little kids. They'd first heard it from their mum as a warning against getting into fights. *Your aunty was the youngest kid in the history of our high school to ever be suspended—for getting into a fight.*

When they went to Nic for confirmation she laughed, said, *How the hell would she know if I was the youngest or not?* And they, wetting themselves with excitement at this seeming confirmation that the story was true, begged for details.

Maybe I was the youngest ever, but I doubt it. It was a rough school back then; it's better now. Be better still by the time you two get there. I can tell you for sure that I was the first in my year group to get suspended, since we were only a couple of weeks into our first term when it happened.

So I was sitting on the toilet one lunchtime (cue hysterical laughter from little Will and Lena) *and just as I was finishing my business I heard this loud voice going, 'Watch what you're doing you turd* (more giggles), *you just sprayed water all over me.' And then I hear this other voice saying sorry and then giving this little yelp. I get out of the cubicle and see this giant girl—a year nine, it turned out, but I didn't know that at the time—holding this smaller girl, a girl from my year, up against the wall. The big one's palm was flat against the little one's chest and she was just eyeballing her, you know?*

So, the little one's friends, two girls I recognised from maths but whose names I didn't know, start begging the big one to let their friend go, saying how she's sorry for splashing water and all that. The big girl kept totally focused on her victim, who was going all red in the face, obviously trying super hard not to bawl. A minute went past. Must have been only that long because I'd rushed to go to the loo with only six minutes before the bell rang and it still hadn't gone by this stage. And then the little girl squeaks out, 'It was an accident, okay? Please.' And the big girl repeated it back at her in this nasty, high-pitched voice. The little one starts crying. One of her friends says she's going to get a teacher and that's when the big one drops her hand. 'Don't,' she says. She stands back as if to let the girl go, then BAM, slams her against the wall again, this time by punching her stomach. Imagine it, right? The height differ-ence would be like if I punched you in the stomach, Leen! ('No!' Lena would laugh-gasp, wrapping her arms around her tummy protectively.) *I'd have to actually bend my knees a little and do an awkward low swing to get you right there* (and Nic would land the world's gentlest punch on Lena's covered belly and sometimes do the same to Will and it would take minutes to stop the gentle fighting and laughing and get back to the story).

So, anyway, she's punched the little one and then she just keeps going, pummelling this little girl, right? By now word has spread, or else there was just a rush of girls coming to the toilet before the bell, because the place is full and as they've come in I've sort of been nudged closer and closer to the action, and so I cannot only see this poor kid's face, all wet and red and with a big bit of snot dripping onto her lips ('Eeewwww!'), *but I can hear this noise. Underneath the yelling of the little girl's friends and the excited commentary of the crowd, I'm actually close enough to hear the sound of the bully's fist smacking into the little girl.* (Here, Nic would slam a closed fist into her own open palm. After the first time, Will and Lena knew to be silent at this point in the story. The *thwack* wasn't loud but it thrilled them every time.)

The bell rings. A couple of girls run out, more worried about being late to class than missing the end of the fight. But most of us stay because it's like the big girl hasn't heard a thing. She's punching and punching and the little one is trying hard to get away, ducking and weaving and covering herself, but the big one just changes her target, going for the arms or chest or shoulders. Never the head, but everywhere else she can land a blow she does and the little one doesn't hit back, just keeps moving her arms around to protect herself best she can and sliding back and forth against the wall trying to escape.

And I didn't know I was going to do it until I was doing it, but I step up real close and say, 'Enough,' and I can smell the foul breath of this enormous girl as she turns on me. The little one takes the opportunity and bolts but she's the only one. The whole room is watching as the bully swings out. First punch connects—POW—with my cheekbone and I can't even think. I'm in it, you know? I'm bigger than the other year seven but still much smaller than this beast, but I give as good as I'm getting. More, I reckon. I go hard, and before I know it we're both on the disgusting toilet floor, each trying to get on top of the other, punching and clawing. People are screaming and cheering. Everything hurts. Everything! All I want is for her to stop but I'm not going to lie still and wait, so I keep going at her and then WHOOSH, she's gone, pulled off me. I lie there, stunned, like the second you first wake up from a really weird dream. And then I'm being dragged up by Mrs Braddon and I see the bully ahead of me being dragged by Miss Carter and that's that.

By now Lena would be almost crying and Will would be air fighting, showing how he would've taken the bully down. Aunty Nic would wrap it up quickly, telling them how she and the bully were both suspended and how the original victim left the school soon after.

They nagged Aunty Nic to retell it almost every time they slept over. It got so they knew it word for word, would jump on her if she got a detail wrong or skipped over anything. But every single time, Lena got all riled up at the end. *I can't believe you got in trouble when you were the hero! I can't believe the little girl didn't say thank you!* The older she got the angrier it made her. *It's so unfair, Aunty Nic!* she would say and, later, *I can't stand the injustice. Heroism should be rewarded, not punished.*

Will knew it was pointless to argue with Lena when she was in a snit, so he never bothered to point out the obvious: knowing you'd acted heroically was the reward. You could hold your head high even if you were doubled over in pain. Your brain would rest easy at night even if your broken skin kept trying to sting you awake. You would always know what you did, and that would get you through a whole lot of feeling you were useless and scared of everything. That was more than most people had.

It was more than Lena had. She wore everything on the outside. Needed you to know when she was hurt and when she was sad and when she was angry, when she'd done well on a test and when the nurse complimented her on helping her aunty. It was like that goddamn scar; she wore it like it was something she'd done on purpose, like it meant something. Like gang colours or a prison tatt. She never considered that keeping things to yourself was not about shame and hiding; it was about not thrusting all your shit in someone else's face because *everybody's* got shit to deal with. Have some dignity, he wanted to tell her. Have some pride.

That's what he'd tried to do when he got sentenced. Maybe he'd done it too well, though. Made Aunty Nic think he didn't need her. Maybe that was why she didn't come.

But actually, given the hysterical—it *was*—howling coming from the bedroom right now, maybe Mum had been right all along. Nic couldn't handle hard stuff. Wasn't tough like the rest of the family. Wasn't good of heart or strong of spirit, either. Maybe she had shown her true colours when he'd been locked up. He should've told Lena about that. Saved her from wasting her week and breaking her heart over the mad, selfish cow.

THREE

NIC

She has survived worse betrayals, she tells herself, but that's self-comforting bullshit. This is beyond anything. Much worse than when she found out that Tony had been getting blow jobs from a woman he worked the closing shift at Maccas with. Coming to pick Nic up, all tired and stinking of lard and her not knowing for months that his dick was coated in some middle-aged desperado's dried spit. Worse than the feeling that time at work, the big staff meeting to say that Samantha—Nic's best mate in the place—had been pilfering from the till and from staff lockers for years. Worse—and she would have until this day said nothing could be worse but here it was—worse worse worse than when Michelle had upped and moved to Brisbane and taken Lena. It was like having a piece of herself wrenched off and her not allowed to be angry or even sad because how pathetic would that be—crying like a bereaved mother just because your niece has moved interstate?

This, today, was that same betrayal playing out its endgame. Something had changed in Lena during those years away. Nic's joy and gratitude at having her girl back was so great it had blinded her to the fact that Lena had turned into her bloody mother. Someone who thought she knew what was best for everyone else, who interfered in things that were none of her business. Someone who took it upon herself to do shit that no one asked her to do and then acted like a blessed martyr about it.

Like mother, like daughter! It wasn't supposed to be that way. From the minute Lena slid into the world she'd been Nic's girl. There in that miserable backyard, that drunk fool too busy performing disgust for his drunk fool mates around the fire to take his perfect baby, and Mum, now that the ambos had arrived, occupied with keeping little Will away from his gore-soaked mother, and so it was Nic who, seconds after the ambo had cut the cord and tied it off, took the squirming little wonder into her arms. Nic who kissed the terrifyingly soft head and rubbed the impossibly perfect little arms. Nic who opened her own shirt and held the baby against her bare skin in the back of the ambulance, just like the paramedic suggested. Nic's skin that gave primordial comfort to Lena's panicked newborn spirit, Nic's heart that set the rhythm of Lena's, her breath that dried Lena's first tears.

They're murmuring out there; the sound of it throbs through the space and burrows into her chest. She can't bear it. Can't. The pain of dragging her busted body up is better than sitting in this crypt letting their conspiring thrum through her.

She's felt this one other time, her body knows, recognises this feeling of being alone in space, plummeting. Fifteen—old enough to wear a junior bra and shave her legs and walk home from school on her own and do her own laundry and cook dinner for the family three times a week. Fifteen, yet younger somehow than thirteen-year-old Michelle, who already had a proper bra and her periods, who had used her birthday money on a perm, who had been sneaking around with a much older boy and, now she'd been caught, let rip, screaming at Mum about her hypocrisies, all the men whose places *she* stayed over at, creeping back in before the girls got up, as if they didn't notice she was wearing yesterday's clothes and stinking of smoke and *you know what else!* Nic did not know what else. She had not noticed the day-old clothes or the smoke or the creeping. And while she was still taking in this new information and what it might mean, Michelle screaming, *Imagine how Dad would feel if he knew!* And Mum screaming back, *Why do you care about how he feels? He doesn't give a shit about you. When was the last time you heard from him?*

Michelle, sobbing: *He's just trying to protect us. When he comes home he'll—*

Grow up, Michelle! I'm the one who protects you! Me! He left us with sweet fuck-all. I chased down the money he was owed and bought this house for you girls. You've got no idea the kind of things I had to do! No idea. And who do you think buys your food and clothes and shoes and everything? Who pays the bills? Me me me me! He's a worthless piece of shit and it's about time you girls realised that.

You're a liar. He loves us.

Mum stormed into her bedroom, came back with a cardboard box. Dumped its contents onto the floor: so many envelopes, thick and unopened. Nic sat on the floor, sifted through them. Every one addressed to Dad in the correctional centre. Some in her neat, precise handwriting. Some in Michelle's impatient scrawl. Older yellowing envelopes in the round, careful, childish hand of someone just learning to write. She remembered doing that: making neat pencil lines with a ruler, painstakingly copying the letters from the paper Mum had showed her, erasing the pencil lines and blowing away the rubber shavings. Wanting it to be perfect for him, to cheer him in that awful place.

I'm sorry, Nicky, Mum said, rubbing her shoulder. *I should've said something earlier. He started refusing delivery years ago. I couldn't bear them coming back with a big government stamp on them so I just . . . I stopped sending. Kept them in case . . .*

Nic gathered up the letters, took them to her room and shoved them in her school bag, too desperate to get away from Mum and Michelle's screaming to find a better place for them in the moment. She zipped up the bag, pushed it under her bed and then walked out of the house. No one tried to stop her. Probably didn't notice her leave. She walked and walked. The world had turned upside down and inside out and no one out here cared. As she walked, she found it got better, the feeling of being tossed through space. Seeing that the trees still grew upwards out of the ground, and that the sky was still very far away and showing no signs of falling any time soon. It helped to feel her feet connect with the earth, her lungs fill with air.

She will do that now. Not as easily, granted, but still. She makes her heavy way to the hallway, each clunk of the crutches on the hardwood floors reverberating through the house, shaking her bones. Clunk clunk clunk down the hallway, the promise of traffic noise, trees and shrubs and walls and garbage bins and telegraph poles and dogs and birds and cats and rats all filling the space, softening the blows, crowding her in.

The betrayer-in-chief and her assistant gape from the living room. Living room, but who could live there? It's a tomb! They're firing off questions and orders, telling her what she can't and should do. She ignores them: clunk clunk clunk. The B-i-C stomps her way across, tries to bar the doorway, but she is a coward in the end. Nic doesn't have to touch her, just keeps clunking forward and the girl moves, crying if you can believe it. Her, the cause of it all, the one who got her way, crying as if a grown woman leaving her own house for a walk outside is a personal attack on her. And him, well, he's obviously chosen his side. He won't even lift a hand to pull the axe from her back.

The door is already open; the children who have taken over her house have a bizarre obsession with *fresh air*, as if the place could hold any more of it. It's all air. Nothing but. And yet they don't want her to go out in it! Nonsensical. She would like to slam the door closed behind her, shut them up in the air-filled tomb of their making, but she would have to break her stride—clunking as it is—and risk falling, so she pushes on, grateful when the racket of outdoors drowns out their yowling.

—

Nic stops in the park where she found the bonnet last time she passed by. It feels so long ago. The jacaranda is in flower, serving its annual reminder to the slippery dip and swings that they are inferior installations. Small, hard and dull. Unable to regenerate or surprise. She positions herself in front of the bench, slides the crutches forward and eases back. The seat is lower than she expected and she lands on her tailbone with a thud. Pain is everything and then becomes only something. She can't stop looking at her pale, chalky nails. Kon swiped off the chipped polish with an alcohol pad when he saw how much it was bothering her, but this is worse. Like when she had bubble gum stuck in her hair as a kid and Mum cut it out and then evened out the cut until she looked like a cancer patient. She remembers the deep, low-down sick feeling she got when she saw strips of her own raw pink scalp, the queasiness of touching flesh that should be untouchable. She'd wanted to rip her own head off to stop that sick, creepy feeling. Wearing her Tigers beanie helped with the dis-ease, but they wouldn't let her leave it on at school and she would never, ever forget what it felt like to have to sit in that already hostile room, feeling the awfulness of it all sink right into her head through the unprotected raw skin.

Her nails are naked now the way her head had been naked then. Her mind flashes to the mole rat Facebook meme that was popular a couple of months ago. Did the mole rat feel like this all the time? Nauseated by its own disgusting bareness? Nic tries to shut her mind off from the horror, but it's useless. The shuddering is well underway. Only thing to do is to force herself up and set off again.

She makes her way to the corner and the universe rewards her efforts. Gifts strewn all over the nature strip: two pine chairs with woven cane seats, a squat footrest covered in pink and black polka-dotted fabric, a single-shelved bookshelf with Disney characters dancing over its sides and back, a cardboard box filled with glasses, coffee mugs and who knows what else. In her distress and haste she forgot to bring any bags, but never mind. Except for a couple of mugs, she wouldn't be able to carry any of this on her own anyway. Not in this state. She'll need help. Will might do it, if she can get him out from under the Betrayer's influence. Or maybe she could get her hands on a trolley. Wouldn't need the crutches if she had a trolley to lean on. Yes. She would push on towards the housing commission flats near the supermarket. There were always trolleys abandoned there.

A memory, sharp and bright, of walking this way to pick up Lena and her friend on a stifling summer afternoon. Lots of afternoons, wasn't it? She'd walk around after work to collect Lena and the other girl, bring them home for fish and chips and ice cream. She couldn't remember the girl's name. Short and broad-shouldered with thick little legs, looked at Lena with total adoration in her wide-set eyes, which made Nic love her. Saw herself in her for that reason and more, if she was being honest.

For one, Nic had lived in flats like those as a kid. Another suburb, further from the city, but same deal: besser block, outdoor walkways that begged you to lean too far over, to splat yourself on the concrete below, leave others to wonder if it was an accident or what. Inside, vinyl sheeting over chipboard, walls so thin you heard every fuck and fight and fart from next door. Carpet that'd give you nasty burns if you forgot your life and rolled around like a kid on it.

Her bedroom had been nice, though. Her half of the bedroom, at least. Michelle was neat to the point of ugliness. Would rather a blank white wall than blu-tacked posters that might unstick at the corners when the humidity was high. Rather a bed made like in a hospital room than one with colourful pillows and friendly fuzzy faces. Sometimes Nic would attempt to interrupt the blandness, poke a single pink feather into the edge of Michelle's mirror or thread a gold-sequinned ribbon around her bedhead. Michelle never commented, just plucked up the bit of beauty and tossed it in the bin in the corner. Nic would go to the bin and rescue it, find a place on her side where it'd feel properly appreciated.

When they moved into the Leichhardt house Mum threw out nearly all the decorations Nic had up around her room. She said it was a *clean start. A home all of our own, girls!* She said they could choose to paint their room any colour they liked, and for weeks Nic and Michelle fought bitterly about that. Pointlessly, too. There was never money for painting. No energy or will. The walls stayed the same dirty cream they'd always been. Nic could have painted it any colour she liked once Michelle moved out. She doesn't remember why she didn't. Nor why she didn't paint Mum's room after she died. It didn't matter, though, because there was so much else to see. Who thought about walls?

Now she had to because they were all you saw when you walked in. Walls and floors. Naked, old and grubby.

A shot of pain up her spine. New pain. Not an intensification of the pain that's been with her since she woke in hospital, not the already familiar tugging that came as the painkillers wore off. Altogether new, like a piece of amber glass from the gutter had leapt up and stabbed itself into her back. Stabbed her hard in the tailbone and then dragged itself towards her heart, digging in deeper as it went. Nowhere to sit and rest a minute here. Can't provide a seat or ledge or anything at all that would encourage people to linger. You might accidentally give someone a moment of comfort. You might allow an injured and broken person a place to rest before continuing on her way in the world. Can't bloody have that, can we?

So this is what you get then, concerned citizens wanting to discourage comfort for the undesirables. You get a mess of a woman collapsed on the bristly, bindi-strewn so-called grass of the nature strip. A mess of a woman, yes, she is aware. Used to walk this street briskly, looking out for forgotten things on the ground, and now she is one, too bruised and crazy-looking for even her own self to want to pick up and care for. Noisy, too, the pain making her mewl against her own will. She hears herself: a cat who's caught her paw on a jagged tin lid.

I am a woman who needs rescuing, she thinks. I am a public nuisance. I am a matter of public health and safety. I am a danger to myself and my neighbours. I am in need of intervention.

Steve is with her again, as he was last time she was laid out helpless. He is reminding her that she will be fine. He nodded off or fell down in the street all the time in his final years and it never killed him. What killed him was being alone inside. No one to stumble upon him and call for help. No one to bash down his door and carry him out, humiliated but alive. She could argue, tell him death is preferable to shame and violation and betrayal. But she only means it for herself. For him, she wishes all the humiliation and agony in the world if it had meant survival. She wishes he'd OD'd right here where she lies and that passers-by spat and cursed at him, but only after calling an ambulance. She wishes he'd had everything taken away from him, been forced to stay in a huge, echoey hospital, prodded and patronised by people who couldn't even be bothered to introduce themselves before fingering your wounds. She wishes, even, for his hatred, if only she'd earned it by saving his life.

A few metres along the nature strip a silver slingback sparkles at her. Too high for a long work day, but low enough you could wear it out to dinner and then walk home without stumbling. Shiny finish, probably fake patent leather. The inner soles would be cheap vinyl that smelt bad after a night of sweat. The sides would cut, the toes pinch. So pretty, though, gleaming out on this rough, unlovely patch of wannabe grass, a moment from a fairy tale fallen exactly where it is needed.

Mum had a pair of silver high heels once. Higher and more expensive-looking than this cheerful gal. Mum's had a textured silk finish and creamy, real leather inner soles. When she wore them she was half a head taller and a million bucks more beautiful. Moving through the house on her way to the door, it was like little bits of glitter and sunshine and joy trailed behind her. Michelle once asked if Mum would leave her those shoes in her will. Mum had laughed and said, *Sure, but I don't plan on falling off the perch any time soon. They'll be out of fashion by the time you get them.* Michelle, who thought herself more sophisticated than anyone, said, *Oh, no, Mum. Those are classics. They're forever.*

One morning Mum came home in bare feet, her eyes ringed with melted make-up, her dress torn at the hem and stockings gone. The blue veins on her shins were gruesome in the early light. *What happened?* Michelle asked and Mum shrugged and said, *Rough night.*

But where are your shoes?

Mum flicked the question away with her hand. *They hurt my feet.*

But where did you—

Enough. I need some quiet.

She trudged flat-footed through to her bedroom and Michelle went on a whispered rant about how careless and embarrassing and stupid their mother was. Nic agreed with everything she said, and when she seemed to be done with the rant asked her, *Should we go and find her shoes?*

Nic would never forget the look her sister gave her. *You poor little idiot,* it said. *You don't understand a thing that's happening here. You will never understand the adult world. You will always be locked out.* What she said with her mouth was, *She doesn't deserve those shoes.*

What's that got to do with it, Nic wanted to say, but the look had made her feel like she did at school when everyone else picked up their pencils and started writing. She'd thought she'd been paying attention, but everybody else had heard something different from her. They all knew what to do. She had missed it. Whatever it was, she had missed it. Again. *Dumb slow retard.*

Someone was saying those things to her now. Not with their words, but with their tone. 'What's happened here then? Let's get you some help.' (*Dumb slow retard, risk to yourself, matter of health and safety.*)

Sirens and then men lifting her and her own terrible cat yowl. When did she become a woman who couldn't control the noises she makes? She manages to say, 'The shoe.' And someone says, 'You're wearing your shoes, darling, it's fine.' And someone else says, 'Does she mean that one?' And no one answers out loud, but she imagines the looks they give each other: *She doesn't deserve that shoe.*

It is a good thing she didn't get the shoe, she realises as they unload her from the ambulance. No matter how much she cared for it—and she would have, giving it pride of place on the TV cabinet, where its shine would be reflected by the trophies on either side—it wouldn't be right. Shoes come in pairs and this one, when she thinks of it, looked more forlorn than fairy tale, there on the nature strip. Somewhere its mate lay just as sadly, waiting, waiting, waiting to be whole again.

LENA

After Nic left, Will slumped on the sofa and closed his eyes. 'I should go after her.'

'She's a grown-arse woman. She can come and go as she pleases.' Her voice sounded normal, which was interesting. Who knew you could speak normally after having been obliterated?

'She's on crutches, Leen.'

'So she won't get far before she realises she's being an idiot and comes back.'

'What if she falls or something?'

She would almost certainly fall. Burst stitches. Faint. Dirty her wounds and get a nasty infection. Shit.

Lena moved towards the front door, remembered the vicious way Nic screamed, *Rape!* and stopped. 'She doesn't deserve our help.'

'You don't help people because they deserve it. You help them because they need help.'

'Righto, Saint Will. Go and help her then. Off you run. Be the big fucking hero as per fucking normal.'

'Bitch.' Mumbled, as though she was barely worth the effort to insult.

Lena turned to yell at him, was punched by the sight of his body curled tight, hands over his face. A child in hiding. You can't see me if I can't see you.

'I'm going out,' she said.

He said nothing, did nothing. Will the Brave. Will the Bold. The New Man of the House temporarily in the Big House. Our Will. Lovely Will. Poor Will. His Father's Son. Our Hardworking Hero.

Fucking *nothing*.

Leaning against the hedge out front, she turned her phone back on. Wished she hadn't. The flood of random messages and penises seemed to be getting heavier. Surely it must be time for them to move on to a new dumb ugly slut? Or should she admit defeat, disconnect her number? Or just leave her phone off permanently, let the creeps imagine what they wanted while their messages sank into the void?

She was about to turn the thing off again, see how long she could go without rechecking it, when the screen flashed up an incoming call: Uni Admin. She answered without thinking. A woman called Mona hoped she was well and needed to speak with her about her failure to comply with her obligations vis-a-vis the fellowship that covered half her rent. Her failure to attend

two exams this week meant she was in breach of her Contract
of Mutual Obligation. She also appeared to be in breach of the
requirement she sleep in her assigned room at least six of every
seven nights unless she has received written permission to do
otherwise. A written notice warning of the consequences of these
breaches had been placed in her pigeonhole.

Lena apologised. Said there'd been a family emergency. Was
told that might be an acceptable reason for a student to fail to
meet obligations, but the student must communicate the circumstances to the fellowship committee, to the university admissions
office and to the residential hall management so that allowances
can be made, ways forward agreed upon.

She would still need to do this: apply retroactively for a leave
of absence she had already taken. She must also attend all her
remaining exams and make urgent applications to re-sit the two
she has missed. Failure to do so would result in the cancellation
of her fellowship, and if that occurred, she would need to pay
her accommodation bill in full or risk eviction. All of this was
contained in the notice in her pigeonhole, Mona told her. Which,
it had been noted, had gone unemptied for the past week.

As soon as she hung up the screen started flashing again.
Annie was ringing her now?

'You have never voice-called me once the whole time I've
known you.'

'I'm growing as a person. Trying new things, you know?'

'Hmm.'

'And you've stopped coming to class. And deleted your socials.
And don't answer my texts.'

'Yeah. Sorry. It's been a lot. Nothing personal. I just need . . .'

'I get it, babe, I do. But I worry. You gotta let me know you're still alive now and then, yeah?'

'Yeah. Sorry. I didn't think.'

'Well, I forgive you, because I'm a really, really good person with an enormous heart, as you know. But listen, actually, I do have to tell you something. Two things. Good news and bad news.'

'Okay.'

'Where are you right now?'

'Why?'

'I need to know if you're in a safe place. Like not standing on a bridge or anything?'

'Funny. I've never heard anyone check for suicide imminence right before they give someone good news before.' Lena began walking towards the main road in case she needed to throw herself in front of a truck.

'It's good news in relation to the bad news, though, if you get what I mean.'

'I don't. Please just tell me.'

'I'm serious though, babe. Where are you? Is anyone with you?'

'You're freaking me out, Annie. Fuck. Speak.'

A big sigh. 'You're on *sydneysluts*.'

'Isn't that . . . Wasn't it shut down?' Lena had read the weekend paper exposé on it a few months ago. This old-school bulletin board-style website where people traded nude pictures and videos complete with full names and home town of the women. Sometimes their workplace or—and this was where most of the media outrage came from—their school. The story ended by saying the site had been closed by the time the article went to press. And if you were dumb enough to believe it would stay down you were probably dumb enough to end up featuring on it. Dumb, dumb, trusting, dumb ugly dumb slut.

'I'm sorry, Leen. They don't have your work or suburb or anything on there at least.'

'But my name?'

'Yeah. And the uni.'

It explained the increase in harassment. Confirmed she needed to cancel her number. Maybe change her name. Uni was definitely over for her even if she could make up for the missed exams.

'So that's it then. No coming back.'

'But, Leen, wait, the good news, yeah? There's this man my dad knows, right? Takes care of problems like yours.'

'Your dad knows a hitman?'

'Ha. No. Well, maybe, who the hell knows. But listen, this dude has a company that cleans all the shit you don't want off the internet. Dad's used them before, says they do a good job. Trustworthy.'

'Wait, why would your dad need—Shit, did he . . . ?'

'Ewww. No. He would never.'

'Of course not. Only disgusting trash whores—'

'Lena, no! I didn't mean that. You know I didn't mean that. Just don't make me think of my dad having—ewww! See, now you've made me think it! Ugh. Listen, listen, listen: his firm uses this dude to clean up after some of its clients. A couple of its employees, too, I think. It's not just sex stuff. Like, this one knob got filmed saying racist shit at a party. Scrub, scrub, scrub and now there's no trace.'

'No trace.'

'None. And this knob was a big-deal knob to start with. Dad reckons a nobody like you—'

'Shit, Annie. I can't believe you.'

'Oh, he didn't mean nobody in a bad way. Just like not famous and—'

'I'm a nobody, whatever. I just can't believe you told your dad.'

Silence, not for long, but any time not talking was a lot for Annie. 'I wanted to help. I knew he'd know how.'

'You told him me specifically or a friend?'

Another, sick-making pause. 'I said a friend, but he assumed I meant me. I had to be more specific so he'd calm down. I'm sorry.'

Lena had never met Annie's dad, didn't know what kind of man to imagine. A rich man, sure. Expensive suit and haircut, clean, perfectly fitting shoes. A man who took time to listen to his daughter talk about a friend, to give advice. But then what? Did he put it all from his mind and return to his newspaper? Talk over the dangers of the smartphone age with his younger kids? Or did he lock his office door and type in her name? He might have. Get the goods before they disappear forever. Only fair.

'Leen? He won't tell anyone, if that's what you're worried about. He's decent like that. And, listen, his advice is good. It's a real solution, you know? I'm going to text you the details, okay?'

'Yeah.'

'Yeah? And if you want I can come with you to the appointment or whatever you need.'

'Okay. Thanks.'

'You're okay? Really?'

''Course. Thanks. I'll let you know how I go.'

───

On the main road, she walked until she reached a strip of four vacant shops. Under the awning, back pressed against the graffitied glass, she pressed call on the number Annie had sent. Pressed cancel right away. Was this how Will felt when he had to call Mum and tell her he'd been arrested? Ashamed and guilty but also furious at the fucking unfairness.

She called again and, before she could cancel, a woman answered with the name of the company. Lena fumbled her way through a version of her nightmare, speaking as quietly as she could in case any passers-by caught a hint and moved closer. The woman listened without interruption and then offered to set up a meeting with the company's head of removals.

'Removals? So he'll get rid of the bloke who did this to me?'

'He takes care of online removals. We don't do real world ones.' Her tone was flat; Lena couldn't tell if she was continuing the joke or missing it. After confirming that there'd be no fee for the consultation, she made an appointment for that afternoon, started the long walk to Central. There wasn't enough on her travel card for a bus and a train and, besides, she had nothing else to do, nowhere else to go.

───

The office was in a rundown shopping arcade near Parramatta station. She used to pass here all the time when she and Mum would catch the train to Parra, walk around the corner to meet Will at his college then return to the station to take the train to Westmead where Dad lay dying. From her seat across from the head of removals, aka Nathan, she could see the back of a restaurant they sometimes ate at, the three of them, pretending it was a normal thing to do—stop off for a five-dollar bowl of noodles on your way to check how much closer to death someone you loved had moved since yesterday. While Nathan behind the desk gave her a spiel about privacy—a little late for that, the voice she used to think of as Aunty Nic said—a tiny boy in a school uniform stopped and ran his hand over some crates stacked by the restaurant's open kitchen door. Maybe the tiny boy spoke, because a man in a white apron stepped out of the restaurant, looked at the crates with his hands on his hips, shook his head and went back inside. The boy stayed there a moment longer then took off fast down the alley, his giant backpack bouncing. He probably wasn't even born last time Lena had been to the restaurant. There were lots of people like that, she realised. More and more every day. All these people who lived in a world in which her dad did not exist.

'I understand it's difficult,' Nathan was saying. 'But the more detail you give me, the better job we'll be able to do.'

'Yeah, it's just . . . I don't even know if I can afford this. So, like, I don't want to . . . to say all the detail and then I can't afford to—'

'I see a dozen sex tapes a week. I'm not going to go looking yours up for fun. If you contract us to do this, we'll find it and get it down wherever we can. If you don't, I'll never think about you or it again. Not being harsh, just real with you. If it's my job to, I'll care that someone is disseminating a video of you without consent. If it's not, I couldn't give a shit about the video and where it is. So, why don't you tell me the situation so I can tell you what it might cost to deal with it and we can move forward or say goodbye. Okay?'

Lena felt like laughing. This gross, ridiculous man with his nineties leather jacket and B-grade cop show patter. *He's got nothing I need and if he did I wouldn't need it anymore,* Nic'd say. *Never take advice from a man who can't even dress himself,* Mum'd say. *I'd fuck her as long as I didn't have to look at her,* the internet'd say and say and say and say.

She told him in as unemotional, clinical terms as she could. He asked for clarification a few times, but never in a way that made her feel he was storing the details away to wank over later. He stabbed at his keyboard with two fingers as she talked, every so often telling her to slow down. Shouldn't a tech expert be better at typing? she wondered, but told herself someone else probably did the actual work; Nathan was the detail and fee collector.

Yeah, so, the fee. She actually laughed. Nathan stared at her, unmoved, unembarrassed.

'I can't,' she told him. 'There's no way.'

'It's only half up-front. You can pay the rest—'

'No, I can't ever. It's . . .' How to explain to this man that even half of what he was asking was as accessible to her as a million fucking dollars? She couldn't even top up her Opal card, had spent her last few bus trips in high anxiety on the lookout for fare inspectors.

'What about the young man? Does he have funds?'

She laughed again, a bark of shock. 'You mean the person who filmed the fucking thing in the first place?'

'Yes.'

'You want me to ask him to give me money?'

'I don't want you to do anything in particular. I'm suggesting options to you. Whether you take them is up to you.'

———

The thing was, she thought, as she clomped down the piss-stinking stairwell to the street, Josh probably could get that much money. She could ask him, but that would mean making contact with him. It would also mean admitting she had thought of it, which would mean admitting she was bothered by it. Which she couldn't do. Or wouldn't. Same thing, in effect.

———

As soon as she turned her phone back on it rang. Three actual live phone calls in one day. Definitely a sign from the universe that she should get rid of the evil thing.

'Will. What?'

'I just got a call from the hospital. Aunty Nic has been brought in by ambulance.'

Lena sat down right where she was. A nature strip it was called, though it was mostly dirt. Dirt was natural, she supposed.

'You there?'

'Yeah.'

'She's going to be okay. Probably. Good of you to ask. Just getting checked over after a bit of a fall on the street.'

Lena waited in silence. Not for long.

'A fall like I said would happen.'

'Like you said would happen while you curled up in a ball and did nothing about it.'

A longer silence this time. Three tween girls in skin-tight jersey shorts walked by, giggled, covering their mouths in mock horror. Lena made a savage face, stuck her finger up, made them laugh harder.

'Anyway,' Will said at last, 'they're going to call again when she's ready to be picked up.'

'Okay.'

'Call *me* again. The person who actually answers.'

'I had to turn my phone off for a bit. Hadn't got to checking since—'

'Yeah, well. Nurse said Aunty Nic was pretty distressed when they had to ask her for a second emergency contact number because the one on file wasn't answering or returning calls.'

'Shit.'

'Yeah.'

'I'll head to the hospital now. Wait there until she's released.'

'Honesty, Leen, I reckon you should steer clear for a bit. She was that wild at you this morning.'

'She was wild at both of us.'

'Yeah, but mostly you. And now you've ignored the hospital—'

'I didn't ignore it! I was just dealing with a different—Fuck, Will, I've got a lot of complicated shit happening right now, okay? And my phone was, like, blowing up. I didn't know she'd . . .' Except I watched her leave this morning, out of her mind. I almost willed this to happen. Maybe didn't know, but should have. Definitely should have.

'Doesn't matter now, anyway. They've got my number. You can just . . . I dunno, maybe stay at your place tonight or something. Come around tomorrow, see what's what.'

She agreed. Hung up. Stood and brushed the dirt off her arse, almost spitting blood when a truck horn blared at her. Texted Annie: *Any chance I can crash at yours tonight?*

Im staying at the olds. If you can get out here I can give you my key?

Lena had never been to Annie's family home. She'd never been to Annie's family's suburb. It would be a train and a bus at least. Maybe a bloody ferry, for all she knew.

It's ok, I'll be right

Really tho? Dad just said I can prolly call the desk dude and ask him to let you up?

Annie's dad. Who knew about—had probably watched . . . And there was Annie casually discussing her. My poor whore friend with nowhere to stay. How can we solve this without leaving our harbourfront mansion?

Nah, I'm good. Don't worry about it

Cool. Did you ring that place? Can they help?

Lena turned off her phone.

—

She'd been back in her room for ten minutes when Jules knocked, called out that she'd love to have a chat. Lena lay frozen, silent. The knocking stopped, restarted. Stopped for longer, started again. The knocking provoked the same physical response as her phone's buzzing: a hard jolt in the chest signalling the start of a few minutes of tight breathing. She couldn't bring herself to turn the phone off in case Nic tried her again.

There was no alcohol in her room, no way she'd be leaving it to get some even if she did have money for it, which she didn't. There was one reliable way for her to calm down, something she'd stumbled upon at twelve or so and honed to perfection since. A series of simple but rapid moves that would take her from agitated to blissed out in under five minutes, every time. She barely thought of it as sexual; it was a physical manipulation to release a naturally occurring relaxant. Self-soothing with three fingers and the heel of her hand.

She stashed her phone under the pillow, slipped off her pants and snuggled deep under the covers. It was harder than usual to get into it—her mind kept straining towards the door and the phone—but within a few minutes her muscle memory took over and everything was building just as it should. The usual images flicked through her head on cue—a pop singer whose music she hated but whose pillowy lips made her hot; a movie star dead before she was born; a teacher from tenth grade; a primary school friend's dad—each of them taking his turn at working the hand between her legs until she was seconds away and then a sound escaped her throat and—

fuckin sexy cum sounds

needs a gag on her noisy bitch

sounds like my cat coughing up a hairball

Who knew a building orgasm could just stop like that? No retreat, or ebbing away. Just killed dead on the spot by the sound of your own pleasure.

—

A noise in the hallway but not knocking. A sheet of paper skittered under the door. Blue scrawl:

Lena,

I am concerned for your welfare as you are not responding to knocks or phone calls. Under the housing rules I am permitted to let myself into your room if I have welfare concerns. I'd rather you simply let me know you're okay. I'll wait ten minutes to hear from you and then I'll have to come in and check. You're not in trouble! This is about making sure you're okay.

Jules

She picked up her phone to call the stupid interfering arse, was interrupted by a text from Josh.

Please give me a chance to make things right. Please

Someone breathing right outside her door, she was sure of it.

Fine, she typed. *Meet me somewhere near uni with no uni people*

Immediate reply. *Shit. Didn't expect this. U mean now?*

Yes, she typed. *You know somewhere?*

Thirty seconds and he'd sent her the address of a hotel bar a few blocks away. Followed by, *I'll be there in half an hour*, then a minute later, *Thank you so much for this*

When she opened the door five minutes later, she felt awful at how genuinely relieved Jules looked to see her.

'God, Lena, I—'

'I was sleeping. Heavily. I've been having family drama and haven't slept much.'

'I just wish you'd let me know. I thought, because of the—the, you know, the thing—I thought you might have . . .'

'I'm fine, as you can see. But just on my way out.' It had been hard to dress quickly in a way that was appropriate for a fancy city bar but wouldn't indicate to Josh that he was worth any effort whatsoever. She'd gone with black work pants, black V-neck t-shirt, black high-heeled sandals. Unwashed hair in ponytail, no eye make-up, slick of true red lippie.

Jules nodded, fake smiled. 'Of course, of course. Have fun! Make sure you check your pigeonhole, though, hey? You know what admin's like!'

'Will do,' Lena said, smiling back as though she was exactly what she claimed to be: someone who was finally well rested, someone who was fine.

The east lawn was busy with people enjoying the late afternoon sun and relative lack of smoke haze. Some studying, but most talking in small groups, or lying on their backs, looking at their phones. Lena passed the spot where Josh had kissed her and she'd believed for the first time that she might get to live the life she'd dreamt of. She was struck with the thought that all these people were contemplating their own possibilities. Every one of them at the start of a story they hoped was a romantic comedy or an inspirational biopic about triumphing over adversity. At the very least a gritty realist arthouse film about finding your place and not selling out. None of them anticipated being the centre of a grubby and maudlin melodrama. Or, for that matter, a low-budget porno.

She wished the best for all of them, these sun-blanketed strangers. Genuinely, wholeheartedly, she put her remaining hopeless romantic energy behind all their stories. Go well, be happy, prove that dreams come true.

'You don't want to be checking that out,' someone said from within a cluster of golden light.

'Shhh. You're so loud.'

'I'm just trying to warn you, man. Could fill a swimming pool with the amount of cum that's been spilt on that one.'

WILL

The cute little social worker looked more intimidating and official than she had at the house. Suit jacket, gold hoop earrings, ramrod straight behind an enormous desk in an overcrowded office. Still cute, though. She reminded him of the girls he hung out with at college. If things were different he might even ask her out. If there wasn't an ongoing family crisis under her supervision. If his body wasn't yearning for Mercy and his heart for the kids. If eighty-eight per cent of his attention wasn't taken up by the excruciating pain in his mouth. If that percentage wasn't going up by the minute.

'We knew there was a risk that making the home physically safe for Nicole would cause distress,' Ada said.

'Yeah,' Will agreed. 'I think my sister might have gone overboard. She does that. Sorry.'

'Your sister has done her best to deal with a very challenging situation. Hoarding disorder is tough. The danger of not intervening can be high, but the fallout of intervening is, well . . .'

She gestured down the hall where his aunty was, presumably, having bandages put over her bandages, stitches over her stitches.

Ada told him that she'd referred Aunty Nic to a service which ran group cognitive behaviour therapy sessions. The success rate was, she said, very good 'for this condition'.

His phone pinged in his pocket. Could be Mercy. Or Nic, of course. Lena. He apologised for the interruption, pulled it out and saw *Anton*, which meant nothing to him. He slid it back into his pocket, picked up the thread with Ada: 'What's "very good" for this condition?'

She smiled, pretty and sad and sorry. 'Traditionally we see under fifteen per cent of people treated for hoarding disorder make any substantial change in behaviour. This group has been reporting over thirty per cent.'

'So even with the best treatment, chances are it's not going to be fixed.' Creepy to hear himself saying such similar words to those he'd said before, in a hospital across the city, his mum and sister with him then, his dad rather than aunty down the hallway. On that day, he'd wondered if it was all just a scam, medical science. These big buildings and well-dressed, expensively trained staff and million-dollar equipment, and still they couldn't do fuck-all to save the life of a father of two in his mid-thirties. Now he thought: psychology, psychiatry, all that's bullshit, too. Nobody knows how to fix anything. It's all just bandaging up and calming down, pills and action plans to make you feel in control of the random and unfixable horror. And for him, not even that. Not even some decent fucking drugs to make him forget his mouth was rotting from the inside out.

'Realistically, we're not trying to fix it,' Ada was saying. 'We're just trying to find a way for Nicole to live safely with her condition.'

'What if we found out what caused it? I read it can start with a trauma. If we knew what the trigger was, would that help?'

'If that's something your aunt wants to explore in therapy she can. I wouldn't speculate. Sometimes there's an obvious trigger, sometimes hoarding behaviour is situational, like in times of scarcity. And sometimes it creeps up over years and it's impossible to say when a tendency to overbuy or under-discard becomes full-blown hoarding disorder. There's diagnostic criteria for the condition once it's active, but not to identify its potential cause or causes.'

At his local up in Mackay the old-timers would sometimes see fit to educate the younger drinkers about the way things used to be and the changes they'd seen. Some were obvious—technology and all that. But sometimes one of them would sniff and wrinkle his nose, say the rain doesn't smell like it used to, and two or three others would nod solemnly, agree that there was something off about the smell this year. Sometimes the thing they'd talk about was the feel of the wind, drier and fiercer. Can't measure it, but it's different all right. The bugs and snakes, they talked about, too. The former down to city levels, the latter slinking up into everyone's houses. No one was counting, understand. But you heard much more often these days about some poor bugger meeting one when he got up in the night for a piss or a kid finding one of them coiled up in their toy box, that was for sure.

The heat, now *that* you could measure, could see the changes on a weather map. The eggheads at BOM had even come up with new colours to accurately show it to those who demanded proof. The deep crimson and purple of imminent death, as Mercy said (cheerfully). The old men didn't need any new colours, any time-lapse maps. They knew there was a time when you could walk on the road without shoes and not scald your soles. At least in bloody August!

What they couldn't tell you, these old men, was when these changes happened. Not like the new Centrelink system which meant you got your pension straight into your bank account every Thursday instead of passed to you over a counter in a yellow envelope. There was a specific date that happened, even if you didn't care to remember it. And not like the internet or satellite TV, which got more common as time went on, but whose introduction you could pinpoint to a particular week in a specific month in a verifiable year. No, the smell and wind and heat snuck up on them all. Which was the day it became definitely bad, no one could say, but bad it definitely was.

Was it like that for Aunty Nic? Day after day after day of one more towel or ornament or pillow or hand cream or book, until she couldn't use the bath because it was full, found herself walking from the bedroom door to her bed without her feet touching the ground, and she genuinely didn't know how it had happened? It wasn't like she was having shipping containers emptied out into her hallway. Just ordinary items carried in one at a time. One thing cannot make such a difference, can it? A single towel or ornament or pillow or hand cream or book cannot instantly transform a house full of belongings into a hoard.

He'd missed the end of Ada's spiel, but it was obviously finished because she was standing and placing a stack of brochures—the same ones Lena hadn't bothered to read, he supposed—in his hands. She said she'd take him down to the area where he was supposed to wait for Aunty Nic, and as they wound through corridors and down some stairs and across a courtyard, then through a large echoey foyer, he was trying to think of a non-addict-sounding way to ask Ada whether a random GP could see when he'd last been to a different GP and that he'd asked for codeine. It was only when she squeezed his hand and said *stay in touch* with a questioning lilt that it twigged she might have thought he was working up the nerve to ask her out, that she wanted him to.

He sank into a squeaky orange chair, mouth hinged open to minimise the pain. He pulled out his phone and it took a couple of seconds to match the name Anton with the idea of a person he once knew. Before prison and Queensland, he and Anton had been mates. Last year Anton had messaged him on Facebook and, after the predictable back and forth about jobs, marriage, kids etc., they'd exchanged numbers on the off chance Anton would follow through on his plan to head north for a bit. Weird that he knew Will was back in town. He'd told no one, been nowhere except this damn hospital.

The message was long and confusing. He needed to stop and reread every few words.

hey mate long time no see still planning to come up and see you in qld just need to sort stuff out here first i feel shit about this and didnt know if i shld tell you but asked around and fellas said you

*should know pretty sure its your sister sorry mate but id wanna
know if it was my sister take care*

He read the whole thing through twice again before he realised there was another message beneath it, this one a link.

———

Back at the house he got Nic into bed, helped her take some
painkillers, said he'd check in on her in a bit. His own pain was
so bad he wanted to die. First, though, he would murder Anton
for sending him that link. Then that smug pubeless fucker in
the clip. If he could even find him. Cowardly shithead hiding
his face while Lena was easily identifiable to anyone who'd ever
seen her in a t-shirt.

That scar. Bane of his cursed fucking life. She was nine and he
thirteen, and they were fighting over something. It didn't matter
what. That year she'd had a growth spurt and he hadn't and it felt
like a personal attack. Four years between them, but her suddenly
so tall that people just had to comment. *Look out, Will, your
little sister's catching up on you!* He felt mocked by her height.
Like she was growing to humiliate him. He found any excuse to
make her cry.

This day he'd been yelling at her in the yard and she turned
and ran for the front door. He thought she was going to dob or
maybe he just felt enraged at her leaving before he was done. He
streaked after her, could have caught her easy but didn't want to
wrestle. She might have been slower but she was strong and not
afraid to bite. He ran past her—it was a matter of seconds, the

yard was not large—and reached the front door of the apartment block, open as it always was during the day. Cackling he slipped inside and slammed it closed.

He hadn't taken more than three fast steps when something hard slapped the top of his back. The sound of glass hitting timber and the realisation he was surrounded by jagged shards of the door's thick yellow glass. One near his bare left foot was as long as his arm. Feet frozen he reached behind him to touch the place he'd been hit. Tender but dry. His shirt was unripped. Must have been struck by a flat edge.

Lena screamed and he turned as fast as he could without lifting his feet off the ground. Swivel, swivel, swivel. She stood with her hands clamped together over her chest. He couldn't see why she was screaming, told her to calm down, but then the blood started running through the cracks in her fingers and he saw the dark patch spreading fast over the centre of her pale pink t-shirt.

It was her left arm, cut deep and ugly when it went right through the slamming door she was trying to stop. It was her arm and it was bad, but just her arm. Still, when he remembers that afternoon he feels the panic, the certainty that she was clutching her heart, that the blood in her hands, on her shirt, was heart blood. It was only her arm, he told himself, told others—the let-down at the end of the dramatic story—just her arm. Only that. Only that.

For over a decade he'd hoped that one day he'd be able to see the scar and not re-experience the five seconds in which he was sure he'd killed her. Hoped and wished and tried and ha ha ha ha ha ha. Good joke, universe! Now when he saw her arm he would think instead of her grinding on top of a waxed and spray-tanned college fuckboy. And so would everyone else she knew and lots of people she didn't.

What the actual living fuck was he supposed to do?

The blister pack in his hand offered a suggestion. Yes. Good. That'd be a start. He swallowed two of Aunty Nic's Endones with a handful of water straight from the tap. Crawled under the blankets on the lounge. Scrolled through Facebook, clicked on a link about a species of antelope nearly wiped out in a month. Bacteria living in their guts ever since the species existed, got too warm and killed the lot of them. Almost the lot of them. It could happen to us. Who knew what lurked inside us waiting for activation. He texted Lena, fast, without thinking, before he faded out to blissful nothing.

NIC

'It's really not as bad as you think,' Will had said when he brought her home the second time. 'All the important things are still here. We just cleared out the older, junkier stuff.'

She hadn't replied because doing so would legitimise his outright lie. Now she lay in her barren bed and stared at the space where her side table used to be. She'd bought it at a garage sale on Catherine Street three summers ago. *French Provincial Style*, the man had said. Nic was going to ask if it was the odd shape— round top balancing on a single leg which split into three curved feet at the base—or the crackly beige and blue paint which made it French Provincial Style, but the man was sweeping his hand over the top and saying, *Antique Finish, Freshly Varnished, Rustic Charm*, and she felt stifled by his words and his closeness, his stale cigarette smell. She started to turn away and he said, *Belonged to my mother, may she rest in peace*, and then Nic saw everything she needed to about the table, saw the decades of magazines and school notes and electricity bills, the wedding and christening invitations, the cups of tea left to go cold while the nappies were changed, the homework finished, the dinner cooked, the phone answered. Saw it cleared of everything but a vase of fresh flowers once a month and then the slow pile up of leaflets and letters and bills, petals dropping, water turning thick and brown. Saw the children's birthday parties where it was dragged in to sit next to the kitchen table and hold the plastic cups and plates. Saw the not-quite-faded texta marks layered over the not-quite-buffed-out cat scratches. She paid seventeen dollars while mentally telling the deceased woman she knew it was worth a hundred times that. She carried it home, a fifteen-minute walk taking almost an hour, changing positions every few minutes: arms stretched wide embracing the round rim, then chin on top, hands gripping the leg, then hanging upside down like a chook in a window, the table banging her shins with every step.

At home she'd stripped to her underwear, let the sweat air dry, while she searched for the perfect place for the table. It hadn't taken long; there was an easel in her bedroom, displaying a painting she'd bought at a different garage sale several years before: a little girl in a yellow dress holding a white vase holding a red rose. It had been painted by the woman who owned the house, which was being cleared out because she had been moved to a nursing home. Nic knew the woman who owned this table would have loved the painting of the girl, and the painter would be happy to know that her little girl had found a friend in a much-loved old table. The boxes that had been next to the easel were happy, too, being snuggled up more closely with their mates further along the wall.

The position of the table was perfect but its emptiness was not. She grabbed the plastic Monstera from the bathroom, giving the table a sense of purpose and the girl something green to look at. The Monstera had been a gift from the receptionist at the medical centre who had seen Nic admiring it and said she should take it as it was being chucked out later that week when they refurbished the office. That receptionist had left years ago and been replaced by someone less friendly and observant, but every time Nic passed the Monstera she felt the woman's warmth and thoughtfulness.

The plant, the girl with the rose, the easel, the table. All gone. Not as bad as you think, her nephew said.

⁓

She drifts into a druggy sleep, wakes to the golden late-afternoon light and doesn't see, on her bedside table, the cherry-sized lump of blu-tack she has opened her eyes to for over a decade. Dried out, sandy-textured, barely stuck to the surface, but at the same time always the fresh, minty-blue strip from when Lena was six and had a habit of tapping her tiny fingers on the desk during class. Another child had told her to *STOP IT, LENA* and the teacher had repeated the order, though more gently; it was distracting the other children. Lena's fingers tapped Nic's arm as she told the story. No rhythm to it, index and pinkie and ring and pointer and thumb playing over her skin in a different order each time. Mummy told her to squeeze her hands into fists instead of tapping. Mummy didn't understand that moving her hands helped her to concentrate and sit still.

Nic spotted the new packet of blu-tack on the coffee table. She had bought it to replace the old pack, which she had used up the week before putting another of Lena's drawings on the wall of her room. She opened it, stripped a full piece off its white paper dressing, balled it up and handed it to Lena, who understood immediately what it was for. Her stubby fingers pressed and kneaded, the crease between her eyebrows eased and then disappeared. *Listen*, she said, and Nic did and smiled, because it was silent, or close enough.

Michelle called the next night. Another child had loudly accused Lena of being a thief, of taking blu-tack from the teacher's desk. The teacher called Michelle, stressed that she wasn't concerned about the *value* of what may or may not have been taken, only that Lena may or may not have been sneaking around and going through her desk and could Michelle please talk to her daughter about whether she did or did not do this thing that— *let me stress*—is not about the blu-tack itself but about a possible issue with sneakiness and lying.

Nic confirmed that she had, as Lena'd sworn, given her the damn blu-tack. And excuse me, but what kind of nasty, punishing place was this classroom where anxious little girls were publicly shamed and accused for rolling a piece of household adhesive worth all of ten cents!

And for once—literally probably the only time ever—Michelle agreed with her. Was furious on Lena's behalf. Made one of the trips to the principal's office she would later become known for. Demanded the teacher apologise to Lena in front of the class and, in fact, thank you very much, congratulate her for finding something so quiet and non-disruptive to help her sit still and concentrate.

The teacher did all that and then let Lena take a lump of which-ever play-doh colour she liked best to roll between her fingers in class. It had been a tough decision, because she loved purple more than anything, but if she chose that she might spend too long looking at it instead of concentrating, and so she chose her second favourite colour—yellow—and when she rolled it between her fingers she felt both calm and proud because she had solved a problem all on her own.

She told Nic all this when she came over the following Saturday and what killed Nic, just *killed* her, was that the darling, earnest little thing actually handed the blu-tack back to her! Said, *So you can have this one back now, Aunty Nic.* Can you believe the sweet-ness of that child?

Did the woman she'd grown into remember any of this when she'd scraped it up and discarded it? If she had, would she even care?

LENA

L ena had walked too quickly and arrived at the bar both early and sweaty. She went to the bathroom, wiped off the red lipstick which she had felt screaming from her lips the whole way here. She splashed her face with cold water, then sank into the plush armchair in the corner of the bathroom breathing in the rose oil-scented air.

A night she'd not thought of for years came back to her. Mum's husband had a big fiftieth birthday bash in the function room of a fancy Brisbane hotel. Lena had been allowed to invite Lou and the two of them tolerated the cringiness until after the speeches and then snuck out. They needn't have bothered sneaking; Mum and the Dick were too busy tipsily dirty dancing across the silver balloon-strewn dance floor to have noticed anything.

They found the hotel bar, strode in like it was something they did every bloody night of the week. It was a walk, an attitude, they'd rehearsed many times at the clubs in the Valley. It had never worked before. Always there was a bouncer stepping in front of them, demanding to see ID, rolling his eyes or not even bothering with much reaction before he sent the obvious sixteen-year-olds away. Here, there was no bouncer, just three model-gorgeous barmen in old-fashioned waiter outfits gliding silently back and forth behind a marble bar. They didn't even glance in the direction of the girls. No one did.

Score! Lou whispered, chin-pointing at a booth in the far corner of the room.

Lena's instinct was to turn and run back to the party before anyone noticed her Kmart black ankle boots, tight red mini-dress and cropped vinyl jacket from Supré. Before anyone noticed that her lipstick was Priceline and her hair Just Cuts. In the function room with all the Dick's gross bogan friends, she'd felt too classy to bear. Now, in this room full of actually classy people, she knew she looked like a hooker from a nineties movie. But more awkward.

Lou urged her on to the booth and she felt a little better sinking into the plush fabric and barely candlelit shadow. Almost invisible here. Good. Then she read the drinks menu. *Might as well go buy myself a new car while I'm at it*, she said to Lou. Seriously, though, the first cocktail she liked the look of was a third of Mum's weekly grocery budget. While they were still flicking back and forth through the menu in the hope of finding something under twenty bucks, a hot barman plonked two enormous glasses filled with pink bubbles and garnished with what looked like fairy floss in front of them. *A gift from the gentlemen*, he said, like it was a frickin' movie. He gestured towards two men in suits taking up half the length of the bar with their widespread knees. They were not as old as the Dick's mates, but not too far off. One of them raised his glass at her, mouthed, *Enjoy, darling.*

The drink was revolting—raspberry cordial mixed with lighter fluid—but they drained them, tongued the sugary floss on the rim. The men sent over a bottle of champagne next, and Lou had the presence of mind, and the guts, to refuse. One of the men came over then, leant far, far over the table, his freckled hands planted flat in the space between Lou and Lena. *Listen, this isn't a transaction, ladies. We've had a win today. Bonuses coming in, big ones. Let us share the luck around, hey?*

So they said, *yeah*, and, *thank you*, and started on the champagne, which must have been expensive because it tasted like air and happiness. As Lou shook the final drops into her glass, the man returned, his mate with him. They slid into the booth without asking, one trapping each of them against the wall. Seconds later another bottle arrived. The girls made eye contact, giggled, kicked each other under the table. Why not? they said to each other telepathically. Why not drink this delicious air and listen to these men talk absolute shit? Better than drinking flat Coke and listening to some different old men talk absolute shit down the hall.

They drank *a lot.* At one point the man squished next to Lena took her hand and ran it up the inside of his thigh. *Armani*, he said. *You can feel the quality, can't you?*

Just so you know, said Lou, who was always watching out for her, and had leant across and tapped the man's arm so he dropped Lena's hand. *Just so you know, she's not going to root you.* The man held up his hands, mock offended. *Hadn't crossed my mind.* Lena had Lou's spirit and the delicious air in her now, said, *Not gunna blow you either, just to be clear.* Both men cackled with laughter at that. *Same here, by the way,* Lou said to the one next to her, which made them laugh more. The man next to Lena put his hand on her back, the bare skin up near her neck. She liked how it felt was the truth, but she shook him off, because she might have been rat shit but she wasn't stupid. It was possible these men didn't expect outer suburban teenagers who accepted hundreds of dollars' worth of alcohol from men in Armani suits to pay them back with their bodies. For all she knew, a couple of hundred bucks to them might be like twenty cents to her. Sometimes she tossed that much into a homeless man's bowl on the street outside the 7-Eleven and it had never occurred to her that he should lick her out in return. So, yeah, maybe this was obligation-free generosity. But just in case, she would not let his hand linger on her skin. Just in case, she would excuse herself to the bathroom. She wanted to ask Lou to come with her, but she was engaged in a savage argument about the quality of the music playing in the bar with the man beside her (Lou said the music made her want to shoot herself; the man said she should do that but in shame at her terrible taste) and waved a hand at Lena to go ahead.

The bathroom was nicer than any she'd seen in her life. Maybe any room at all. She sat so long on the padded stool in front of the softly lit mirror that Lou came looking for her, worried she'd passed out or was yakking. Who knew there were bathrooms like this in Brisbane and that you could sit in their gentle light and barely-perceptible-yet-soul-lifting scent clouds, use their hand lotions and impossibly soft hand towels, all for free? How did people who came to places like this handle ordinary bathrooms with their stiff brown paper towels and ammonia stink? How could you live in the rough and fluoro-lit world once you knew there were places like this? Places like this were why girls her age fucked old men in Armani suits. Why people smashed up luxury shopfronts and dragged their keys down the side of BMWs.

Sitting in this hotel bar bathroom in Sydney, which was even nicer than the Brisbane one—the padded chair softer than her bed, the light golden—she looked at her hands, turned alien from the harsh chemicals she'd used to clean Nic's bathroom. Skin rough and splotchy on top while the palms and fingertips were flaky white with angry crimson cuticles. She'd worked so hard, clearing and soaping and rubbing and scraping. When she'd finished, had sat back on her heels drinking water which she had been keeping in the living room fridge but which nonetheless seemed laced with detergent, she was confident the room had never, ever been cleaner. She'd even used a high-end brand of toilet duck (salvaged from the hoard) in the hope the scent would be more floral than chemical. She'd salvaged, too, a fluffy, peach-coloured bath mat with tags still attached, chucking the old one which was caked with dried lotion and soaps and fuck knew what else. She'd replaced the threadbare, scratchy towels on the rack with soft, thick, brand-new ones she found in a Kmart bag under the sofa. And even so, the room was grim and nasty. The cleanest it would ever be and the kind of person who came to hotels like this would take one look and decide to hold their pee in rather than use it.

Josh was waiting in a dim, narrow booth close to the bar. He was wearing a navy blazer with a crisp pinstriped open-necked shirt beneath it. His hair was freshly cut and immaculately styled to look ruffled. He froze when he saw her, pressed his lips together and raised one hand. The other was wrapped around a half-drunk beer on the table.

She backtracked to the bar and bought the cheapest beer on the list, taking a huge gulp before she approached Josh again. It was bitter and gassy and made her eyes water, which was a great way to start things off.

'You look amazing,' he said once she was seated across from him, and it was all she could manage not to tip the beer over his head and leave.

'Thanks. Is that what you were so desperate to say to me?'

'No. Sorry. Lena, I . . .' He began tearing a burgundy napkin into thin strips. It must be hard for him, trying to sit still, pretend to focus on her and her alone. As though hearing her thoughts he dropped the napkin, pushed it to the edge of the table, folded his hands in front, looked her in the eyes. 'I fucked up. I disrespected you and betrayed your trust.'

'Yes.'

'I've never regretted anything so much.'

'Same.'

'Not being with you! I could never regret that. It's why I needed to see you, to talk. I haven't been able to stop thinking about you. About us.'

God, was he for real? She kept her face blank.

'I know you probably can't forgive me, but can you at least admit that you did have feelings for me? That we were *good* together.'

Her body betraying her, the liquid heat flooding her lower belly, replacing the hunger cramps and beer bloat. The warmth spreading out and up, probably turning her face red. Probably making her pupils enlarge. She slugged more beer because she would not lick her lips to salve the sudden dryness there.

'The thing is . . .' He picked up the table-talker—*$15 cocktails Wednesday and Thursday 4–5pm*—smoothed it flat against the table, his hands working the folds out, hard along each seam. 'The thing is, I've been under all this pressure at college. Like, you know the shit that's been going down, in the news and all. I wasn't involved in any of it, and you'd think that'd be a good thing, but it put me under suspicion. People were saying I was the leaker. It got so I was piling furniture in front of my door at night, I was so scared they'd come and . . . I don't know. Some act of retribution or whatever. I mean, you have no idea the kind of stuff these guys are capable of.'

'I have some idea.'

He paused in his work, left his hands flat on the table-topper, looked at her properly again. 'Yeah. That's what's so fucked up. I became the monster so the monster wouldn't hurt me.'

'My heart bleeds for you. Is that it? I'm really busy.'

'Yeah? I wondered about that. You haven't been at uni, so . . . I wondered what you were up to, if you were staying away because of me, or—'

'My aunty had an accident and I'm her only family in Sydney. I've been taking care of her.'

'Oh. Thank god. Not that your aunt—obviously. I was worried you'd, like, dropped out of uni because of . . .'

'Do you really think I'd chuck my whole life away because of your bullshit?'

'No, of course not. Sorry. I guess I can be pretty arrogant.' Those damn hands, raised up now, like the fucking what-can-you-do emoji.

Lena finished her beer. She needed to walk away. Now.

'How is your aunt doing?'

'Not great.'

'I'm sorry. And it's only you taking care of her?'

'Yeah.'

'Hectic. Can I help at all?'

'Yeah. Delete the video and then leave me alone forever.'

'Lena.' He looked like he was going to cry, for god's sake. 'I deleted it, like, an hour after I posted it. I've been going after every fucker I see sharing it. Look!' He held up his hands, scabbed-over knuckles out. 'I haven't punched anyone since I was fourteen, and I've been in two fights this week.'

'My hero.'

'I'm not saying that, Lena, Jesus. I'm just trying to show you that I *know* I fucked up badly. If there was any other way to fix things I would. I'd do anything.'

My pride fell with my fortunes. Who said that? Someone who understood what it felt like to choose between eating shit once and being covered in it forever.

'There's this company,' Lena said. 'They scrub the internet of stuff like this. Find it all and get it deleted.'

'I've heard about that kind of thing. I don't think it works very well. Impossible to stop the—'

'You know it's on *sydneysluts*? My full name, my uni. All up there now.'

'I'll find who did that. I'll get it off. I promise. Just . . . Fuck, I'm *so sorry*. I can't sleep with thinking about what I've done. I'm going to fix it. I'll look up that internet scrubbing company. I'll . . .' Tears. Actual frigging tears. He swiped them away with the back of his hand, flinching as his bruised knuckles made contact. 'Whatever it takes, Lena. I promise.'

'Okay.'

'What?'

'Okay. I accept your apology and your promise.'

A smile. Such a smile. 'Thank you. That's just . . . It's everything, Lena. Everything. Thank you so much. You're amazing.'

'I need to go.'

'Already? Let me buy you a drink at least. Unless your aunt needs you, of course.'

'She'll be okay a bit longer, I think.'

A showy little air-punch. 'I'll be right back.'

While he was at the bar, she turned her phone on, felt the familiar sick drop of her stomach as the screen filled with notifications, shoved it back in her pocket without looking at any of them.

Josh put a beer in front of her, slid into the booth. 'Tell me about your aunt. Is she the one from the rose garden, the one who held you after you were born?'

Ooof! What was this feeling? What was happening right now? Falling and falling while sitting still, bursting and bursting while trying to stop her face from showing any of it. Failing, obviously, by the way his gaze was locking on to hers, his own falling and bursting clear.

'Can't believe you remember that.'

'Best origin story ever, Harris—of course I remember. So it's her? The same aunty?'

Lena nodded. 'Nic.'

'So you and her have been bonded from the start. No wonder you feel like you need to be there for her now.'

She was going to burst open and who knew what would come out? There was too much in her and he was too good at knowing it. Oh god. I have to go. I have to go and sit in a pile of sticky dust and throw out other people's garbage that my aunt has collected. I have to go and clean up after the woman I've looked up to my whole life while she cries and rants like a mad person, while she accuses me of theft and betrayal.

'I really do have to go, actually.'

He touched her hand. Fast, but oh! Damn. 'Finish your drink at least. Tell me about Aunty Nic. What do the family legends foretell about her?'

'I don't want to talk about her,' she said.

'Okay. Tell me something else. Tell me about the music that was playing when you were born. What song was it?'

The song Dad had sung while she was born and that he'd sung to her every year on her birthday and that would sometimes come on the radio or be playing in a shop and wrench her grief up to the surface within a few notes. The song was a massive hit that year and was loved by a lot of people, but no one would expect it to be the most important song in the world to someone her age. No one except Mum and Will and Nic, who knew and who silently reached for her if it ever came on when they were nearby. *I just want you to know who I am.*

'Do you think we're friends?' she asked Josh.

He bit his lip. 'I wish we could be.'

Lena finished her beer. Too much, too fast. Her eyes and nose watered. 'I'm going.'

'Okay. But . . . can I see you again? I mean, I know it's . . . I know I'm asking a lot, but . . . I *really* like you, Lena. I can't stop thinking about when we—'

'Thinking about? Or watching?'

'How many times can I tell you I'm sorry?'

'I know you're sorry. I'm sorry, too, because I *really* like you. Or I did. I can't trust you, though, so that's it.' She slid from the booth before he could speak again. God, she liked him. It was pathetic.

As she walked out she saw Will had sent several texts, clicked open the first.

I've seen the video. You need to get back here. Now.

Lena turned off her phone. Josh was where she'd left him in the booth. He looked up with an expression she could only describe as fatally thirsty. Made her feel like a cockroach was scurrying up her spine.

'This is a hotel, yeah?'

'Yeah.' Up out of his seat, moving towards her.

Josh apologised that the room was *corporate* and *bland*. Lena's word would be *immaculate*. She touched the smooth stone bench to the right of the door—empty except for a sparkling stainless-steel kettle and a glossy white dish filled with individually wrapped teabags. She touched the dust-free top of the big-screen TV, then the slippery, flawless ceramic of the lamp on the desk, and then the black leather folder with *For Your Convenience* embossed in gold on the cover, then the desk itself. A light touch, skimming past with her bare fingertips. Touch by touch the rope inside her uncoiled.

She headed for the bathroom, wanting to press her hands against the un-smeared tiles with no mould in the grout, run her fingers over the hairless drains. But Josh was a step behind her, his breath on the back of her neck. *Do ya take me for a pirate?* Dad would've said. *Bloody big parrot on my shoulder.*

She turned, tried to look at his face instead of the crisp white sheets on the queen-size bed.

'It's okay,' he said. 'You do what you need to do.'

A lurch in her chest. How did he know the filth she had come from? But then he held up his phone and said, 'It's off. Look. You keep it until we leave.' She took his black, dead phone, realised she should have asked for it immediately, should have been doing what he assumed and checking the room for hidden cameras. She really was asking for it. *Dumb cunt.*

'Thanks.' She made a show of double-checking his phone was off, shoved it in her backpack and continued her circuit of the room. Part of her wanted to ask him what it felt like to be the kind of person other people needed to check for spy equipment before they could relax around. Another part of her wanted to jump out of the streak-free window because what kind of a person hooks up with the kind of man you need to check for spy equipment? The biggest part—right now, anyway—wanted to scrub herself raw in a clean shower then climb into a clean bed, have a fast orgasm with a clean man, shower again and sleep through the whole night without waking to cough up dust.

She finished her inspection of the bedside tables and the wardrobe and strode to the bathroom, Josh behind her the whole way. The shine coming off the tiles made her feel like weeping. The tiniest bit of dirt or dust would show up like an oil spill.

She stood facing him, their doubles looking on from the wall-sized mirror. She had grown up believing that men who took care of their appearance were soft, dressing in the clothes Mummy laid out on the bed. But there was a manliness to Josh's neatness; a confidence and certainty. He did not expect to be changing a tyre or digging a ditch—or ending up in one, for that matter. But if physical action was called for, he would be up for the challenge, his pants not too tight to squat in, his jacket easily slipped off.

And what kind of woman would you expect to find in a nice hotel with someone like him? Not some *scrawny bitch nastiest in this series yet good tits but arse like my granny 6 out of 10 are you kidding mate thats a four at best.*

'All clear?' he said, moving towards her.

'I'm hungry.' She left the bathroom, flipped open the room service menu, nearly choked at the prices.

'What?' He was behind her, breathing on the back of her neck.

'Nothing.'

'You made a noise.'

needs a gag on her noisy bitch

She turned, shoved the menu at him. He sighed, already reaching for the room phone with his other hand. 'What do you want then?'

She'd been so distracted by the prices she couldn't remember any of the items they referred to. 'I'll have the forty-seven dollars ninety-five with a side of eighteen dollars and a glass of twenty-four,' she could say. Nic'd laugh at that, reply, 'Oh, forget your diet. Go for the thirty-eight seventy-five with the eighteen *and* the twenty-three dollars on the side and a whole bottle of a hundred and ten.' But Josh wouldn't get it so she said, 'I'll have whatever you're having,' and he ordered two Wagyu burgers with beer-battered chips and a bottle of something she'd never heard of.

'What'll we do while we wait?' he said, coming at her again, touching her this time, his lovely, clean hands on her shoulders.

'I need a shower.'

'Shower after.' His hands moving down her arms.

'Shower first.'

'Okay, but I can help.' Hands moving around to her back now. 'Scrub the places you can't reach.'

She pulled away, turned too fast to see his reaction. 'Nah, I'll be right. I'm very flexible.'

'Oh, I know that.'

'Yeah, you and the entire internet.' She was in the bathroom by then, shutting the door. She locked it, stripped, turned the shower on full. The water came from a silver disc in the ceiling above and covered her so completely it was like being submerged, but with deliciously hard water darts striking her all over. She lathered her hair with shampoo that smelt like freshly squeezed lemons, lathered herself with body wash the texture of whipped cream. Blood and grime swirled at her feet, then was gone.

If she told Josh she had her period would he be disgusted and leave? Would her relief be more powerful than her shame? She watched the water run clear over her feet and down the drain, imagined having that clean bed to herself all night.

Maybe he deserved to be bled on without consent, to know what it was to feel violated and stained.

He might not even notice.

―――

The towel was softer than her good sheets, almost as thick as her pillow. It wrapped around her twice, hung past her shins. She never wanted to wear anything else ever again.

Josh was on the bed, stripped to shimmery grey boxer shorts, watching a screeching high-speed car chase on the TV. 'Finally she emerges.' He glanced at her, smiled, turned off the TV. 'Sorry to tell you, Harris, but you've wasted your time.' He got to his knees, his hard-on obvious. 'I'm going to get you filthy.'

It wasn't normal to feel like throwing up right before you had sex with someone you were attracted to. Wasn't right to feel torn between kissing or stabbing the near-naked hottie reaching out to you from the biggest, cleanest, softest-looking bed you'd ever seen.

'Seriously, you need to get over here now. You're so fucking gorgeous I can't stand it.'

Cover that ugly wound next time don't know whether to barf or wank nice nips pity about the rest

There was a knock. Josh strutted to the door, adjusting his shorts as he went. Lena hovered near the edge of the bed, out of view. A voice said, '*Good evening,*' and Josh said it back and then there was a man in a waiter's uniform three steps away from her. 'Good evening,' he said in her direction, though not, thank god, looking at her. He placed a gigantic silver tray on the table and had Josh sign something—called him *sir*, told him to *enjoy*—and floated out of the room like it was nothing.

It *was* nothing, she understood. Just another rich bloke who needed feeding; another dumb cunt without her clothes on in the background.

Josh carried the tray to the bed, smiled at her as he put it down. 'Picnic in bed.'

She stood, frozen in her corner. 'I didn't know you were going to let the guy in. I'm not dressed.'

'So? He doesn't give a shit.'

'I do.'

A sigh. 'Here we go.'

'Where?'

'To the place where your body is so precious and special it needs to be locked away in a fucking vault.'

'Wow.'

He lifted the silver cover off the tray, put it on the bedcover, not even checking if there was sauce or something clinging to it. 'Listen, you have a nice body. Gorgeous. I mean it. But hot girls are everywhere. People on the internet don't care about your hot body. That dude out there doesn't care. Stop acting like the world's going to end if someone sees your precious tits.'

Lena perched on the edge of the bed, picked a chip off her plate. It was barely warm, soft and soggy. She ate it because otherwise she might scream so loud that the people in the next room would call security. She might punch Josh until his face looked like the chopped salad in front of her. She ate another chip and then another. She hadn't eaten potato for years. Hadn't eaten anything fried for months. The chips were starchy and salty and slicked with fat. She had to concentrate on chewing and swallowing each one completely before picking up the next. If Josh wasn't there she would have been shoving them in by the handful. *I'm so fucking easy. Josh's hand on my leg and I'm a senseless whore. One not-even-good chip and I'm a greedy pig.*

Josh was making fast work of his burger. He didn't look like a greedy pig, though. He looked like a man with a well-earnt appetite. A man in a hurry, but not so much he couldn't enjoy his food. He was near naked, too, and not self-conscious about it. Not self-conscious about anything. In his skin and in this room and everywhere else. What must it be like, to be so at ease?

'So, ah, I think my brother knows.'

He stopped mid-bite. A millisecond but she saw it. Ha. Good. He chewed, swallowed, said, 'About this?'

'About the video.'

'Shit. Should I be scared? Is he gunna come at me? Bash me farkin' 'ead in.'

'What is that accent?'

314

Josh took another bite. Chewed aggressively. Swallowed. Smiled. 'That's how he talks, right? Like you, when you get upset or turned on and forget to posh up.'

'And the way you talk when you're turned on? Is that how your family speaks back on the porn set where you grew up?'

He laughed at that, loud and surprising and real, a bolus of burger flying out and landing on the bed, all red and brown and wet and gristly. He covered it with a napkin and swept it out of sight like it was nothing. Everything was nothing with him. It was a superpower.

'Is your brother as funny as you?'

'God, no. He's earnest as fuck.'

'Pity. I wouldn't mind him bashin' me 'ead in if he did it in a funny way.'

'Nah, most humourless head bashing ever, I'm sorry to say.'

'I better stay away from him then.'

'Yeah. Me too.'

'Is that why you're here?'

'Yeah.'

'Great. Thanks.'

'No, I mean . . . I could've gone somewhere else. I wanted to be away from him, and I wanted to be with you.'

Josh pushed the tray to the side, leant in and kissed her. 'I don't even care why. Not really. I'm so into you, Harris, it's not funny.'

'Not laughing.'

'You laughed all the time when we first met. Now, barely at all.'

'You talk like we've been married seventy years. You hardly know me. Don't know how often I laugh.'

He bit her lip, held it there between his teeth until she ached all over. He pulled away, said, 'I can't bear it that I've made you unhappy.'

'You have to.'

'When you walked into the bar it was like seeing someone at a funeral. I wanted to bash my own head in.'

'You should do that, for sure. You've got it coming. But not too hard. Only some of the funeral face is because of you.'

'I'm sorry for that, too, then. That I've done this to you when you've got other hard shit going on. Do you want to talk about it?'

'No.'

He nodded, kissed her, soft and chaste. 'You can, you know. I'm not only here for the sex.'

'What if I am?'

'You do want to have sex with me then?'

'Yes,' she said. It had been good, hadn't it? Would feel good again if she could shut all the other stuff out? And after, she could have another shower, wrap herself in another fresh, clean towel like this one, go to sleep in this clean, soft bed.

'With me?'

'Is there anyone else here?'

'Right. See.' He sneered. Face of a college boy who scores you out of ten while you pull on your undies. 'You don't even like me. You just want to get fucked and I'm the only one who'll do it.'

'Get over yourself, mate. You are not the only one who—'

'Since the thing, though.' Smug, superior, shit-eating grin. 'How many queuing up to take you out since they've seen you riding me?'

Her body was too used to crying. The tears came easily, hot and fast. She tried to get up, but he held her by both arms.

'I mean, you're damaged goods now. No one wants to drive a car some other bloke crashed. Even if it's been cleaned up okay, you know it's not right.'

'Let go or I'll kick your fucking teeth in.'

'I love it when you talk houso, Harris.'

She kneed him hard in the stomach, sprang off the bed. He was doubled over, gasping. 'Psycho bitch. That hurt.'

She should pick up the bedside lamp and smash it over his head. Kick him. From this height she could land a good blow on his ear, set the bells ringing. 'Lucky I didn't do worse.'

'Jesus, calm down. You said mean shit to me, I said mean shit back. No need to get violent.'

'You're a nasty, spoilt little cunt.'

'And you're a foul-mouthed houso slut, but I still want to be with you, so why don't you calm down, come back over here and kiss me better.' He lay back, eyes closed, pointing to his lower stomach.

Like nothing had happened. It hadn't, had it? Not for him.

'You want to be with me? Really? Even though I'm damaged goods. Wow.'

'You say that a lot. *Wow*. It's irritating. But, yeah, Harris, I actually do want to be with you and not just like this, either. I'm *into* you, you psycho.'

'Sure you are. So into me you want to fuck me then take me to your college parties so everyone can see how much you've owned the six-out-of-ten bitch with the ugly arm wound?'

He flopped back on the bed. 'You're not ever going to let it go, are you?'

'Seriously? It happened, like, ten days ago!'

'I don't see how we can be together going forward if you're always harping on about this one mistake I made.'

'How about this: I'll get over it when the file is no longer anywhere on the internet.' She walked to the bathroom, dressed fast. Didn't even look at the heavenly, purifying, life-affirming shower because she didn't want to change her mind.

When she went back into the room, fully clothed, his face fell. 'You're seriously leaving?'

'Yeah. Don't contact me again.'

'Fuck you. You're the one who asked for this.' He spread his arms wide, taking in the whole fresh-smelling, dust-free, smudge-less, uncluttered loveliness.

'Yeah, well, I'm a psycho bitch, like you said.' She pulled his phone from her backpack, chucked it hard at the wall. Didn't hear the crack of glass, which would be just his sweet luck. And she left, hair still wet from the magic shower, tongue still tingling with salt and fat.

———

When she turned her phone back on, there were no new messages from Will. Nothing from Nic. But there among the unknown numbers and caller ID unavailable, between a message from Annie and one from college admin, was Kylie.

Whatcha up to girl Bubbas at mums tonight wanna hang

The message had come in two hours ago, at 7 p.m.

Lena texted back: *Sorry just got this. Are you still up and keen to hang?*

Kylie answered straight away: *Come now I have sambucca* 🎉 *Do you reckon I can crash there? Okay if not . . .*
👍🕺🍻

NIC

Nic wakes to pitch-black and silence, terror squeezing her throat closed. A few seconds until she remembers where she is, what's happened. Not silence, really: water is dripping somewhere, the building creaking, someone snoring aggressively. Not pitch-black, either: she can see the cracked open door to her room, the bulky dresser against the wall, the lighter blanks of the windows. She can see all the nothingness in between. She listens. How long since she's heard someone sleeping in her home? Ah, not so hard to remember. These same world-busting children, back when they were all easy hugs and ear-splitting squeals. When they fought to sit on her lap or next to her at the table, and wanted nothing more than to listen to her tell them stories until their determined little eyelids gave up, fluttered closed. When she could tell which was which from the night sounds of them: Lena's fast, short little breaths, as though she were jumping up and down on the spot even in her dreams; and Will's breaths so slow and deep that Nic sometimes held her own breath waiting to hear the next one kick in. It always did, just when you thought it really wouldn't this time, that something catastrophic had happened, that you'd lost the most precious of treasures even as you stood there sending every bit of love you ever had and then some. The certainty and horror and then—ahhhhhhh—there it was, slow, soft miracle breath. It always came.

Tonight there is only the drone of his snoring, loud enough that you'd think it was on purpose just to piss you off. If he would stop for a minute, turn down the sound at least, she could listen harder, find Lena. She strains, willing it. Like old times, except now she can't tiptoe light as a pixie and lean weightlessly over the sleeping child. Now she is heavier than the world and just as stuck.

A wave of nausea and she rolls to her side and dry-retches onto the floor. How can throwing up nothing hurt so badly, like all her insides are being scraped raw by the same razor wire squeezing her ribs and digging deep into her spine?

'Arnienic?' Will's voice, sleep-slurred and young. 'Youkayarnienic?' His outline in the doorway, bare-chested and with a bed-hair halo. A memory like a punch in the heart: the full trusting weight of his head in her left hand as she scooped warm water over his sudsy, baby-soft hair. My beautiful little Will, she wants to say to him, there's nothing harder than loving a child who is not your own. Nothing.

She can't speak, is racked with failed vomiting.

'Shit. Are you being sick? You need a bucket or . . .' Light on and her big little boy by her side, touching her forehead with his rough, working man's hand. His eyes keep fluttering closed as though it hurts to see. 'I'm gonna get you some water, 'kay? And a cloth or something. Hang on.'

He does as he says, wiping her sweaty face and feeding her some water. It helps and it makes her wish for death. This shouldn't be.

Will presses the same washcloth he used on her face to his own forehead. His eyes flutter and flutter as he studies her painkiller packet and checks the time and scrunches up his face, calculating. It hasn't been long enough; she can tell by his lip-biting. She lets the moan she's been holding in escape. He wipes her forehead again, but the cloth is dry and warm.

'It's a bit soon for more tablets.'

'How soon?'

'Should be another hour and a half, I think.'

'I can't wait that long.'

'Hang on.' He plods from the room, comes back with eyes and thumbs on his phone. 'I'm just . . . Okay, I think it'll be . . . Your dose is at the high end but not . . . A little early won't cause . . .'

Does he know he keeps trailing off, that she can't actually read what he is reading?

'Yeah, 'kay. Then hopefully you'll sleep long enough to . . . So the next one won't be . . .'

She swallows the pills, asks him for help to the bathroom, is grateful he waits outside the door for her. Hates that he waits outside the door for her. When she's back under the covers he surprises her by sitting on the end of her bed.

'Is it okay if I stay here a bit?'

'If you like.'

'I'm not bothering you?'

'Not at all,' she says. 'You don't need to watch over me, though, if that's what you're doing.'

'Nah, nah, I know.'

She waits for the tablets to take effect. Even wide awake and in pain she feels better having Will here. The weight of him there by her feet is what's been missing.

'Have you ever found out something and just wished so hard you could un-know it?' he says after a little while.

'Hmm. Yeah, I s'pose so. Must have. Why?'

'Nothing. Just thinking.' He shifts his weight and the movement ricochets up her leg into her hip. 'Up at Mercy's place we had this neighbour, a few doors down. Neil. He'd sit on his front porch, sunrise to sunset, with this massive thermos, a crossword book and a blue heeler called Winky. I got in the habit of stopping by most days on my way home from work. I'd take a six pack of VB or Neil'd bring out a mug and share the coffee from his thermos. Strong whisky-flavour to that coffee, which I didn't mind. We'd talk a bit, but not about anything really. I just liked hanging with him there because, see, he never talked about it but I knew from Mercy that Neil had done serious time. Twenty years at least, she said. It was inspiring. Shit word, that one, but it fits. Inside for more than twenty years and still, here he was, acting as if his life was a sweet and worthwhile thing. Every new day worth lingering over and enjoying. Never talked down about stuff, or like he was ruined or a failure.'

She needs to tell him he is not either of those things, never will be, but the medication is kicking in, has filled her mouth with chewy toffee.

'One arvo Neil wasn't on the porch. Didn't take long before the whole street knew that he'd dropped the dog at the pound then gone home and hanged himself. People said it was no surprise, he couldn't stand the guilt, and I realised I'd never thought to wonder what he'd done to be locked up so long. I should've wondered, don't you reckon?'

You were just minding your own business, she attempts to say, but it comes out garbled and, anyway, he's continued speaking as if she's not even there.

'Once I knew what he'd done, I felt . . . I felt like giving up on everything. Knowing that crimes like that even happened was too much, let alone that this nice bloke who loved his dog and his crosswords and watching the neighbourhood go about its peaceful business could be responsible . . . I was so angry. Fucking furious. And I said to Mercy that it was because I felt tricked by him, his kindness. But being honest, for real I don't think that was it. I think I was angry because I'd been forced to know about this awful thing and I'd rather not. I'd rather have kept being his friend if he lived or kept a nice memory of him when he died. It's not like I don't care what he did; it's that once I knew I *did* care, and I didn't want to. You know what I mean, Aunty Nic? I don't want to have to care about everything all the time. You know?'

She is cold and hot at the same time, tries to tell him, *I didn't ask you to come.* It is very important that she make this clear and so she says it again, more slowly and with great concentration. 'I. Didn't. Ask. You. To. Come.'

'What?' Will stands. Without his weight her bed is a flimsy thing, likely to float away. 'I'm not talking about you. It's nothing to do . . . Forget it. Go to sleep.'

Anger in his voice, and for the first seconds after he leaves the room her blood itches with worry for him and for her and for what has passed between them. Gratefully, she remembers the narcotics have been waiting for her to stop resisting. She lies back and lets the surge take her.

LENA

Two beers and three sambucca shots in, after Kylie had filled Lena in on Lacey's birth, and then working backwards, her gestational diabetes, her miscarriage, her escape from an abusive relationship, her mother's breast cancer and her various high school flings and suspensions, Lena blurted out that there was a video of her having sex online.

'No way!' Kylie said, slapping her hand over her mouth. 'Kim Kardashian in the house! Woot woot!'

'Shhhh,' Lena said. Ty was sleeping in the bedroom, which was one very thin wall away from where they sat.

'Serious, though. Can I see?'

'No! It's not something I want to, like, *share*. I didn't do it on purpose.'

'Your bloke uploaded the vid without you knowing?'

'He took the vid without me knowing. Then he uploaded it.'

'Fuuuck. What a cunt. Sorry, Leen, but that's a seriously cunty thing to do. Do ya need someone to smash him? Is he big? Ty does

326

all right, but if your bloke's big we can get Ty's karate teacher to do it. Brick shithouse.'

'Don't karate teachers have some honour code or something? Not allowed to use their skills on randoms?'

'Yeah, probably, but this bloke's not proper. He just fucking loves karate, teaches some mates in his mum's basement. And anyway, this wouldn't be a random. It'd be *targeted*.' Kylie karate-chopped the air, dropped the empty shot glass she'd been holding. It bounced off the carpet and Lena caught it mid-air. The two of them couldn't breathe from laughing for several minutes.

They calmed down by knocking back another shot each. Lena's stomach felt dangerously queasy but the rest of her felt better than she had in weeks.

'So tonight, earlier, I went to a hotel with the fuckwit who filmed me.'

Kylie slammed her fist on the floor. 'What are you telling me? Fuuck, Lena. Spill, spill.'

Lena told her what had happened but with more violence and kick-arse repartee on her part and more grovelling and crying on Josh's.

'You, Lena Harris, are a fucking bad bitch. For real you are. But listen, hey . . .' She leant forward, forehead touching Lena's. 'Next time, get him starkers and excited and all that, right, and then kick him hard as you can in the dick. While he's down, whining and all that, you film him. Spread the vid of him being a little bitch all over the internet, see how he likes it.'

Lena opened another beer, drank deeply. If she could kiss Kylie all over her face without it being weird, she would.

'Won't be a next time,' she said. 'I'm all business from now on. Gonna make him pay for a scrubbing service and—'

'A what now?'

Lena explained about the internet removal company, told her how much it cost.

'Wait wait wait wait wait!' Hands in the air, voice so loud the whole street had to be hearing it. 'You're telling me you're going to pay some bloke in Parra more money than I make in a frickin' year to look for your hoo-ha on the internet?'

'Not just look for my hoo-ha, mate. Delete it.'

Kylie shook her head, pulled herself to a standing position using both hands on the lounge. Clomped three or so steps to the bedroom door, pushed it open. Lena would've stopped her but she was helpless with laughter and booze.

'Ty, babe, Ty, wake up a sec. Come out here a minute. It's important, come on, yeah, just for a second.'

'Kylie, no. What are you doing?'

Kylie had the best look on her face. Kid on Christmas morning. She poured them each another shot. They downed them as Ty stumbled out, wearing a pair of bottle-green footy shorts and nothing else. His hair was halfway to the roof. Lena and Kylie couldn't stop laughing. It was beginning to hurt.

'How pissed are youse?' he said, dropping onto the lounge next to Kylie. 'What ya got there? Fucking sambucca? Bloody hell.'

'Listen, listen.' Kylie struggled to get herself under control. Ty shook his head, but warmly, Lena could tell. Like how Dad used to shake his head at Mum when she drank too much Lambrusco and got all clumsy and loud.

'So, listen. Lena's got a job offer for ya.'

'Shut up, ya bitch!'

'Nah, Leen, he'll do it heaps cheaper for you. Serious, Ty, listen.'

Lena leapt on Kylie, clamped a hand over her mouth. It was better than kissing her, jumping on her full-bodied, wrestling and laughing like they were eight years old.

'Youse are fuuucked.' His tone said, *Youse are glorious.*

Somehow they calmed down. Kylie told Ty, brief and crude, what had happened.

'Right. You want me to fuck him up? He big? I can get some fellas together.'

'I thought maybe Wayno,' Kylie said.

'Yeah, yeah. Could do it, could do it. Where's this grub live?'

'No. Thank you, but no. I don't want him bashed. I just want to forget I ever met him.'

'Not being a dick or nothing,' Ty said, 'but that's gonna be hard when there's footage of you rooting him all over the internet.'

'Yeah. So, my plan is, I think, move back to Brissie for a bit and—'

'Boo! Queensland!'

'Shush, ya boofhead.'

'Just to get out of the intense sort of, ah, scrutiny and that. Meanwhile, I'm going to make him pay for the removal service, if I can. And if I can't do that, or it doesn't work, then last resort is I change my name so anyone who googles it doesn't get an eyeful of my tits.'

'That's what they'd see if they googled you now is it? Just type in, what? Lena—what's your last name?'

'Not funny, Ty. Gross. But listen, Leen, honestly, fuck that plan.'

'What? No good?'

'Fuck, no. Get your hands on that amount of money you buy yourself a car or a holiday or something. Don't pay some weirdo to spend weeks watching you screw. And your name, Leen. Come on. You can't let this fucker take that from you.'

'It's just a name.' But even as she said it she knew she could never do it. If Dad was alive maybe she wouldn't care. But she had so little of him now. She couldn't let his name go.

'So what then? Just accept that everyone I meet for the rest of my life will know what my come face looks like?'

'Jesus,' Ty said.

'Yeah—I mean, nah,' Kylie said. 'Like, some people will and so what? I bet your come face is bloody gorgeous.'

'Fucking hell.' Ty rubbed his head. 'Should I leave?'

'But there's so much porn on the internet, Leen. Like, for real. And do you know who all those women are? Would you have the slightest clue if the chick who serves you at Maccas or your teacher at uni or, hell, your mum is one of those eighty billion videos?'

'Her mum! Settle, Kyles. Jesus.'

'I'm just saying. It feels like everyone is—what'd ya say?—got you under scrutiny, but it's just fresh and that. Plus you're living right among these idiots. Time'll go on and your bits will be just another set of bits bouncing around out there, and if someone does match 'em up with the real-life Lena Harris they know, then lucky fucking them, I say. Getting to know this cool chick for real and seeing her hoo-ha as well.'

Lena was drunk and nauseous and teetering on the verge of another bout of hysterical laughing, but under all that she felt a pocket of air opening in her lungs. Clear, clean air which swelled her chest, helped her sit up straighter, made her feel like she could take a deep breath without hyperventilating. Without choking.

—

Kylie and Ty went to bed. Lena crawled under a blanket on their lounge which smelt like pot and chicken noodle soup. She didn't think she'd sleep, for the usual reasons plus sambucca wooziness, but next minute it was daytime and a shower was running, a kettle boiling. Ty was singing one of those shithouse glam rock songs that Nic loved so much. Kylie yelled, 'Just going to pick up bubba,' and the front door slammed.

The shower stopped and then Ty was on the armchair across from Lena, dressed in a pale pink towelling robe that stopped at his knees. He raised his steaming mug. 'Help yourself to coffee or whatever else in the kitchen.'

'Thanks.' If she moved she'd spew. She closed her eyes, hand over her nose to block the coffee smell. Listened to him sipping, flicking his lighter.

'Listen,' he said, after a bit. 'Serious, hey. We've all done stupid shit. I walked over hot coals once and burnt the fuck out of my feet. Dickhead mates filmed the whole thing. That's out there on the YouTube. Maybe worse. Used to get blackout drunk and that before Kyles and bubba, you know. Coulda done anything.'

331

He took a sip, smacked his lips together. 'Point is, but, everyone's a fucking idiot.'

'True, yeah,' Lena said.

'Everyone's a fucking idiot,' he repeated. 'Remember that and you'll be right.'

WILL

A scuttling in the corner woke him. Took a few seconds for
him to make out Aunty Nic crouched by the bar fridge,
pulling out bottles of drink and dropping them on the carpet in
front of her.

'Aunty Nic, let me . . . What do you need?'

Nic closed the fridge door, put both hands on the top and
hauled herself to a standing position. Will leapt from the sofa,
but she muttered, *I'm fine*, and so he stood back, watched as she
wedding marched from the room. That was what Dad called it.
His way of moving, towards the end, from the bed to the bathroom, sometimes the living room to watch TV. One foot out.
Pause. Bring the other foot to meet it. Pause. Step out. Pause.
Other foot to meet the first. If any of them told him to sit down,
said, *Let me help*, he'd brush them off, fake cheery voice: *Just
practising me wedding march*. It'd made Will want to knock the
old man to the ground, kick him in the crumbling lungs. *Stop
pretending*, he wanted to scream. *Admit you're fucking dying on*

us. Of course, he never did that. Never did anything to show Dad that he knew how hopeless it was. Even the pot was a way to continue the pretence: *Give you your appetite back, help you get better quicker.*

Watching Aunty Nic wedding march out of his sight didn't make him want to knock her down or kick her. Didn't make him want to do anything except call Mercy and ask her what he should do. What was the right thing? Aunty Nic was clearly not fine on her own, but she refused to let him do anything other than dole out her painkillers. Lena had apparently pissed off back home, and it was only when he imagined Mercy asking, *Where does your sister live?* that he realised he'd never asked, and that made him feel even more fucking helpless and useless.

He checked his phone: no messages or missed calls. Nearly midday. Shit. He remembered, then. Around 6 a.m., desperate enough to yank out the tooth on his own if he could find some pliers, he'd taken two more Endone. The relief hadn't been instant. He'd lain still for what felt like days, listening to cats yowling under the window, almost gone back for a couple more pills, but then all at once the warm syrup swooshed through him and his jaw relaxed and next thing was waking to Aunty Nic scrambling at the fridge.

He crouched where she'd been a minute earlier, put the drinks back, leaving out a small bottle of orange juice to take in to her. He'd love some himself, but everything except water and milk took his pain to the next level. Yesterday at the hospital he'd bought a pot of sweetened plain yoghurt and managed to suck it down okay. Why hadn't he thought ahead, bought an armful to keep him going? Like he didn't know he'd need to eat again within the next twenty-four hours. And he thought he could be a dad, take care of vulnerable kids when he couldn't even—

Shit. Shit shit shit. He raced to the bedroom. She lay with her back to him. 'I'm so sorry. You must be starving. I'm going to go get something now. What do you feel like?'

The rise and fall of her back.

He tried again. 'Aunty Nic? Whatever you feel like, I'll head out now. Or I can get us some Uber Eats.'

She mumbled something to the wall.

'Sorry, I didn't hear—'

'I don't want anything from you.'

'You must be hungry, though. I'm really sorry, Aunty Nic. What can I get you?'

Silence. He fetched her tablets and a glass of water, put them beside the bottle of juice on her bedside table. He waited while she took the pills. She swallowed, glared at him. 'What?'

'I just . . . I'll go get some groceries and that, but . . . I'm out of money and I need to—'

'If you know where my wallet is you're welcome to whatever's in it. It was on the kitchen table when I had my fall. That thieving sister of yours might have emptied it already, though.'

'I'll have a look. I wouldn't ask, it's just . . .'

'I don't care, Will. Take what you want. Do what you want. Leave me alone.'

Will called the first emergency dentist on the list, confirmed he could get in today. Aunty Nic's wallet was not on the kitchen table. He kicked the wall, downed another Endone. Even water hurt almost too much to bear. When he recovered enough from the pain to focus again he saw a handbag on a hook by the door. Inside was a wallet. No cash but two credit cards. He pocketed both and headed out.

NIC

Afternoons in this empty, alien place are long and full of terrible sounds. Like in the hospital, noises convulse through the space, working on Nic's nerves like a sustained electric shock. The planes overhead are as loud as everyone always complained they were. She'd never noticed before. Like death swooping in to scoop you up, changing its mind at the last second. Meanwhile the cars and trucks and bikes are outside but they sound—feel to her shivering limbs—like they are in the room, or at the very least right outside her bedroom window, revving calmly before charging through to crush her where she lies. She asked Will yesterday what they were all doing out there, revving and revving and beeping and revving, barely ever seeming to simply drive on past.

'A lot of deliveries around here. Groceries, postie, couriers. I've seen a lot of those motorbikes with the big heat packs on the back. Uber Eats mostly.' And he went on to explain what that was as though she were a visitor from the past.

She could tell him that she orders food and groceries and other
bits and bobs on a weekly basis. Sometimes more often. He could
have guessed that if he'd had the slightest curiosity about how
she managed to fill her home and her belly when she has no car
and lives blocks away from the shopping centre.

Now she doesn't even have her phone or wallet, thanks to him
and his sister. Now she is hungry and scared and unsure what to
do about it. Moving means pain without any certainty that satisfaction of her needs will come at the end of it. Moving means
experiencing the rest of the disaster site. It's too much to contem-
plate when she is still confronting the losses in here.

Like how always from her bed she has been able to reach out
and touch with her fingertips the top that she had worn the first
time Tony kissed her. It had been draped, always, from a Freedom
Furniture, cow-spot-patterned swivel chair, the first big purchase
she made after she started work at fifteen, and which had taken
three months to pay for using lay-by, and which is also gone.
Screaming Slut Red, Mum had called the colour of the shirt. Nic
knew it was Revlon Fire & Ice Red. She couldn't afford to buy
the lipstick but she could pop in to the chemist on Norton Street
and slick it on from the tester tube. Perfect match. The fabric was
like layered cobwebs. Tony had commented on it, the delicate
softness. He was sorry, after, when he noticed the back of it all
fuzzed up from the friction of the brick wall she'd been pressed
against for so long. So long kissing like that. Fully clothed and
his hands mostly on the wall at her sides, her hands on his back,
and it was almost too much. In bed alone that night she couldn't
shake the feeling he was inside her. Not the usual way men got

inside women; not the temporary pushing in and out of a dick. This was cellular.

Of course the top was wrecked by that. Who wouldn't be?

And long after she'd said goodbye to him for the final time, she could put her hand on the top and be twenty again. The cold brick against her kidneys, hot mouth against hers, hard-on making promises into her hip. The sound of him—the throaty tormented groan—when the security guard flashed a torch at them, told them to clear out. All of it right there in the fuzzy weave of that ten-dollar top.

Older, junkier stuff, Will had said.

She can't wait any longer. Has to piss, to eat and drink and take more painkillers. She manages the first with an ease which boosts her confidence but then whacks her hip against the kitchen table, which has been pulled out from the wall for no apparent reason except to cause her both insult and injury. There is no food in the kitchen, and when she makes her way back to the empty lair Will slept in last night and checks the fridge she finds only two bottles of Fanta. She hates Fanta but bought it because it was on sale and the next time someone she knew mentioned that it was their favourite drink she would have a surprise bottle or two ready.

Her tablets, at least, are easy to locate. Sitting on the kitchen table next to her open handbag. She takes only half of what she has been prescribed. She is tired of feeling foggy and uncertain, of letting herself be helpless.

Without the children to stop her she walks through the house, using walls and furniture instead of crutches, taking in the remains. The echoes of her slippers on the floorboards conjure ghosts. Lena and Will running wildly up and down the hallway in their school uniforms, Lena as tall as her brother, Will determined to run faster to make up for it. The narrow space taking the sound of their slapping feet and broadcasting it to the rest of the house.

They are in the kitchen, too, the ghosts of her sister's children. Summer-brown legs swinging, skinny forearms on the tabletop, sunburnt faces intent on the plates of food in front of them. Always ate like they hadn't been fed in a year. Those children died when their daddy did, is the fact of it. What if the ones who took their places had been here instead of the ghosts? Been here all these years, running up her empty hallway, scraping plate after plate clean. In that version of reality, the house stays as it was in the years between Mum's death and Joe's. It is as it's always been, a family home. Space to play, to cook, to make up beds for whoever needs them.

Nic makes her way to the only room she hasn't seen since she returned from hospital. The door is difficult to push open, which is exactly exactly exactly right. The room is exactly right. She closes the door behind her and inches forward, nudging bags and baskets and books with her feet as she goes. She whispers apologies, hopes they'll understand and forgive. She cannot bend to move them more gently, has to get to the bed before she drops. Once there, she lowers her bum, drags up one leg at a time. The bears and pandas and rag dolls squish together to accommodate

340

her. There's no way to get the blanket up now that she's on top of it, but it doesn't matter. The room is warm and her cuddly friends nuzzle her back, stop air creeping down the neck of her nightie.

What would've become of these snuggly fellows if the children had had another week or two to wreak their havoc? Charity bins if they were lucky. More likely the forever hell of the tip. And she would be living in a tomb without a soft, safe space to lay her head.

The irony is that Nic rarely came into this room before, but now that they've destroyed everything else it's the only place she can breathe easy. The toys behind her, and piled-up clothes behind them. The lumpy sea between her body and the door patrolled by a fleet of misshapen boats. A stripy travel bag containing gifts and cards from boyfriends and workmates over the years; a shoebox of certificates from school that proved she was polite, was kind, was conscientious; laundry bags holding outfits she'd worn on days and nights that had been particularly sparkling; photos (in albums or in yellow envelopes waiting to be put in albums) of birthday parties and christenings; the treble recorder she played at the Opera House (in a group of one thousand school kids but only seventy of them with the treble recorders and Nic was in the front row with a bottle-green ribbon in her hair and when the audience applauded it was the proudest she'd ever felt up to that point).

A whole plastic laundry basket filled with all the letters and paintings and drawings and craft projects Lena made her in the years between birth and Brisbane. Snuggled in there the locket with a snippet from Lena's first haircut, snatched from Michelle's kitchen drawer, where it lay in a ziplock sandwich bag nestled with rubber bands, paperclips and lockless keys. Shamelessly snatched and right to do so, as Michelle had evidently never noticed it missing whereas Nic feels its protective presence every day and night.

A smaller basket, woven cane, not full, but almost, of the cards and pictures made by Will in those same years. He drew less, gave less, than his sister, but the things he did make and give were heart-busting. A pastel-coloured, pencil-drawn, comic strip in which he is Super Will, with cape and tights and all, rescuing his aunty from a snarling dog and dropping them both into a vat of whipped cream at the end. A paper clock with the words *Time for kisses* across its middle. She remembers him explaining it to her, his little face thrilled with the cleverness: *See, whatever time you want a kiss, you just move the hands to the time it is! See?*

And at the far shore of this lumpy, lovely sea, in the middle of the top shelf of the wardrobe, is the box she needs to have but never needs to open or touch. She knows its contents by heart.

Dear Daddy Dear Daddy Dear Daddy Dear Daddy Dear Daddy Dear Daddy Dear Daddy and never a *Dear Nicole, Dear Daughter, Dear Nicky, Dear Nic* in return.

In the first little while after Steve found their family, he would take Michelle and Nic up to Norton Street for gelato and ask them endless questions about their father. Michelle always said she didn't remember anything, tried to change the subject. Nic didn't remember much either, but what she did—a big, hard belly you could play like a drum; a laugh that sometimes turned into a coughing fit and, just when you thought he was going to choke, back into a laugh again; thick, furry arms that would lift you up until you could touch the ceiling with your fingertips and then bring you down onto his wide, fuzzy shoulders so you could bury your fingers and sometimes face in his thick, brown, curly hair—she gave to Steve. Michelle glared at her—they weren't meant to talk about Dad, not ever, to anyone—but hearing about him made Steve smile. He said that maybe there'd been a mix-up and the man he met in the prison meeting room wasn't their dad at all. That man was scrawny with wispy, white hair and gave the impression he'd never smiled let alone raucously belly-laughed in his life.

After a few months of this Michelle slammed her little palms on the plastic table, sending gelato cups skittering close to the edge. *The only thing we need to know about our dad*, she told Steve in an end-of-conversation tone, *is that he loves us very much and can't wait to get out and see us again.* Nic had agreed, of course, and poor Steve must have known it wasn't true, but he'd hugged them both to him, one under each arm, and said, *True words, last words, yeah.*

It was only after their mum dumped the letters out on the floor that Nic brought up the subject of their dad again with Steve, who was by then twenty-five or twenty-six and already in the grip of his addiction, though she didn't yet know how irredeemably. She told Steve how for years and years whenever she did anything good, like get 10/10 in a spelling test or come first in the fifty-metre sprint at the sports carnival, she would write about it to Dad as soon as she got home. If a whole week passed in which she'd done nothing good (and this was lots of weeks, even though she tried very hard all all all the time) then she'd write a letter anyway, because otherwise he might think she'd forgotten him. In those letters she sometimes told him good things Michelle had done (there were lots of those) and sometimes good things Mum had done (not as many), but mostly she just told him whatever she could think of that wasn't bad: the funny dog she saw on the way to school; the chorus of the song that was her favourite that week; the colour of the new dress Nan had given her for her birthday; the funny show she and Michelle watched on Saturday mornings while they ate their Rice Bubbles. Just all the things that, if *she* was the one in prison, would make her think, *Hmmm, that sounds pretty good, I'm going to be very well behaved so I can go home soon.*

She told Steve how she *stupidly stupidly stupidly* imagined the letters Dad was writing back to her but for some reason not managing to send. She imagined his letters said, *My precious girl* and *I love you more than the world* and *I think about you every day* and *I'm very proud of you.* And she imagined what it would be like when she finally saw him again. How she might come out of school at the end of the day and he'd be there waiting at the gate, and even though she hadn't seen him since she was tiny and they both had changed a lot since then, they would recognise each other straight away and she would run run run and he would run run run and then in the middle they'd nearly crash into each other but he would grab her hard but not hurting-hard around the middle and lift her into the air and spin spin spin and all the other kids would be watching so that she felt embarrassed but at the same time prouder even than at the recorder concert at the Opera House.

Or if it was longer away, the day he came home, it might be even better. Because good things come to those who wait. And if she waited, then the day he came home might be when she had finished high school and was wearing a straight black skirt that stopped at her knees and black shiny high heels and a white shirt with a sheer collar and short, puffy sleeves, and Daddy would say, *Who is this grown-up beautiful young woman?* And Nic would say, *It's me, Dad! I'm just off to my job in an office in the city,* and he would pretend to nearly faint with amazement but it would be pretending because of course he recognised her with love's gaze and of course he wasn't surprised at her city job because he always knew she was smart and would make something of herself.

Or maybe one night—any night! Maybe this one!—she would fall asleep like normal but then a racket would wake her and she'd stomp into the living room to rouse on her mum for being so noisy and there he'd be, a beer in one hand, ciggie in the other, like he'd never left. He'd say, *What are you doing up at this time?* And even though her heart would be bursting she'd be so so so so cool and she'd say, *Some noisy bugger woke me up,* and Mum'd say, *Nicole! Language!* and Dad'd laugh and say, *Can the noisy bugger get a hug or what?*

She spilt all this out to Steve as they sat with their backs against a wooden playground fort, her sipping the beer he'd given her, him halfway through his third already. He was silent, listening, and when she was finally done he said, *Geez, I'd love to have a read of those letters, Nicky. Catch up on all the stuff you done before I knew ya.* And even though he never mentioned the letters again, and the few times she thought of giving them to him without his asking, her whole body cringed with embarrassment and so she never did. Even so, every time she looked at the little box after that a wave of love washed over her.

The wave still comes when she looks at the box now, but it's polluted by the pain coming from the plastic bag nestled at its side. The ordinary, standard-sized white plastic shopping bag containing all that is left of the brother who never read the letters but made her believe he wanted to. It was the worst thing she owned and the most important, this pathetically small and crumpled bundle of 'personal effects' deemed worth keeping by the people who cleaned Steve's flat after he died. (*Crime scene cleaners* they were called. As though being fatally weak and sad was a crime.)

As she lies here closer to the bag and box than she has been in years, she remembers that they once caused only shallow surface cuts when she'd glimpse them as she moved around sleeping bags and pillows, board games and tape recorders, all the things kids needed for sleepover fun.

Something happened. Something terrible.

She remembers pulling down Lena's sleeping bag, knowing it was the last sleepover before her mother took her to Brisbane. And that made her sad, of course, but it wasn't the thing she had forgotten. The thing that happened.

It hurts hurts hurts but it's important.

Something happened here, to do with the bag and the box.

Her blood itches and she sees her boy, her Will, heading off to court in the suit he wore to his dad's funeral, his hair cut too short, showing the prickly heat rash on the back of his neck.

She didn't see him after that and it was months along, that last sleepover with Lena, pulling down the sleeping bag and seeing the space it left on the shelf and a thought slammed into her: *I can put Will's stuff alongside Daddy's and Steve's.*

Treacherous mind, killing off her nephew when he was alive, if not necessarily well, fifteen kilometres away in Silverwater. Treacherous space provoking her to imagine it filled in that way. Imagine the things that might happen to him in prison. The things that might happen to him if he made it out and had to live in the world with an unscrubbable stain on his life.

It had been a moment and it passed and the shelf filled with other things. Soft and kind and sweet things. The box and bag surrounded by so much goodness there is no room for anything else. It is a good place now. Safe.

It is important to acknowledge gratitude in even the hardest times, Mum used to say, having learnt it from Oprah. Here is what Nic is grateful for, lying alone in the dark on her child-hood single bed in significant physical and psychological pain: the room in which she kept the most important things—painful and lovely both—is the room the children left alone. They had tried to erase her life but here she was embedded in the best of it, more in touch with its aching, profound, important beauty than she had been for years.

WILL

Air quality worse than Beijing, the news said yesterday. Today was clearer but still hazy enough to scratch at your throat and nostrils. His eyes were streaming by the time he reached Dead Man's Park. His and Lena's private name for it, since every time they passed Dad would remind them that it used to be a cemetery. Imagine, ten thousand bodies under that dirt a hundred years back. Then council decided a park'd be nicer and the families had to scramble to rebury their beloveds' bones. Some didn't bother, Dad said, and so they rested there still beneath the roses and bandstand and playground equipment. Geez, they used to love it, Will and Lena, when a neighbour or friend's mum would suggest going to the park for a picnic or run-around and one of them—naughty shits—would say, *Oh, yeah, Dead Man's Park? Sure, sounds fun*, and the other kids and most of the adults would get all freaked, want to know what they meant.

Dead Man's Park was heaving with living bodies today. Weird how quickly people adjusted. A week of smoke so thick you can't

348

see the sky and the first sign of visible blue everyone rushes out to enjoy the day. They'll all come home clothes stinking of smoke, tell themselves at least there's no ash streaking their windows, no blackened leaves dropping into their backyards today.

'Hey! Watch it!' Will was jolted backwards. A horn blared. A bus sped by a fingers-width from his face. He stumbled, tripped, landed hard on his arse. Pain right up his spine into his jaw.

'You all right?' A suited pair of hips in his face.

'Yeah. I don't know what—'

'You almost walked in front of a fucking bus, ya tool!'

Had he? He tried to remember the second before he was pulled back. He was long past the park, almost to Parramatta Road. Looking around he couldn't tell where he'd got to, couldn't remember deciding to step onto the road.

'What street is this?' he asked.

The suit disappeared. 'Fuckin' druggo,' a voice said.

Standing felt too risky. He might fall. Or walk into traffic again. Next time there might not be a rude but strong businessman to pull him back. Another red bus whooshed past and even here on the footpath he felt its weight and speed. He sucked in huge gulps of air, every one of them like a punch in the tooth. Couldn't stop shaking. Feet stomped past. If someone called the cops about the quivering, drooling man on the footpath he'd be fucked. Mumbling like a smackhead, someone else's credit cards shoved in his pocket.

Least in prison they pay for the fucking dentist. Probably not right away, but. Probably he'd have to spend hours at the station, maybe get sent home anyway, seen for what he is: a pathetic non-man, so broke and useless he's resorted to swiping his injured aunty's medication.

Concentrating hard, he managed to get up on his knees and then, after a minute or so, to stand. When he'd done that long enough that it felt safe he walked very slowly to a bus stop he'd spotted from the ground. Not far, but he didn't trust his legs and the traffic kept whizzing past, reminding him how close it was. How close he was.

—

Hours later when he'd got to the dentist alive and his mouth had been anaesthetised and the tooth pulled and he'd taken a proper dose of painkillers prescribed just for him and sculled a cup of lukewarm pumpkin soup from a 7-Eleven across from the dentist, when he felt more grateful even than the night he'd met Mercy, more relieved than the day he was released from prison, *then* he remembered the video.

Anton had thought he'd want to know but he didn't. Hated knowing. Knowing meant he had to *do something* about it and he had no fucking idea what that something might be.

Mum would know what to do. But Mum could never find out. Mum who had worked herself to the bone making sure her kids had a better life than her only to have one of them end up in prison at the age of eighteen anyway. Never, ever, could she find out about this. It would be the end of her.

Dad . . . What would Dad do? As usual it was a puzzle with too many pieces missing. He knew that Dad had watched porn;

he'd asked Will to help him clear his computer history and cache not long before he died. *Hate to ask but best spare your mum,* he'd said. Will didn't try to see what his dad had been into, just showed him how to click, click, click here here here to get rid of every trace. Sometimes when Will had a wank he'd get distracted by wondering what would happen if he had a heart attack and died before he could delete his browsing history. Mercy wasn't anti-porn, but as with her coffee and eggs and meat and clothing she needed a lot of information about its origins and who was being paid how much at every point of the supply chain.

What did he know about the supply chain of this piece of horror? Amateur, obviously, so chances are no one got paid. Did the performers consent? Did the performers even know they were performers? The pubeless wonder clearly did, given the nasty little scoring skit, but Lena probably didn't. Would've hidden her arm as well as her face.

He was almost back at the house. The last of his post-dental bliss evaporated as he realised Aunty Nic had been here all day without food or anyone to get her medication or help her to the bathroom. He pulled up Uber Eats on his phone, ordered several serves of spag bol from a local Italian joint along with garlic bread, salad, lemonade and a serve of tiramisu. He used the Mastercard in case he'd maxed out the Visa at the dentist.

Aunty Nic would know what to do. Or maybe she wouldn't but, fuck it, she would have to figure it out. That's what Lena had done for her and, yeah, maybe she'd gone about it wrong, but she bloody tried, didn't she? Didn't move states or flee north and find another family. Didn't plug up her ears and close her eyes and build a fortress made of memories and two-dollar-shop tat. She turned up and she gritted her teeth and she tried. Only one in the whole damn family who still knew you could do that. Only one until now.

FOUR

WILL

He'd found Aunty Nic wide-awake on the spare bed. It was a miracle she'd made it there without another serious accident. He nearly stacked it trying to get across to help her up, then again fleeing when she barked at him that she could move on her own, thank you very much.

True to her word, she made her own way to the kitchen when the food arrived. She was sulky at first, refusing to look at him, shrugging or grunting when he offered her a drink or bread or salad. Eventually, though, the spag bol worked its magic and she began to answer his questions with more than one-word answers. He learnt that the pain was better than yesterday, that she had slept half the day or more and that her phone was missing. Her tone suggested that he might have something to do with its disappearance; he told her he had no idea, promised to find it for her after dinner.

'Weird thing happened today,' he said, as he was clearing the plates. 'Nearly got hit by a bus. Fella pulled me back just in time.'

'Will! God! Where were you? You all right?'

'Yeah, good now. I need to confess something, though.' He kept his back to her—cowardly, he supposed, but he didn't know how else to do it. 'I was spaced out because I've, um, I've been knocking off your tablets. The Endone. Had this killer toothache and couldn't afford to get it looked at. So I've been—'

'Why didn't you just ask, for goodness sake? I would've given you some. Would've paid for the damn dentist.'

'Yeah, that's the other thing. You did pay. I mean, I used your Visa. Emergency dentist costs a shit ton. I'm really sorry. I'm gonna pay you back soon as I get another job. Or sooner if you need the money. I can call Mum, ask her to transfer it.'

'Don't be silly. It's fine. I'm happy to pay for my nephew to not be in excruciating pain! I just wish you'd asked me. I don't understand why you felt you had to sneak around. You know I would've helped.'

He wished Lena was here to appreciate his amazing self-control in this moment. No laughing in disbelief. No: *Are you fucking kidding me?* Not even a sarcastic smile, though that was as much to do with the post-dentist ache in his mouth as it was the desire not to let Aunty Nic know how ridiculous she sounded.

'Didn't want to bother you,' he said, filling the sink with water and dish soap.

'Haven't I always treated you and Lena like my own kids?' Aunty Nic's voice broke like a thirteen-year-old boy's. 'Who makes their own kids pay back money for a dentist's bill, for god's sake?'

Will turned off the tap, leant against the kitchen counter. She *had* always treated him and Lena like her own. Dropped everything to mind them, stepped forward with the cash if there was a school excursion Mum and Dad couldn't afford, always took the time to crouch or sit at their level and hear their winding, pointless stories or mediate their petty fights. Except.

Maybe the strong gear he'd been taking was still in him because he couldn't stop himself from saying it. 'You know, I used to imagine moving in here with you.'

'I know. You kids used to say it all the time. *Why can't we live with Aunty Nic?* No wonder Michelle'd get the shits.'

'Nah, I mean later. When I was in prison. After Mum moved. I thought about it a lot. But you never came to see me or rang or anything. Figured you didn't want much to do with me.' Will plunged his hands into the hot suds, washed their dinner plates and cutlery. Dried each item, put it away.

Finally, her voice small and scared behind him: 'You have to know, Will, that I'm not a very strong person. And that's what you needed.'

He turned, saw she was crying silently, said it anyway: 'I needed whatever kind of person I could get.'

'If I thought about you, I couldn't bear it. So I stopped.'

'You didn't stop thinking about Lena when she went away.' He hated how whiny his voice was. Might as well have been five years old, complaining that Lena always got first pick of the iceblocks.

'That was different. Your mum took her away and it hurt. I missed her, but I knew she was okay. I knew she was safe. Like you and your little ones, Will. Those kids, I know you miss 'em, but they've got their mum and their dad and that. They'll be all right and so you can ... can ... You can think about them without . . .' She threw her hands up, grimaced, stopped the motion short of a full arc.

'It's okay.' He was afraid she'd burst a stitch. 'Forget it. It's okay.'

'It's not. I should've . . . I'm not good in a crisis. Never know the right way to help.'

'You do, though. You did.' He took a breath, sat across from her. 'Remember the story we used to love, me and Lena? The one about you getting suspended from school?'

Flicker of a smile. 'You'd beg for that one. Funny kids.'

'We'd beg for it the way Haymish and Taylah beg to rewatch *Moana*. You were our hero, Aunty Nic. You were who we wanted to be when we grew up.'

'Pity my heroism peaked at twelve.'

'Bullshit. You stuck up for us all the time when we were kids. Remember the nit incident?'

There was a head lice outbreak in fourth grade, and when the teacher lectured the class about it she stood behind Will and said that long, dirty, messy hair made a perfect nest for nits. His hair *was* down below his collar because he wanted it to be like his Dad's, and it *was* dirty and messy because he refused to wash or brush it more than once a week, but he didn't have nits and when he told Mum and Aunty Nic what happened they went bananas. Yelling and slamming fists. Mum started writing an angry letter but then Aunty Nic had the idea to borrow a nurse's uniform from a work friend's sister and march up to the school herself. And she did it! Mum called the school, said her *sister the nurse* had kindly offered to do a *factual* presentation on head lice and the principal let her. Aunty Nic up there all prim and proper, explaining how nits love shiny, clean hair and then, with the teacher's help, she inspected all the heads and found nits in nearly half and none of them were Will's.

'That was your mum, egging me on. Never would've had the guts otherwise.'

'Only time the two of you got along was when you were defending me or Leen. But listen, point is, you didn't have to do that stuff but you did. Do you remember the other day, what you said to me about Haymish? How he'd always remember I stuck up for him? That's me and Leen. We always knew you'd have our back.'

Aunty Nic was red in the cheeks, her eyes streaming. 'That was easy stuff, though. When things got really hard I couldn't deal with it. I let you down.'

'Yeah, you did.' Tempting to leave it at that, leave her to feel the ache of it. But Lena. 'Now we've got something else really hard to deal with and I need you to do better this time. Need you to be the Aunty Nic we worshipped as kids, okay?'

'Will, please. Please don't touch Lena's room. The spare room. Please, it'll be the end of me. You can't.'

'No, that's—we can talk about that later. Right now, I need your help with a different hard thing. With Lena.'

She swiped at her eyes. 'Your sister can look after herself.'

'I don't know if she can. She's in trouble.'

Aunty Nic flicked her gaze at him, the rest of her stock-still. 'Tell me.'

It was hard to know how, what language to use. He wasn't sure if she knew about internet porn or file-sharing sites or any of it.

But after a couple of awkward, euphemism-loaded sentences she interrupted with a firm hand in the air.

'Enough. I get it. The turd taped them doing it and put it online for other turds to share.'

'I don't think you . . . It's really bad. Like . . . I don't know how to describe to you—'

'You didn't watch it, did you?'

'I skipped through it. Fast. I needed to know what was on there so I could . . .'

'So you could what?'

'I don't know. I don't know what to do.'

'Does she know you know?'

'If she's checking her messages she does, but . . . God. I keep thinking about how glued to her phone she's been this last week. Pissed me off how much she was staring and poking at the thing.'

'Does your mum know?'

'Nah. I mean, I'd have heard from her if she did. She can't find out, Aunty Nic. That's the one thing I'm sure about.'

'It's not up to you. It's up to Lena.'

'I don't particularly trust her judgement right now, though. If it was any good she wouldn't be in this situation.'

'Bad judgement, you reckon?' Too slow, too calm. Shit. 'What, the decision to have sex with a boy she liked?'

'Come on, Aunty Nic. She let herself get filmed. Not real smart, you have to admit.'

'Tell me, Will. Last time you got busy, did you check the room for recording devices first?'

Will pressed his palms together, trying to find the right way to say it. 'Girls need to be more careful about this stuff. I'm not saying it's fair, but it's reality. She should've known better.'

Aunty Nic was quiet for an alarming amount of time. Will refilled her lemonade, got himself a glass of water from the tap, sat back down and she still hadn't spoken. He opened his mouth to ask if she wanted to lie down again but she cut in before he could speak.

'I don't disagree she should have known better. The repulsive bullshit those college boys pull has been in the news on and off for a month. If I knew about it there's no way she wouldn't have. I can't imagine what she was thinking, hooking up with one of those grubs. But the thing about Lena is . . .' Another deep, long breath. 'The thing about Lena is that she expects the best from people, expects they'll be as up-front and generous as she is. She thinks well of people and opens herself to them and, and, it just sucks, doesn't it?' Her voice broke again. 'This world where someone like her has to be guarded and suspicious and, and, and make these small scared choices so as not to be *brutalised*.'

'Have some more lemonade. It's important you stay hydrated.' He didn't know if that was true, specifically, but it was never a bad idea.

She sipped, breathed, settled more calmly in her chair. 'Do you remember when you were little and you came home from a sleepover at a mate's place carrying on about the glow-in-the-dark stars on his bedroom ceiling?'

'Yeah. Ronnie. You turned the lights out to sleep and it was like there was open sky above.'

'Yeah. And you remember that almost a year later you climbed into bed and your mum turned off your light and there they were, all those stars shining away?'

Of course he remembered. When had he ever, ever, ever felt joyful surprise like that before or since?

'You know it was your sister did that. Saved all of her car-washing money since you told her about the stickers. Finally had enough to buy two packets, because one wouldn't give a flash enough result. Spent hours sticking those tiny stars up, crawling back down the ladder and pushing it a few centimetres before climbing back up, over and over and over again, refusing to stop for a break because she might not finish before you were home from cricket and she was determined to give you the full, glorious surprise of the night sky in your room.'

'I know. She did well. She did.'

'Your face when you saw it, and hers seeing yours—brighter than all the stars that had ever shone. That's what your mum told me. Brighter than all the stars, the two of you that night.'

'She was a good little sister.'

'And you were a good older brother. You *were*. Don't give me that look.'

'Tell that to her arm.'

'A stupid accident. And it wouldn't have been nearly as bad if your bloody father had got her stitched up properly.'

Will's stomach lurched. 'Wait, what are you saying?'

'That damn scar. Your dad was at the medical centre with her and the doctor said it didn't need stitches even though it clearly bloody did. And your dad—not having a go, truly, I know he loved you both to pieces—but he wasn't good at talking to people in authority, standing up to them. He knew Lena needed stitches but the doctor said those stupid damn sticky butterfly clips would do the job and Joe didn't argue, took her home with a great bloody crevasse in her arm, useless little stickers pulling the edges together. If they'd sutured it like they should've, all you'd see now is a tiny neat trail, like an old bit of spiderweb or something.'

'I didn't know.' Made horrible sense. Dad so scared of doctors he didn't go see one until his body was already swarming with cancers. All his comments about Mum being a firebrand and a troublemaker, about her insistence on arguing over incorrect bills and parking fines and people pushing in queues. Someone had to do it. Pity for Lena Mum'd been at work when Will slammed the stupid glass door that day.

'Mum would know what to do with this situation, I think. She would. But it'd gut her.'

Aunty Nic sighed, looked pretty gutted herself. 'When Lena comes back,' she said, 'we'll find out what's what, sort it out.'

'She's not going to want to talk about it.'

'No, but that's too bad. She's going to have to whether she wants to or not.'

Will raised his eyebrows and Aunty Nic raised hers back. 'That's what you two said about chucking all my stuff out, wasn't it?'

'Something like that.'

'Well, there you go.'

'It wasn't right, though. You were devastated.'

'I was. *Am*. You understand that, Will? It's all still . . .' Aunty Nic inhaled, tilted her head from side to side, exhaled. 'So let's try to handle this situation a little better, hey? We'll talk to her, *listen*, not decide we know what's best and go behind her back? Yeah?'

Will nodded. Felt hot shame at what they'd done to her.

'And just for the record,' she said, 'I would have loved you to move in here after you got out. Entirely my fault you didn't know that. My fault, my loss.'

'It doesn't matter now, Aunty Nic. It's in the past.'

'Maybe, but I'm feeling it in the now so it needs to be said. I would have loved having you here and even with everything that's . . . Even with everything, I'm glad you're here now.'

Hot shame surging but something else, too. A shadow of hope, cool and kind.

LENA

Lena had stayed all day at Kylie's napping, playing with Lacey and ignoring her phone. Ty brought out the Jim Beam around four and by the time she thought about going home she was drunk enough to laugh at the fact she didn't have one. Wasn't so funny on Saturday morning when Kylie and Ty both had to go to work and she had to decide which site of misery and failure she should return to.

The idea of talking to her brother about a sex tape while hungover was unbearable and so she caught the bus to uni, collected the notices from her pigeonhole on the way up to her room. She'd decided sometime the previous day that she would defer, go back to Brisbane for a bit. Even so, reading the letter threatening to cancel her fellowship and accommodation subsidy got her blood up. Other people skipped loads more classes, were allowed to make up exams they missed. Some never went to lectures at all. Prided themselves on it! Evidently slacking was for people whose parents could pay.

She spent the morning working her way through the online forms to withdraw, emailed the accommodation office to give notice she'd be leaving before the end of the exam period, texted Annie to let her know she was alive, would meet up for a drink soon. Then, still at her desk, upright and business-like, she called Mum. Told her everything. Not about Josh and all that, but the truth about the house, how bad it had been in there, what it had taken to clean up. How awful it was when Nic came home.

'You should've told me, Leen,' Mum said when she was finished. 'I would've come. I'll come now. Tomorrow.'

'No, that'd make it worse. No offence, but you know it would. The two of you . . .'

A sigh. 'We rub each other the wrong way, yes, but we don't abandon each other. And it's really not right that she's got my kids dealing with all this. Not right at all.'

'The thing is, she didn't want us dealing with it. I insisted and then Will turned up to help, and . . . I should've listened when she told me to leave it. I should've let the social worker handle it.'

'Taught you too well, my girl. Never abandon family.'

'We did, though. When we moved. Abandoned Nic. Abandoned Will.'

'Oh, Leenie. That was a bad time for all of us.'

'When wasn't?'

Mum made a sound that might have been a laugh. A very small and quick one. 'I needed to get you away from Sydney. Get you a fresh start. And Will agreed, wanted that for you, too.'

'I know. I'm glad, but . . . I've been thinking that was when this all went wrong for her. When she started losing her shit. Or keeping every bit of it. She was pretty devo when you told her we were leaving. That was a bad fight, even by Miller sister standards.'

Another pause. Lena would do anything to be in the room with her mum right now, be able to read her face to understand the silence.

'It was Will.'

'What was?'

'Him getting locked up. She took it very hard. We all did, obviously, but . . . Nicole's always been so fragile, especially when it comes to you kids. It's been . . . It's been difficult. She was a great help when you were growing up. A spare parent, you know? But always so judgemental of us, me and your dad. She thought—still thinks, I guess—I'm a shit mother. Maybe I am.'

'Mum, you're not.'

'I have been at times, I'm sure. It's been hard. *Hard*, Lena. I've done my best.'

'I know you have.'

'But it was never good enough for her. She always acted like I was failing you both, and so when Will . . . I knew he was dealing, Leen. I didn't like it, tried to talk to him, but you remember how it was then. It was *hard*. I'm repeating myself, but, god. Sometimes I can't believe we got through it. I know I didn't do all I could. Didn't do enough to stop him, protect him.'

'No one did.'

'Who else should have, though? Your dad was gone, you were a kid, Nic had no idea. Will was . . .'

'On his own.'

'Like I said, shit mother.'

'Shit times.'

'Anyway, Nicole was devastated and it pissed me off, to be honest. I'd lost your dad and then, not lost, but it felt like I'd lost my son. And she was carrying on like—like she always has, like you're her kids. I had no patience for it. She was hysterical.'

A ridiculous sting of jealousy. Nic wasn't supposed to care so much about Will. She was Lena's special person, and Lena was hers. Upset, sure, but devastated? Over Will?

'She told me something once, long after he was out. We were having a rare, proper sisterly chat. I think it was her birthday. I'd called and she'd had a couple of wines, wasn't all prickly and defensive, like normal. I said something about how I wouldn't be getting to sleep any time soon because I'd had a cappuccino after dinner and she said—God, it's so ridiculous and sad, Leen—she said she hadn't had a cappuccino since Will went to jail.'

'What?'

'That was Will's drink, remember? Thought he was Mr Slick getting his takeaway cappuccino on his way into college, sipping it with all his little girlfriends tagging behind. Nicole loved her cappuccinos, too—might have even been her that got him on to them—but she said she couldn't drink them from the day he went to prison because all she could think about was Will not being able to do what she was doing, sitting in the sun before work, licking the chocolate and froth off the top. She couldn't bear that she was doing something he'd like to be doing. And it spun me out, because—I mean, not to be harsh, Lena—but there are worse things about jail than not being able to drink a bloody Italian coffee! But that's what she's like, you know? Obsesses over this stupid drink, as if not having it was a tragedy beyond the telling of it. As if her having or not having it made the slightest bit of difference to that poor kid.'

'Bloody hell.'

'My whole life, she's stumped me. Not you, though. You always seemed to get her. Which also stumped me.'

'I thought I did. I didn't know her, though. All this time she's been . . .' Lena had been going to say she'd been living a double life, but she hadn't, had she? She'd never lied or pretended to be someone different. It was just that Lena didn't really bother to learn who she was. As though Aunty Nic—as though *anyone*— was simple enough to understand through sharing a boozy lunch once a week.

Lena had made the call with the intention of asking if Mum could pay her fare back home, but in the end she held off. Said she'd think about coming up for Christmas. Said she'd let her know once exams were finished.

Another missed call from Will. She moved to the bed, lay on her side and tucked her knees to her chest. Hit 'return call' before she lost her nerve.

'Will, the thing you saw—I don't want to talk about it.'

A breath. 'Okay.'

'I think we really fucked up with Nic's place. I fucked up. Threw out her whole life without even trying to understand.'

'Don't know if we can understand, Leen. I mean, up to a point we can. I definitely get not wanting to let certain things go.'

'Like Dad's vice grips.'

'Like Dad's vice grips. And don't think you can have a change of heart on them now by the way. They're mine.'

Lena wanted to hug her brother very, very much in this moment. 'I don't know how to make it better.'

'Come back here and we'll figure it out.'

'She hates me.'

That tongue on teeth noise that Dad used to make when he was losing patience. 'She doesn't. You two just need to clear the air, set some boundaries. It's important that you make up. Strong relationships and regular visitors can be an incentive to maintain a less cluttered home.'

'Jesus, you sound like that social worker.'

'I've been talking with her, yeah. We've set up a treatment plan. Haven't convinced Aunty Nic to follow it yet, but we're working on it.'

'What the fuck, Will? When I took off you were in a puddle and now you're Mr Fix It.'

'Yeah, I haven't been firing on all cylinders, I know. I'm starting to get it together, though. Thanks to Aunty Nic.'

'God, I should've pissed off earlier. Sounds like everything's going much better there without me.'

'I mean, she has gone from screaming at me to get out to more or less saying I should move in with her, so.'

'Well, then. No need for me to come back at all. Sounds like she's already got her strong-relationship-clutter-management-incentive blah blah whatever person.'

'First, stop being a crayon-for-brains. You know you have to make up with her sooner or later. And second, I can't keep moping around like this. I need to get a move on. Find a proper job or do some training or something. Start over. Again.'

'Can't you do that from Nic's?'

'I guess, but . . . it's hard here. Too much history. Too many people know me. I need to be somewhere that . . . somewhere that I can walk into a pub or a party and not have anyone already know the worst thing I ever did.'

'People don't care, though. Probably see you as a hero.'

'Selling drugs to kids. Real heroic.'

'That's not what people remember. They remember Dad. That you were helping him.'

'Dad woulda been wild if he'd known I was dealing. Woulda disowned me.'

'Please. He would have frowned for a couple of hours then forgiven all. You were always the favourite.'

'That's why Aunty Nic refers to her spare room as "Lena's room". Because I'm the favourite.'

'Mum and Dad's favourite. Plus all the teachers at school. *Everyone* at school. All my friends had the hots for you.'

'Yeah? You still in touch with any of them? I could do with a—'

'Ew. Stop.'

A pause. 'Hard to imagine now. Being anyone's favourite.'

'Maybe if you stayed in one place more than five minutes.'

'Tried that. Didn't help.'

'Maybe if you stay in this place more than five minutes.'

'What? I'll be your favourite?'

'Don't ask for miracles. Nic's, though. With me out of the way you've got a clear run.'

'Don't be out of the way. Please, Leen.'

She sat up, tried to make her voice steady. 'I think I have to be. I've stuffed everything up. What you said about people knowing the worst thing you've done? That's me right now. And there's no heroic angle to my—'

'Come home. To Aunty Nic's, I mean. Come back and we can deal with all this.'

'That's the thing—I've tried dealing with it. Didn't work. Plan B is ignore it and hide.'

'Not to throw your own words back at you, but can't you do that from Aunty Nic's?'

'Not as well as I could do it at Mum's.'

'Mum doesn't need you right now. We do. Come back, Leen. Please.'

WILL

Will and Nic were watching *The Block* when the front door opened and there was Lena standing in the doorway looking twelve and fifty all at once.

'Listen,' she said, 'I meant it when I said I want to ignore it.'

'Ignore what?' Aunty Nic said, not looking away from the TV. 'My hoarding, Will's pill thieving or your porn career?'

A second of shocked silence and then, 'What did Will do?'

'Thieved my painkillers, the bugger.'

'What, to sell? You back on that bullshit?' Lena chucked her backpack in the corner next to the TV, propped herself on the edge of the sofa he was sitting on. She was all jutting elbows and knees and he wanted to punch his younger self in the face for being so angry at the height of her. Imagine ever wishing she was smaller!

'Settle down, you. I had a bit of a toothache, needed some relief. Meanwhile, you didn't even notice Aunty Nic used the H word.'

'I noticed. It's just that I think your return to criminality is the headline here.'

'My criminality? So porn is legal in New South Wales, is it? I wouldn't know.'

'May or may not be,' Aunty Nic said, still watching the telly. 'But what's not is hacking the balls off a college boy.'

'Who's done that?' Will asked, finding it hard not to smile, suddenly.

'No one yet,' Aunty Nic said, finally cutting a glance at Lena. 'But soon as Leen gives me a name, I'll be on my way.'

'Sweet,' Lena said, face softening at last. 'As long as you don't bring those filthy things back here. Last thing this place needs is more clutter.'

''Course not! They'll be going right down his throat.' Aunty Nic made three sharp movements: slice, slice, stuff.

'Sickos,' Will said, and Lena scooted across so her side crashed into his. He lifted an arm, let it fall on her bony shoulder.

'How's your toothache now?' Lena asked, resting her weight against him a little more.

'Gone. Thanks to Aunty Nic's generosity.'

'You should've told me you were in so much pain.'

'Look who's talking,' Aunty Nic said.

'Look who's talking,' Lena and Will said back.

———

Later, after Will had helped Aunty Nic to bed and was waiting for her to swallow her pills, Lena came into the room, hovered near the door. 'Listen, Nic, I need to tell you . . I'm sorry. It was stupid of me to just get rid of everything. I really did want to help, but . . .' The tears started flowing before she'd finished speaking. It was the worst thing of all, seeing his sister cry. It had been what broke him at Dad's funeral, Lena sobbing into Mum's shoulder. He'd cried until he couldn't see then.

'Forget that for the minute,' Aunty Nic said, placing the water glass on the bedside table, patting the bed. 'Tell me, for real, how are you?'

Lena on the furthest edge of the bed, as stiff and straight as a ballerina. Will ached to reach out and pull her close, stroke her sweaty hair. It wasn't his place, though. This was between her and Aunty Nic. Still, he couldn't bring himself to leave them to it.

'I feel,' Lena said, voice so soft he had to hold his breath to hear, 'like everything is ruined.'

'Nothing is ruined.' Aunty Nic's voice was stronger than he'd heard it since he'd arrived.

'I am.'

'I know it feels like that, but it's not true. Some rich little turd has done a shitty, shitty thing and it's knocked the wind from you. Of course it has. It'd do the same to anyone. But you'll get your breath back. It'll be okay.'

'If Mum finds out, she won't cope. She won't.'

'You don't give her near enough credit if you think that. It's your decision to tell her or not, but you two know better than anyone that your mother's a strong woman who loves you both to the moon and back. There's nothing either of you could do that'd change that.'

It was the kind of thing an aunty was meant to say, Will knew, but he also knew it was true. Mum was gutted when he was sent to jail, but she never once made him feel like it was the end of anything, least of all their relationship. She called every single day. Wrote almost as often.

'Mum aside, there's a whole world of . . . How can I be a teacher? As soon as the school searches my name, it's over.' Looking at Will now. 'And if I did manage to get a job, and one of the kids in my class googles me! Can you imagine? God! Not to mention when I have kids myself. Not that I'll ever get to that point. Blokes google before they go out with someone, right? Good luck ever having a date with someone who hasn't already seen all my bits! It just goes on and on. I'll always be her now. The girl in the video. The dumb whore who—'

'Stop it!' Aunty Nic's voice like a whip, cracking through the rising panic. '*He's* ruined, the kind of person who could do something like that. Only him.' Nic pulled herself upright, closed her eyes for a second. She was in pain and they should leave her alone, but before Will could intervene she went on. 'Listen to me: when we're out together, having lunch, I can't believe everyone in the place isn't staring, pointing, asking for pictures. I want to call out, tell all these clueless people what they're missing. Boast that I'm your aunty, actually related to this extraordinary creature. I can hardly stand it that they're all sitting there oblivious, like they're eating alongside just anyone, when there you are: Lena! You're *magnificent*! And to think that this, this, this *boy* has treated you like you're some ordinary—no, worse than that! An ordinary girl shouldn't be treated like this either. No one should. He's treated you like you're not real. Like you're a thing. But, my god, the thought that someone like him could *ruin* you even if he tried his very, very hardest is ridiculous. Can a mosquito ruin a dragon? Never! It's an irritant. That's all, Lena. That's all.'

Lena's face streamed with tears, but she made no sound. Will felt his heart would never stop breaking. He wanted nothing so much as to climb onto the bed and snuggle under Aunty Nic's arm like when he was little. Feel the solid, pure certainty of her love. But even if he wasn't a grown adult man he couldn't do it. She was breathing heavily after her outburst. What he needed to do was calm things down, let her rest.

'Aunty Nic's right, Leen. It's going to be okay.' Relieved his voice came out normal.

'You know that's not true, Will. You know there's no way to truly get rid of this thing.'

And she was right, of course. It was the fucking internet. They'd been taught since they were six years old that you don't put anything online you're not willing to have out there forever. 'Maybe not. But you'll find a way to live with it.'

'Listen to your brother,' Aunty Nic said, soft now. 'He knows what he's talking about.'

'That'd be a first.' But not meaning it, he knew. She was listening, looking to him.

He didn't know what Dad would do, or Mum, but he knew what he needed to. He punched her arm.

'Let's take this to the pub, give Aunty Nic some rest.'

Tiny tired smile. 'Okay.'

'You're paying, but. I bought dinner.'

'With Nic's money, I bet.'

'I'm unemployed.'

'Same, though.'

'Bloody bludgers. Take my Mastercard and bugger off, will you? I'm exhausted.'

They kissed her goodnight, crept out like she was a lightly sleeping baby. In the hallway, Lena took a great heaving breath and Will thought she would start sobbing again, but she righted herself quickly. Gave him a nod. And on they went.

NIC

Every morning, after feeding the cats, Nic makes a cup of tea and goes through yesterday's mail. Most days she's done with the sorting and chucking and filing before she's halfway through her tea. She thinks she might switch the task to weekly to allow a decent pile to form. More satisfying that way.

Today there is only one piece of addressed mail, a letter about her follow-up appointment at the hospital. Dutifully she places it into the red plastic in-tray Lena has put dead centre on the dining table she deigned to leave in the living room. It still makes Nic's stomach churn to think about what happened to the others: dropped into the stinking rotting maw of the council tip, obliterated by a woodchipper or some kind of futuristic crusher. Her beautiful, useful, friendly tables of different colours and materials and lengths and heights, each bringing its unique personality to the room, each crushed into anonymity. Made indistinguishable in a mass of colourless, shapeless waste.

It was this table's weight that saved it. Too heavy for those skinny kids to lift or even tip on its side and push across the floor. Wouldn't even fit through the door unless you took the legs off, Nic bet. She had no idea how it had got there in the first place, but it didn't matter now. It was built to stay put, this one. Never had matching chairs but she liked it better that way. Matching chairs would've made it a formal kind of thing, the type of table rich people sat at to sip their seafood soup or whatever. Over the years Nic had introduced the table to an assortment of odd-bod chairs she'd bought or found here or there and they'd made a cheerful set. You never felt worried you were using the wrong-sized fork for your entree when sitting in those chairs. Never used words like *entree*. You plonked in any one of them and smiled at all the others and ate or drank or did whatever else the hell you wanted without any airs or graces. If your back got achy or your bum numb, you could slide over to a different chair and neither the one you left nor the one you landed in would mind. It was that relaxed.

Now there are four chairs left. Four! Around a table that demands eight at least and had previously accommodated three times that. Four chairs that the kids must have decided looked like the best fit for the table and each other, not seeing that by removing all their cheerful mates they'd left these ones painfully visible in all their try-hard matchiness. One, the same wood as the table but polished to a weird sheen. Two, a shade lighter and matt. Three, the same wood as the table and polished to a weird sheen but half a head higher than the first two. Four, the same colour as the table and chairs one and two but made of some kind of hard plastic with wood-veneer paint. They each look so embarrassed standing around like this it makes Nic's heart hot, reminding her of turning up to ballet that first time and seeing all the other girls had their hair in slicked-back buns while her own was in a high ponytail, and even though she twisted the pony around on itself and stretched and doubled her hair elastic to hold the bun, everyone could see it for the pathetic attempt at covering up an error that it was.

The in-tray, too, looks all wrong, although it is a thing she loves dearly. A serendipitous find. On the way home from the hairdresser on a Saturday morning three years ago the sky had opened up and she'd ducked into the nearest open door to avoid getting her freshly blow-dried hair drenched. Found herself in the midst of an office supplies warehouse's annual sale. Oh, the things she wanted to buy! But she was on foot and in dodgy weather so had to restrain herself to what would fit in her spare plastic carry bags. Pretty pastel-coloured pens she could use to spark up her evening Sudoku; dry-erase markers that would be useful when she unpacked the whiteboard she'd bought months ago to use as a wall planner; three keep cups so she would have one for home, one for work and one spare. And this beautiful, beautiful in-tray. Extra length and with high sides and made of an opaque red plastic with a slight opalescence.

When the rain stopped she rushed home, filled with purpose. Better organisation was the secret to an easier life, and who wouldn't want to stay organised if it meant interacting with this gorgeous, glowing tray? She remembers the feeling: like after her first solo day on the register at work, knowing she'd nailed it, that her dreams of a different, better life were not only possible but actually not even that hard to reach.

But now, in the middle of the stripped-bare giant table all alone, the tray looks small and cheap and incapable of doing much good at all. She is looking at a wooden thing holding a plastic thing holding a paper thing. She is looking at utility and practicality and administration. She is looking at emptiness cradling a reminder of pain. She is looking at her future.

No! She must not think that way or it will *be* that way. The past cannot be undone, but she is back in control now and can change the course of things. For example, look! The letter is in the red plastic tray but its envelope, still in Nic's hand, is not empty, not if you know what to look for. There, there: the lining which government departments put inside the envelopes to prevent the postie or snooping neighbours from holding it up to the light and reading the contents. Or no, it's probably not the government departments who put the lining in, but the envelope company, knowing that government departments can and will pay more for envelopes containing the extra security of a rectangle of thick, printed layers inside.

Nic goes to the kitchen and opens the second drawer and immediately sees the lone pair of scissors lying between the lone sticky-tape dispenser and the lone tightly wound ball of packing string. The scissors are sharp and precise and the lining comes away from the envelope beautifully. It is a small work of art: cross-hatched navy blue against a paler blue background. She is sure—if her memory serves her correctly and it usually does—that she has seen and not bothered to keep envelope linings printed with tiny flowers, with noughts-and-crosses, with diamonds, with wavy and straight lines intersecting. If you could collect enough

---

of these tiny works of art you could make a . . . a . . . a . . . a . . . mosaic! A mosaic, yes.

She will need some wallpaper glue. Or will that be too heavy for the delicate square fluttering so prettily in her right hand? She takes out her phone, googles *making a paper mosaic*, makes a list of items to buy, feels swollen with hope.

Walking to the shops takes twice as long as before the accident, but it barely hurts anymore. As she passes the neighbour's house she notes with satisfaction that the three fancypants cars out the front—the cars Will reckons are together worth as much as her house—each have a perfect row of muddy paw prints across their bonnets. It brightens her day to see them, truly.

Nearing the shopping centre her excitement builds and she wonders how long it will take to make a good, wall-hanging-sized mosaic artwork given how little official mail she receives each month. Lena, bossy as ever, signed her up for emailed bills for the phone and electricity. 'No point bringing extra paper into the house and it's less likely you'll put them aside and forget to pay. Just click through when it comes and it'll be paid in seconds.' Nic wanted to tell her that she *never* forgot to pay her bills, not once, but she was trying this thing Will suggested of letting the past be past and only arguing if it was to help create a better future.

But now she thinks of it, the lack of mail doesn't matter, because if you walk through the fire escape next to Target and pass the three doors on your right and then push through the sticky, dirt-speckled, heavy plastic doors leading to Dock 5 and follow the trail of cigarette butts along the wall to your left you'll come to the paper and cardboard recycling bin. As big as the regular rubbish skip but nowhere near as stinking, and although it would be impossible to find individual envelopes in among the large slabs of packing cardboard and broken-up boxes, it happened that most of the occupants of the centre used cardboard boxes as recycling bins for their office papers which they would drop directly into the skip rather than bother to empty.

Today there are four such boxes propped on the cardboard piles, two within leaning distance. Nic pulls the first out onto the dock and plunges in. Mostly advertising brochures and torn-up letters, but there are half-a-dozen envelopes. She won't check their linings here; she is alone now but that could change any second and it would be awkward to explain why she is out here on her knees. The second reachable box is a treasure chest. Four thick, neat stacks of envelopes, apparently unused. Perhaps TPB Realty had a logo change or someone ordered the wrong size. Their stuff up is her wonderful win. She shoves greedy handfuls into her carrier bag. It's hard not to look inside the envelopes so she can see the beauty, begin imagining the mosaic in detail, but she has to be disciplined about this, take her bounty and get out before someone comes along to ruin it all.

———

Walking home, arms laden with bags, the footpath reverberates up her left leg and provokes the hip which used to only bother

her at night. This was how her mother walked, not quite a limp but a list to one side as though her left foot was squeamish about the floor, unwilling to fully plant itself there. Mum never climbed on a desk and took a tumble. Mum never worked in a shop on her flat feet for eight hours a day for decades on end. Mum wore high-heeled shoes and went dancing and the next day soaked her feet in balsam salts and sometimes went weeks without leaving the house and sometimes went out all day and night and came home carried in the arms of a man. When Steve died, Michelle said, *What chance did he have with those doomed Miller genes?* and Nic argued so hard, but here she is in her mother's body after all.

———

At home she empties the carrier bag with a thrill of anticipation but it's a dud lot. Almost transparent as soon as you lift one side of the envelope off the other. Of course, that's why they'd been dumped in the first place. Her blood itches with the new dilemma. They will be no use at all for her mosaic, but if she discards them she'll be as callous as those snobs at TPB Realty. They're lovely envelopes, when you really look. Smooth, stark-white paper. Thin, yes, but sometimes that's what you want, isn't it? She isn't sure, not having sent any mail for years. But now she will! Because these unassuming, abandoned little things have found their way to her and she will not let them down.

Nic stacks them neatly on the left-hand edge of the big table. The table is instantly more solid and homey, the red plastic tray in its centre redder and friendlier. The envelopes have transformed it all into a buzzy little office space. Everything feels more useful and alive. She empties her shopping bags: lays out the glue pot and paintbrush, measuring tape, backing cardboard, ribbon (to trim the edges of the mosaic) and twine (because you always needed twine sooner or later). The right envelopes will come to her, she knows, and when they do there will be this happy little set-up to welcome them.

When Will comes home from his shift at the servo he doesn't comment on the mosaic supplies or envelopes, though Nic knows he's clocked them. It's the central part of their agreement: no nagging or judging as long as the shared spaces stay uncluttered enough to remain functional. Each of them has a room of their own with which the other cannot interfere, no matter how much irritation it provokes with, on the one hand, its fullness and on the other sparseness. Nic's mum always said compromise means nobody gets what they want. Which is true when it comes to how the house looks, but not true when it comes to who is living in it. Compromise means they both get exactly what they want on that front.

Getting to this point has meant walking over a lot of broken glass and they haven't finished pulling the shards out yet. Will remains hurt that she abandoned (his word) him while he was in prison and ghosted (Lena's word) him afterwards. In the damn therapy group (which she attends because she promised Lena and only because she promised Lena) it's been pointed out that one person's avoidance of pain often creates more pain for others. Like so many things said in therapy it is both eye-rollingly obvious and very difficult to accept that it might apply to her.

The injuries are not all Will's. There are days when the broken glass seems almost gone and days when it pierces her with every step. Times she looks across the kitchen table and can't believe this is her life, this dream: both kids free and safe, eating food she has cooked, chatting and laughing like they've never felt or caused sorrow in their lives. And there are times when she can't stop thinking about what they've taken from her, can't compre-hend how people she loves could do such a thing, could roughly bundle up her world and chuck it in the bin.

Tonight, Nic and Will are in the kitchen chopping vegies when Lena calls out from the living room. She's staying at a friend's place in the city for the summer, but she visits a few times a week to eat dinner and check that order is being maintained. *She comes and goes like she owns the place*, Will says, and Nic reminds him that it's Lena's house as much as his whether she's living there or not.

'You two, quick, come look,' Lena calls, and so they wipe their hands and walk through the unnecessarily, gapingly huge doorway into the spikily bare living room.

Lena is at the window, which is wide open to the street. Nic doesn't like the way she exposes the place so casually. You'd think after everything that had happened she'd be more careful about being on display.

387

This thought followed immediately by another: Why shouldn't she show herself to the world? Lucky world!

Nic and Will have worked hard, recently, to convince Lena of this. That she is not the one who should feel shame and hide away. That she has every right to stride through life with the sun on her face. It took a bit of arguing, but eventually she agreed to let Nic approach the college boy's parents and tell them what the turd had done, get them to pay for a content removal service. Will was sceptical about the removal thing, reckoned it was impossible to find every trace of anything, but if it helped even a bit while also meaning the dickhead's parents would know what he did *and* that it would cost them a shitload, then that was win-win-win in his book.

An unexpected benefit of that stoush: the pornographer's parents made him withdraw from uni and stay on the farm to learn the family business in a more hands-on, constantly supervised manner. It was the boost Lena needed to reconsider quitting. That battle was ongoing. Nic and Will had to admit cluelessness when it came to battling university administrations. Pushing computers off desks or pretending to be medical professionals wouldn't cut it, unfortu- nately. But Michelle and her husband were coming down to have Christmas in the Family Home (and now there weren't enough chairs for them all and she'd have to get more! See!!!) and staying in Sydney long enough to storm the admissions office when it reopened. Lena had worked so hard for her place at that univer- sity. Nic knew that her irritating, overly confident, bossy-boots little sister would work just as hard to make sure she could keep it.

'Come on,' Lena calls again. 'Look!'

And so Nic looks, and there outside her window is the most

extraordinary sunset of her life. Colours she didn't know existed in nature bleeding into each other. If she saw a painting of this sunset she would think it unrealistic. If she saw a photo she would assume a filter. But here it is, live and unfiltered and changing by the second.

Will hovers at her shoulder. 'Sunsets get more vibrant the worse the climate—'

'Chemical haze rapid climate catastrophe we're all going to burn up Anthropocene something something disaster death despair,' Lena says.

'And here I was thinking you never listen to me.'

'Seriously, Will. How does destroying our ability to enjoy a sunset help the planet at all?'

'I'm not destroying your enjoyment. Enjoy away. I'm just saying the vibrant colours are because of the smoke and ash, the air pollution. Doesn't mean you can't enjoy the result, just, like, be aware how it got that way.'

'That's my brother, always pointing out the cloud attached to the silver lining.'

'Doesn't stop me appreciating the silver lining, though.'

'Shush, you two,' Nic says. 'However it got like this, it's ephemeral. So pay attention.'

'Ephemeral. Good word,' Lena says, wraps her arm around Nic's back, lets her head fall on her shoulder. Nic reaches with her free arm, pulls Will in to her other side. They stay like that while the clouds drift, the gold and red bleed together, turn purple, lose their edges, become part of the night.

ACKNOWLEDGEMENTS

Most of the research for this novel was undertaken thanks to the Judy Harris Writer in Residence Fellowship at the University of Sydney's Charles Perkins Centre. This fellowship allows a creative writer to spend a year working side-by-side with medical researchers, encouraging fresh thinking and imaginative leaps in both art and science. Thank you to patron Judy Harris and to CPC Academic Director Professor Stephen Simpson for your expansive vision and continued support.

Thank you Joel Smith, Helen Splarn, Gemma Ashton, Fernanda Miranda, Alessia Pagano, Hendra Wijaya, Katia Kullengren, and everyone else at the CPC who welcomed me and facilitated my research. Thank you Michelle St Anne for nourishing conversations about rage and art and the beauty of clutter.

Thank you to all of the researchers, clinicians, academics and students at the CPC and in its connected communities who helped me untangle the various threads that make up hoarding behaviour.

Your willingness to take a novelist's endless what-ifs and but-whys so seriously was a true gift.

Special thanks to Denise Milicevic at the Nepean Anxiety Disorders Clinic for your insights into treating people with Hoarding Disorder and to Gayatri Anand at Westmead Hospital for your enthusiasm about my project and for introducing me to your team of incredible social workers who are on the front line in situations like Nic's.

To my agent Grace Heifetz: your guidance makes the things I find hardest a little easier and your unashamed enthusiasm gives me life. Thank you, thank you, thank you.

Thank you Jane Palfreyman for your excitement about, and commitment to, this novel and your spot-on editorial insights. It's truly a dream to be published by you.

Ali Lavau, this novel is much stronger thanks to your meticulous, wholehearted editing. I'm so grateful for your care and attention.

Indeed, the care and attention of everyone at Allen & Unwin has been exceptional. Thanks to every one of you.

Large parts of this novel were written at Writing NSW, an organisation that has been central to my writing life for well over a decade. Thank you to the staff, board and members for creating and maintaining such a nurturing and inclusive organisation. Special thanks to the students and mentees who've come into my life through Writing NSW's programs. Working with you all on your novels-in-progress has enriched my own practice immeasurably.

Thank you Natasha Rai for giving excellent advice on an early draft and for your friendship. You, along with the rest of the brilliant women who (occasionally, messily) gather around that upstairs table at the Newtown Hotel, are helping to create a writing community I'm proud to be part of and a literary future that thrills me. I'm grateful for you all.

Thank you dear Weedy Writers. May we continue to drink rather than write and talk about everything except our work on many, many more nights to come.

Thank you to my aunties, none of whom are at all like Nic, except in that they are loved deeply by their niece.

Thank you to my nieces and nephews, none of whom are at all like Lena and Will, except in that they are loved deeply by their aunty.

Thank you to Jeff, the only home I've never wanted to run away from.

Finally, my unending gratitude to every single person who spoke to me about their own experiences with hoarding behaviour or their experience loving or living with someone who hoards. The stories you trusted me with will remain private, but the insights I gained from hearing them suffuse every page of this novel. It could not exist without you.